A WORK IN PROGRESS

A Novel

Ebonii Nelson

Ebonii Nelson

Copyright © 2020 Ebonii Nelson

ISBN-13: 9798688476682

Cover design by: Ebonii Nelson

Printed in the United States of America

For the hopeless romantic…never lose that hope.

Acknowledgments

In beginning acknowledgements, I would be remiss if I didn't start with my friend, unofficial editor, accountability champion when it came to active writing, and of course a beloved irritant at moving toward publishing – Esther "No Middle Name" Lamarre, back then, but now Dr. Esther L. Jean. Second, I must acknowledge my friend and surrogate little sister, Ashlee Peoples. Both of you have not only been immensely supportive of my storytelling, but gracious supports and cheerleaders for bringing Noe to life. In the times when I begged folks to just read a few chapters, you both willingly obliged reads and re-reads, and for that spirit I am evermore grateful.

I thank my mother, who unwittingly saved the first drafts of this story by taking my demolished thumb drive to the computer guys following my theatrical breakdown of 2010. Thank you, Natalie, for your desire to read it. Many thanks to anyone who has ever encouraged me to continue to write. And lastly, I thank my Heavenly Father for the gift placed in me to be able to tap into such worlds and create that which I do.

A Work in Progress
Ebonii Nelson

Chapter 1

"And I said to him, I'm Noe Marie Cortes. N-O-E, but pronounced like Noah, the man with the boat. I know that's a boy's name, but it's an abbreviated anagram of my mother's name, so she was willing to make a sacrifice," I breathe quickly before continuing.

"Noe," a voice says, stirring me from my quick-paced jabber.

"I always feel compelled to go into that story whenever I say my name. And that story is generally followed by me telling whomever that person is that my family calls me MC —for Marie Cortes of course. I feel like using MC makes you an insider because not everyone knows what MC means. Though I guess you would if I told you my story," I close, sealing my eyes shut as I place my hands behind my head and reminisce.

"Noe," the voice calls again, through gritted teeth.

"Yeah?" I ask opening my right eye to reveal Dr. Logan Hale – my therapist.

He's sitting in his rolling chair, red leather pad folio and pen in his hand, with both feet firmly planted on the floor. He's looking at me rather quizzically with his gray eyes, over his sleek, rimless glasses, preparing to speak.

Today he's wearing a light blue button down, black slacks, and his favorite black Ferragamo loafers.

"What has any of this got to do with why you're here today? Seeing me? I already know your name."

I open both eyes, sit straight up, and address him almost yelling.

"You asked me to tell you how I'm going to feel about whatever this new boss is, so I'm telling you." Deflated, I slink back down.

"But Noe I asked you for feelings and you've offered me a wonderful narrative and many thoughts, but no feelings."

"I feel like I've been living a nightmare. And this is

the worst kind of torture because I can't wake up," I seethe.

"Tell me more about that."

"This is life. This is real life. It's happening and I can't do anything to re-write it, stop it, or pause it. I can't rewind or fast forward. I can't skip to the next scene. I have to be here," I add using my fingers to sign each clause.

"Where do the new boss and your feelings fit into that?"

"Dr. Logan, what are you talking about?" I snap up, eyes ablaze. "For the love of all things sweet, Dr. Logan, are you hearing me?" I whine throwing my hands up in mock exasperation.

"Are you serious today?"

Though his voice is laced with skepticism, I sense he's anticipating a less than predictable answer. I settle further into the couch, readjusting my hands, palms up, savasana position, and take three deep breaths.

A little perturbed, Dr. Logan adds, "Tell me why you're here today. Why Noe, can't you sit on that couch and just talk to me about what's going on?"

I rise and turn to face him and mirror his demeanor. I put pretend spectacles on my face and slide them down to the tip of my nose. I sit upright, not touching the couch's back, with my feet resting on the ground, legs equidistance from each other. I clasp my hands, left thumb over right, laying them neatly in my lap. Slowly, methodically, and making sure to enunciate I start speaking in my best Dr. Logan voice.

"Breathe Dr. Logan. Just breathe." I wink as I've just said one of his favorite lines for me.

"Alright Noe, have it your way. As you were. Do as you must."

"Thank goodness!" I toss the imaginary glasses behind my couch and lay my head back.

I can feel his eyes piercing the side of my face as he rolls his chair beside me and taps me three times on the nose.

"Yes?" I ask surreptitiously.

"At some point if you're going to keep coming here and if I'm going to help you, you've gotta show up. As much as I love our weekly sessions..."

He often complains about my "repetitious behavior", avoiding his questions and posing a threat to my own success, but he has managed to give me this same speech at least twice before without different results. He's so stodgy.

"Dr. Logan...," I say.

He stops, awaiting the rest of my statement. I look at him and he looks at me squishing his face in confusion until finally he peers at the clock behind me and says dryly, "Oh, it's that time. I suppose, I'll er, um...see you next week."

"That you will," I say as I stand. "Don't get frustrated Dr. Logan. I'm a work in progress," I add patting him on the shoulder, picking up my bag, turning on my heels and walking out his office.

***

Leaving his space today and strolling through downtown, I can't help but replay Dr. Logan's words and wonder exactly why I'm in therapy.

I was sent to Dr. Logan on referral by my mother. She wanted him to reign in the free, creative spirit, trapped within a slightly obsessive compulsive, spacey, yet anal retentive body, that is me. Truthfully speaking, I always have so many different things going on in my mind that having his rigid structure in my life has been a Godsend, so for my persnickety mother I am grateful.

I remember how beside herself Mama was when I moved back to Texas. I'd just finished the first four years of my PhD program at the University of Georgia after I graduated with my Masters, and I was looking for work while I wrote my dissertation. Being back home was amazing and I was high on life until I found myself opening five rejection emails from large private universities and three rejections from some community colleges, and the icing on the cake was my denial for a job at Blockbuster. Much to my mother's dismay, I took a vow of silence and then I went to sleep from July until September – enter Dr. Logan. It really wasn't that big of a deal. I was tired. I mean three months of rest in exchange for 20 years of non-stop schooling. I think I deserved it.

Mine and Dr. Logan's first year together was really a time when we got to know one another. When I walked into his life that fateful Wednesday, there was no way for me to know that he was such a special breed of man. At first glance he looked harmless – normal and upstanding, but I soon learned that he was much more than his physical appearance.

I pause a moment and stretch out on a bench in a park. I close my eyes and as the sun beams down on me I return easily to my first day with Dr. Logan. That day I was just leaving the movie theater. I'd gotten a private screening of the new Jennifer Lopez movie, The Back-up Plan. Well actually it wasn't so much a private screening as it was a first screening on a Wednesday, and no one was there but me. That day I hadn't gone into the office, so I wore my favorite pair of dark wash seven jeans and a white racer back tank. I donned black low top converse without the shoelaces and had my hair in a loose side ponytail. Oh, and the best part, I wore my sparkly lotion. I used to love that lotion. In the sun it shimmered and looked so nice on my beautiful brown skin.

I left my movie with a Dr. Pepper and red vines, and I moseyed along to Dr. Logan's office. It was right off Main Street in Downtown Dallas, on the third floor of this antique house. It was so old that the elevator was one of those with a door and it had buttons that stick like the buttons on a typewriter.

The ride up was rickety, adding to the anxiety bolus that welled up in my throat as the car slowly climbed the shaft. I stepped out of the elevator and met the door. Deadpanned I searched the door for some nerve. Piper &

Hale. That's all it said. Piper and Hale. What did that even mean? There was nothing anywhere that said Psychiatric or Psychologic...wait, that's not even a word. I had to keep reminding myself, 'MC, you're thinking too much. Open the door!'

"Okay, fine," I muttered aloud.

I walked into the lobby and felt...nothing. It was very clean and, and sterile –very minimalist. The walls were painted this weird white. It wasn't hospital white; it was more like neon white – very strange. There were two sea foam green armchairs flanking an apricot orange sofa. In front of the sofa the coffee table was a cherry wood with a natural powdery finish. On the table, there was bonsai tree, a little sandbox thing with a claw, and a box of tissue. It made me nervous to know that those tools might be useful. Looking left and right the one thing I was excited for didn't exist. There were no books, and after signing in I sat in awe wondering how that could be.

"Good morning. How can I help you honey?" A woman with a deep southern drawl called out to me.

I walked back up to the window to the receptionist, Julia Charbrow her nameplate said. She was a brunette with tight ringlets that just about overtook her smiling chubby cherub-esque face.

"I'm here to see a Mr. uh, Dr. um...er Mr. Dr. Hale."

Geez could I have been more awkward; I laugh aloud at the thought.

"Darlin', d'you have an appointment today?" Julia asked clearly oblivious to my phonic blunders.

"Er...yes. What do I need to do?"

"Calm down sweet pea. Take this clipboard and fill out these forms; bring them back to me and we'll send you in for your visit."

There were about 40 pages to "these forms". I could feel a migraine coming, imagining the types of questions. Seated left-justified on the sofa, pulling my feet from the ground to use my knees as a table, I surveyed the forms.

Patient Screening Demographics:

Okay. These are the easy questions. So the pen was a good choice. Crap! Maybe I should read over the whole thing so I can know if the rest of it is this simple too. There's no eraser on a pen. Right…so…this just got hard. Forget it. Go MC. Go.

Name.
Last name, Cortes.
~~First, middle, Noe Marie.~~

~~First, middle, Noe (pronounced Noah, like the man with the boat) Marie~~

~~First, middle, Noe (noh-uh) Marie.~~

Do they care how it's pronounced? Probably not. It's just I hate it when they call your name out and they say it incorrectly. I know it's not their fault, but this way I can save myself the irritation and help them in the process. That's being too selfish. I thought this was the easy section. Ugh, this is stressful, and my paper makes me look like I need to be here, but I know this is just something to get mama off my back. This is taking too long. Okay, fine. Name…

Cortes, Noe Marie
Race/Ethnicity

I never know which box to check. What's the difference between race and ethnicity again?

Black, or African-American.

Kind of. Well, half.

Are you Hispanic or Latino?

Well. Kind of, half. So which one do I choose? There's nothing that says that I have to choose just one, but they don't have those instructions that say "choose all that apply" so does that mean that isn't an option?

Other (Please specify.)

Okay, that one will work

Black & Puerto Rican

Good geez. I've been on this thing for 20 minutes already. Julia keeps looking over at me. How can they expect people to fill this thing out? It's like a book. Let me flip to the back. Maybe some of the other questions are less intense.

I feel sad.
~~Sometimes.~~
~~Rarely.~~

What's the midpoint between *sometimes* and *rarely*...because that's where I am. I don't feel sad right now, but I have felt sad. It's in present tense, yes, but is that what they really mean? Couldn't be what they meant because then the responses would be different. So the pen was definitely a bad idea. New question.

I think about death.

Um.... no.

Who do they think I am? Why isn't there a flat out

"no" on here? "Almost never" is hardly the proper response. Dang it. Julia is looking at me again.

"Almost done," I said peering over the peaks of my knees.

"Oh, well…"

"I promise I'll be done soon. It's just some of these questions are kind of. Well you know. I mean, is there a different questionnaire? Prolly not, huh, no I'm working. It'll just take a minute."

"I'm afraid, Dr…"

"Ms. Cortes," a voice said.

I looked up and I saw this guy. He was wearing ebony slacks perfectly pressed and freshly shined Salvatore Ferragamo loafers to match. He wore a belt with a silver buckle, a slate grey shirt, and a perfect full Windsor in his black tie. His hair was cut low similar to the guys in the Navy, but he had the ever slight 5 o'clock shadow left behind by his beard and mustache, by far the only thing out of order. He donned an almost white pair of rimless glasses that gave rise to his intense gray eyes. He looked like a walking, talking ad for hues of gray.

I guess I was staring a bit and not moving because Mr. Gray served as his own echo, "Ms. Cortes? Are you alright?" he asked unassuredly.

He sounded just like Matthew McConaughey, though I could tell he was trying to hide some of his South. I finally got up, dropping my clipboard twice on the way, and met him in the doorway.

"Hi, I'm Dr. Logan Hale. Pleased to make your acquaintance," he said quickly offering his hand before ushering me through the hallway into his office.

As we walked, I dove right into introducing myself, "I'm Noe Marie Cortes. N-O-E, but pronounced like Noah, the man with the boat. I know that's a boy's name, but it's an abbreviated anagram of my mother's name, so she was willing to make a sacrifice. I always feel compelled to go into that story whenever I say my name," I paused to take a quick breath.

"And that story is generally followed by me telling whomever that person is that my family calls me MC. For Marie Cortes of course. I feel like using MC makes you an insider because not everyone knows what MC means? Though I guess you would if I told you my story."

Suddenly feeling quite red, I quickly put my hand to my mouth.

Taken by surprise but quickly straightening his face again Dr. Hale said, "That's quite a mouthful. If you'll come in and have a seat, I'll explain to you how our time will be spent, and you may ask questions about anything I've said. Then we'll get through what we can before our hour comes to a close."

I couldn't believe that after my quasi involuntary attempt to go out of my way to give him a proper welcome he stayed all businessy and 'if you'll have a seat' blah, blah, blah.

Of course, I didn't have a seat. There's no way I could've had a seat without properly exploring and taking in my surroundings, so I proceeded to inspect this office, and of course Dr. Stodgy proceeded with his doctor protocol or whatever.

"Noe?" he asked.

"That's my name," I said still surveying.

"I guess…. I er, um, I'll just go forward with an explanation of…"

"Ok, I'm listening," I said smiling at him and starting toward one of the bookshelves behind him on the opposite side of the room.

Even though his lobby was a bit bland, his office had some serious potential. It was very contemporary. He actually did a great job matching it to his persona. All the walls were a sienna color except for one. It of course, was gray. On the gray wall there was a huge window that overlooked the Dallas skyline. The curtains that covered it were a wonderful cream color and on either side the wall was adorned by these two Manet-looking paintings. His furniture was an espresso color. Very deep and dark. His desk was flush with his gray wall and its top was simple, with just a phone, computer, slender vase filled with cream colored rocks and perfectly white calla lilies, three pencils, and a very peculiar item – a picture frame, with a picture of a guy taking a picture in it. His desk chair had the same espresso legs and the cloth of the chair was the same cream as the curtains.

The office was rather spacious, and in front of his desk, facing away from the large window was the biggest, most plush red couch. It looked to stretch for miles. He had a small coffee table fashioned with a ton of toys and gadgets – stress balls, play doh, dice, and those cool Asian balls with the sound in them. He had his own personal chair. It looked like a mini-love seat, of course with espresso legs and cream body, but it was on wheels. He had wall-to-wall, floor-to-ceiling shelves, full of books. There was only one small space on the back wall that had an exquisite silver clock, complete with no numbers, just three hands.

Lost in my exploration I heard none of his explanation. He kept droning on and on and eventually I started to hear the Charlie Brown teacher before I couldn't hear his voice at all. After surveying his bookshelves, I had a seat cross-legged on the couch.

"Will that work for you Ms. Cortes?" he asked.

I nodded and said, "Actually you can call me Noe or MC, whichever you prefer. You can save all that Ms. Cortes and formal business for the real crazies."

"Very well then Noe, where would you like to begin? What brings you here today?"

The rest of our session was forgettable. The most important thing that happened that day was I'd come to learn that Dr. Logan actually prefers that you call him Dr. Hale. During our subsequent sessions I noticed that he always wears slacks and more than likely always has on a tie. I

15

know he's had a really rough day when he isn't wearing one.

His gray eyes seem to match his gray personality as he never talks about himself, which I think is so unfair. I've never understood how I'm supposed to build trust and all that if I don't know anything about the person I'm speaking with. And unfortunately, he's never been in a rush to change his approach.

This antagonistic truth manages to wake me from my memories. I pull a new tool from my bag – my journal. Since I have a habit of running long, Dr. Logan wants me to use this so he can get the information he needs, and I can float through sessions as I feel. I'm supposed to write daily. His only instructions were to write everything that's in my head.

I pull a pen from my bag and open to the first clear page. Today with all this time of remembering his and my beginning, it definitely feels like Prague.

From the Desk of _____Noe Cortes_____

May 23, 2010

Prague. On a couch somewhere in Prague. That's where I feel like being right now. I don't know why Prague, except that I was just reading an article about travel in Prague and life on the Vltava River. This journal thing is becoming a space where...I don't know. It's back again. The itch. In the most inopportune time too. One can't suddenly discontinue their dissertation writing, can they? I bet they can...but I suppose they shouldn't...they meaning me. I don't know what's wrong with me. I finally have a job and it's actually rather good. I like the people I work with...well...I like Joyce my admin. She's the only person in my office really. I love my condo. It's nice and it finally feels like home. Mama has finally stopped hounding me for a while about what I'm doing with my life, which is all the more reason for me to not give into the itch. But Prague. I mean, come on. Google it. It's absolutely amazing. Maybe if I could get away for a week it'd help with itch relief and it'd help with my writing too. It'd get my creative juices flowing. I am finding it supremely difficult to write 300 plus pages on how students experience transferring and how colleges and universities can better help them if I can't even stay in one place. I can't figure out how to make myself stay so what would I know about getting anyone else to stay? What is it that I am supposed to be accomplishing with this whole life thing? I think maybe that's the problem...I like need to be totally fulfilled to stay in one place for a long while, but I haven't quite gotten to that passion place yet. What am I passionate about? Books. Staring at people...ok, so that one doesn't count. What I meant was being observant. Dancing. None of that adds up to a profession.

AHH! Ok, I need...a...Dr. Pepper.

Chapter 2

"Buenas m'ija. ¿Cómo estuvieron tus sueños?"

"Bien Papí. ¿Dónde está mama?" I said, joining my dad as he sat in the sunroom reading his newspaper and drinking his café con leche.

"Maaaaa…where's my sock? The one with the blue stripes?" My baby brother JJ whined, trailing behind my mom moving past us.

"Jamal Joaquin…I," mom began.

"JJ," he gruffly corrected.

"JJ…if you put your socks in your drawer then you'd…."

"Ahh…I don't wanna hear it."

My brother JJ, a lanky 5'8", with his curly brown locks, brown skin like mine, with beautiful charcoal eyes had the youngest sibling role mastered. He was habitually looking for the mate to his sock while trying to run out the door to catch the bus. One day maybe the concept of pairing will pop into his head and all will be right with the world.

I chuckled at my brother and resituated in the kitchen to make breakfast just in time to have my hair mussed. Only two years my senior my older brother, Jackson, is completely opposite JJ, and will forever be a pain in my you-know-three-letter-what. He towers well over everyone, except my dad, standing robustly at 6'5". He's quite fair-skinned, with long sandy brown hair. He has eyes of blue – which is weird because no one in our family has them…and it's also annoying as it seems every girl in the world is madly in love with him. Jackson is what you'd call a…a, wh…er, um…oh, who am I kidding; he's a pompous a-hole, who thinks himself an irresistible Adonis who should be worshipped and waited on hand and food, which is incidentally why he lived at home.

"Thanks jackass. Shouldn't you be gone already? Pass me the eggs."

"Love you too," he said with a smarmy grin. "One day, my darling sister, you too will enter into a final year of school and know how it feels to not have class every day. Right now MC, I just woke up from siesta time. You want bacon too?"

"Siestas happen in the middle of the day, not before 9:30 in the morning. Yeah bacon. And Mr. Muscles, I'll have you know that I am being cultured by my many travels and my knowledge base will be far greater than the likes of yours nincompoop. Gimme some jugo."

"Oh wow, nincompoop? So fictitious words count as the knowledge you've supposedly amassed? You're even more delusional than I thought."

"Nincompoop is a word. Look it up."

"Whatever. Oh and I was up this morning at 5 to work out then I returned for my siesta if you must know. Anyway, I'd love to stick around some more and chat, but the time is now like you said, 9:30 and my chariot awaits."

"Who is it today? Jennifer? Mandy?"

"Actually her name is Melanie if you must know," he added, sticking his tongue out at me.

I rolled my eyes. "Right, as if her name makes a difference."

"Never know she may be your future sister-in-law," he finished grabbing his bags and with a kiss on the cheek he added, "Tell mama I said bye."

Upon his departure I joined mama and papí in the sunroom, bringing mama some tea and mentally preparing for an unavoidable life chat as I made my attempt to leave and drive to campus.

"Mama, Papí, Jackson said goodbye and I'm on my way out too," I said as quickly as possible trying to make it to the door before my ears met my mom's tut tuts.

Like clockwork as soon as my foot hit the doorframe she got started.

"Marie Cortes, did your brother tell you he's got a job lined up at NASA after graduation this year?"

"Yes mama; so great; gotta go," I tried.

"I hope what you're doing everyday will allow you to one day come home with such good news," she said, staring out the windows.

Must we do this every day? I thought to myself.

"Ay mama. I'm staying in school and out of trouble and I get good grades. And I've got a plan…"

"I've heard this plan before," she interrupted, violently swinging her hair as she turned toward me.

"So why don't you believe me?"

She picked up her tea and took a drink tacitly informing me of her discontent with my life's choices.

Just looking at her you'd never know she could be so taciturn. My mom is a fairly petite woman – only five feet tall. Everyone says we're almost a spitting image of one another. She's got black hair that comes just past her shoulder blades, a beautiful caramel complexion, and deep dark eyes of brown. She's very slender because she used to be a dancer. She was really good too, traveled all over Europe all on her own. Now she's a dance instructor and co-owner of La Pura Vida dance studio. She's feisty and headstrong and everyone tells me they see a lot of her in me.

My dad…my papí, is the salt to her pepper. He's 6' 6", with an olive complexion. He has green eyes, and the most perfectly shaped bald head. He's an almost retired investment banker. I thought investment bankers were a type – fast-talking and unavailable – but not my papí. He's quiet and caring, and has more books than I could ever imagine, but not money books, all kinds of everything else. Though no one says it, I've always thought I was more like my papí. We have a special language and he's the person I always go to with my secrets.

"Papí, please, can you talk to her?"

She hated when I did that.

"Don't try and bring your father into this. I'm talking to you."

Actually, you're shutting me out, I thought to myself,

sighing and smacking my lips.

"Go on," she finally said, "Or you'll be late."

As I turned to go, my dad caught the door before it slammed, and called out to me, grabbing my hand just before it escaped the doorframe.

"Mi'ja…" he began, giving my hand a tug slightly, turning me toward him. He swept a hair from my face and continued, "Your mother, she only wants what's best for you."

Summoning all my strength to stop the tears from stinging my eyes, "I know," I said "I just wish sometimes that…"

"I know. ¿Tú sabes qué?"

"¿Qué?"

"Tú eres mi orgulla y te amo con todo mi corazón"

"I love you too papí."

He grabbed my face with both of his hands and kissed me atop my forehead. Closing my eyes, I smiled.

"'sta luego."

"'sta luego papí."

My dad always made that drive to class so much better. This would be the last time my family would re-play our morning activities because after today I'll officially be moved into my new apartment. I'll be in my own little patch of heaven. Nestled in a quaint area full of young professionals and graduate students, my apartment will be a great way for a great start.

***

The day before classes began allowed me to really take time to get comfortable with my new home. To my west about a block was a cool little Spanish-style coffee/book shop –incidentally named "Café y Libros". On the east side was a little walking park. And about a mile north was campus.

Full of excitement on the eve of the start of classes,

and a little nervous at the memories of my past decisions, I decided to take a self-guided walking tour of campus. Grabbing my messenger bag and my sunglasses I headed out.

The walk was about fifteen minutes of gorgeous house after gorgeous house. Eventually the houses parted and became a lush campus. As I approached, I could see a beautiful boulevard lined with lazy oak trees as far as the eye could see - each oak tree leading you further into the heart of campus. Walking up the path, I couldn't help but make up stories about all the many activities that occurred in each building.

"Meadows Museum. Betwixt these hallowed halls you'll find exhibitions of Rubens, Renoir, and Van Gogh. You'll see classic sculptures and, and, and a gift shop. And on your left, we have Perkins Chapel," I said, turning to point as if I were conducting a tour.

"Students attend weekly chapel, and in the spring and summer months you'll see beautiful brides who leave in wedded bliss. Oh and directly right is McElvaney Hall. This is your underclass residency. This place full of excitement and fervor is how SMU welcomes its students to their home away from home."

The campus was awfully quiet despite class beginnings being one day away. I supposed since move-in was earlier in the week, and it was a Sunday, everyone was well...resting. I quickly made it to an open area near the flagpole. Just beyond the pole I could see a large fountain and from it emanated three different pathways, each going in a different direction toward a different destiny. The most stunning of which was the one smack dab in the middle of the grassy knoll. Adorning luscious stairs leading to a six-column domed building, this place was undoubtedly a noble place of learning.

A wave of joy rushed over me. I placed my bag on the ground and found myself dancing. Jeté here. Rond de jambe à terre then en l'air. Plié. Relevé. Chaîné turn.

Double pirouette. Fouetté en tournant. Triple soutenu. Double pirouette. Getting a bit dizzy, I stopped. Brushing my hair from my face, I looked up and saw a very tall specimen of a man looking back at me, standing with his hands in his pockets.

From the Desk of _____ Noe Cortes _____

May 25, 2010

I watched that movie, Tuesdays with Morrie the other day. It was incredibly sad. It made me start to think about carpe diem. I need to seize the day so I can be like Morrie. Totally content with life because I've done everything that I have ever thought of doing. I haven't really done much of anything. Not really. There's so much else that I want to experience. I want to learn more languages. I want to travel and take my dancing overseas. How awesome would it be to dance Tango in Argentina? To do Flamenco in Spain; Meringue in the Dominican Republic; Rumba in Cuba; Samba in Brazil or Salsa in Puerto Rico. I want to learn to play an instrument.

I think it'd be cool to play the guitar or something more traditional like the cello. Maybe I'll play something like the harp. I don't know. But I want something. I still want to write a book. I feel like there are a ton of stories in my head that would definitely be appreciated by

26

the masses. I think I want to paint or take up photography. Or make movies. Being able to capture things on film – still or moving – is really you know awesome. Awesome's not exactly the word, but I'm definitely going for a cousin of it; something stronger. I think I want to join the FBI or the CIA. I want to solve crimes and mysteries and save lives and really contribute to society.

Well don't I sound like a child? I can see myself being all frivolous and without guidance, as my mother would call it. Reckless and without consideration for the consequences of my young frittering. I have her speech memorized. But it's okay, because really, I am a work in progress. And I have a plan. I do. I will finish this dissertation and I'll be the Dean of Students and then....and then.... I need.... I need.... a Dr. Pepper.

Chapter 3

"Good morning Joyce."

Joyce is my administrative assistant. I love her. She's always so festive, even on the rainiest of days. She's 57 with a salt and pepper bob like Diane Keaton. She has two daughters – Morgan and Heather. I've never met them, but I hear about them all the time. They're not too much older than me, in their early 30s. They both have families and they're Joyce's pride and joy. Morgan lives in North Carolina with her husband and two young boys, and Heather lives not too far from here, in Cleburne with her husband, three daughters and two parakeets.

I've worked with Joyce since starting at Texas International College. It's just a small school, only about 1200 students and Joyce and I are the Student Conduct dynamic duo. I'm like the judge here, and she's my bailiff. Joyce has worked for Texas International for over 20 years, so she knows everybody here and everyone loves her just as much as I do – maybe more.

"And what a lovely morning it is MC."

"I brought us quesitos today. My dad made them."

"I love your dad's cooking. I wish you'd bring some of your mother's famous cheesecake," she smiles patting her stomach. "I just put on a pot of coffee, and I'll bring out the orange juice for you," she finishes.

"Great. Lemme turn on my computer then I'll meet you en la sala," I look at Joyce expectantly.

"Sala. That one means…ah, uh…sala…"

I'm teaching Joyce some Spanish. She wants to go to Spain and run with the bulls in Pamplona, but she wants to know the language first. We learn new words each week, and I test her vocabulary by throwing in a few words in our sentences every now and again.

"It's another word for room, right?"

"You got it Joyce," I say, calling from my office space.

I sit rather gawkily, crack my knuckles, and pull up my email. Alright, inter-office email, what do you have for my life?

TIC ITS>>>Subject: Your password will expire in 30 days.

What am I going to change it to? All the good ones have been used before. No time for this now. Next.

Harper Harrison>>> Subject: Brunch Friday

Mental note: put that in your calendar. Read this email post-breakfast.

Hayley Martin>>> Subject: I must know where we're going to eat brunch...

I need to remember to let her know the proper usage of the subject line. There are way too many words here.

Raymond Dinet>>> ON BEHALF OF THE VICE PRESIDENT'S OFFICE

Nervous, I am.
"You ready?" Joyce calls out to me.
Careening into the corner of my desk on the way to the breakfast area I say, "Sugar, honey, iced tea. Crap. Joyce did you get an email from Ray in the Vice President's Office?"
"You alright hun?"
"Yuh huh."
"Yes. I got it. The one about Mr. Callado?"
"The Matthew, Mateo guy?"
"His name is actually Matias. He's from..."
"Matias..."

What kind of name is Matias? Where is that from? It sounds awfully...um, well...like Matias. I think that's proper. What's he doing here?

"What's he going to be doing again?" I ask Joyce waking from my trance.

"Well, he's from Spain, and over there he worked at a University. He's here on a teaching fellowship and he's going to be the new Vice President for Academic Affairs."

"That's a drinkful," I say staring into space and reaching for my orange juice.

"You mean mouthful dear."

"Oh right. Isn't that what I said? And why is he coming over here?" I ask attempting to drink my juice but missing the opening of my mouth.

"He is deciding where he would like his office to be. Since he will be supervising our area it might make sense to come here but being an AVP it might also make sense to be in the Administration building with all the others."

"Joyce, I think I.... I think I need to take a walk for a second. I...uh, I'll be right back."

"Okay, hun. You okay?"

"Everything is the picture of copacetic. Just got a little winded or de-winded.... or something...I just need some air."

I give up drinking, deposit my orange juice on Joyce's desk and fumble with the door a bit as I go to leave.

"Turn the knob dear," Joyce says to me.

"Oh right. I think I forgot."

Retreating to the front porch I feel light-headed and nauseous. Why am I reacting this way? It's just a new person. Boss. New boss person. It's no big deal. Change is a good thing. Dr. Logan said so. It's good. It's normal. It's healthy. It's.... it's deal-with-able. I take a seat on the wood paneling, pull off my shoes and place my head between my knees flinging my hair forward. I take slow breaths in and quick breaths out.

"Excuse me," a voice says.

Breathe quieter, maybe they'll go away.

"Pardon," the voice asks again.

"Yep?" I ask, my voice muffled betwixt my knees.

"Oh. Well that's peculiar. Ok, well, could you direct me to the Office of Student Conduct?"

"You're lookin' at it. Well, it's back there," I say pointing backward.

"Might I ask whether you're alright?"

Technically you've just asked, I think to myself.

"No, I'm totally wonderful."

"Well, alri..."

"It's just that, change is happening, and change means, you know.... never mind. Please delete that from your memory. I am great...good even."

I see his penny loafers begin moving, and I feel a slight breeze as he squats down and settles near my face.

"I have absolutely no clue what you're speaking of," he says, "but how's about I have a seat with you, and we can figure it out?"

"I would hate to bore you. I mean, you don't even know me."

"Well you know what, I think I might like to. What is your name?"

"My name?" I ask sitting up to take in this nameless, penny loafer-wearing guy.

He moves to sitting composed just next to me with the most excellent posture. He's wearing a perfectly pressed white button-down shirt just barely hidden beneath a tan tweed sports jacket with those weird elbow patches. As I scan him, he sits looking back at me. Staring into his sea blue eyes and seeing his cocoa brown hair, I feel myself forget my name and trip over the words competing to stay lodged in my throat.

"Yes, your name. What is it?" he leans in, giving me a whiff of lavender and jasmine.

"It's uh, um…. Noe?"

"Of this, you are unsure?"

"Um, no. My name is Noe. Noe Marie Cortes. N-O-E, but pronounced like Noah, the man with the boat."

You do not have to do this. You don't. You can stop right now. It's okay.

"You're staring at me. I, uh, I know that's a boy's name, but it's an abbreviated anagram of my mother's name, so she was willing to make a sacrifice."

Stop talking. S-T-O-P. This is a concept I need you to know and know well. Please don't finish this speech, I shout internally at myself.

"I always feel compelled to go into that story whenever I say my name. And that story is generally followed by me telling whomever that person is that my family calls me MC. For Marie Cortes of course. I feel like using MC makes you an insider because not everyone knows what MC means. Though I guess you would if I told you my story," I finish quickly, frustrated with myself, immediately dropping my head back between my knees.

"That's quite an incomparable introduction," he says without even a hint of a laugh in his voice.

Muffled again I say, "I've never heard it put quite like that. I'd like to say I have mild OCD that causes me to do that, but it's more like an intense addiction to habit, which I promise is different."

"I see, so you are inherently ordered, with an affinity for vomitus verborum."

"Come again."

"Word vomit."

Tickled, I sit back up focusing intently are those sea blue eyes again, as he says "Hi."

"Hello," I say.

"My name is Matias. Matias Collado," he says extending his hand to shake mine. "I'm new here, and I'm looking for a place to set up my office."

"Mr….Dr…. Dr?"

"Just call me Matias."

"Matias, I uh. Oh, I've already said my name. Hi?"

"What do you say, we both go inside, and you tell me what goes on here. You do work in here?" he asks with a slight laugh.

"Of course," I say matching his laugh. "For me and Joyce, this place is a little like home."

He helps me to my feet, and I grab my shoes from the ground. As we walk up the stairs and into the building I smile thinking about how I always manage to make peculiar introductions to people that end up being primary supporting characters in my life and I wonder what, pray tell, Matias will become.

Back inside, Joyce had already put up breakfast but was buzzing around with other work.

"Joyce? Where are you Joyce?" I call out.

"I'm 'round here hun. How was your breathing?"

Trying to maintain my composure, while biting my lip I say, "Oh, it went fine. Er, um, come here I've brought someone in to meet you."

"Oh, alright, I think we should be expecting..." she stops interrupting herself with a cough as she sees and makes some quick assumptions about the man standing next to me.

"How do you do?" she says and bobs a curtsey.

"I am well, how are you?" Matias asks with a slight snicker and a bow.

"You two are something else," I join in their playful laughter looking back and forth between the two of them. "Well, Joyce this is Matias."

"I think I may like working here. Everyone is so pleasant," he says looking back to me and then to Joyce. "Ms.?"

"Oh, just call me Joyce. Joyce works fine."

"Would you mind giving me a tour of the space?" he asks energetically.

"No problem. Right this way. We'll start in the

sala," Joyce says to him giving me a wink.

"I'll just be in my office," I call out to them, as Joyce starts the story of her Spanish lessons.

Alright, back to email.

To: "MC Cortes"<noe.cortes@tic.edu>
From: "Harper Harrison"<hharrison@texlegends.com>
Subject: Brunch Saturday

Sent on the Sprint® Now Network from my BlackBerry®
MC –

Because I know you'd forget your head if it weren't permanently attached to your body, I know you've forgotten about brunch with Hayley and I Saturday. Put it on your calendar. Actually, I'd love for you to give me your pin so I can put it in your blackberry. Why do you refuse to learn how to use technology? That lecture will be for another day. Stats are listed below:

- Brunch.
- Saturday.
- May 29th
- 11:30A.
- Long Island's Pier.

-HH

To: "Harper Harrison"<hharrison@texlegends.com>
From: "MC Cortes"<noe.cortes@tic.edu>
Subject: RE: Brunch Saturday

Harper,

I really feel like you may have the makings of a future heart attack patient. A little morbid, I guess, but you're seriously stressing me out with that bulleted list sentence thing. Anyway, I have the brunch on my calendar

so take a chill pill. Oh, can you score me some tickets to a game of some sort? 'kay thanks, bye. See you Saturday!
MC

Ok, next email…

To: "MC Cortes"<noe.cortes@tic.edu>
From: "Hayley Martin"<hayleym@baylorhealth.net>
Subject: I must know where we're going to brunch Saturday because I am supposed to also meet Connor that day too.

MC,

Good morning! I hope you are doing well. I am writing because I really must know where we're going to brunch Saturday because I am supposed to also meet Connor that day too. Did you forget about brunch Saturday? I feel like you might have. MC, you really must make use of all of your resources. Put your dates in that fancy phone of yours. Well, I suppose Harper has already harped on you for this. Haha. Get it? Harper, harped? It's funny because that's a part of her name. Well, don't forget. Please email me back with the details of the day. I can't wait to see you.
Hugs, Hayley

To: "Hayley Martin"<hayleym@baylorhealth.net>
From: "MC Cortes"<noe.cortes@tic.edu>
Subject: RE: I must know where we're going to brunch Saturday because I am supposed to also meet Connor that day too.

My Dearest Hayley,

Have I told you how much I absolutely love reading emails from you? Especially when I see that in your subject line you pretty much put the entirety of the email contents. You should have no worries about me and my memory. The brunch is totally on my calendar. Details are as follows (directly quoted from yours truly, Harper Harrison, Esq.)

- Brunch.
- Saturday
- May 29th
- 11:30A.
- Long Island's Pier.

What is this business that Connor is breaking up our girl's brunch? Doesn't he know this is our time together? Or better yet, what are you doing allowing him to schedule something during our day? I'll expect your explanation at brunch. Alright, so I'll see you there, or rather you'll see me since I know you'll be there a bagillion hours early.

MC

"And this is where MC does all of her work," I hear Joyce say as she rounds the corner, Matias following close behind her.

"Hi again. How's the tour going?" I ask Matias.

"It's going great. This though is where Joyce has told me is my last stop," he says with a smile.

"Well, I guess, Mr. Matias, I need for you to have a seat. Let's take a look at your file," I say mock sternly with a wink before I turn to Joyce. "Please buzz me when it's 2 o'clock."

"Sure thing. You want me to order us lunch?"

"Of course. We'll treat Matias to the Student Conduct special."

Which is code for a Grilled Chicken Club, side of tortilla soup and a sweet tea from McAlister's Deli.

"I'll expect you in the sala at 12 sharp."

"Buen trabajo Joyce. See you in a bit," I say closing the door to my office and turning my attention to Matias who is busy investigating one of my bookshelves.

"Find anything you like?" I ask walking to join him.

"Well that depends. Looking from left to right I thought I was smitten with your extravagant collection of Cervantes and García-Márquez," he says dragging his hands in the direction of his words along the book spines.

"But then looking from top to bottom, I am nothing but intrigued by this *The Tao of Pooh* flanked by *Art of War* and *Love the One You're With*. Please explain to me, Ms. Cortes how can one have such an eclectic library?" he turns to me, eyes locking unnervingly on mine.

"Please, call me MC," I say stepping closer to the books he's examining. "I like books of all kinds. Anything that takes me on a journey belongs on my shelf," I add with a slight stutter.

"This Cervantes was a gift from my dad, who's also a lover of literature. It is the classic Don Quixote. Who doesn't love Don Quixote? He's the original dreamer. A personal role model of mine," I say hugging myself a little at the thought of my father.

"Pooh. He's the most underrated stuffed animal that probably ever was," I continue returning to my shelves. "People always assume that Owl is full of wisdom, or even that Piglet with his stuttering holds the answers, but really it's Pooh. In his book, Hoff says 'the surest way to become Tense, Awkward, and Confused is to develop a mind that tries too hard - one that thinks too much.' That mind that he's describing, is the very opposite of Pooh, you know, which is why Pooh is truly the intellectual."

I quickly squat to eye level with my next novel not waiting on a response from Matias. "And, *"Love the One You're With"* .... I mean who doesn't love Emily Giffin? She offers more reason than one to get into the art of Chick Lit."

I stop speaking just enough to look to my right and

see a quaint smile spring onto Matias' face. He's peering down at me covering his mouth with his hand, and his piercing eyes stir my insides.

"Oh, I'm sorry," I say shaking his gaze, rising, and stepping slowly away from the bookshelf. "I would lie and say that doesn't happen often, but it probably happens more than I'd like to admit. You are definitely here to talk about what it is that I do in this office, so if you'll come and have a seat," I say back peddling toward my desk and pulling out the guest chair, "I'll do just that."

His eyes follow me intensely as I find my chair and get situated. His gaze continues to be unsettling, causing my heart to beat a little faster and I start to feel what I hope are fictitious beads of sweat beginning to form on my brow. I try smiling, but my left upper lip starts to twitch as Matias' face goes a little blank and he begins walking toward the chair I've pulled out for him.

"You sound as though you are in some way embarrassed, which I assure you, you shouldn't be. I will have a seat, but only if you continue your mesmerizing description of your literary collection."

"I could resume your book tour I suppose....... after I tell you at least a little bit of what goes on in this office," I say pleased with myself for having exercised some self-control.

"Deal," he says offering a hand for me to shake. "So, Ms. Cortes?"

"MC is really more than fine," I interject retracting my bargain-making hand. "I wouldn't encourage it if I didn't mean it."

"Oh, MC...I feel as though someone may have mentioned a short story in passing about that name. It's wonderful being able to be on the inside," he says a hint of sarcasm. "Well, MC what is it that occurs here in this building?"

"Well Mr. Collado, I am the Assistant Dean of Students, and here is where I meet with students who have encountered a few moral compass dilemmas, and unfortunately it has been alleged that they have chosen the least preferred path."

"I see. And what types of paths are these? Generally speaking," Matias asks seeming genuinely interested.

"Well statistically speaking, you know speaking statistics," I find myself getting tongue-tied as I've gotten lost in his blue eyes that seem to be staring at me quite intensely, studying my face almost as if something important depended upon making its memory.

"Well um, right, so…most of the students I see have presumably violated one of three policies: alcohol, curfew, and computer usage, respectively. TIC is a dry campus; however, there are times when our fraternal organizations host gatherings and in the midst of their excitement for good, clean fun, they forget this policy," I say dropping my head in disappointment.

"Alcoholic beverages are purchased and consumed, and things happen that apparently no one can recall. The only things people do seem to know is that as a result of so much 'dancing' they have developed sensitivity to light, sound and smell. It's really quite fascinating," I giggle awkwardly noticing Matias' unblinking eyes.

"Our computer usage policies also manage to get broken when one of our many highly intelligent students finds a mode of using whatever the most hip downloading software there is," I continue, turning my eyes away from his.

"They upload a song or film or two and then it gets exloaded, or exported, or whatever it's called, to other people, which is in direct violation of TIC policies and not to mention a host of copyright issues," I add tossing my hands into the air.

"And as far as curfew is concerned, TIC wants to offer its students the best opportunities for success, one of them being the encouragement of students getting the appropriate amount of nightly rest. One way the institution works toward this goal is requiring our students be in their residence halls no later than 11pm Mondays through Thursdays; 1am on Fridays and Saturdays; and 10pm on Sundays," I recite as if reading directly from the student code of conduct.

"For our lovely students who violate their curfew no fewer than 5 times over the course of a semester, they inevitably come to visit me," I close jabbing my index finger into my chest.

I pause. Only quasi unnaturally because technically I've said a ton so it would make sense to break, but not so much because my inflection at the close of my statement definitely sounded as though something else was to come from my mouth. But still I am deep in pause as Matias begins to speak.

"My, oh my, what you do sounds…. important," he says.

"Er, um…I…yeah."

Pulling his chair nearer and placing his elbows on the desk, his chin in his hands and leaning closer, he asks, "Are there times when you eh, um, leave this building, no?" doing that walking thing with his fingers on his hand, before replacing his chin to his upward turned palms.

"Oh, sure. At the beginning of the year I go to the orientation sessions and I speak to parents and incoming students about being responsible and making good decisions," I say miming some big boss judge guy I've created in my head, but looking more like an awkward robot, swinging my fisted arms, pointing and scowling.

"If student groups invite me to speak at their meetings I will sometimes do that," I continue, "or go to the activities fairs and hand out brochures, otherwise, since I'm just a one- person office, outside of orientation I only speak one-on-one right here in this space."

I stop, only because he's doing that weird staring thing again. I don't know if it's on purpose, but it's definitely mesmerizingly intimidating. He makes a noise like he's going to speak, but he doesn't. He drops his hands from beneath his chin and as they fall, his left-hand grazes mine. I reflexively pull away and stand just as Joyce enters.

"Order up!" she says spritely.

"J-Joyce. Yay. Matias. Come. Go. Lunch. In the there."

"Are you alr…," Joyce begins.

"Yeah Joyce. Just a little undernourished. I'm gonna go…yeah, bathroom."

As I side-step Joyce and head toward our bathroom, I hear Joyce laughing and telling Matias that with me, occasional erratic-ness sort of comes with the territory as she ushers him into our lunchroom.

In the bathroom I can't help but berate myself.

"What is your deal? Stop being weird. He's your new boss. So what, if he is endearingly handsome with his impressive sea blue eyes and cocoa brown hair."

Auditioning a new up-do I sigh, looking at myself.

"And so what, if he's got an entrancing Spanish accent and has forgiving crinkles at the corners of his eyes and he could so be your George Clooney…except younger," I continue painstakingly.

I let go of my hair and move really close to the mirror, inspecting every section of my face. I whisper, "snap out of it," and turn on the faucet spritzing my face with the cold water. I study my face in the mirror again and begin mentally psyching myself out for my return to lunch. I take a paper towel from the dispenser and dab the still wet places and try breathing.

"You've got this. You're Noe Marie Cortes. Built tough, you know like that one truck. The Chevy or the Dodge, or something. Go out there and eat your food and interact normally with your boss."

I step back, lightly tousle my hair, toss my paper towel in the bin, and leave the bathroom. Back in the lunch area Joyce and Matias look as though they've been waiting to devour their food upon my return.

"I hope I wasn't too long."

"Certainly not," Matias says, rising from his chair as I join the table.

"No dear, Matias has been helping me with my pronunciation, while we've been setting the table. Are you okay?"

"Me? Weh...sure. I'm just...uh...great. So let's eat," I say about 2 octaves higher than I intended.

Joyce hands out our sandwiches before turning to Matias, "We've spent most of the day sharing our stories, tell us about you."

"It's so boring, my story."

"No, we really want to know. Tell us. We don't keep secrets in this office, do we MC?"

I take a huge bite of my sandwich nod my head and say, "Un huh"

"Don't talk with your mouth full, honey. So Matias..."

His eyes find mine and linger a little too long before he begins, "Well, if you want to start from the very beginning, I was born to my mother and father in a small town in Spain called Segovia."

"Tell me, is it wonderful?" Joyce asks.

"Oh, it has beautiful summers. It is the only place in España that offers refuge from the sweltering heat. In the winter it is, well it is quite, how do you say desafiante?"

"Arduous or challenging," I say looking up with wide eyes, as I have unintentionally engaged in the conversation.

"Yes. Challenging," Matias says meeting my eyes, smiling, and running his fingers through his hair.

"Why are they challenging?" Joyce asks Matias, genuinely intrigued.

"Well, it's just that the winds that make the

summers so welcoming become forces to reckon with in the winter months. The winds are so strong that they offer frigid lashes to all who brave the outdoors."

"It must be awfully romantic," Joyce adds with a doe-eyed look complete with mushy smile.

"Some say, yes," he says quickly before returning to where he'd bookmarked his story. "Well, there I grew up a boy who was always filled with many stories. Eh, my father he was a professor at the University, which was in Salamanca, so I did not see him always, but I always looked forward to when he'd take me to the campus and I could get lost in all the books my heart desired."

"You sound a lot like MC. She's always buying new books, and when work is light around here, she's always caged up sitting in her window seat reading. She thinks no one knows, but I know," Joyce adds to the story.

Laughing, Matias continues, "Well, my mother owned a pastry shop and after school that's where I would spend most hours. Growing up I loved stories and languages, so when I finally went to University that's what I studied. I traveled all over France, Italy, Portugal and Spain embracing the language and reading everything," he says glancing over at me.

"I was teaching literatura and idiomas, until I applied and received the teaching fellowship over here. One of the big tasks that came with the fellowship is the chance to work with other departments, like Student Conduct."

"That's an amazing story Matias. Don't you think so MC?"

"It's definitely the bee's knees," I say as I stand up to clear the lunch dishes.

"Would you like me to help you?" Matias asks standing and collecting his dishes as well.

"Well, I mean, I- I…" I stammer.

"Why sure, she could definitely use the help. Thank him MC for his hospitality," Joyce urges.

"Thank you, Matias, for your, er, um, hospitality. Trash is this way," I say turning to walk toward our kitchen.

"You know, Joyce is quite an amazing person to work with," Matias says placing a hand on my right shoulder.

Trying to suppress a jump caused by my stomach flip-flopping, I say, "Oh, yes. I love her. She's like a second mother to me."

I turn into him over my shoulder as he leans into me tossing his handful of trash in the garbage.

"So, have you decided where you're going to set up your office?"

"Well, I must still take a tour of the administration building tomorrow, but after today I have some thoughts."

I am trying harder than ever to overcome this sudden dry mouth that has assailed me, and my insides feel like they are gasping for air because it seems as though Matias has somewhat encroached upon my bubble of personal space.

"Thoughts…that's nice," I say, looking down and focusing intensely on a spot I've found on the floor.

He's standing there looking again. He's got that thing mastered. It's like an art form. Oh, I'm suffocating. Must….get….out.

"What? How's that Joyce?" I say sliding past Matias back into the main lobby.

"I didn't say anything, MC."

"Oh, I thought I- I…"

"Well I think it is time for me to get going," Matias says from what I feel like is in freakishly close proximity to my back.

"Well, if you must," I say turning around to confirm my suspicions of his closeness.

"It was a pleasure Joyce, and MC. I will see you both another day."

I am standing. I am physically stuck as he turns on his heels and departs our building. I am still standing as

Joyce buzzes around me continuing to clean and babbling on about how nice and incredibly handsome our new boss is. I am still stuck when Joyce reminds me of the 2 o'clock hour and my departure time.

***

"Dr. Logan, we've got a lot to talk about," I rush in cannonballing on his sofa.

"Well hello to you too Noe. Please, come in. Have a seat," Dr. Logan says without looking up from the book he's reading and being his usual uptight self.

"Out with it. I'm ready. Let's get to work," he says flatly.

"Dr. Logan, come roll next to me. I need you to look into my eyes as I speak," I plead. I can feel his confused and judging eyes on me, and I know he's about to ask why.

"And don't you dare say what you're thinking right now because for number one in this relationship you totally work for me so on some level you gotta do what I say, and for number two because you're my doctor please try to remember, or convince yourself that you truly want me to get better and not need your services any more, and in order to make that happen you must succumb to a few of my seemingly meaningless requests. Please and thank you."

I hear him rolling towards me, but he stops near my feet.

"Come closer."

He inches near my waist.

"A little bit closer."

Now his feet are at my left shoulder.

"Dr. Logan quit playing games with my heart, and come here will you," I demand grabbing hold of his chair, rolling him toward me. I yank his tie until we are staring one another in the face.

"I'm here," Dr. Logan says breaking free from my vice grip.

"Okay, so today I met my new boss."

"That wasn't exactly a surprise Noe; we've been talking about the possibility of you getting a new boss for a month or so now. And, change is good," he says readjusting his tie.

"Oh I know all that…"

"Well then, why are you troubled?"

"It's just that he…. he, well he…he…. looked at me."

Dr. Logan settles further back in his chair, closes his eyes briefly and starts massaging his temples.

"You know, Noe, people generally look at others. That's what's normal. I'm sitting here, looking at you, and likewise you're looking back at me, and we are having no problems."

"No, Dr. Logan, it's not the same. You look at me like I'm crazy. Don't think I don't know that, but that's beside the point. He came to my office today, and that's when he looked at me."

"Wait, what? Start at the beginning, but please skip the part that holds your introduction," he says quickly putting his hand out as if to say stop. "Tell me what you're talking about."

"Ok," I say sitting up, rotating his chair toward me, and sitting cross legged on the center sofa cushion.

"I went into the office this morning, 'cause it's a workday you know. I brought in quesitos that my dad made for me and Joyce to have for breakfast."

"Do we have t…"

"Dr. Logan, I need to recreate the scene so you feel like you're there, like you're me.

Come ride with me for a minute," I say flailing my hands about.

"Ok. I'm in the car. Drive."

"As I was saying, me and Joyce were about to have breakfast but first I checked my emails," I continue, starting to ramble fidgeting with my hands.

"I got one from Ray in the Vice President's Office

about our new boss, Matias, and something happened to me, and I kind of…well…I kind of…"

"You freaked out," Dr. Logan says pausing the writing he'd been doing as I have been telling my story and removing his glasses.

"I had a minor lapse in good sense," I say flatly.

"So, I went outside you know to catch some air and get my breath and get a different perspective and then some random guy started harassing me."

"Harassing you?"

"Just checking to see that you were listening," I sneer.

"Ok, so this guy, who really was wearing penny loafers, comes up and interrupts my time of composure and I just start telling him things, everything in my head," I pause reminiscing in it all.

"Okay? What happened next?" Dr. Logan asks expectantly.

"It's weird."

"Weird how?"

"It's weird because despite my oversharing he just stayed there," I continue staring out still confused by the occurrence. "We eventually go inside, and he inspects my office."

"Are you going to get to the looking at you portion any time soon? I am not trying to rush you," putting his hand up to stop me from speaking, he continues, "I know that's how it seems. I'm just monitoring our time and I want to see if I should interject with some other information regarding your journals, because some of your behaviors are similar and can be addressed. Ok, I'm finished."

"I am getting there. It won't be too much longer. I almost promise," I say batting my eyes quickly.

"He's checking out the bookshelf and confused by my choices. I get caught up explaining myself. When I finally get control, I turn to face him and he's already looking at me."

"He was maybe listening intently. People look at others as a sign of interest and engagement."

"Dr. Logan, are you listening to me? I mean like really hearing me. He looked at me, but it wasn't the regular looking. We talk about work some and then at lunchtime I made a mad dash for the bathroom. Dr. Logan, am I boring you?"

He opens his mouth to speak, but stops, puts his right index finger to his pursed lips, scribbles something quickly on his pad, and then says, "Continue."

"In the bathroom, I gave myself a pep talk and back in the kitchen I fed my face while Matias and Joyce talked so I didn't have to really be in the conversation," I say mock shoveling food into my mouth.

I pull my legs from underneath me and slide to the end of the couch in anticipation.

"Lunch ended and he helped me clean, and then when I turned into him after we were done, he's doing it again…LOOKING AT ME! Argh," I say with disgust.

"But thankfully, he excused himself and bids both Joyce and I adieu. And I just…then I came here," I finish breezily.

Dr. Logan slides his chair back to his desk and deposits his glasses and his notepad. I watch as he takes off his shoes, one at a time. First the left. Then the right. He walks toward me and pushes his coffee table away from the couch where I'm sitting. He sits cross legged on the floor right in front of me, places his elbows on his knees, clasps his hands and rests his chin atop his knuckles and he just looks at me. I see him, and he sees me. I look left and right and re- situate myself on the couch matching his body positioning, and he never drops his gaze from me.

"Dr. Logan, what are you doing?"

He says nothing, just scoots a little closer to the couch.

"I don't really know what you expect me to do about this right now," I add.

He stands up, still not dropping his gaze, and turns my knees left so when he sits, we're facing each other.

Seated on the couch in the same position he was in on the floor he continues looking at me.

"How do you feel right now, Noe?" he finally asks.

"I mean. I don't know what's going on. I don't know what to do with this…this…this," I say pointing between the two of us afraid to drop my gaze from him.

"You're telling me thoughts, and what I asked you was how you *feel*. Give me a feeling. Just one is all it takes."

"Feel? Well how would you feel? How am I supposed to feel? I don't know, nervous, anxious, ill-at-ease."

"Alright, that's good," he yells clapping his hands, still not breaking eye contact.

"Now, why does it bother you to not know what to do right now? Why do you feel like there's something that's *supposed* to be done right now?"

"Because there is. Isn't there?"

He looks at me still, not responding to my question.

"Isn't there? You're looking at me and it just makes me feel like there's something expected of me. Something that I don't know. Something that makes me feel…. because I don't know what it is…I feel…like I don't know," I sigh heavily.

"Noe, what don't you know? You're telling me an awful lot about thoughts you have as a result of my looking at you, or dare I say it, Matias looking at you, but you're not saying *how* it makes you *feel* and *why* you feel that way."

"I don't know what that means Dr. Logan. I thought I was telling you what you wanted. I don't know. I…I…"

"It's ok," Dr. Logan says touching my knees with his hands, finally breaking the visual trance.

"We're going to work it out. There's no time now. This week, even though I don't like structuring your journals, I'm going to. Try and use one of your entries to talk yourself through your feelings. Write freely; try to let go."

"We both know that's easier said than done."

"That is true, but we also both know that you are capable of doing what you must.

Okay…out with you," Dr. Logan says twisting me front as he starts standing.

"I don't think I can get my brain to shut up long enough to listen to the 'get up and leave' command," I say staring dumbfounded, at the door.

"I'm certain this task isn't too daunting for the likes of Noe Marie Cortes. N-O-E," he says placing a can on the edge of the coffee table closest to the door. "And if it feels like that right now, take this, and I'll see you next week."

I finally get up, slide my feet into my shoes, walk around the table grabbing the Dr. Pepper Dr. Logan placed on the table's edge and open the door.

"I can do this," I said before crossing the threshold and quietly closing the door.

From the Desk of _____Noe Cortes_____

May 26, 2010

I used to think I was like Winnie the Pooh. I thought my approach to life was to not think too much and have that bring clarity to life. But, I suppose as I definitely learned from my last session with Dr. Logan, that I am most certainly not Pooh. What if I'm Piglet? Oh, I don't want to be a worry wart. So...my assignment...how do I feel about not knowing, and why do I feel that way? I just think everyone has everything all figured out and I don't, and I don't know when I will. But why should I? I should, I know I should. I go home and it's expected of me to know what's next. These aren't feelings...Dr. Logan would say, where are the feeling words. Okay: nervous, anxious, stressed-out (is that an emotion), scared (a little...ok, a lot). Why? I don't know. I feel this enormous pressure to be as "good" as I seem. Where's the pressure from? Me, mama, me...what is so wrong with not knowing? I don't know. Ah, there it is again. It's just that...I thought there would be some point in life where there were just some certainties. Not that there would be complete clarity, but some lucidity, about...something. I am 28 years old and I don't know anything...and that scares the hell out of me.

Dr. Logan...I can't finish this. I'm in desperate need of a double shot of the 23 flavors that make Dr. Pepper so wonderful.

Chapter 4

I stood there a little bit paralyzed, a lot a bit shell-shocked. And when I thought he was going to speak, I had to first.

"Right. Okay. So…I promise I don't usually do that," I said speedily.

He took a few steps toward me, undoubtedly so I wouldn't mistake his slight chuckle for a colossal laugh. As he stepped, I turned around to grab my bag, tripping as I did.

"Oh, and I am generally not this clumsy," I said as I hopped around trying to disentangle my foot from the strap of my bag.

Bouncing about I could see that he had removed his left hand from his pocket and placed it over the smile he was desperately trying to cover.

"Oh good geez," I said as I finally freed myself, my back now to him. I turned briskly over my right shoulder yanking my hair from my mouth to say, "Yeah….so…'kay bye," And ran as fast as I could back in the direction I'd come.

I never knew what it was like to run an 8-minute mile, but I think this particular mile, I'd done in under 5. I ran until I couldn't see the campus anymore landing just outside the bookstore. It wasn't open yet, so I sat on the curb a while to catch my breath. Feeling safe and alone I put my head between my knees and scolded myself aloud.

"For the love of all things sweet Noe, what were you thinking? You looked like a complete idiot back there flailing about. How long had he been there?" I asked peering into my hands as if they held the answer.

"Oh goodness, I may be thinking about the possibility of feeling like I have to vomit in the near future," I continued grabbing hold of my stomach.

"No, you don't. It's cool. You'll be fine. The school is big enough. He probably won't remember you. And you'll probably never see him again anyway," I resolved.

Disrupting my self-inflicted chastisement, I felt

three small taps on my right shoulder.

Slightly frightened I sprang to my feet and turned to see him…again.

"And I also don't make a habit of talking to myself…while sitting on the curb…alone," I instinctively retorted.

I went to run again, but he gently grabbed me forcing me to halt. He held my left hand cupped in his, his thumb lying firmly across the back of mine.

"Before you run off again," he said "want a cup of coffee? Not that you need it."

I did an awkward half smile and he continued holding my hand as he unlocked the door to Café y Libros. Pushing the door open, he tugged my hand a bit and asked, "So what'll it be?"

Not having the strength to tear off again, I shook myself free from my daze, and sighed a little.

"Sure."

"Alright then," he said releasing my hand, "after you." And he guided me into the café.

I walked in without a word, absorbing all of my surroundings. He began his own routine changing the door sign from closed to open and then off behind the coffee counter he started turning on life.

"Is decaf okay?" he said with a wink and a smile.

"Decaf is fine. If you can do con leche I'll be immensely grateful," I said with a sweet smile.

"You got it."

Listening to the churning of the coffee machines, I surveyed the landscape. The shop was small, but it was bursting at the seams with books. I touched many of their spines finding new worlds that I had yet to explore, melting in the smells of cinnamon and jasmine, poking each of the cushy chairs spaced sporadically about the shop until eventually I found myself at the coffee bar.

"Here you are. Café con leche," he said laying a small red cup and matching saucer in front of me.

"Thank you."

"It's nothing. The name's Luca by the way. Luca Bianchi," he said looking at me expectantly.

Luca Bianchi. Almost as tall as Jackson, he stood at about 6'3". Dark brown eyes that crinkled at the corners when he smiled. Dark brown hair with an ever-slight bang parted to the right. The most perfect pearly white teeth and I saw from his smile that he only has one dimple in his left cheek. Peculiar maybe, but definitely attractive. He wore loose fitting jeans and black and white pumas. His short-sleeved tee had sort of a snug fit that hugged his prominent biceps and made his abdominal ripples beneath it easily identifiable.

Sensing I dropped the conversation, I shook myself from my reverie to hear Luca asking, "and you are?" probably for what could've been the 3rd or 4th time. Oops.

"Oh, I'm Noe Marie Cortes. N-O-E, but pronounced like Noah, the man with the boat. I know that's a boy's name, but it's an abbreviated anagram of my mother's name, so she was willing to make a sacrifice. I always feel compelled to go into that story whenever I say my name," I say taking a quick drag of breath.

"And that story is generally followed by me telling whomever that person is that my family calls me MC. For Marie Cortes of course. I feel like using MC makes you an insider because not everyone knows what MC means. Though I guess you would if I told you my story."

Shoot, I thought. Why do I always do that? And judging by the mouthed gaped look of shock Luca was giving me, I could tell he was thinking the same thing.

"Yeah a little over-share mixed with a little non-diagnosed OCD will yield that kind of look. I get it."

He laughed.

"So if you would, just lemme know how much I owe you. Better yet, here's a 10 for you know…I don't know. But I'll just be going now."

He laughed kindly as I began slinking off the stool.

55

"The drink's on me," he said placing his right hand over mine, "if you stay."

I looked up, "Is that something you're sure about? 'Cause that probably means you're in for hearing a ton of information you never knew you never wanted to know."

"I wouldn't have it any other way. Besides how else am I going to get to know you...MC?"

A smile broke across my face and I returned to where I was seated.

"Sorry about that."

"Don't be. So...where'd you learn to dance like that?"

I could feel my ears get hot. I'd almost forgotten about our ill-fated first encounter.

"Um, well. It's just that my mom. My is, or wu, uh." Breathe. "Try it again....ok. My mom was a dancer, and she owns a dance studio. And I'm the only girl in my family, so I've been dancing pretty much since I was out of the womb."

"Right. And what inspired your choreography earlier today?"

"Oh...well that was not supposed to be witnessed..."

"But I saw it, so come on, out with it."

"Ugh...'kay so can I tell a story? I feel like I have to go back to go forward to make it all make sense."

"Continuare."

I told him of my travels from school to school and about how excited I was to be at a new place. I told him I was to be a Psychology major this go 'round along with my Spanish studies.

"Learning about the mind and people is a good idea for any profession," I said.

"What is this 'any profession' you've got in mind?"

"Let's surprise the world with that response. What about you? Tell me about you."

"Well, I don't suppose there's all that much to tell. I'm an import to the states. My parents, Roma and Giovanni were vintners in Italy. And that's where my older sister, Giana, and I were born – in Rome. Giana came to the states for university and before my 10th birthday she asked Mamma e Babbo if I could come to stay with her and her husband Marco."

"How exciting! You call your mom and dad Mamma and Babbo, that's cute. How did you manage to adjust? Were your parents furious? Was Marco, terribly romantic? Ohp. Don't answer that last one."

"Unless, you really want to know," he said laughing sprightly. I offered an encouraging nod.

"Well, my parents were not upset because they felt like coming to America was a great idea, and they themselves eventually brought their winemaking over here too. They live in California. Napa Valley."

He paused briefly, pondering his next statements.

"Adjusting wasn't so hard. In Rome we learned English and living with Giana and Marco I learned about everything else. Marco was born here in the states, so he helped me out a lot."

Listening to Luca was like listening to the best bedtime story you've ever heard. It was soothing because of his accent, but it was exciting – or at least, the story lines I created in my head made it so – and simply mesmerizing. I was so lost that the only thing that managed to wake me was the loud roar that erupted from my stomach. Apparently contagious, my roar was a purr in comparison to his stomach growl.

"If you want, I can go out and grab us something to calm the storms in our stomachs," I laughed.

"Is it normal for there to be no customers? We've been here for about four hours, and no one has come to visit," I continued, looking around at the empty café.

"You sure have a way with words," he said amazedly.

"My dad says I'm a word miser, which I think is meant to be a compliment," I responded staring down at my hands. "Whaddya want to eat?" I added quickly, trying to move the conversation.

"Word miser? That's a new one for me," he said looking up, eyes roving through his mental dictionary.

"It's Sunday," he continued, "so we really don't usually have too many people coming in. One or two might come grab a cup of coffee, but to answer your question, yes, this is normal. As far as food, there's a really nice bistro just down the street. I don't really know the menu, but I'm not picky. Let me just give you something to pay, and you can surprise me with the entrée."

"Nope. This one's on me. Repayment for all the yammering I've subjected you to, and payment for your continued silence about my awkwardness."

I headed out, about four buildings down to Buon Giorno Bistro. The day was suddenly brighter. The sun was much warmer, and the smells, oh, the smells of late summer, and fast approaching fall were more aromatic than I had ever experienced. There was something about Luca that was so refreshing.

I returned to the café and our conversation picked up right where we left off. In between bites I told him about my brothers, and he even said he'd had a class or two with Jackson in grade school. He told me about Giana and Marco's daughter, Bella. Marco is an attorney and Giana is an orthodontist – wonder who worked on Luca's periodontal splendor? I told him about mama and papí, and how they met in a diner, her working hard for the money, and him reading his life away.

That whole time, Luca stayed engaged. Asking me question after question. His hand brushing across mine ever so slightly – and methodically, I'd hoped – all through the day. He's also studying psychology and I guess that's why he was so easy to talk to – though later I will have to tell him that he should refrain from laughing at his patients.

"Well…it's quitting time," he said as a clock in the café began to chime. "I suppose we better lock up."

"Seriously? It's only been," I say looking down at my

watch, "Good geez…9 full hours."

"Time does pass when you're in good company," he said catching my eye and maintaining contact just a little too long to be called natural.

"Um, can I help? What do we do? I wanna know all the secrets."

"I've never known someone to get so excited about some of the smallest things."

"Oh," I said bashfully "I'm sorry."

"No need for apologies. It's just that…. it's well…kind of...well, how 'bout you help me with the dusting."

Unsure whether to press him about what he was about to say, I nervously grabbed the feather duster for another tour of the store. We worked in a loud silence until I heard the jingle of the keys and met Luca at the door.

"Would you mind if I walked you home?" he asked.

"Oh, it's not too far. So you don't have to. So…no. Well…yes. I mean…only if you want to."

Oh brother, I made everything so much more difficult than it probably had to be.

"Think of it as me repaying you for spending your entire Sunday keeping me company. If it hadn't been for you, I'd have been all alone today."

"Ok then. It's this way," I said turning in the direction of the setting sun.

"Mind if we take a walk through the park?" he asked grabbing hold of my fingers. "The sunset is always really pretty over the trees," he added, releasing my hand, and nervously forcing his own in his pockets.

"Where you lead, I will follow," I said sidling up next him, offering a reassuring smile.

We took paths all through the park. I chased a chipmunk after naming him Alvin. We named the different colors in the sunset naming things like cinammony-amber and hunter- fuchsia. When we finally made it to my apartment, he deposited me at my front door and for the first time since we began our conversation, I was speechless. Being a true gentleman, Luca watched as I successfully let myself in – after dropping my bag on the ground three times and flinging my keys across the pavement.

Finally, opened, I turned from the door to make an audible attempt at goodbye. Sensing my apparent spontaneous bout of muteness, he took my hand into his and lifted it to his lips. My heart skipped a beat and I couldn't find my breath as he kissed my hand and said "Buona sera, signora" before he turned on his heels to leave.

Not until he was clear out of sight could I convince my brain to let my mouth speak.

"Okay."

From the Desk of   Noe Cortes

May 27, 2010

'Member that movie? It takes two. But the second one. You know, it had Kirstie Alley and Steve Guttenberg. And the twins. The um, detective ones...full house...the Olsens. But there's that one scene where Kirstie and Steve were in the mess hall and there was that food fight and then they go outside to like clean up in the lake/ocean/body of water. Then wait...either before, or after the ocean play they – or maybe just Kirstie – say this whole descriptive thing about a grand slam homer. And that play was their metaphor for what love is. That's what I ~~need.~~

Thought I was going somewhere with that huh? So much has happened. So much is whirling and whizzing around in my mind that I'm not totally sure I can funnel them out through my arm, clear of my fingers, pass the pen and onto the paper. Matias. Really awesome boss (so far). Really awesome features. Really awesome life. His life is like a compilation of travel books. We had lunch today accidentally on purpose. Yeah I know, but I...I can't figure it out. I want to get to know him, and I don't know why, and since I can. I don't know. There are no hard-fast rules, but it's frowned upon. My happiness is frowned upon. I wrote 500 words of my dissertation this week. That's like 2 pages. A typical dissertation is like 500. What's that math?

```
  250
2|500          250 x 500 = 125,000 words
 -4
  10           125,000
 -10           -500
  00           124,500 words left
 -00
   0
```

That's a lot. My life hurts so much right now. I need to revisit my feelings check and make sense of the way Matias makes me feel. I need a Dr. Pepper.

Chapter 5

I'm pacing. Barefoot and wearing a hole in the floor. It hasn't even been a week yet. It's only been 2 days. That's 48 hours. It's 1440 minutes. Broken down to 864,000 seconds. There've been 6 different greetings and salutations. I've had 7 mild panic attacks. In two days there've been 2 dirty fantasies, 8 cans of Dr. Pepper and half a Granny Smith apple...and I am still disheveled by Matias.

I check the calendar again and see that evil red exclamation point – my indication of an important event.

Today is Friday and per Matias' request we will have a one-on-one meeting. Just the two of us. Alone. The last time we were alone I tripped over my words and I couldn't help but feel like he was one comment shy of a sexual harassment suit...maybe I'm exaggerating a bit...but there were definitely waves of attraction crashing toward me. And we mustn't forget how he kept LOOKING at me. Ah. Weird thing though...I may have liked it.

I plop down in my chair, arms sprawled along either side, legs and feet unnaturally entwined with the leg and wheels of my chair, and my eyes cast upward toward the ceiling.

'Just breathe,' I remember Dr. Logan saying. Maybe I'll try this breathing thing.

I close my eyes, placing my thumb, index and middle fingers on each of my temples, envisioning and hearing Dr. Logan as he says, 'Focus on the breath. Think about how fast it moves, where it is in the body.'

Breathe in. Feel it in your nose and down your throat. *'Focus on dispersing it evenly throughout the body,'* I hear him saying. Send it to your limbs and out through your fingers and toes.

'Feel it as it cools and calms the body,' he'd add.

"MC?" Matias peeps in.

"Huh? Who? Wha-?" I ask in haste nearly becoming

airborne at this interruption. "Um…yes, how might I help you?"

"Ow-were meeting today…"

Gosh I love his accent.

"Yes?" I squeaked.

"It is now, no?"

"Oh gosh, is it 12? Yes…it is 12. Let me just…"

"Please, I will await you at the front door."

I will await you…who says things like this? Ah, I swoon.

"Oh, ok. I'm coming," I respond thinking to myself, get it together MC.

First find your shoes. Oh, and you need to seriously re-think walking around this place barefoot. The carpet is disgusting. What is your hair saying? Did you comb it at all this morning? I walk over to my closet and open the door to my full-length mirror. Oh gosh, I look ill slept.

I pull a pencil from my pocket and use it to quickly sweep my hair into a bun. From my closet caboodle I extract and apply a nude gloss to my lips, pinch my cheeks for a little natural rouging, remove eye boogers, quickly grab a pen and pad from my desk and join Matias at the front door.

"I am so sorry I wasn't ready," I apologize brushing imaginary lint from my clothes.

"This, it is okay; just don't make a habit of it," he says flashing his pearly white smile, his eyes crinkling subtly.

Oh. I. Love. Him. STOP IT! NO YOU DON'T!

"So, where might we be going?" I ask as we exit the building. We're on foot, so I can tell we aren't going anywhere too fancy.

"Bella Vita. I heard they have soups and salads and they have a patio we can sit on since the day it is so beautiful."

"Bella Vita. That place is really quaint and subdued."

Intimate and amorous is what I want to say.

"I haven't been there in years," I add.

Though I really want to include that I last went there for a secret Valentine's rendezvous with an all-too memorable ex-boyfriend, but I resist.

"Is that so? I think this will be the best place for a special conversation."

"Special? Why special? Today, aren't we discussing my role in the office?" I ask nervously.

He stops walking, so I do as well. And he furrows his brow a little staring blindly into the distance. Though I did manage to stop with him, I find myself uncomfortably close to his left shoulder. Instinctively, I hold my breath and wait for his response.

"Especial," he says, turning over his shoulder until he stands squarely in front of me.

He peers into my eyes so absorbedly that I can feel him exploring the inner depths of my mind's eye. I do my best to shake free, but his gaze temporarily restricts my brain from sending the message.

"Shall we?" he calls, and our stride continues; my question unanswered.

I trail behind him the rest of the way in silence. Just a boy, and his shadow.

"Benvenuti a Bella Vita! Welcome to Bella Vita! Party of two?"

"Yes. Thank you. Might we be seated on the patio?" Matias answers.

"Certainly. Right this way."

I don't know that I have ever maintained this level of silence since the laryngitis episode of 2004, and even then, the volume of my pen writing fervently on the pages of my notepad could be considered surround sound in comparison to this.

I finally break silence to say, "Sweet."

"What is that MC?"

"Oh nothing. I, I, I'm so glad that it's not busy today."

"Wonderful. I-"

"I. Uh, you. Oh. Excuse me. I need to ladies. The ladies' room, I'm going. I'll be right back."

I stumble my way to the bathroom and bury my face in the washbasin.

"Noe. You have got to get a grip on today. You're here. You're eating. You're discussing. You're discussing…work. Then you will pay for your meals. Separately. And back to the office you go," I say aloud.

For a moment I think I'm mentally prepared with this agenda for our meeting, but as I brace myself to return to what I imagine is our romantically positioned table on the patio, I instead slide to the floor and tuck my head in my hands.

I envision a better place. Dr. Logan's couch with my Dr. Pepper. His strangely soothing drawl forcing me into a comfortable stupor. Safe among my thoughts because I know his reality has a stronghold on me. Alright. Let's go.

I get up and amble back to the patio and to Matias Collado. My boss and secret crush.

He stands as I return to the table.

"Welcome. I took the liberty of ordering you a beverage. I hope that is okay."

"That is perfect. So, where should I start with the standings at the office?" I ask, eager to get the afternoon over with.

"Actually, MC I wanted to take a moment to better understand you. Your hopes. Your dreams. Your, how do you say, eh, what brings you inspiración to do the work that you do?"

"Oh. I don't know that I've been asked anything so abstractly pointed. Let me think. Well, I was hired because –"

"Not why you were hired. What brings you here? What wakes you up every day?"

"On a daily basis you might find me –"

"MC," he says covering my hands with his and peering down at me.

"I want to know more than what your job description says or what your daily agenda looks like. What about the things you do speaks to your soul?"

Sitting across from him, my hands still nestled beneath his, I'm dumbfounded. I'm, for the first time, lost in a sea of thoughtlessness. I tuck my chin, and staving off a torrential outpour of tears, I hear myself whisper, "I don't know."

I sense Matias' presence overtake me in slow motion. He raises his right hand and lifts my chin until my tear-filled eyes meet his.

"This is okay. It is why I am here. For you, no?" he says beaming. "With me, we will find what it is that lights your world on fire, and through that all else will be well."

Our meal continues fairly quietly. I pick over a Cesar salad before the rest of the day passes in a blur. Sometime around 4:30 I stagger off campus and drift to Dr. Logan's.

***

I stand staring at Dr. Logan's door for what feels like an eternity. I don't have an appointment, and I know that he's all about routines, so here I am with my fist prepared to knock. As much as I will it, I can't make anything happen. My impulses are stuttering so I'm left, arm raised, unmoving.

The door moves swiftly and the rush of air from Dr. Logan's force blows my hair a little.

"Noe?" He asks, as if he feels he's seeing a hologram.

"I- I- I. I uh," I say stuttering, my arm still raised.

"You don't have an appointment today do you?"

"I- I- I-. I-uh."

"Come inside," Dr. Logan says forcefully, glancing quickly at his watch, and taking me by the hand into his office.

"I- I- I-. I-uh," I continue as I take a seat on the couch.

67

"You what?" Dr. Logan asks. "What happened? Why didn't Julia tell me you were here?"

"I just came back. She wasn't around. Bathroom probably," I say breathily.

"It doesn't matter. What's happened?" he probes voice full of worry.

"I was at work today. I was at work today and I was pacing, but then I was breathing, and you were in my head," I begin, staring out raking my fingers through my hair and panting slightly. "I was at work and pacing and breathing and you were there, but then he asked?"

"Noe, you're incomprehensible. Breathe. Just breathe. What happened today?"

"Dr. Logan, I don't know what happened. I went to work. I was supposed to have lunch with new boss Matias. I was in the office and I was freaking out, then you came," I say frenzied and maniacal.

"Wait, what do you mean, I came?" Dr. Logan asks. "Noe, please put your hands at your side and look at me."

I do as he says and find myself in his eyes. As crazy as he makes me, something in his eyes calms me instantly.

"Now, can we try again? How was your day today Noe?" he asks coolly.

He leads me to have a seat on his couch and he sits in his rolling chair next to me. He takes in a few deep breaths loudly so I can hear. I follow his example and we're quiet until I'm ready to respond.

"Today when I went to work," I begin, "I went in knowing that I was to have lunch with my new boss Matias. I worked myself into a tizzy because of the last time we shared space. Remember Dr. Logan, the look?"

He nods in agreement.

"So I was in the office and I was pacing, and my breathing was hurried, so I thought to myself, 'breathe.' You know, just like you always say. So I was breathing and calming down and then he came in and startled me."

"I'm listening, I assure you. Please, go on," Dr.

Logan says leaning over to his table to grab his notepad.

"We walked to Bella Vita. and all I think of is how the last time I was there I was with Luca, and that can't be a good omen," I say shaking both my hands as if I've just touched something really hot.

Dr. Logan peers at me with quiet resolve and nods encouraging me to continue.

"We get seated on the patio and it's too much. Too gorgeous. Too not platonic. Too reminiscent. I leave to give myself a pep talk. When I return, he asks me why I go to work every day and what speaks to my soul. Who talks like that?" I nervously ask Dr. Logan.

"What was your response?" he asks, skirting my inquiry.

"I don't know."

"You don't know what you answered?"

"No. I said I don't know. Then I got into a thoughtless panic. How can I not know? What am I doing with my life? What have I been doing with my life? I felt lost and I needed to be found, so I came here."

"How are you feeling now?" Dr. Logan asks as he sits next to me on the couch.

"I don't know. Dr. Logan, I feel like the only thing I know for certain is I don't know. I can't answer his question. I feel like I can't experience his presence, and that makes me feel like I can't be at work. I can't. I don't. I am so exhausted," I whine, leaning my head back and closing my eyes.

"In one of your last journals you wrote of this feeling of not knowing and how disconcerting it is for you," he says tugging on one of my hands and pulling me up. "Why Noe do you *have to know*? What makes knowing important to you?"

"What do you mean? Don't **you** know? If someone were to ask you why you do what you do every day could you not answer that?" I spit pulling my hand from his.

"If someone asks you what your soul's work was

couldn't you give them an acceptable answer? I don't have an answer Dr. Logan. It's the only thing in life that I probably have no thoughts about. I have no words for it. So who am I? I am nothing," I say exasperated and angry.

"Noe, you –"

"And I am **not** catastrophizing. This is real. This is truth. It's based in fact. Evidence," I say yelling, looking directly into his eyes.

"I wasn't going to say that you were catastrophizing. I was going to validate. You are correct, there are many who can without a doubt answer these questions when asked," he says calmly, sliding closer to me before continuing.

"But what does that have to do with you?" he asks hands finding mine on my lap.

"How does comparing yourself to someone else's ability to vocalize their life's passion help you? You know that our process together is solutions-based, so how are you going to discover your passion?"

As I listen to each of the words, the syllables, the letters that Dr. Logan is speaking I can't help but imagine myself as one of those ballerina dolls forever stuck in the same position in a jewelry box. I'm spinning and spinning with no recompense and no cause, and I just want to stop. What am I going to do he asks? What am I going to do?

"The red light."

"Yes, Noe?"

"Your red light. It's blinking."

"Would you be –"

"Answer it. I don't have an appointment. I know the rules."

"But I –"

"Push the button," I say forcefully, feeling a sense of quiet calming rage as I peer penetratingly beyond the red light to somewhere far off.

"Yes, Julia?" Dr. Logan obliges.

"Dr. Hale, your 5:30 is here, what would you like for

me to tell them?"

"Send them in," I respond. "We're finished here."

I stand and move swiftly toward Dr. Logan's door. I pause before placing my hand on the doorknob and turn to see Dr. Logan who's looking at me with fear I've never seen.

"I'm okay Dr. Logan. I promise. I think it's time for a change. I am going to deviate. I'll see you next week."

I disappear and walk home. Aimless I am not, but lost in a sea of telling uncertainty, I hope I will not forever be.

From the Desk of _____Noe Cortes_____

May 28, 2010

Have you ever paid attention to the Harvest Moon? It always happens in October...around Halloween. It's the biggest, most orange moon one could ever see. When I was younger, I thought it meant there were frightening things to come, that as long as it was so large that I could be in some uncertain, certain danger. Now as I sit and write and think about my life's everything, I think it's something totally different. It's not about fear, which I think drives many people's actions. It's instead about new beginnings.

When I write I always feel like if I write enough, I will reveal some things about myself that I'm usually too busy to notice. My truth is I think the same way I was afraid of the moon...I'm afraid of myself and the thought of letting me out. Today that all changes.

Chapter 6

"Buona sera" is what he'd said, and in my dumbfounded stupor all I could muster was "okay". Four almost inaudible letters were the only things to fly from my mouth. Such an anticlimactic end to a seemingly perfect afternoon. After that night, I kept replaying that moment in time. Recapturing the way his eyes caught the auburn glow of the setting sun. Rewinding and playing it in slow motion, I analyzed all that led up to Luca's departure hoping it was more than him taking pity on a poor awkward soul like myself.

I wanted to be a mature and reasonable person, so I made a pro/con list to solidify my decision to like him.

Luca Bianchi
Pro:

Wait; is it wise to start with a pro? Don't you usually start a pro/con list when you secretly want something but you're trying to systematically prove that you should in fact have it? Which means that pros are easier to come by…so…

Con:

But wait, who wants to be a Negative Nancy, always quick to point out the negatives? That's just so…insert a word that's essentially a synonym for cliché. Ah…let's consult Robert. Robert's Rules of Order begin their debate with…Survey says…Pro…so….go.

Pro…he's chivalrous.
Con…he makes me lose my words.
Pro…he's easy to talk to.
Con…he laughed at me…. twice!
Pro…he has a job.
Con…we've only just met…

The pro/con list was a stressor. I'd become functionally debilitated until it only made sense to shut down. Who was I kidding anyway? The school was huge and there was no way I'd see him nor was there a high likelihood that he'd even remember a chance-encounter with a dancing fiend. For my sanity's sake, I abandoned my list and I focused on school.

Being at SMU was undoubtedly the best decision I ever made. My coursework was enlivening and enriching. Being a psychology major I decided was the best way to understand myself and hopefully help me have better experiences with others.

My first day on campus was everything I'd imagined and more. Maybe my imagination was a bit developed because of my slight addiction to literature but walking back onto campus made me feel very scholarly. I knew that my destiny was awaiting its discovery and I was on the prowl to find it.

My schedule was light and fairly easy. My classes started early and went until lunch, and after class I'd eat under the most perfect magnolia tree. Its trunk curved almost perfectly to my body shape and there I could dine and read and just be.

One Wednesday nestled 'neath my tree I was pinged on my shoulder by a flying acorn. I looked up to no avail and asked myself when magnolia trees began housing acorns.

I started to read again when another acorn found its way onto one of the pages of my book. I ignored it until a shower of acorns covered me from head to toe. Flustered, I stood, shook acorns from my hair and scanned the horizon in search of the acorn source. Finding nothing and no one, I returned to my seat.

"You missed one," A very familiar Italian accent said from behind the tree.

I turned over my left shoulder, to find Luca holding an acorn he'd just released from my hair.

"Where'd you come from?" I asked, genuinely surprised and intrigued.

"I've actually been buzzing around you for the past 20 minutes. You read rather intensely."

"Oh gosh, I feel so embarrassed," I said feeling the warmth of my shame radiating up the nape of my neck.

"Please don't be embarrassed. I am actually quite impressed and a bit envious of your ability to focus. How's your time here been so far? I've noticed that you've made a bit of a home in this spot," he said rounding the tree and squatting in front of me.

"Oh, well, this tree is just so perfect. Its trunk is exactly my body shape. School is gr- Hey wait?"

"Huh? Yeah?" he asked almost falling from his feet.

"How'd you know that I'm here often?"

"Oh, it's just that well. I mean, I dunno, I guess I. Okay, you got me. I get out of class, I guess at the same time as you, and I see you on my way to the gym," he said sitting squarely on the ground, legs sprawled into a vee.

"You have sort of a routine. You come out and brush away any misplaced foliage. You lay your bag on your left and pull out a book, a sandwich, and a bottle of water. It's strange though, because of all the days I've passed I don't think you've ever taken a bite," he laughed quietly reminiscing.

"Oh my, you're very observant," I said, afraid of my interruption to his playback.

"Oh, wow, so I hope I didn't just sound like a stalker."

"Goodness no. It's definitely okay. I think I'm just very predictable so it's not hard to pick up on my behaviors."

"I wouldn't consider you predictable. Strangely, amidst your routine there is an air of mystery that's quite captivating."

"Hmp. And you said I have a way with words. You are all too kind. That is a nice thing to say."

"It's not a thing to say. It's the truth," he said peering at me then quickly settling his eyes on the ground. "Anyway, you never told me, how have you been adjusting to life here at SMU?"

"Well, things have been really awesome. I love my classes. My classmates seem nice, and until today I didn't fear death by acorns," I said laughing quietly.

"Hey, if you're interested and you have some time, I'd love to show you some pockets of campus that are seldom seen. Only if you have time you know."

"I'd love that. You want, right now?"

"Oh, I wasn't. If you have time," he said, his eyes lighting ever so slightly awaiting my response.

"Sure. Let's see the sights."

I packed my belongings and re-set the foliage in its natural spot. Luca leaned down and offered his hand to help me rise. On my feet he didn't release me, so we continued hand-in-hand to the unusual and secret escapes SMU never knew it had.

***

"Jackson!" I called as I searched the house aimlessly for my brother. "Yo! Jaaaaaaccccccckkkkkkkkkssssssssoooooooonnnnnn!"

"WHAT?"

"Hi!"

"No. That is not all that you have to say when you've been violently bellowing my name for the past 20 minutes."

"20 minutes, really Jackson. Exaggeration, much?"

"Whatever. Whaddya want?"

"So I need some advice from a decent guy, and you're the best thing I've got," I asked as charmingly as possible, vehemently batting my eyes.

"MC, you know I don't help with guy issues. Besides you're more than a lost cause and I dunno why you're trying to get involved with a guy. You're probably going to transfer in another 3 months so it's practically pointless."

"First, sir, I'm not going to transfer again. I think I've

finally found my home," I commented with a timbre much more staid than my previous remarks.

"Secondly, don't think of it as helping me with guy issues, think of it as a sociological field experiment. You're helping me with research regarding those of your same gender. You're like my guide. My insider to understanding all that I am seeing in nature as it relates to men."

"I have absolutely no clue what you just said. Why do you always use so many words?" he looked at me quizzically wanting an actual answer.

"The first thing I can tell you about dudes – we don't care about the color of the sky or the smell of the air when you stepped outside this morning. Just give us the facts. Plain and simple."

"So glad you're going to help me."

"I never said I was going to he-"

"Right, so his name is Luca Bianchi," I quickly interrupted.

"Why does that name sound vaguely familiar?" Jackson asked simultaneously peeling a banana and scavenging in the refrigerator.

"It should. He said the two of you went to school together at some point."

"Okay? That totally doesn't help me, and right now his name isn't registering a whole lot in the database. Continue," he smacked.

"Can you please close your mouth?"

"Hey, if I'm helping you, I'm going to do it on my terms. Any other complaints and you can consider this sociological field guide a thing of the past. Got it?"

"Got it," I murmured. "Well, I just met him like a week ago. We'll say I ran into him on campus during my self-guided tour. Then I hung out with him for a couple of hours at this bookstore coffee shop he works at and then he walked me home. Okay, so today he found me reading under this tree –"

"Reading? Under a tree? MC, why are you such a

loser?"

"Shut up Jack! I'm not a loser. And I'd like to think he thought it was awesome of me to be immersed within the written word. So there," I said and stuck my tongue out at him.

"I don't care. Get to the good part."

"So he found me and then he offered to show me around campus to some little-known cool spots. And that's it."

"So, where's the question?"

"What does all of that mean?"

"What does what mean? You didn't tell me anything. You saw him once. Then you saw him again. What am I supposed to do with that?"

"Ugh," I huffed. "Jackson Antonio Cortes, what is the matter with you? You tell me that I give too many details, so I don't; now you say you don't have enough to tell me anything. I'm annoyed."

"I said to use that technique when conversing any other time. You're coming to me to examine a situation; duh you give me every minute detail. I thought you were supposed to be the smart one. I guess you and JJ are both one nugget short a 4-piece."

I spent 45 minutes describing my interactions that afternoon with Jackson. He told me that Luca definitely appeared into me, but that he wanted to do some reconnaissance work to see if he were a professional or pure in his intentions.

I started to see Luca on campus every day. On Tuesdays and Thursdays he would show me a new place on campus that was seemingly hidden from the world. Each one was more incredible than the one before it. Jackson and I made time to recap each Sunday during dinner clean-up and all of Luca's behaviors appeared to match with his words and according to Jackson he was showcasing genuine signs of interest and honorable motives.

I was falling hard – definitely in like. Not in love – quite yet.

From the Desk of _____Noe Cortes_____

May 28, 2010

So earlier I wrote, and I was deep in pensiveness. Thinking thoughts I've never thought before. I think honestly, I've always shied away from my wants and desires because to me they have never truly mattered. I've always wanted to make a difference in other peoples' lives and make sure that those around me and those I serve are happy and well that somewhere along the way I forgot that I may have needs and latent desires too. I guess I'm scared of what that means. I'm frightened of paying attention to that person that lives within — my id. I'm scared because what if she's much more selfish than I have grown to be? What if I can't control her? What if everything about her is the antithesis of everything that I have come and am known to be? What if?

I think my future goals will be centered more on me refusing to succumb to the fear-filling essence of the unknown that lives within me. I think today at brunch I'll see if Hayley and Harper can help make sure I don't backslide. I know I can be more than the sum of my parts. I just have to open my eyes and actually acknowledge **all** of my parts.

Comienza ahora. Vale!

Chapter 7

"You're gunna love this!" I hear Hayley say before I even make it into the restaurant.

"Good morning Hayley," I say kissing her cheek and leaning in to hug her before taking my seat. "What's up? What will I love?"

"Well, Connor –"

"I have arrived, so all is right with the world," Harper boasts as she does a slow spin showcasing her undoubtedly new black dress.

"Yes, ladies it is Roberto Cavalli, and yes, you can be envious. How is everyone doing today," she finally asks as she sits.

"Hayley was just about to tell me something I'm 'gunna love' and then you barged in, in your most ostentatious style," I say.

"Well grr, claw and scratch to you too," Harper responds.

"Oh geez, I'm sorry Harper. Hayley you want to tell your story now? I'll check my attitude before something else foul comes out of my mouth."

"If you're sure," Hayley hesitates until I give her a gentle nod to move forward.

"Well, like I was about to tell MC, Connor got us three tickets for Cirque du Soleil!" She wails to two almost blank stares.

"That's, just... Well, that's," I start.

"Who cares?!?" Harper finishes.

"What do you mean, who cares," Hayley asks folding her arms and burying her chin in her chest.

"Well, Hayley it's just that," I start again.

"When you start off with that 'you're gunna love this' business we naturally assume that we actually won't be able to believe what's going to come out of your mouth. Instead you *surprise* us with a non-surprise like tickets to Cirque," Harper begins her cross examination looking inquisitively, almost accusingly between Hayley and me.

"Hay, we've been talking about going to their show for the past two months, and you said that Connor probably got an arts and education discount on account of he's a teacher. So forgive me for not being exactly ecstatic over this announcement. This was planned," she finishes.

"Hay, are you okay?" I ask after Harper's ever eloquent closing argument.

She has such a harsh way with words knowing that Hayley is softer than an over ripened banana.

"I'm fine," Hayley replies tersely.

"Hayley, really, I don't think Harper meant what she said as harsh as you may have heard it. It's just because we all speak so frequently and this has been a big topic of discussion, we weren't as surprised by this announcement as we were expecting to be. But we're super excited that Connor was able to support our girls' nights," I offer, my voice squeaking subtly.

"Thanks MC for trying to make it better. Harper, you don't always have to go lawyer mode you know. You *can* humor me every once in a while."

"Right, I'll think about that the next time you prepare me for spectacularly unforeseen information and deliver lackluster and understood news. Duly noted," Harper responded with a half-smile to follow her less than necessary pedantic sarcasm.

"Okay, now that that's all said and done, thank you again Hayley. We're stoked about our night together. Everybody, high-low. Harper, you first," I hurriedly try to move the conversation.

"Alright, well my high is definitely this new Cavalli ensemble. I bought it with my bonus."

"How'd you get a bonus in June? I thought it was an annual thing. What kind of system is that?" Hayley asks.

"Oh, it's not so much a bonus as much as it was my winnings from an office pool. Goodness I am good at what I do."

"Okay, I am going to save Hayley the trouble of asking you to clarify that terribly vague response and just ask you to continue with your high or proceed on to your low."

"Whatever MC. You're using too many words. That's all for my high. And the high leads me right into my low. So our office pool was about the players from the D-League that were going to move into the NBA. I won because the idiots in my office have no clue about anything related to the game of basketball or sports in general," she sighs. "I need to be out of this space. I should be with real colleagues and in a place where people know just as much about their clients' career field as they do the law," she adds throwing her hands up in mild ire.

"Harper, I thought you had a contact that you were working with to move you beyond where you are," I state rather quizzically.

"Right, Gutten-pretty eyes or something like that," Hayley adds.

"His name is Güttenpris, pronounced goo-ten-pre-uhs, not gutten pretty eyes. It is German," she informs. "And unfortunately I learned that my lead was contingent upon me using my feminine wiles to make a very pleasured Güttenpris so I had to decline."

"Oh," Hayley gasps with the force of a tornadic gale wind, lifting her chubby cherub fingers to her mouth.

"Harper, I'm so sorry. I know you're trying to get somewhere you can feel appreciated. It'll come. I just know it will," I try at consoling her.

While Harper acts all tough and mean, and she often times uses her Brazilian sensuality to get her out of situations and sometimes into situations, I have learned that when it comes to her work and her intelligence she feels hurt by the world that only sees her for her lady parts.

"This I know. Such is life. Hayley you're up next," Harper chimes.

"Well, I already gave my high. I was so excited that Connor got us the tickets. But oh, I also found a new knitting pattern and that was definitely a high. Oh gosh," she continues almost jumping out of her seat

"And I think for summer vacation I'm going to spend at least a week at an adult – knit – camp complete with famous instructors and a jamboree at the closing ceremony. Oh yeah!"

Hayley says putting on her rapper face as she leans to the side a little bit, bobs her head up and down, her eyes squinty, puckers her lips and does this weird roof raising motion.

"Harper, spare us," I snap quickly. She always likes to rain all over any of Hayley's parades. Sometimes she can really be a Hayley hater. "Hayley, what's your low?" I try to move the conversation.

"Oh gosh. Wait, what's the rule again? How many highs to how many lows?"

"Hayley, you ask this all the time and you know that you're going to have to give a low. That's just how it goes. You can have as many highs as you want, and we give you those freely, but you have to have at least one low. It's just natural. You can only have one low because aside from that it's considered excessive and pessimistic," I say.

"Right. So my low," Hayley repeats clearly stalling.

"And you can't use part of your high in your low," Harper adds.

"Wait. Huh? Didn't you do that Harper," Hayley asks.

"Well, technically, but not like you always do. You said your high was about finding a new knitting pattern and then you'll turn around and say that your low is you haven't started it yet. That doesn't count," Harper barks.

"Why not," Hayley asks defensively, clearly wanting to use that as her low.

"You know why not, don't act all doey with me," Harper retorts.

"I dunno what you're talking about. And, **doey** is not a word for your information," Hayley says.

"Doey: of or like a doe; dumb. There, straight from Harper's dictionary. If you want to see the entry, look in the mirror, your picture describes it perfectly."

"Ladies, to your corners. Hayley what's gotten into you? This is usually me and Harper," I proffer.

Usually it's Harper and me that fight like cats and dogs. It's strangely how we make sense of our world. Seeing Harper and Hayley exchange words is truly abnormal. They are categorically opposite, and I guess today their differences have them repelling like magnets.

Harper is undeniably hard and sometimes callous, and Hayley is sweet and charming. Harper wants some of that, but she's afraid to embrace it for fear of how it could taint her image in the corporate world. Hayley likewise wants to be tougher, but she cares too much about how people perceive her.

"My low, if I must have one, is I'm on the next 2 weekends at work and I'm not excited. I agreed to volunteer some time in the ICU and now it's turning into a bad idea. Eek. I feel bad for saying that," she finishes returning to her usual joviality.

"Hayley don't feel bad. That's your truth. You're fine," I say.

"I guess. Um, ok, it's your turn MC. You go."

"Well my high is that I have a new perspective on life, and my low is that I am thoroughly confused about life," I say with a questionable smile.

"So, this means what exactly to the normal human adult?" Harper asks.

"Well, okay, so it's like this," I start and briefly describe the lunch with Matias, my breakdown, and my impromptu visit to Dr. Logan.

"So what you're telling us is that you're crazy and you want us to keep tabs on you so that you don't go too far and end up in an asylum?" Harper says.

"Really, Harper of all I told you that's what your assessment of the situation is?"

"Pay her no mind MC," Hayley starts. "I think it's very noble of you to decide that you want to learn more about yourself. Does this mean that you're going to go to school again?"

"No, I'm not going back to school," I frown.

"Thank goodness. This whole finding yourself in academia is getting pretty old anyway."

"Thank you for telling me how you really feel Harper. Also, thank you so much for sparing my feelings," I say sarcastically. "But no, I'm not going to make a sharp turn this time, I'm going to yield a bit and really pay attention to the way the traffic is flowing so I know which way to go and when. I don't know exactly how to do that yet, but I want everyone to know so that we can work on me together."

"I'm totally in," Hayley obliges sprightly.

"I'll await the contract before I appease you," Harper says unsympathetically.

"Glad you're all on board."

We ordered our regular, a pitcher of margaritas, grapes and crepes, and we continued our friendly chatter about new guys in our lives, which really meant Harper told us the explicit details of her less than fulfilling sexual escapades. Hayley updated us on her and Connor's boringly appealing courtship and I tried to shy away from the mounting feelings I have for Matias.

***

"Dr. Logan, today is a good day."

"Is it? What is making it so?"

"I'm ready to take this seriously. To be very honest I've been avoiding most, if not all talk about me. Please tell me you didn't know this."

"Noe, I –"

"Lie to me! Or better yet, don't say anything. I'll just finish."

"Humph. Okay?"

"Right, so I'm ready to dive into my head. Or rather, I'm ready to open up my head to you. I pay you a lot you know, so you should've probably been in here already, but we won't discuss the why, we'll just go ahead and move forward now. Are you ready?" I ask with wide eyes and a jovial tone.

"As ready as I'll ever be, I suppose," he murmurs. "But before we begin, since you're running this session, do you need me to sit anywhere special? Are you going to let me know what things I should take notes on? I need to know where we are," he says with a smirk and a wink.

"Don't be a jackass Dr. Logan. I'm just saying that I am an open book and I no longer have my mur de la résistance up. So let's go. Woo!" I cheer and sit upright at the edge of the couch.

"Okay, well welcome to treatment Ms. Cortes, so nice of you to finally join me. Before we can get to your prosperous future, we have to I'm afraid re-visit some elements of your past. One of the best ways to understand our current condition is to examine the path we took to get here. Is that ok?" he asks sounding much like a flight attendant.

"Proceed," I say hesitantly and slump a little into the couch.

"We don't even have to go back that far. Let's just re-assess the last time we shared each other's company," he starts returning to his own voice.

As he does, I can feel my palms getting sweaty and massive beads of sweat forming along my brow.

"You'd come in a little distraught and uneasy about a lunch with your supervisor," he continues.

Just having him re-cap causes my saliva to dry, forms a large mass in my throat, and blurs my vision.

"Are you ready to take over the story?" he asks.

"I think so. Being with Matias that day threw me off balance," I croak.

"Good. Off balance how?"

"I prepared for the conversation to be strictly about work. I mean what average supervisor comes in and wants to discuss their employee's life passions?" I continue. "Work vision, career aspirations, and stuff like that, yes, but something so personal and intimate, I never thought to prepare for something like that."

"Okay, so he questioned you and you were thrown askew. Walk me through what came next. Internally, why did you shut down? What brought you to me?"

"Remember Dr. Logan how I said that the first time I met him he looked at me in a way that didn't sit well with me?"

"Yes, I remember," he says with a nod, not looking up from his notepad.

"Well, when he looks at me it's like he looks straight through me. Like deep to my core and he sees the parts of me that I reserve for myself. He sees the parts that aren't strong enough to stand alone and the parts that aren't nearly as developed and ironed as those that I readily show," I say rising a bit anxiously.

"Not everyone can do that. Actually most no one can do that. They see what I show them and they're perfectly fine with that," I add softer, lowering back to the couch.

"But not him?" Dr. Logan asks.

"No, not him. But here's the thing. He can see that the undeveloped side exists, but he can't really see all that it's made up of," I continue drawing up my legs and resting my chin on my knees.

"Instead he asks me to describe it for him. It freaks me out because aside from the fact that he shouldn't be able to see that part of me, I don't take much time to explore and define the areas within so it's difficult for me to say to him, to anyone, or even to myself that I don't know exactly what's going on in there myself. And his questioning makes me feel hurried and inadequate," I finish hastily, panting much like an asthmatic.

"Good job Noe. And when you were here, when you visited me, where were you then?" Dr. Logan asks excitedly.

"I was in a lot of different places with you Dr. Logan," I proceed coolly. "When I first got here, I was lost and confused. After I finally got my story out, I was calm, and by the time I snapped at you and Julia I was resolved to be a different and better me. Matias gave me this inadvertent push to introduce me to myself and I'm glad to know me, or at least I'm happy to be *getting* to know me."

"I like your optimism. Have you spent time deciding *how* you're going to get to know you?"

"Well, not exactly. I don't really know where to start. This is where you are supposed to help. Give me an assignment or something. I don't know where to go next"

"I think this is a good start. You're acknowledging that there is work to be done. The only assignment I can give you is to take this next week to spend some time with your thoughts. Confront those questions that instill fear in you. What is your passion? What brings you joy? Why does it bother you not to know? What about not knowing makes you anxious?" he recites using his hands to drive his message home.

"I know there are endless amounts of questions that make you feel on edge. Write them down and answer them aloud. Answer them aloud," Dr. Logan repeats looking me squarely in the eyes.

"I hear you," I whine looking down and staring at my feet.

"Answer them aloud and then and only then write down a couple of options for overcoming them. We'll discuss where you are with them next week when you come in. This will be a pretty extensive process, so be honest with yourself in knowing that nothing is going to happen quickly, and you may feel yourself want to run from whatever truths are revealed to you. That type of honesty will help you stay focused and it will help you reveal the most," he finishes rolling his chair back to his desk and starting to compose more notes.

"Okay Dr. Logan, I think I can do this. I have a question for you.".

"Yes?"

"In the office I have been able to avoid everybody because I was really bogged down with work. Tomorrow when I go back in…wha-…what will I do when Matias comes in to greet me?"

"Noe, this is an answer I cannot give you, and you know it. If you're working to confront fears, this will be the best time to start," he says dropping his pen and rolling back toward me in his chair.

"You can't prepare for everything. In times of distress just remember to breathe."

"Just breathe," I repeat.

Our session ends and I leave hoping to find solace on my walk home. All is serene and I honestly feel like I am on a good path, a work in progress.

From the Desk of _____Noe Cortes_____

May 29, 2010

Today I will construct my list of questions to answer as Dr. Logan instructed. I am more than definitely a work in progress, and this is the only way I can put all the pieces of my life together.

1.   What is your passion?

2.   What do you do that speaks to your soul?

3.   What wakes you up every day?

4.   How does it feel to say, "I don't know"? Why does it feel that way?

5.   What scares you about you?

6.   What scares you about releasing your parts to others?

I think that's all that I have for now. I'm sure there are a ton more inquiries that I should ask myself in search of myself, but this is somewhere to begin.

Here we go.

Chapter 8

"Tell me again, what brought you to SMU?"

"I've been in search of the perfect academic home for what feels like an eternity. I have been looking for somewhere that welcomes me as much as I embrace it and that naturally paves the road to my destiny," I said staring wildly into the distance.

"MC?"

"Yes," I asked looking at Luca to find him staring at me intensely.

"Who are you?" he asked.

"What do you mean?"

"I mean, the way you speak about pretty much every facet of life is unlike any person I've ever encountered. You're here in search of something that paves the road to your destiny?"

"I know that probably sounds flighty. My mom always tells me I'm too based in fairy tale. I'm working on that."

"No. Not flighty. And don't change a thing. You're refreshing. I love that about you."

"You do?" I asked uncertain whether he meant to say love in relation to me.

"I absolutely do," he confirmed. "In fact, I think that's one of the things I love most about you."

There it was again, that word – love. Twice in a row couldn't possibly be accidental. I didn't think.

"Well, I appreciate and love that you love that about me," I rambled fearing that I was developing a skin rash because of all the nervousness I was feeling.

"MC I –"

"What about you," I quickly asked unsure and frightened of what he was about to say, "Why are you here?"

"Oh, well I love the area and I know that the Psychology program here is good. I know it's not nearly as existentialistic as yours, but it's my story."

"Luca, don't rain on your own parade. I think your being here is pragmatic. It's sound; and it makes sense for you, which is all that matters."

"See, you did it again. Sounds so much better when you describe it than when I do," he said sliding closer to me on the bench we were sharing in the plaza outside the chapel.

"MC?"

"Yes?" I responded avoiding eye contact and expanding the space between us.

"Noe I - I've been meaning to talk to you about something," he said scooting closer to me.

"Sure, what's going on?" I asked glancing briefly at him before sliding to the furthest edge of the bench and peering again in the opposite direction.

"It's just that," he said closing the final gap between us, raising my chin, and turning my face toward him.

"We've been spending a lot of time together you and me. And I would be lying to the both of us if I didn't say that I really like it, and as you like to say, I appreciate you," he began cautiously. "Everything about you – the time you give me, your energy, your enthusiasm for life, has helped me see that I really want for all of you to be a more permanent and exclusive part of my life."

"Oh my goodness you scare me," I said gently dislodging my chin from his grasp.

"What? Why?" he asked genuinely disturbed.

"I don't know. Maybe it's all this premature honesty. Or maybe it's just I've never been so directly appreciated, that I don't even know what to say."

"MC," he said turning, pulling my legs across his and taking both my hands in his.

"If you'll have me, I'd love to be your boyfriend. You're the only thing that crosses my mind each day and though we've only just begun to learn each other these two months, I can already imagine an exceptionally long future with you."

"I –," I hesitated briefly to catch my breath.

"Now, please don't respond in haste. I know I've sprung this on you, and I know that you're methodical and you like to have time. But I just had to say it and so I said it."

"I –"

"It's your decision."

"I –"

"I don't want to pressure you."

"Luca," I snapped and grabbed his face with both my hands. "Shut up will you," I asked and released his face.

"It's just that, this is kind of serious, and I'm totally nervous because I don't know what you might say."

"Luca, of course I'll be your girlfriend. You speak my language indiscriminately and that's what I love most about *you*. I'm so glad to know that we're on the same page of the same book because I seriously can't get enough of you either."

I barely finished my last sentence before he brushed the hair from my eyes, cupped my face with each of his palms and planted the supplest caress upon my lips. It temporarily paralyzed me, and I felt like I was floating on air.

"Oh my gosh I love it when you talk. I love you," he said leaning slightly away from me, my face still in his hands.

"I, I love you too Luca," I said peering into his eyes as we sat quietly, longingly gazing at one another.

I looked away from him as I started crying ever slightly from our innocuous staring contest. Luca grabbed my face again and gently kissed where the tear'd started down my right check. He kissed my nose and then the freckle beneath my left eyelid. Most don't notice that freckle, so I gasped a bit at his discovery.

"You hungry?" he asked looking at me, distracting me with his unexpected inquiry.

"Starved."

"Shall we," he said as we stood. He led me down a

small path alongside the chapel to a quaint dinner setting. I couldn't believe how perfect it all seemed.

We dined alfresco. It was bliss from the pasta salad right to the very last drop of wine.

***

"You're gunna love this!" Hayley said as she always does, welcoming us to our once a month girls' brunch.

"Good morning Hayley," I responded leaning in to hug her and kiss her cheek before taking my seat. "Thanks for ordering the lemonades. I'm dying of thirst. What's up? What will I love?"

"Well–"

"I have arrived, so all is right with the world," Harper egotistically boasted as she walked in – late as usual, wearing something new and overpriced.

"Yes, ladies it is from Express which will one day be Carolina Herrera, and yes, you can be envious. How is everyone doing today," she finally asked as she joined us at the table.

"All hail Queen Harper. You're late my friend. You almost missed a most important memo from Hayley," I said.

"Oh, well that sounds to me like I'm right on time then. Almost isn't missing is it? So we're good," Harper responded. Full of witty yet plausible rationalizations and she wasn't even in law school yet.

"I apologize on Harper's behalf," I said to Hayley. "Please, tell your story now. We're really eager to hear it."

"If you're sure," Hayley hesitated briefly until Harper fluttered her hand encouraging her to move forward. "Well, like I was about to tell MC, I got my first choice in clinicals!" She wailed to two almost blank stares.

"That's just... Well, that's," I started.

"We already knew you would, Hayley!" Harper

closed my sentence with a hint of annoyance.

"What do you mean, you already knew?" Hayley asked fidgeting in her purse searching for her needle and yarn, like any nervous knitter would.

"Hay, you can't possibly be that dense. You always get As, and didn't your advisor tell you that she was almost certain that you were going to get matched with your first pick; she just couldn't tell you formally? Right?"

"That's technically what she said Harper. But she said *almost* certain. Not certain, certain," Hayley retorted.

"Well, surprise or not, we're both happy for you and we're glad that you are sharing this great and special news with us. Aren't we Harper?" I growled and pinched her arm.

"Okay," she yelled jerking her arm from my clutches. "That's really, really, almost insanely –"

I held up my pinching fingers threatening Harper.

"– great Hayley. You know I bruise easily MC," Harper finished through gritted teeth.

"Okay, now that that's all said and done, everybody, high-low. Harper, you first," I chided.

"Aside from my new ensemble, I just got my LSAT scores back. Drum roll please."

"Brrrrrrrrr," Hayley hummed as I pounded on the table.

"176. Wah-kish," Harper sounded as she snapped her imaginary whip on the side of the table. "I made that test my bitch."

"Harper! Your language!" Hayley piped.

"Hay, I'm sorry for stinging your virgin ears. I felt it was appropriate considering."

"That is just fantastic news Harper. We knew you could do it. So when are all your applications due?" I asked.

"Now that my scores are in, I can go ahead and submit all of the applications. Columbia, Yale, and my fall back, SMU. All due by December one. They'll be in before Thanksgiving. I'm prepared. I know."

"Awesome. Okay, what's your low?" I added.

"Well, my low is Bradley Cooper look-a-like is no more. Large sigh."

"I thought he was the perfect guy. Cute and stupid," Hayley laughed and snorted quietly in between chortles.

"Good one Hayley," I said. "What happened Harper? It's been what, two weeks? I thought he was going to make it."

"No, he got clingy and boring and was all like, be my girlfriend and meet my mom. Eew, no. I have a lot of life to live and I'm not going to waste it on a cute face and a teeny-weeny brain. Besides, graduation is fast approaching. That whole college love thing doesn't work."

"Oh no," Hayley gasped.

Hayley'd been with her boyfriend Connor since second semester of our first year. He was in love with her. They got giddy just holding hands. They were the cutest things.

"Not for you Hayley. She means for others who are man-eaters like her," I said through gritted teeth.

"You and Connor are definitely going to go the distance. He's smitten with you," I added, afraid that Harper's obsessive pessimism would cause Hayley a panic attack.

"Right, not you Hay. You and Connor are good as gold," she said offering a cheeky smile.

"Hayley, it's your turn."

"Well, my high was about first choice for clinicals. But oh, I also found out that my knitting club for nurses has an alumni branch and that was definitely a high. Oh, gosh and I think for Thanksgiving Connor and I are going to do a blended approach with both our families. Oh yeah!" Hayley said nearly jumping out of her seat with each new piece of good news.

"Harper spare us," I snapped quickly to stop her from retorting some snide comment. "Hayley, what's your low?" I worked to move the conversation.

"Oh gosh. Wait, what's the rule again? How many highs to how many lows?"

"Hayley, you ask this every time and you know the rule. You know that you're going to have to give a low. That's just how it goes. You can have as many highs as you want, and we let that happen – against my better judgment, but you have to have at least one low. So quit stalling and get on with it," Harper bayed.

"I just like being cheerful," Hayley murmured. "Right, so my low, if I have to give one, is that because I got my number 1 choice for clinicals then my good friend Hilary couldn't get it so she's sad."

"Who cares?" Harper bluntly asked.

"What do you mean, who cares?" Hayley asked concerned.

"Well, Hayley it's just that…" I started.

"Why would you be sad that you worked your ass off for the top clinical spot and you got it and the girl who puts the duh in dumb got whatever she deserved?" Harper responded gruffly.

"That doesn't make sense Hay. You should be freaking ecstatic because you're freaking awesome. Not wasting a low on some loser."

"Hayley, it's weird that I'm saying this," I started, "but Harper makes a lot of sense."

"Thank you," Harper nodded in my direction.

"You should feel good about your hard work and not let it be soiled by someone who didn't work nearly as hard as you have."

"I guess," Hayley answered coyly, barely making eye contact with either of us.

"Hay, we're only saying this because we love you and we want you to be happy for your successes. It's okay to be bummed that another friend didn't get what they'd hoped, but don't belittle your accomplishments on their behalf. It's not fair to you," I added.

"Um, okay, it's your turn MC. You go," Hayley

responded guiding the conversation away from her.

"Are you sure?" I asked in disbelief that that portion of our conversation would be over so quickly.

"Geez, oh peet. I didn't mean to cause a stir. It's really okay. When you agree with Harper it scares me a little. But I'm sure, MC it's your turn."

"Well my high is that yesterday Luca asked me to be his girlfriend," I said quickly before chugging my now watered-down lemonade.

"SHUT THE FU –"

"Harper!" Hayley snapped. "That is so wonderful. I could just- I could just-. Oh gosh now I'm crying. How'd it happen?" Hayley asked fanning her eyes to stave off the already falling tears.

"Okay, so it's like this," I started and described in detail the moments on the bench with Luca, my nervousness and confessions about the fear that he incites and the dinner he had planned.

"So what you're telling us is that against my better judgment you're going to continue seeing this kid?" Harper asked starkly.

"Really Harper I can't believe you're still on this? Did you not hear what he said to me? He told me he loved me."

"Yeah Harper," Hayley started. "Guys who are up to no good don't say the l-word. It scares them."

"No Hayley, my naïve friend, that's exactly what the bad guy does. He disarms you with phrases like "I love you" and "I see you in my future" so ultimately when you are completely open they can rob you of your treasure and move on to the next unsuspecting victim," Harper prophesied.

"Harper, I appreciate your concern for my well-being, but I don't think you have anything to worry about. This whole, something's not right with Luca is getting a bit old," I said using an eerie voice and waving my arms about.

"You don't know him. He's done nothing but adore

101

me since I met him, and when he met y'all our time went swimmingly well."

"She's right Harper," Hayley added cleaning her face from her quick cry. "You are doing an awful injustice to him considering we don't really know him that well. He clearly cares about MC so we should be happy for that. Besides love is so absolutely wonderful," she finished hugging herself.

"I think that speaks volumes," Harper said coldly. "Why is it that he has only been in our company once when he claims he sees a future with MC? Does he not know we're a package deal? What about his friends? Does he have friends? Have you met them? Have you heard of them?" she looked to Hayley for responses.

"If he were truly invested in her life, he'd want to show her off to his friends and he'd not only spend time with her, but also with us and her family too. MC, have your parents met or even heard of Luca?" Harper asked accusingly turning back to me.

"Not exactly, but that's because -"

"That's because you're ashamed of him or something is awry," she interrupted. "It's been two months and you're telling me that you haven't had time to alert your 'rents. You go home every Sunday MC. Give me a better lie than that."

"You didn't even let me finish," I said.

"Right, but you're not arguing with me because you know I know you well enough to know what falsities you were going to pull."

"Harper, you're being way too harsh on her. Now that it's official I'm sure that it will be more natural to bring Luca to more things," Hayley spoke cautiously.

"We'll see him when we come to town and I'm sure he'll get involved with the family in some way. Right, MC. You were just waiting on timing, right?" Hayley asked hopefully.

"That's so right. Just waiting to see where we were

going, that's all. Now our two worlds can merge," I responded softly, lost in Harper's convictions.

I sat in vacancy thinking to myself. Asking myself: Was I really omitting my and Luca's world from the actual world I live in? Was there something fundamentally wrong with our friendship or our new relationship; with me or with him, that I wasn't acknowledging? I hated when the things Harper said resonated with me in a way that I didn't understand. They're always telling, and I'd learned that when I walk antagonistic to them, I always end up telling her she was right, and I was wrong. And on this I didn't want to be wrong.

"We always get so worked up over the smallest things. This is a joyous occasion, we all have wonderful highs," Hayley sang attempting to brighten the mood. "MC, I hate to ask, but they're your rules —"

"What's your low," Harper growled.

"Oh, my low," I whispered, searching for a low aside from the blaringly obvious one that my best friend is in opposition to my newfound love. "I lost 3 chap sticks this week. I'm starting to think there's a lip balm thief in my midst," I finish with a small forced smile.

"It's not that I want you to be unhappy MC," Harper started not looking at me. "It's that I care too much about you to shut my mouth when I have an inkling. You know in 'Valentine's Day' when Jessica Alba gives Ashton Kutcher his ring back?" she closed nudging my arm.

I nodded yes.

"Then Ashton talks to George Lopez and got mad at GLo because GLo said that he knew it would happen because he had an 'inkling'? You remember?"

"Yes, I remember," I answered.

"Well I just didn't want it to get to that point where the inevitable happens and we fight because I kept my inkling. So I apologize for being harsh, but I'm your friend. I'm supposed to tell you these things."

"Thank you, Harper. And I'm not mad because of

your message delivery. You're Harper; scathing is your second middle name. I was saddened because I don't know where to go from here. I know I can't erase the feelings you have about Luca. I don't know where they came from, and if I knew I'm not even sure it would matter," I began peering down at my hands, tracing the path of my veins with my fingers.

"But I think as my friend in addition to looking out for me you're also supposed to support me," looking up with more confidence I continued.

"If at the end of the day you're right about Luca I will be angry with myself for not listening, but if he does turn out to be a gem and I dismiss him because of your feelings I'd harbor resentment toward you. I love you too, and I'm so glad that you're my friend," I said grabbing hold of her hand on the table.

"Me too," Hayley blubbered crying again and leaning in to engulf Harper and me in a group hug.

"Alright, enough of this sentimentality," Harper said releasing my hand from her clutches and tying her hair into a bun. "Let's drink and dish about something else. When's the shopping and what movie are we seeing tonight?"

We ordered another pitcher of lemonade, some grapes and crepes, and we continued our friendly chatter about the new films at the Cineplex. Hayley and Harper talked about graduation weekend plans and I figured out where I was staying and when. I tried to push out of my mind any thoughts of my failing fledgling relationship with Luca. It was too perfect to already be doomed.

From the Desk of _____ Noe Cortes

May 30, 2010

If I'm at all serious about this plan of mine I have to tackle at least one of my questions. My questions force me to confront me and grow stronger and more confident in me, and I need all the strength and confidence I can get.

- What scares you about releasing your parts to others?

I am scared they will reject what they see, and I might not be strong enough to pick up the pieces afterward. That's crazy I'm sure and it's really stressful. I know it's an implausible fear so that should help me move forward, but then, what if it's not. What if I'm actually onto something and people are inherently terrible and when they learn you, they are actually seeking to find out information about you to use against you in the event that you wrong them or they use it to judge you so harshly that you'll feel so terrible being yourself.

Stop thinking MC. Just stop thinking. Try it again.

I am scared they will reject what they see, and I might not be strong enough to pick up the pieces. I'm also scared that *I* haven't completely discovered all the parts of me. I don't know me yet. I think that scares me **more**. And discovering myself **with** other people is a separate concept. What if we both don't like me. Then what? What if they like me but I don't? There are so many more questions to answer and so much more that's in the air. So much more spontaneity required that the parts of me that I definitely know are not ready for. Can't do this anymore. My brain is on fire. Dr. Pepper and a nap. That's what the doctor ordered.

Tomorrow is Monday and I will have to come face to face with the immutable truth that I am not only attracted to my boss, but I'm attracted to and frightened by the controlessness he makes me feel. This is the truth and I have an inkling if I don't address it here in my own space I will fall apart again tomorrow when I have no safety from my work.

Chapter 9

To: "MC Cortes"<noe.cortes@tic.edu>
From: "TIC ITS"<its@tic.edu>
Subject: Your password will expire in 27 days

** IMPORTANT NOTICE ** ACTION REQUIRED **
This message is from the Texas International College Department of Information and Technology Services.

Noe Cortes –

This note is to let you know that your password is about to expire. Your current password will expire in **27 days, on 2010 – 06 – 24.** If you allow your password to expire you will not be able to receive email or access institutional systems.

To change your password, please visit the ITS homepage at www.tic.edu/its/password/.

If you have any questions, please contact the ITS Help Desk at 214.828.1029. Sincerely,

Your ITS Team
Next...

To: "MC Cortes"<noe.cortes@tic.edu>
From: "Hayley Martin"<hayleym@baylorhealth.net>
Subject: I had this thought this morning of you and I wanted to check on you.

MC,

I had this thought this morning of you and I wanted to check on you. It was weird. I was having a dream about peanut butter and jelly and then I saw a flash of you sitting on the edge of a bridge, drinking a Dr. Pepper, and dangling your legs. I'm no dream interpreter, but I can't imagine that dream means good things are a coming. Please call me and let me know if you're up to any bridge dangling this week.

Hugs, Hayley

Hayley is so special. I'll call her after work to assure her that I don't plan on jumping off any bridges any time soon. I wonder what's up with the peanut butter and jelly.

To: "MC Cortes"<noe.cortes@tic.edu>
From: "Ricardo Cortes"<rcortes@gmail.com>
Subject: Have a good day

I love you…
…con todo mi corazón.

This makes me want to call him. I've been at work nearly a half an hour and I can't manage to wake up. I know that all will be better just hearing my dad's voice. "Bueno."

"Buenas mamá, puedo hablar con papá?"

"Well, good morning to you too my daughter. I'm so glad that I haven't seen you in so long and the first thing you want to do is to speak with your father," my mother says bitterly.

"Mama, you know it's not like that. I have a specific question for him, so I wanted to – you know what? I'm sorry mama for being so disrespectful. How are you? I am planning to come by for Sunday dinner this week."

"I know you prefer your father. Your mother is doing well. This year we have some great talent at the studio. You really should think again about doing a Master Class with the level threes," mama says.

"Mama, I promise I'll consider doing a master class. Let me know when you're thinking and I'll see if it fits in my schedule," I say avoiding her pointed commentary regarding my relationship with my father. I hate when she does that.

"Okay, I will chat with you when I see you Sunday for church about the girls and the Master Class. Let me go get your father. Ric!"

I hear my mother call out to my dad and think through all the new expectations of me, knowing I'll never hear the end of it if they don't happen.

"Buenas mi amorcita," my father answers.

He's the only one who can call me sweetheart without sounding condescending.

"¿Papí, cómo te sientes?"

"I am doing well, my love. Pero tú, ¿Cómo te sientes, tú? Why the call today?"

"Nothing. Why does something have to be wrong?"

"Noe," my dad calls knowingly, "I know you. I can hear it in your voice, and I know that something is going on with my little girl."

"Dad, really… I'm fine. I got your email and wanted to hear your voice.

"I love you too, my darling," my dad obliges knowing as much as I do, that I'm withholding some truth.

"Okay, well I just got to the office," I say, though I've been at work for the past 20 minutes.

"I'll see you Sunday when I come for church and dinner."

"Your mother will be very pleased to have all of her children at church. You're doing a good thing. Te amo con todo mi corazón."

"I love you too papí."

I deposit my phone in my drawer and lower my head to my desk. Today is the day I face my fears. I will face them, and I won't be scared. I will. I must. If nothing else, I will definitely breathe.

"Good morning sunshine!" Joyce calls out welcoming me.

"Hi," I say, quickly lifting my head from its perch on

my desk and splashing on the most palpable fake smile I can muster.

"How was your weekend? Have you been able to rest? I know you've been super busy. I've barely seen you," Joyce jabbers quickly.

"Oh, well, you're right. I have been bogged down a bit with lots of case files. I've barely seen myself," I laugh coyly.

"Well dear, Matias wants to have another staff lunch. I put it on your calendar, but I wanted to make sure you got the memo personally."

I can feel myself disengaging from the conversation at the mention of Matias.

"Are you sure you're doing okay?" she asks.

"Joyce, that sounds just wonderful. I've just about completed my cases, so this is actually quite perfect. Just…. perfect. Lunch it is."

"Well…I'll come for you when the food arrives. Don't work too hard. I'm starting to miss your spirit," Joyce finishes before backing out of my office and returning to her morning duties.

Have I really lost my spirit? Have I let so much overcome me that I am not being myself? I work steadily much of the morning, listening to a strange mixture of Adele, Justin Timberlake, John Mayer, and Jay-Z. I'm not sure how they all fit together, but I am definitely in my groove. I am so far gone and relaxed that I don't even hear when I'm called to lunch.

"MC?"

"Yes," I say looking up puzzled by the newfound bass in Joyce's voice. "Oh…Matias! You startled me."

"Did I? You startle quite feebly," he says with a wink and sparkle in his eyes.

"Well, maybe startle isn't quite the word I meant. You did take me by surprise. I was expecting Joyce."

"Ow-were Joyce is afar bouncing as the bee setting the table for the lunch feast."

"Right. I am ready, if we're only waiting on me," I say preparing to stand as Matias moves briskly toward my desk. "But of course I could stay," I add, mid-stand, slightly alarmed by his sudden movements.

"It is just, I wanted to speak with you," he says inching his hand nearer mine on my desk. "Just a quick moment prior to lunch," he continues this time brushing my hand ever slightly as he adjusts his glasses and returns his hand, so our pinkies embrace slightly.

Still mid-stand, I get absorbed in him and say nothing. I say absolutely nothing. I just stare at him – unafraid – staring and staring more.

"MC?" Matias calls moving his hand to my left shoulder jarring me from my trance.

"Yes. Oh, yes. You wanted to speak with me," I respond as we both rise with eyes still locked.

"Yes. It is just, I – what beverage would you like with your lunch today?"

His hesitancy disconnects us, and I am finally able to walk from behind my desk. Next to him I say, "Dr. Pepper please," and leave him still standing as I head toward our break room.

Can he feel what I feel? Could he be inexplicably paralyzed by even the thought of conversation with me, just as I am with him? Impossible. He's Matias. He's worldly, and, and, and Spanish. He could never get discombobulated by me.

"Hi hun," Joyce practically shouts as I round the corner into the break room. "I was about to eat without the two of you. Where's Matias?"

"Oh, he's just getting us some bever – uh, something to drink. I love how you have the table set. It makes us look like a family."

"I agree," Matias says entering with my and Joyce's drinks.

"Wow, you're fast. What about you? What will you be drinking?"

"Me? Oh, I have. I had. I see."

"It's okay," I laugh. "It happens to the best of us. Always the best intentions, but sometimes that memory gets the best of us all. What would you like? I'll fetch it for you."

"Pues, gracias. I'll have a Pelligrino."

"You're more than welcome," I respond with a small nod. "One sparkling water coming up."

Lunch progresses smoothly and Joyce has a ball using her newest Spanish words 'brillante' and 'maravillosa'. With her, everything was doubly awesome. Matias appears rather contemplative throughout our dining session. He grins every now and again, but something in his eyes shows that he's lost in thought, which in our short time together I've gathered is a feeling even he isn't used to experiencing. Joyce doesn't seem to notice, so I work on not drawing any attention to it and after cleaning I move to my office and work silently until the close of the day.

"G'night hun. Please don't stay here too much longer," Joyce rings as she heads toward the door with her work luggage in tow.

"Oh, and grab Matias too. I saw him frown today, and you know how I feel about frowns. He's only just moved into our space. We have to help him maintain his sanity."

"No job is ever worth permanent markings in your face," we say simultaneously.

"That's right. He's working too hard," Joyce grins.

"Have a good evening Joyce," I giggle thinking about Matias' frown. "I will rescue him from hard work, and I'll make sure I get out of here too."

"You're maravillosa MC!"

"Buen pronunciación Joyce," I respond, "And really, you're más brillante because you noticed that Matias needs saving. I'll see you tomorrow."

"Hasta mañana," she says hugging me and departing.

I walk discretely down the hallway to just outside Matias' door. I can't help but watch and observe him in his natural habitat – sitting squarely at his desk, hair tousled but perfect, an unsharpened number 2 pencil nestled behind his right ear, a mechanical pencil dangling between his teeth, and a black RSVP pen amidst his death grip hoisted above a stack of papers. The stress frown Joyce spoke of is tattooed across his brow as he stares too intensely at the information sprawled atop his desk.

"Anything I can help with," I ask, rapping softly and walking just beyond the threshold.

"Joyce?" he calls, loosing the pencil from his mouth as it closes into a smile.

"No, 'tis I MC. I have come to rescue thee from whatever perils you're facing. I come at the behest of your surrogate caretaker – Joyce," I say gallantly walking further into his office.

"How nice of her to think of me, and how much better of you to come to my aid."

"It's quitting time in case you didn't know. We have a strict policy that no one stays past 5:00 pm and no one frowns. And my good sir you are guilty of both."

"I think that may have been one of the few things you left out of my orientation," he says, smiling bigger, beginning to stack his papers.

"I try to be thorough, but sometimes even I mess up. Can I help you with anything?" I ask as I make my way to his desk.

"If you are sure," he says pausing to search my eyes for truth. "I need to just put those books back and then I'm done here. I promise it."

"I am sure. And never fear, I am an excellent shelver," I wink, grabbing all but one of the books from his desktop.

I make my way around his office rather quietly, moving swiftly from shelf to shelf. If I were thinking, I would've alphabetized them before I started, but nonetheless I accomplish my task.

"This last one goes with that one," I hear Matias say before turning and finding myself standing directly in front of him – my nose inches away from his pectoral muscles.

Ebonii Nelson

"I – yes, it appears it does," I say leaning as far back as I can to read the book and create some space between the two of us.

"I feel so useless when this is supposed to be my job. Can I help with this one?" he asks as he places his hand on a shelf just above my right eye to brace himself and leans into me to re- shelve the book.

I hold my breath trying not to give into the hedonistic urges I feel welling up inside me. I know in other countries that whole personal space thing is non-existent, but seriously, I can smell the conditioner in his hair, the soap from his hands, and the sweet-smelling cologne burrowed beneath his chin.

"So, um –" I start attempting to ease my way from between his arms.

"MC?" Matias asks sliding his arms down the shelves until they're like rope barriers corralling me amid them.

"Okay," I say, unable to make full eye contact with him because of the ultra- compromising position I find myself in.

"Look at me please," he asks sweetly.

"It's just, this…I mean…I…" I stammer before realizing how close we are, Matias relinquishes the wall of books and steps back.

"I apologize. I did not realize."

"It's okay, really. What can I help you with?" I say a little more relaxed now that breathing room has been restored.

"I wanted to apologize for the lunch that we shared last week. I did not mean to make you feel, uh, how do you say? ¿Incómodo o um, uncomfortability? ¿No?" He asks looking fearful that his message is not getting through.

"Entiendo. I understand."

"It is just… in you I see that you have an intensity, and ironically a timidity. I can tell that you have so much to give but you ration it carefully, and it intrigues me. So

114

sometimes I get overwhelmed and I want to learn all I can of you instantly, and I realize that that may be more abrasive than I intend."

"I –" I start, unable to fully collect my thoughts.

"It is…I am too much?" he sighs.

"Oh, goodness no. Can we sit?" I ask moving toward a bench he has on the wall adjacent to his bookshelves. "I don't think I've ever had anyone say such things to me, so I just needed a moment to translate all that you said."

"Have I far overstepped my boundaries?" he questions sitting so our knees to kiss.

"I don't know that I can honestly answer that question. Matias with you I am so nervous. You draw out of me parts of my psyche that I've never seen or explored and it's as if every time you need my words my mind skips a beat and I am unable to speak. Does any of that make any sense?"

"Yes, very much sense. It makes sense because at times I feel it too, and I don't know what to do with it. You, MC, you are different," he says, his accent heavy with clarity as he enunciates the word different with three syllables.

"I am?"

"Yes, and especial. So special that sometimes it is hard to ….MC?"

"Finish your thought," I plead.

"Not here. This, it is not the time. Do you think we might be able to try ow-were lunch another time? I would really like to learn more of you, this time without the virulence and vigor of ow-were last time together."

Just breathe.

"Let's."

"It is written."

Matias and I stand – him first, and with his left thumb and middle finger wrapped lightly around my left wrist, he guides me out of his office with the palm of his right hand against the small of my back. We silently saunter to the parking lot where he trails me to my car. He opens the car door for me, and I turn to him before sitting. No words are audible, but there's definitely dialogue being shared between our eyes, our wayward hands, and in the ways we moisten our lips. He takes a breath and I simultaneously close my eyes and feel him breathing in my tenor. He leans into me, places his lips at the crook of my mouth and kisses my left cheek. As he tears his lips from my face, I float into my seat. He closes my door and I place my hand on the window, palm flat signaling my departure.

From the Desk of _____Noe Cortes_____

June 3, 2010

I always find it interesting that the moment that you decide to create change in your life, the universe opens up and helps you achieve your goals. When I started this week, I focused on my first question to myself: what scares me most about releasing my parts to others. I talked it out and of course I revealed that a huge driving factor in my life is fear of acceptance, or not understanding, or of just something so different that I don't know how to grapple with it initially. Today I had an unprecedented experience with Matias. He revealed a side of him that reminds me of me in that he wasn't as collected as I imagined he always is. In his revelations I was also able to verbalize some internal anxieties I have with him and our shared time. We had quiet moments full of deafening information sharing and I don't know, but I think we're moving into a space most unbecoming of a supervisor and an employee...but I like it, and I think it's where we're **supposed** to go.

This self-discovery thing isn't so bad. I know I have so much farther to go, but from the start of things I think I may have recognized my counterpart in a one Matias Collado. I've never had someone speak to me using all of their body in ways that you can only dream of. The passion is there, I only hope I can maintain control of myself appropriately. Tomorrow we will share lunch once again. Only time will tell.

Chapter 10

"You've called."

"Jackson?"

"Yes, younger sister?"

"Who answers the phone like that? It's obvious I called."

"Did you call to nag?"

"No actually I called to talk to dad, so can you?"

"I suppose."

There were times when Jackson and I spoke that I knew we were made of the same genetic gunk. Then there were others, when I was certain that one of us was nothing of my mother and father. Which one it was is debatable.

"Ciao."

"JJ?"

"Yeah. MC, where've ya been? You're like a ghost. You missed my last game. I scored the winning goal – diving header for the win. They never saw it coming."

"JJ?"

"I'm getting so much better. Hey, you wanna help me go to the camp at Indiana?"

"Jamal Joaquin?"

"Seriously?" he asked annoyed.

"Sorry, I just wanted to get your attention. Why are you talking to me? Wait…no…that didn't come out right."

"It came out right," JJ answered still huffy.

"No, I'm serious. I meant, I asked Jack to put papí on the phone, so I wasn't expecting to hear your voice. I really do love speaking with you JJ. And you're right; I haven't been around like I should."

Frightened by his silence, I continue. "And, I don't know what a diving header is, but I know it's amazing and really hard to do. I don't know what I can do with the soccer camp, but that's not because I don't support, it's, it's, it's, because…"

"It's okay, MC. It's okay. I'll go get dad," he

119

grumbles deflated.

"Are you sure? I'm serious. I love you bud. I just put my big foot in my mouth, and you know…. this happens."

"MC, I'm serious too. I'm fine. You're fine. We're fine. I'll get dad."

"Love you."

"Quit being weird."

I never knew what to say with JJ. Even though Jackson and I fought incessantly, somewhere in our fighting we were actually having a quality conversation. With JJ I constantly said the wrong things and I always knew like he felt like I ignored him.

"Mi'ja?"

"Hi papí. How are you?"

"I'm doing well. How are you?"

"I'm fine."

"What's the matter?"

"Is it that obvious?" I asked confused as to how he always knew when I had something specific I wanted to talk to him about.

"I'm waiting."

"Well, I just have a question for you."

"Yes?" with continued quick responses to shorten my diffidence.

"Okay. What if…"

"No, what-ifs. Tell me Noe, what *is*?"

"Daddy, I feel so much pressure. You're making me nervous."

"How am I making you nervous?" he asked affronted. "Don't be nervous. Just tell me your story rather than another plausible story. This way I can help you instead of offer advice to a hypothetical young lady."

"Okay. I guess you're not making me nervous. It's the situation and I've never talked to you about this before, so I don't really know where to start."

"Why haven't I met this potential suitor?"

"First of all, who uses the phrase 'potential suitor',

and secondly, how could you possibly know it has anything
to do with a boy?"

"Mi'ja?"

"Alright. Yes! It's a boy. I like him a lot. And he told
me last week that he likes me too, and then I told Harper and
Hayley and Harper's all like, 'I have an inkling' and I'm
nervous that she might be right and I don't know what to
do," I said hastily.

"Should I listen to her? Should I listen to me? I
don't know what to do," I continued, getting lost in my
own thoughts and endless sets of questions.

"What is it that you want?"

"I don't know."

"Noe, what do you want? No one can tell you this
and no one can give you what you don't first identify."

"But daddy…"

"Why do you argue with me? I could go back and
forth with you, but we both know that it would not help.
What's your hesitation? Why don't you trust what's in your
heart?"

"Because it could be wrong. I could be wrong and
everyone else could be so right and then where will that
leave me?"

"It won't leave you anywhere. You will have pursued
a path that you really believed in, and there's never any
wrong in that."

"Papí you always make everything sound so easy –
so uncomplicated. But nothing ever is. How would it look if
Harper is right? How would I make it?"

"You'll make it. And again, what does it matter
whether or not Harper or Hayley are correct about how
things progress in your life? If it's something you truly
want, you should go after it. Haven't I always told you
that?"

"Yes," I answered meekly.

"And this boy, the one I will surely meet soon, he
makes you happy?"

"Yes."

"Y también, ¿te respeta?"

"Yes, he respects me."

"So where could the harm be in any of that?"

"I guess there is none."

"Alright so let's make sure I get acquainted with him sooner rather than later."

"Thanks dad."

"I'm serious about meeting him."

I laughed before adding, "I will make sure this meeting happens. I promise."

"Con todo mi corazón."

"Love you too dad. Bye."

I loved my dad, and as hard as I felt it was going to be to just go with the flow and completely follow my heart, I knew he was right. He was always right.

***

"Cucciola mia," Luca called kneeling down, kissing my cheek and sidling next to me as I sat beneath my tree.

"What does that mean," I asked with piqued interest unable to tear myself from the current paragraph I was reading."

"Do you really want to know?"

"Of course; why do you ask?"

"Well…" he began, fingering the pages of my book.

"Oh gosh, I'm so sorry," I said immediately closing my book and placing it on the ground. "I'm here now," I added leaning over to hug him.

"There she is," Luca added gaily. "I always get a little jealous when you are off in your worlds of fiction."

"No need to be jealous. I'm only ever in those worlds for a short time. You have me in yours for forever. So what does it mean?"

"Huh?"

"Cucciola mia. What is that?"

"Well…the English translation isn't awesome sounding."

"Okay…then don't give me the literal translation, give me your meaning."

"It means my love or my pet."

"Ah ha…como amor mio," I whispered to myself. "Luca?"

"Yeah."

"Never mind."

"No, ask me."

"How do you know it's a question?"

"Well…are you going to ask it?"

"What did your friends say about us becoming an item? Have you ever talked to your family about me? Do you think it's weird that we've only interacted with one another and not really included others in how our relationship has progressed?" I asked searching his face trepidatiously awaiting his response.

"Wow," he responded, a bit dumbfounded by the barrage of inquiries.

"See, that's why I wasn't going to ask," I huffed, folding my arms and burying my chin in my chest.

"No, no, no," he protested leaning into me, lifting my chin, and gently kissing my lips. "It was just a bit unexpected. I thought it was just one question; but it's not a problem."

"I don't want to force you to do anything you don't want to," I replied gazing apprehensively into his eyes.

"It's not a problem, I promise. I didn't ask my friends their opinion of us. I feel like this is our thing, so their commentary is unnecessary," he offered before gently laying his arm around my shoulder.

"I have mentioned you before to my family, and I hope that at some point you will meet them. They will love you. And no, I don't think it's weird that we've kept our relationship between us. It's about us, so who else should matter? Did I get to everything?" he closed giving my arm a slight squeeze and peering down at me.

'At some point.' 'Who else should matter.' Over and over again I replayed small bits of his response. 'At some point.' 'Who else should matter.' He was right, right? 'At some point.' 'Who else should matter.' But I wasn't certain. I could see Luca's mouth moving, but I couldn't lift myself from my catatonia. 'At some point.' 'Who else should matter.' What was I doing? I thought, and before I knew it tears began streaming down my face and all I could see was Harper's prophesy manifesting itself and it hurt to know that I'd been so blind to whatever harm Luca was going to bring to me.

"MC?" I finally heard Luca's troubled yell as he grabbed my shoulders and began shaking me gently.

My mouth opened, but I couldn't will the words to fall. The harder I tried to speak, the harder I cried, and the more Luca called out to me willing me from the dolor that was slowly overtaking me.

I cried for what felt like an eternity. Luca just pulled me into a loving embrace, rubbed my arm and let me release. At some point we fell asleep nestled in the security of the tree.

***

We slept until it started to rain, and we were jarred from our slumber. Alert, we got up and ran to his car and drove to Luca's apartment. He came around to open my door and covered my head with his jacket as he led us inside. We sat on the couch, still wet, and Luca looked at me searching for meaning in my eyes. I was still mute with angst so I couldn't ease his pain with an explanation.

"MC," he began, brushing hair from my face. "I want to help you, but I don't know how. You're frightening me and I don't know what to do with that. You're safe with me. Whatever it is that you need, I am willing to do; but you have to talk to me first."

"Are you sure," I whispered.

"You never have to ask that again. It is a permanent truth with us." I took his hands in mine and I started my story of the girls' brunch.

"Harper was just so upset that I hadn't included them or my family for that matter in our courtship and she said that it was telling of how I felt about our relationship subconsciously. And I don't know, something about what she said stuck and resonated so loudly with me that I started to question whether or not it was true."

"Meaning?"

"Well, Harper has known me since I was 10, and as introspective as I am there are certain things I don't notice until someone brings them to light. So what if what she's saying is a reality that I was immune to? Then what?"

"Do you honestly believe that?"

"I don't want to."

"But do you? Because if you do, if you have pause for concern then maybe we shouldn't…I don't even want to finish that statement because I don't want to give you ideas and I don't want that version of life."

"You think I'm totally crazy, don't you?"

"I don't. I just. I don't know. What do you want?"

"I love you Luca."

"So that's all that matters. It's the Noe & Luca show. If we're in this, no one else matters."

"I appreciate you so," I said leaning into him.

We shared a hug before pulled away a bit to examine me. He took my face into his hands, kissed the freckle beneath my left eye, before tracing a line of tears on my face to my lips.

***

I hoped Harper's prophesy would be the first and last big scare that Luca and I had. After that day I started working

125

really hard not to let the fear of the unknown prevent me from pursuing and enjoying my present and things that I desired.

Being fearless meant taking him home to meet my mother and father, a contender for our next big hurdle. Mama was of course displeased by the sight of Luca. She barely said much to him. With her it was,

"Are you aware of Noe's life plans?" and "Are you prepared to allow her to concentrate on her studies without interfering with the path she must take in order to be successful?"

"I am well aware of what MC, or Noe, I apologize," he quickly amended, noticing my mom's raised eyebrows. "I know what she is capable of, and I only have plans to support her in any way that I can," he responded, unwavering and unafraid.

My papí was a little more subtle, and he really wanted to learn more about Luca and his personal goals.

"How do you envision your life over the next 3 years? What will you do upon graduation?"

"When I finish my schooling, I will be a Licensed Professional Counselor and I hope to use my current internship to gain employment at a marriage and family center. My family is here so I plan to stay in the area, and I'm confident that these plans will not change," Luca said calmly speaking pointedly and clearly.

Meeting Jackson and JJ was anticlimactic. I almost wished that I would've omitted it altogether.

"So are you using MC here for her body? As a sexual pawn? Or are there actual feelings involved?" Jackson asked trying to sound serious, while shining a flashlight in Luca's face.

"Do you play FIFA? JJ inquired anxiously.

"I actually care very much for MC because of her intelligence and our friendship and have no mal intentions sexually, not that I think that's any of your business," Luca responded to Jackson, not even squinting from the unnatural light.

"And, JJ, I've never played FIFA, but I'd be willing to learn."

Luca was so calm and collected and said all the right things. I felt like even though he got the third degree he really connected with my family and it brought a smile to my heart. My meetings with his family were a different story. I was acquainted with everyone one weekend when his mother Roma, and father Giovanni were in town visiting with his sister Giana, her husband Marco, and their daughter Bella. And I failed miserably – embarrassing myself and only saying the wrong things.

"So…Noe, that's a very interesting name; how did you meet our son?" his father asked.

"Oh, well, thank you for the compliment. My full name is actually Noe Marie Cortes. Spelled, N-O-E, but pronounced like Noah, the man with the boat. I know that's a boy's name, but it's an abbreviated anagram of my mother's name, so she was willing to make a sacrifice," I began taking a quick breath.

"I always feel compelled to go into that story whenever I say my name. And that story is generally followed by me telling whomever that person is that my family calls me MC. For Marie Cortes of course. I feel like using MC makes you an insider because not everyone knows what MC means. Though I guess you would if I told you my story," I closed with resounding embarrassment as my face turned beet red.

"That's a sweet introduction. So how did you meet our son again?" his mother added trying to soften her rumpled face.

"Oh, right. I'm so sorry, sometimes I get caught up and I digress. Actually he stalked me," I added swaying my legs.

"He stalked you?" Giana shrieked, nearly spitting her lemonade across the table.

"No, not stalking so much as the word stalk means,

127

but more or less watching from afar without my knowledge," I corrected.

"So, what distinguishes that from stalking?" Marco inquired.

"Marcel, what is the meaning of this," his mother asked using his middle name.

"Yeah Luca, why are you such a creep? And Noe, or MC, I'm still not sure which you prefer, what could be endearing about that?" Giana asked.

"MC is fine. Most everyone calls me MC," I mutter.

"That's not actually when we first met, MC. And...I did not stalk her, like she said," Luca nudged me while trying to explain through gritted teeth.

"He's right," I added. "I can't believe I misspoke again. Our first meeting was an accident. I was wandering on campus and I was overwhelmed by its beauty and the newness of it all and he caught me during an impromptu dance performance. I ran away to escape embarrassment but ended up right with him at this bookstore and I kept him company for the day."

"You're a dancer," his mother asked genuinely intrigued, her face forming a real smile for what seemed like the first time all day.

"Yes mother and she's incredibly good too. I was mesmerized," he beamed, catching my hand.

"Well one day you must show us," Giana harked.

We rode a rollercoaster for the rest of our time together. I would say something idiotic and Luca would help me out of my hole and then everyone would be pleased. Someone would ask a new question and the cycle would continue in that way. After leaving I was sure that they hated me or thought that I had some mental disorder. Luca assured me that it was nothing of the sort, but I guess I'll never know.

We decided to have a joint meeting with all of our friends. So me, Hayley, Harper, Luca and his friends Justin and Simon enjoyed each other's company over a couple of games of bowling – a harmless meeting, on neutral territory.

"What do you all do?" Harper asked condescendingly of Justin and Simon.

"Well I'm a 1L at Texas Wesleyan," Justin answered.

"Hmp, subpar," Harper murmured.

"What was that?" he asked.

"Oh, nothing, what about you Si?" she continued.

"It's Simon actually; I've never been one for nicknames."

"Well alright, what do you do on a daily basis? How is it that you spend your time *Simon*?" Harper continued rudely.

"I'm obtaining my Master of Education and I teach 5th grade math."

"So you're a homosex-"

"That sounds wonderful Simon. You must have patience beyond any of our wildest dreams," I interceded.

"And ladies, why don't you tell us about yourselves," Luca encouraged.

"Well, we're both finishing school this year. I'm getting my BS at UT and in the fall, I'll start nursing school. Harper is also graduating in May with a BS in Political Science and a BA in Sociology and she'll be going to Yale Law," Hayley cheered.

"How do you all feel about this MC – Luca thing? Did it come as a surprise to you? Does he generally peruse the undergraduate pool for prospects? Are there things about your friend that either Hayley or I should be concerned about? If so, speak up now. Quite honestly, I don't have time for the bullshit," Harper asked, face stern, looking blankly from Simon to Justin.

"I –" Hayley started, unsure where to take the conversation from there.

I looked at Luca frightened and then back at Justin and Simon struggling with how to properly apologize for

Harper.

"Wow. I don't know where to really go from there. I want to think that you're joking, but your face and the tone of your voice say you're serious. You definitely have the chops for law school," Justin started through his slight laughter.

"Are you flirt–"

"She does; doesn't she?" I chimed in and mouthed to Harper 'cool it'.

"Justin and I have known Luca since we were at space camp together in the 3rd grade. We all wanted to be astronauts until we found out that very few astronauts actually get to go into space. That dream ended really quickly," Simon noted.

"Aw poor guys," Hayley whimpered.

"If you're seriously concerned Harper, don't be. Luca is one of the best guys we know. His mission in life is to help people. For fear of sounding too sensitive, I will refrain from discussing how much he cares for others, but just know that MC's in good hands," Justin rejoined the conversation.

"Why do I feel like your response is biased or somehow swayed because the subject in question is in our presence mentally documenting your every word?"

"Harper these guys would tell you the truth even if it painted a terrible picture of me. I assure it."

"You would," she spit.

"Well what about MC? If you're going to question us, I feel like it's only fair that we cross-examine you," Justin continued.

"Fair game. Honestly, MC is kind of flighty. She's got lofty goals, but her head and her heart aren't on the same page most of the time, so she usually deviates when the end is near. Hayley, am I leaving anything out?"

"Really Harper? Don't spare my feelings. Tell me how

you really feel," I bellowed.

"Oh geez oh pete Harper, you're so funny. MC's really a sweetheart. She loves love and she's artistic and really smart. So you all don't have anything to worry about either," Hayley added cheekily.

The rest of our outing was so scarring that I put most of it out of my head. Harper continued biting everyone's head off, offending them and purposely belittling them. Hayley was oblivious to life – as usual. Justin and Simon were simply perfect, and Luca managed to handle himself with just as much dignity and grace as ever. He was so hot. I was a nervous wreck trying to intercept the verbal violence Harper continued to spew.

After our meet and greet hurdles we managed to find a rhythm during our first year. We were together constantly, and Luca even became a staple at spaghetti Tuesday with my family, and I at his parent's home for their mid-week lady's tea. We never subjected our friends to one another again. I thought it was best not to subject Simon and Justin to the likes of Harper unnecessarily. I gradually made time for Luca to join forces with the girls and me, but it was never easy. As Luca moved into his second year of grad school and I into what would be my true final year of undergraduate studies. We started to discuss our future and I learned more and more of myself.

From the Desk of ___Noe Cortes___

June 4, 2010

My brain is on fire. For some strange reason I can't focus the way I should. I had a random déjà vu moment during my dream. I definitely dreamt my break-up experience but instead of Luca's face it was Matias'. Luca's voice and Luca's words, but it was all Matias. It was weird and I don't really know what to make of it, and I don't really want to think of it much. Matias and I have only just connected. Why would this type of dream creep into my brain space? The subconscious – it will forever be a mystery, even to the person who houses it.

Let's go back to the list. My self-discovery.

- What is your passion?

~~Actually, I don't know what to say to this right now. Too much on the brain.~~

No, you don't get to not do this. That's not an option. This is your life, and in life there are distractions and you have to work through them. So answer the question.

132

This is clearly unhealthy. Tomorrow. This is for tomorrow.

Chapter 11

"Morning hun!"

"Hello Joyce. ¿Cómo te sientes?"

"Como te," Joyce audibly ponders the translation of my inquiry. "Ah, how am I doing? Right?"

"Sí. Bien Joyce. Now dime. ¿Cómo te sientes?"

"Oh yeah. Me siento…. excited!"

"Excitada."

"Ex-ee-tah-da. Thank…uh, uh…. gracias."

"De nada. What do we have going on today?"

"It should be fairly quiet today. I think you have a follow-up meeting with Julius Cravens."

"Joyce…anonymity please!"

"No one's here," she starts to protest. "Alright. You have a follow-up appointment with an academic integrity case. Then at some point the Deans will request a meeting with you. You know, it's the end of the year they want to insert themselves in pretty much everything. But other than that you're free."

"What's Matias' calendar looking like?" I ask, immediately regretting it.

"Well aren't we a nosy Nancy?"

"I am not. It's just…it's weird having someone else around here. We hardly see him so I can't help but wonder what he does all day."

"If you say so," she says laughing a bit, not yet responding to my question.

"Okay well…I guess this nosy Nancy, is going to head on back to her office. Buzz me when Mr. Cravens gets in," I say winking as Joyce gasps at my lack of discretion.

"Well I'll be," Joyce adds placing her headset on.

Even with a relatively small suite, the walk to my office is long and boring. Our suite is set up similar to a right triangle. Matias and Joyce's offices are side by side along the short leg and my office is almost directly across from Joyce's down the long leg. Because of that I always have to ask Joyce about Matias' whereabouts.

After our interlude I'm a bit anxious about the relationship that has seemingly developed out of thin air between me and Matias. It doesn't seem natural that I can feel the way I do about someone I've basically just met, but I do. I think I have since passed the healthy infatuation phase and I'm now securely in the 'I like him for a reason' phase. It's eerie. I wonder if he might be anywhere near a similar phase with me. I've always thought that men began to listen to their feelings much later than women did. It's like we're so much more in tune with all the voices that are in our heads than they are. They only think about one thing at a time...or at a maximum two things.

"Good day," Matias' voice interrupts my train of thought.

"Hi," I say looking up to greet him with a smile.

"How is your day so far?"

"It's just wonderful. How'd you get past Joyce? I didn't hear her call out to you."

"I came through the loading dock behind the kitchen. Joyce has not yet seen me."

"Wait, what? We have a loading dock?"

"How long have you worked here? How do you not know of that? I'm certain it is your fire exit."

"I don't know. I suppose that's one more reason I appreciate your being here. You're teaching me things I probably should've known," I beam.

"How does your day look today?"

"It's pretty light. I have one academic integrity follow-up appointment and...that's about it. How about you? What does your day look like?"

"I have a meeting with the Vice President and then I too am free."

"Well look at that," I say flirtatiously, batting my eyelashes as coyly as possible.

"Would you like to go to lunch this afternoon seeing as we are very free post meridian."

"Post meridian," I reiterate. "Does that? Is that? Oh geez. That's p.m.? Again with the teaching. Your brain astounds me. I am definitely available for a midday meal, but I don't think we should."

"Why not?" he asks, worry lines overcoming his face.

"We shouldn't be...I mean an us...this is..." I struggle to explain.

"Just say it. What is wrong?"

"You and I...we're illegal," I whisper.

"Illegal, how?" he asks moving closer and drawing me in.

"No," I begin, trying to separate, "our relationship would not be condoned if others knew."

"But no one knows," he growls some and nuzzles my neck.

"Matias I'm being serious. If we keep up like this, then Joyce will know," I wriggle, freeing myself from his clutches.

"Just this once," he makes puppy dog eyes.

"Ma-ti-as."

"Please. You *need* this as much as I want this. It'll be good for you. Joyce won't know. I promise it," he adds crossing his heart with his fingers.

"She can't know," I reemphasize.

'She won't,' he mouths

"Okay," I relent.

"Then it will be. I will come for you at noon," he says releasing me.

"Sounds perfect."

"Adieu," he voices as he turns on his heels and makes his way up the corridor toward Joyce.

"Well hey there! Aren't you stealthy? I see you found the back door. Did you see MC back there?" I hear Joyce say in a louder than normal volume.

How is it that everyone knew about this back door but me? Hmh. Alright. Lunch. I'm so excited about our postmeridian meal.

"She is busy at work," I hear him answer. "I will see her later."

He is amazing, I think to myself. I sit at my desk quietly humming as I work my way through a ton of case files and my end of the year report for the Deans and the Vice President. My meeting with Mr. Cravens goes well. Since being convicted of plagiarism on three counts – he literally copied the text from two books in three different political science courses, he was ordered to take some remedial writing courses. In our meeting we discuss his progress with his course work, his understanding of what he's learning, and any apparent improvement. He says little to nothing aside from 'yes' and two blinks which I sometimes take as 'no' or as a sign of confusion. He is in and out and my report about our meeting complete in a matter of 30 minutes – including the time it took to walk him to the front door afterward.

I continue my reports and impatiently await the noon hour, passing the time checking my emails to no avail. I check Facebook and after three failed attempts I realize that I no longer have an account. Restless and distracted, I go exploring to find the hidden back door and much to my dismay it's less than 50 feet from mine. I stare at the gateway and can't help contemplating the various ways my office could be infiltrated without my knowledge at the behest of the loading dock door.

Noe, shut up! I shout inside making my way back to my office. Bouncing and marching up and down my floor I continue, practicing small talk and rehearsing reactions to whatever Matias might say.

"MC!" Joyce calls over the buzzer.

"Ma'am," I call breathing heavily running toward the phone.

"You're to meet with Matias this afternoon is that correct?"

"Me…meet with Matias?" I start trying not to seem so obvious that I have no clue what she's talking about.

I thought Matias and I were going to lunch today; I didn't know that he put it under the guise of us having a meeting. I'm so confused, and my heart feels like it's trying to jump from my throat.

"You seem confused. I'm just doing some reconnaissance work and I see that Matias has blocked the next two hours off on his calendar. And then I saw on your calendar that you have the same time frame, so I figured that you two were meeting and neither of you decided to be descriptive in your scheduling."

"Joyce, did anyone ever tell you that you should be a detective?" "That might've been my calling in a former life," she chuckles.

"Well, what makes you think that our calendars coincide strategically? We just both have meetings at the same time."

"That is very possible, but not very probable," Joyce pauses inciting a bit of fear in me. "Aw, I'm just messin'. I just want to stir up some sort of excitement around here. But I know that's not what goes on."

"Oh ah ha," I attempt to laugh. "Well I'll actually be going out for a long lunch today. It's the end of the summer you know, so I want to take advantage of all this free time. I might not get much more you now with the school year just around the corner," I start to ramble.

"Okay, bring me something if it's good."

"Right. 'kay bye," I say hanging up the phone.

Me: 'Remind me to give you a lesson in strategic scheduling.'

I type, sending Matias an inter-office instant message.

Mr. Callado: 'Beg pardon?'
Me: 'Nevermind. Forget I said anything.'
I try at amending, desperate not to imbibe him in potential drama.

Mr. Callado: 'Of this you are certain?'

Me: 'Of this I am.'

I type a beat later, desperate to usher us away from the previous conversation.

Me: 'Is it time yet?'

Mr. Callado: 'Anxious, are you? Where shall we go?'

Me: 'I'll ignore that first question and just say since it's your idea to dine you should have the location. So…where are we going for lunch?'

Mr. Callado: 'I appreciate your wit. I will meet you beneath the magnolia tree in 2.5 minutes.'

Me: 'two point five minutes it is.'

I shut down my computer and make my way to the front door.

"Heading out now MC?" Joyce asks.

"Yes. I'll be back after I'm done."

"Alright. I'll see you later."

I walk anxiously toward the magnolia tree at the edge of campus nervous that Joyce will figure out what's going on.

"Alo"

"Uh hi," I say turning to find Matias lingering, clearly unscathed by Joyce and the interrogation I assume he underwent.

"Are you ready?"

"I am. Did you get out of the office okay?"

"Why, but of course. What makes you ask?"

"It's just that Jo- …actually nothing," I stop, wrestling to overcome my sudden nervousness. "Did you decide where we're going?"

"This is true," he states definitively and starts toward the south end of campus arms crossed behind him.

"Matias?" I ask, peering at him as he makes swiftly across the lawn.

"Yes?" he asks, pausing his march, turning toward me looking quizzically and uncategorically handsome.

Sheesh I think, just his turn makes me weak in the knees. "After you," I say smiling and walking to catch up to him.

Our walk to this undisclosed location is in comfortable silence. The breeze is cool causing my dress to dance gracefully as we move. Matias walks with ease, floating next to me, our strides matching and our hands playing tag with each sway of the arm. As we walk, I can't help but stare at this gorgeous man who for some reason is besotted with me. He's dressed more casually than usual with a deep purple polo, snuggly fitted jeans, and some cowboy boots. I can see he has the beginnings of what will be a 5 o'clock shadow as the sun kisses his face. He actually reminds me of a Stetson guy. I don't think there really is a Stetson guy, but if there were, he could be him. Rugged and masculine, and oh…calmate Noe.

I sense he can feel my eyes and maybe even hear my impure thoughts because every so often as I pull my eyes from him, I can feel his on me.

"Alright, we are here," Matias announces proudly, interrupting my recent erotic reverie.

"Um," I begin, feeling a bit embarrassed. "I think, um-" I continue and start looking around at the open area.

We're in the middle of a park and the only things around are a small bench, a lamp post, and a small running trail.

"I don't think we were thinking the same thing when lunch was mentioned."

"You are very comical. Come on," he says taking my hand in his and pulling me in front of him. Wrapping himself around me, maintaining possession of my hands and leaning his face next to mine he adds, "look a bit closer."

I do as he says and squint past the bench to see a basket and a folded red blanket.

"How did you?" I respond turning my head toward him. "I mean, wha-?" I ask astonished and looking around to see if there are any accomplices in eyesight.

"I have my ways," he remarks devilishly. "Sit. Get comfortable," he finishes giving me a slight nudge.

I step around him away from the bench and prepare to sit.

"Wait," he calls out with a quiet sense of urgency as he lays the red blanket onto the ground. "Now it is appropriate to sit."

I take my seat atop the blanket and watch as Matias prepares a romantic feast around me. I am awestruck as he walks, floating, humming to himself in a world all his own. Witnessing it all, I can envision throwing myself at him in an embrace of gratitude. He's absolutely ravenous.

He finally finishes and has a gorgeous place setting around me. Along with the food in his basket he set up and 'lit' three flameless tea lights and they seem to flicker in the wind. The ambiance mixed with the summer sun serves as an unexpected hotly aphrodisiac.

"Bon appétit," he utters pouring wine in the stem-less glasses to go with our warm chicken sandwiches. After the main course we have frozen grapes and chat in a perfect halo of bliss.

Our lunch marks the first of many. Once a week we escape to 'the bench'. I learn more of his life and solidify what makes him so desirable. If he could be anything in the world it would be a travel journalist so he could backpack through Europe, Thailand, and the Canadian outback – whatever that means. He says he'd see the sights and write as much as he could. I love hearing all of the stories he has – of his childhood and all the books he's read. He asks many questions of my history too. I tell him of my brothers, mama and of course my papí. We talk dancing and languages – of which he knows five. I tell him that my only dream is to be happy doing whatever that means. Somewhere in our time together we become an us and I find my happy again.

Ebonii Nelson

From the Desk of _____Noe Cortes_____

June 28, 2010

I think I know more about myself knowing absolutely nothing about myself. What is your passion?

Making other people happy and being happy. It's very abstract which ordinarily makes me nervous and anxious because of the uncertainty of it all, but this is the only truth that I have. The 'what' is relative and flexible and ever-changing and that's okay.

Who is this person that I am becoming? I can't help but think that Matias is having a freakishly positive effect on my life. Every week going back to the bench I learn more about him and in return I think I learn more about myself. I just want to be engulfed in his aura. He is fantasmic...and all with his clothes on.

I want to say, with this Dr. Logan you should be pleased. No Dr. Pepper tonight. We're all good. Next question: What do you do that speaks to your soul?

Chapter 12

"Luca, where are you going?"

"I have an appointment this afternoon."

"Where? With who? How long are you gone?"

"What's with the interrogation?" he snapped.

"Oh, I'm sorry," I said wandering into his room where he was dressing. "I didn't realize they were coming out like that. I just wanted to know how long I'm on my own today," I finished, sitting on his bed.

"Right," he added tersely.

"So…. where then?"

"It's with Dr. Levi."

"Who's that? I don't think I've heard you talk about him before. Here let me help," I said pushing off the bed to help as he struggled with his tie. "Why so dressy?"

"It's not a *he* it's a *she* and she's a therapist that we have to start seeing this year. It's for graduation. I got it," he added swatting my hands away from his tie. "I'm not dressy. I'm just professional."

"Are you nervous? You seem really tense," I said reaching up to massage his shoulders

"I'm not nervous and I'm not tense; I'm just focused," he added with a large sigh, shrugging my arms away before pulling his tie from his collar and stalking to the closet.

"You want me to…I don't know…how can I help?"

"Just leave it, MC. I'm fine. I just need to find a new tie."

"Are you sure?"

"Noe!" he affirmed sternly and succinctly.

"Okay. I'll just leave then."

He didn't respond.

"Call me later?" I asked slowly making my way toward the door secretly hoping he would beg me to stay.

"Right. Later," he finally spoke emerging from his room and meeting me at his front door.

"Are you sure babe," I asked grabbing his chin and searching his eyes for truth.

"I really am good. I promise," he conceded and leaned in to hug me, giving me a hard kiss on the mouth. "I'll call you when I get back in."

"Okay, bye."

Luca, I think was slowly becoming bi-polar or depressed or a mixture of the two. We were happy, but then there would be outlandish moments where a switch would get turned on and he was aloof and angry and there seemed to be nothing I could do or say to snap him out of it. Times like that were spotty, so I figured he was just stressed about school. I refused to let myself worry about him going to that place and staying there without me.

***

"Harper, you there? Pick up. Pick up!" I yelled over her voicemail willing her to hear and answer.

"What is it?" Harper answered voice raspy and full of sleep.

"You busy?"

"Is this some kind of booty call?"

"Searching for things to say. I seriously have no words," I said stunned by her comments.

"What do you want MC? Stop being weird."

"Oh my gosh you sound just like JJ. I'm not being weird. I'm bored. Want to go see a movie?"

"No. I can't. I have LSAT prep later today. I'm teaching this section."

"Oh. Right, well I'm off then," I faked cheeriness.

"MC, what's wrong?"

"Nothing," I paused, second guessing my lie. "Just bored," I finished, deciding to commit.

"You're lying but I don't have time to coax it out of you."

Thank goodness.

"When I get done with LSAT I'm going to ask you again and you better be mentally prepared to tell me the truth by then. Understood?"

"Bye Harper."

"Ciao."

Suck. Round two.

"Good afternoon dearest best friend of mine!" Hayley answered the phone gaily.

"Hayley, hi. How are you?" I said with an awkward jauntiness that I've never used.

"You sound weird. Are you sure you're okay?"

"I'm fine," I said trying to figure out how everyone knew I was out of sorts. "What about you?" I tried at diverting the subject.

"Well Connor and I are about to go thrifting. It's going to be superb. Our theme for this trip is holiday scrabble party. Isn't it kitchy?"

"Kitchy? Is that even a word? And what exactly is a holiday scrabble party theme?"

"Sure kitchy is a word. It's like neat or something. Look it up, I'm sure it's in a dictionary. The holiday scrabble party theme is all about funky sweaters and letters and cups of tea and hot cocoa and of course scrabble. It's all just so....so..."

"Let me guess.... kitchy."

"Exactly! We're actually on our way out now."

"Hi MC!" I could hear Connor yell from the background.

"Connor says hi!" Hayley repeated. "Don't you want to join us? Connor would love it. Right Connie?"

"So right, Haybabes. Come on MC," I could hear Connor's reply.

"First I can't make sense of Connie and Haybabes," I began mock disgustedly, "but seriously thank you both for the offer. I'm good. Have fun."

"We will," they both answered.

"I'll talk to you later."

"Love you. Mean it. Buh bye MC!"

They are seriously the most awkwardly perfect couple. Connie and Haybabes? It's just strange. Ugh. Strike two.

"Bueno."

"Jackson, stop being weird. We're totally an English-speaking household."

"It's you. Don't have time MC I've got shopping with Felice right now. Get off the phone."

"Jack don't hang up," I spoke speedily trying to avoid a click.

"Hello?" I heard a confused JJ speak.

"JJ?"

"Yeah. Hey MC. Mom's out shopping and Papí's golfing with the guy's club so no one's here."

"No. You. Well."

"What? Are you speaking English? Is the phone breaking up?"

"No. JJ do you want to hang out?"

"Are you being serious right now? We never hang out. Am I being punk'd? It's not funny," He said growing more irritated with each new clause.

"No. I'm serious. What do you have going on today?"

"Well, only if you're serious," he added his voice laced with hushed excitement. "I was going to hang out at the park and maybe kick the ball around, but nothing serious. You wanna come?"

"Actually…"

"It's okay if you don't want to," defeated he interrupts.

"No, JJ I was going to say, I would love to. I'll be there in as long as it takes me to drive."

"Sweet. See you in a bit."

***

"So what's going on with you," JJ asked lightly kicking the

soccer ball my way.

"Nothing much little brother. What makes you ask?" I continued, lobbing the ball back toward him.

"We never do this. If I was your last resort, something has to be wrong."

"JJ don't say that. I'm sorry that I make you feel like you're my last option. I actually never thought that you'd enjoy just hanging out with me."

"Don't get all mushy. It's all good. But seriously, I can tell something's wrong. You're just more different than usual today."

"Well if you must know, I think Luca is going to break up with me and it's wearing a hole in my gut."

"Why do you think that?"

"I just have an inkling," I retorted and dropped to the ground with exasperation.

"You think too much," JJ told me, walking closer and grabbing a seat just in front of me.

"I don't think I'm thinking too much."

"See you did it again. Life is a lot simpler than you make it out to be. It's probably because you read so much."

"And how would you know?"

"Well, maybe I don't I guess, but I can see that you're making your brain work too hard and you probably need to just chill out and let things happen," he said tapping my leg, making me look up at him. He slid just in front of me so that our knees touched, then he nudged me again with his legs. "I can't speak for Luca, but I can speak as a boy, and honestly if I wanted it to be over, I'd make it so. Since that hasn't happened stop thinking about it."

I looked at him unable to speak, trying to process his words.

"Besides," he continued, "from the times he's come over I'm fairly sure he's crazy about you. I think he tries to seem more grown up than he is, but even with that he's okay. Ride it out MC."

I was stunned. I'd never heard JJ say more than seven

words at a time and the seven he'd utter usually had something to do with soccer. It confused me to hear him talk about relationships as if he'd had one with something other than a soccer ball.

"Thanks for the perspective. When did you get to be so wise? I thought I was supposed to be the one offering you words of wisdom," I gushed leaning over giving him a hug and planting a huge, slobbery kiss on his cheek.

"You're so gross you know that," he added, gently pushing me away and wiping his face. "I don't talk all the time, but I know a thing or two," he finished with a rarely seen smile.

We got up and kicked the ball around a bit more. He told me about a couple of scouts that were supposed to come to check him out. He said he hoped to get a scholarship to go to a soccer camp and maybe even a preparatory school for soccer for the next school year. He came alive out there and we shared a bond like we'd never before. When the sun started to set, we made our way back to the house, and there we cooked a quick meal before everyone arrived from their day's activities. Dinner with the full family was raucous as usual, but the familiarity of it all was soothing and something I desperately needed.

***

"Hello?"

"MC?"

"Luca, hi. How are you?" I asked awkwardly.

"I'm fine. Look can you come over?"

"I mean I-…. I guess I-..."

"Are you at your apartment?" he asked hurriedly.

"Yeah. Luca, what…"

"I'm coming over."

I didn't exactly know what to expect when Luca arrived. I was frightened but eerily exhilarated because he's never been so insistent. I found myself pacing and talking aloud – having a fictional conversation with Luca, or how I imagined a real conversation would go with him. It wasn't until I heard his boom on my front door, the scalding splash of water on my kitchen floor as the macaroni noodles I was boiling overran their pot, and was violated by the piercing screech of the fire alarm which signaled the overcooking of the biscuits I'd placed in the oven that I realized I wasn't fully focused.

"MC? Ew, what's that smell, why's it all smoky?"

"Oh, I'm sorry," I began rushing back to the kitchen to rescue the food.

"Were you asleep?" he asked fanning the smoke detector with a pillow from the couch.

"No, I was just a bit distracted I guess," I added turning off the stove, oven top and dragging all the paper towels to the floor.

"Here, use this," Luca said handing me a towel as the alarm siren waned. "Let me get some more."

"Thank you. I don't know what happened really. It was supposed to be a simple meal. Just some mac 'n' cheese and you know a biscuit. And then there was fire, and water and booming and craziness," I muttered quickly. "I'm sorry. Thank you."

"It's fine," he voiced returning from the linen closet with more towels. "Sit down. I need to talk to you."

"I'm mentally prepared for this Luca. I know things are weird and I can understand if what you need just isn't here. I get it I do," I started quoting the speech as I'd rehearsed.

"What are you talking about?"

"Well that's what this talk is about isn't it?" I inquire, planting myself on the couch.

"You think I came to your house to break up with you?" he asked puzzled staring down at me.

"Yes?" I answered my voice quaking. "No? I guess. I don't know."

"No, that's not it at all," he added wiping his face

in frustration and joining me on the couch. "I can see how you managed to almost burn your whole kitchen down," chuckling a little he continued, "oh my gosh I love you. I am not trying to break up with you MC."

"I love you too and I'm so glad to hear you say that. I think I was going a bit crazy trying to figure out what on earth you needed to talk to me about. You sounded so panicked on the phone. I didn't really know what to think."

"Well, after my meeting with Dr. Levi today I think I know how to save our relationship."

"How do you mean?"

"Well, you always say that you don't feel like I'm telling you what's going on with me, and I always tell you you're nagging me, which don't say it, I know you hate that," he said before I had a moment to speak. "Well, I think I figured out a way that we can both get what we want."

"And…"

"What do you mean 'and'," he asked his voice filling with anger and disappointment.

"No, not the bad and, the anticipatory and. What's the thing you figured out?"

"Oh right – compromise," he spoke boldly and prideful.

"Compromise," I repeated. "The big plan is for us to compromise? Forgive me for being a bit confused. Where do you propose we start with this plan to compromise?"

"I don't think I like your tone MC. You just don't get it."

"Don't get upset. I don't mean to come across however I'm coming across. I just want to understand. Tell me. Talk to me. Let's rap it out."

"I'm not upset, it's just…I don't know, I'm not communicating it well. When Dr. Levi said it, it all made perfect sense. Maybe next time I'll take notes," he said almost to himself a bit deflated by the situation.

"Luca we're capable. We can make sense of this. Okay? Compromise it's not such a hard thing to work toward. We each give a little to get a little. Right?"

"No. It's all wrong. I need to ask Dr. Levi. She said everything just right."

I hated my new relationship with Dr. Levi and Luca. It was terrible. She was always suggesting different things that Luca and I should do to *better* our relationship. Luca would always bring back these 'magic fix' plans that she'd craft and if they were a success Dr. Levi was a genius and a saint. When they predictably failed it was my fault and I was 'purposely trying to prevent forward progress'. This *help* was making me resentful of Luca and I started speaking my opinion a lot less. It was disarming how much faith he was putting into this new relationship and how much he seemed to tell Dr. Levi that he was never telling me. She brought him joy and I was always good to unintentionally rob him of it whenever we were together.

From the Desk of _____Noe Cortes_____

July 7, 2010

What do you do that speaks to your soul?

Okay, so I was hot last week but I've gone cold so far. Dr. Logan has been saying that my journal entries aren't very focused. Or rather, they're focused but not on my personal development. They've mostly been about Matias I suppose, but that's what's been occurring in my life. I think with him I am developing personally. I am definitely opening up and for the first time in a long time I am willing to let someone in. I feel like I'm sharing parts of myself that I have kept hidden for so long and I honestly don't know if I want to stop writing about that. The thing I do that speaks to my soul is enjoy time with Matias. I told Dr. Logan that and he said it wasn't acceptable for my happiness to hinge upon a person. He said it's not healthy and it could potentially send me into a dark depression if and when Matias was no longer a character in my life. I told him he was just being pessimistic and that he should be happy that he'd helped me so much and that I wouldn't have been this person if it had not been for him. And he's all 'what happened to that dream you had with the déjà vu moment'...ugh, you'd think he didn't want me to end up with Matias the way he talks.

I'm stressed out now. I don't know how to right what's apparently wrong. I can't think of anything else that speaks to my soul. Whenever I start thinking my thoughts always wander to Matias.

23 flavors of Dr. Pepper stat.

Chapter 13

"You're going."

"Harper, why should I?"

"Because you need this. And I need this. And you're supposed to be my wing woman at all costs. You're supposed to have my back."

"I do have your back; but I think speed dating is stupid. What could you possibly learn from someone in five minutes? This is a waste of time."

"Don't be such a party pooper MC. I don't really understand how you don't see this as an opportunity for you too. I mean you're single too. We need to catch up to Hayley. I need a plus one for the wedding that's coming in the not so distant future. Oh wait and you do too," she rants. I can feel her disapproving eye roll her as she closes.

"What if I don't want to worry about a plus one right now? We don't know that Connor's going to propose."

"MC what planet are you living on? Connor is so gonna – hold on. Hold the phone. Hold the motherfu–"

"Vulgar much?"

"Look at me."

"Harper, we're on the phone."

"You can work some magic. Look at me dead in my face. What aren't you telling me? The only reason to avoid this kind of experience is because you have a prospect. But you couldn't possibly have a prospect that you haven't yet told me about, right?" she asks rapid fire.

"Harper, I don't even know how to respond to your line of questioning. You're getting into that lawyer babble and it's always a bit hard to follow."

"Noe Marie Cortes," she adds slow and methodically.

"You're three-naming me?" I ask slightly piqued.

"And you're avoiding my questions. Wasting precious time and words on unnecessary statements regarding the supposed perplexing nature of my inquiries, when we both know you know exactly what I'm talking about. Use your words and speak," she continues plainly enunciating each new word.

I honestly don't know what to say to her. Maybe if I wait long enough, she'll just let it go.

"I know you hear me. I know you're hiding something. And I'm not going to let it go, so out with it," she retorts as if she can hear my thoughts.

"For the love of all things sweet Harper…it's not that I have a prospect necessarily. It's just that…I don't know."

"You're not saying anything. It's a black and white issue. Either you have one or you don't. So what do you have?"

"Do you remember me saying anything about Matias?"

"Matias?" she asks pausing a bit roving through the numerous files in her head. "Wait, your boss?"

"Technically he's not my boss. Well, he's sort of temporary. But it doesn't really even matter because there aren't any rules that say that we can't be friends."

"What's with you and all these shades of gray? He is your boss and if you want to jump his bones, I'm certain he's not in the category of 'friends'."

"Harper what is it with you? You are so crude. Who said anything about bones? And I think we *are* becoming friends."

"What has happened for you to think that you are becoming quote-un-quote friends? You've clearly been a terrible friend to me because I haven't been made aware of some goings on in your life."

"What do you mean what has happened?" I ask ignorantly.

"You've got this playing dumb thing down really well, and I want to know when you became *that* girl because she is getting on my nerves."

I can hear her smacking her lips and the anger bubbling inside as she berates me.

"If you don't give me the information I desire, please know you will find that your schedule has been booked from 1:00pm until close. I have no problems making home or work visits," Harper says her attitude changing from calm and resigned to borderline exasperated.

"I'm not playing dumb. It's just...I don't want to have this conversation over the phone," I whine.

"Okay, well I will take a late lunch and I'll see you this afternoon around 2. Clear your schedule and mentally prepare to tell me every last detail. I'm telling you now...I will be relentless in my pursuit," she adds resolutely.

"Does it have to be that serious?"

"It didn't have to be, but you've been trying to cover things up, so I don't want to take any chances. See you later."

And with that the line goes dead.

"Is everything alright hun?"

"Huh? What? Joyce, yes...why do you ask?"

"Well you're just holding the phone, and I can hear the dial tone way over here," Joyce shouts from the doorway. "Did you forget who you were calling?" she adds in a hushed, semi-condescending tone.

"Right. Yes, I momentarily forgot," I laugh and return the receiver to its base. "I don't know where my head is sometimes."

"I think you just have a case of the Mondays," she laughs. "Hey, Joyce?" I call as she starts walking away.

"Yeah?"

"Is Matias in yet?"

"I hadn't checked. I can rustle him up if you'd like," she says with a quick wink.

"No, it won't be necessary. I was just asking."

"Well okay. If you change your mind just gimme a holler," she says making her way toward the front of the suite back to her desk.

I should probably add the hostile Harper takeover to my calendar. She said 2, which really means 3, and

156

she'll probably stay 'til close. It's going to be a long afternoon.

"Buenos días, querida."

"Matias," I say, surprisingly. "Hi. Good morning to you too."

"How was your weekend?" he says walking in, closing the door, and leaning over my desk to give me a hug and a small kiss atop my forehead.

"How was my weekend? Hmm…well I spent a most glorious time with this dark and mysterious Spanish gentleman. I think he may be smitten with me," I almost sing, strumming my fingers on my desk staring up longingly at him.

"What makes you think that? Please, do tell me. What activities did you engage in this weekend?" he asks sidling next to me seated on my desk.

"For starters that very handsome Spanish gentleman met me at Hideaway Park for lunch. There we dined on grapes and other delicious berries, wine, and the best roast beef sandwiches I've ever had."

"What else did you do?" he asks truly intrigued by these already known facts.

"What happened next will astound you," I continue lifting my right index finger to Matias' lips before he could ask me another question. "After the wonderful lunch this very handsome Spanish gentleman turned on his portable jukebox. Some also like to call this an iPod," I whisper.

"And what is it that was playing on this como se dice, jukebox?"

"It was a most beautiful waltz. And with the very handsome Spanish gentleman I began to dance," I say starting to sway a bit in my chair.

"How is it that you danced? Do you mind showing me? I am sure I am not as good as this Spanish gentleman you speak of but–"

"The very handsome Spanish gentleman," I

157

emphasize.

"I will amend. Do you mind showing me how you danced with the very handsome Spanish gentleman?" he asks standing and offering his hand to me. "May I have this dance," he adds.

"Why of course you may," I say as I come to my feet and bob a curtsy.

We float around my office for at least one full stanza, re-playing the waltz from the weekend before, our steps in perfect sync.

"You might actually give the very handsome Spanish gentleman a run for his money," I say to Matias as we come to a stop.

"I'm glad to know that you enjoyed yourself this weekend. I had a very pleasant time as well."

"Pleasant. That's a nice word to use. I suppose I've been having a pleasant time every day for the past three weeks. You're an amazing person in that way," I hear myself saying before I can compel it to stop.

Un-frightened by my unsolicited praise he comments, "You are even more incredible than I, with each passing of the day I find more and more reasons to adore you. I am glad to have met you," he says, arms still wrapped tightly around my waist.

"I always thought I had a way with words but in you sir, I may have met my match," I declare pulling away from him and having a seat on the corner of my desk.

"MC," Matias starts as he joins me at the edge of my desk. "I think I would like to be very honest with you."

"Yes? You're making me incredibly nervous with your phraseology. You don't have to state that you want to be honest. You should just let it out."

"Do you know you ramble a lot when you are nervous? It is one of the qualities that I…"

"That you? That you what? You can't just start a phrase and stop and stare off into space like that. It's, it's indecent," I say nervously fidgeting, my heart rate quickening. "Maybe indecent is the wrong word," I continue my ramblings, "but it's definitely a cultural no-no, and I owe it to you to make sure you don't do that again. But –"

"MC, calmate. Calm down," he says "I wanted to make sure that I had your attention and that I was saying the proper words. You interjected before I had a moment to fully collect my thoughts."

"Okay. I will sit still and be quiet."

"I don't know if I am overstepping some boundaries, but I can't help the feelings that I have. You have helped me learn the area where we work, and we have learned a lot about each other over the course of my two months here."

"Yes. Nothing about that is overstepping any bounds. I am confused."

"Still and quiet," he whispers, lightly touching my hand sending an electric pulse up my arm.

"Oh right," I silence myself and steady my eyes on the floor.

"I find myself thinking about you often in ways that are probably not very becoming of a supervisor. Nothing inappropriate, I assure you," he stresses, lifting my chin and turning my face toward his.

"You just manage to consume many of my thoughts, most of the time."

Matias truncates his conversation and stands almost in slow motion. He walks over to my door and locks it, before returning to me. He pulls my chair from behind my desk and sits squarely in front of me. He takes my hands in his and continues his half of our colloquy.

"MC, it is just, I have grown to care for you quite a bit and I would like to advance our relationship. And with your blessing I would like to curtail my work as your interim supervisor, take up full residence in Academia and court you," he pauses to slow his breathing.

"I know that we haven't had a lot of time together and it probably seems unreasonable to be so enamored so quickly, but I have learned in life that when one knows what it is they desire, they should grab hold of it when they find it."

"Oh my goodness," I say, my thoughts starting to race and my palms getting sweaty.

"What? What is it? Have I said too much?" he asks searching my eyes for a promising answer and a sense of calm.

"No, no, no. It's not," I start, words getting caught in my throat as I'm staving off unexpected tears.

"I do not understand what is happening. I have upset you. That was not my intent."

"I–"

"It is your decision."

"I–"

"I do not want to pressure you."

"Matias," I snap and grab his face with both my hands. "It's time for you to be still and quiet."

I drift off very quickly, having this strange feeling of déjà vu. The words Matias said – our banter, it reminded me of...oh gosh, I can't go back there. "Matias," I repeat.

"Yes? I am listening. I am waiting patiently for you."

"Are you sure you want to make all those changes.... for me?"

"Why would I not? You are unlike anyone I have ever experienced, and I appreciate all that you are and all that you give not only to me but to everything. I don't think you see all that you are. You are much more than the sum of your parts, and for you I would do it."

"I've just never had this experience before...nor had anyone tell me things like this in such a short while."

"I cannot deny the concise process, but I also cannot deny that which I feel. If you do not want it or me, I do not have to...how do you say..."

"It's not that at all. I too appreciate you in more ways than I know how to express. You've brought me to life in a time when I felt so lost. You bring out my creativity and I'm always excited for what new life you will send me to each day we talk about Proust or Kierkegaard, dance or modern art, or even when we're talking about what's going on here – it's never venerable."

"So, what is it that you are saying?"

"I think it's okay that you want to switch sides and it's okay for us to pursue…us," I say my face turning up into a smile as his eyes meet mine.

Suddenly Matias stands, dropping my hands as he does. He rises in front of me and looking down he takes my hair and puts it behind my shoulders. He squats subtly so that our eyes meet, and he grabs my face with each of his hands. He caresses my lips more passionately than I can ever remember being kissed. Getting lost in this place of passion, we only find ourselves at the untimely ringing of my phone.

"I have to take it," I say, breaking from our trance, eyes still closed.

"But why?" Matias asks kissing my bottom lip and then my top.

"I have a meeting at 3," I continue indulging in his continued kisses.

"But it is only 2."

"What?" I yell, snapping back into reality, opening my eyes, and feeling very exposed.

"What's the problem?" Matias asks, nervous at my outburst.

"She's never on time. What's happening?"

"Who is she? I am confused."

"Harper."

"Harper?"

"Yes, Harper, one of my best friends, Harper. The best friend who is never on time for anything in her life, Harper. The one who is here at this very moment, Harper. Oh my gosh. I don't know what is going on. We've got to stop. To be continued," I say hopping off my desk, kissing him again hard on the mouth, and then ushering him forcefully out my door.

"Will I meet this Harper?" he asks before I close the door to answer the still ringing phone.

"When the time is right Matias, you will meet them all."

"Okay, I suppose," he says through the crack of the door as I draw it closed.

"Really it's true. I am not prepared for her though, which is why I'm forcing you out."

"I understand. I will go."

I press my back against the door, and I slide to the floor mouthing 'I love you' as he walks away. I spend a moment to myself until I am pulled to the yet still ringing phone.

"Student Conduct, this is Noe," I answer.

"MC, what took you so long? I'm nearly at your door. I like to be welcomed. You know that. Come on out won't you."

This is going to be the longest visit ever.

From the Desk of ___Noe Cortes___

August 2, 2010

So tomorrow turned into three weeks, but I think I needed the break. A mental break, and that release has opened the door to more time with Matias, who I think is inadvertently helping me return to my question of passion. I am passionate about love, and right now I feel a ton of love or something very love-like with and for Matias. I don't know what it is, but I know it has a lot to do with the fact that he and I communicate in a different way. Well...in every way. We talk with our words. We talk in our smiles. We talk with our looks. We talk when we dance. WE DANCE! That's something new. His upbringing in Spain has undoubtedly made him a gentleman unlike any other American idiot I've ever dealt with. This weekend we waltzed, and it was heavenly.

And today, today he professed a level of love for me. On the love continuum we're not at a 10, but he's definitely past 5, and as quickly as it came and as strange as it seems to also feel so overwhelmed by him I am.

Where I will take this conversation is that I am more than smitten with Matias and I am so excited to enjoy this ride with him.

Where I will not travel in this conversation is Harper and her scathing approach to finding out why I didn't want to accompany her to speed dating. I despise her investigative nature. Why can't I have my own escapades for only myself, my imagination and right now Matias? Why do there have to be rules for everything? Why should anything matter to anyone? This is my life.

It's mine and I should be able to indulge however I feel and wander down any path of my choosing free from judgment and chastisement when others disagree. I agree with Matias — this is nothing inappropriate, I assure you.

Chapter 14

"MC?"

"Un, huh," I answered softly.

"MC?"

"Yeah?"

"Noe," Luca practically yelled from his kitchen into the living room where I was snuggled up with a blanket and a new book.

"Yes?" I answered, confused at his abrasiveness.

"Why haven't you answered me?"

"I have. Every time you've called me, I've answered."

"Maybe you just thought you answered. You're always so caught up reading that you probably only imagined responding to me."

"I resent that. Yes, I read a lot, but that's not new. I've always read a lot, and I definitely know what's real and what's not," I began, slamming my book shut and looking directly at him. "And I know that I responded to you when you said "MC" question mark, "MC" question mark, and then finally yelling my name." I paused and awaited a response. Hearing none, I added, "Your apology will be accepted," before rolling my eyes and returning to my book.

Luca and I had been in a funk for over three weeks. We engaged in more than the occasional lover's spat. These loud conversations generally erupted out of nowhere, and they always became obstacles that we side-stepped and never really seemed to deal with. We'd been exclusive for one year and six months before all of this started and it just seemed like we were in too deep to implode

"Luca," I called more calmly, laying my book down.

"What?" he answered with disdain, not moving from the doorway of the kitchen.

"Luca, can you please come and talk to me?"

"What for? I'm tired of doing this."

"What do you mean? What is this? Can you come and sit down?"

"I don't want to sit," he added standing his ground from the kitchen.

"Please sit with me here. Please," I pleaded. He obliged and sat next to me on his sofa. "Thank you."

"MC, I'm so tired of this," he sighed running his fingers through his hair.

"What is this? You keep using that phrase and I don't understand what you mean. You're done with me? What is it? Are we breaking up?"

"No, no, no. We've fought every day for the past month. I don't want to anymore. I'm tired of always being angry and yeah...I'm tired of it."

"I don't think either of us likes to argue," I began.

"Oh really, if that's the case, why do you start them?"

"Are you being completely serious right now," I asked huffily. "I rarely, if ever start our arguments. We can use today for example. That was all...you know what? Actually, I'm not. I refuse. This is what you want, I think. Luca, what is the matter?"

"Nothing."

"It's obviously something. I feel like you're picking fights with me, so I'll get angry enough to walk out. Which unfortunately, my track record says I will, but not today. What's wrong with you? Talk to me."

"The only thing that's wrong with me is I'm tired of fighting with you," he said, his eyes blank and glazed over as I searched them for hidden meaning.

"Okay then. Clearly, I can't win here. I'm going to go," I started and made my way to the door.

"This is not a contest, it's a —" he instigated before I interrupted him.

"You're so right. It's not a contest."

"Actually," he began as I stepped out the door, "here, you forgot your bag."

Luca came close, handed off my messenger bag and

closed the door behind me. He didn't walk me to my car. He didn't ask me to text him when I made it to wherever I was going. He didn't even ask where I was going. I walked what felt like 500 miles to my car, got inside and just started to weep. I didn't know what was happening. Luca was talking to me less and less, and he was starting to be more and more ornery. I sat with my face buried in the steering wheel, and he didn't come to see if I was okay. I didn't talk to him the rest of the weekend. I wanted nothing to do with him and I hated that. He was becoming my unhappiness. I didn't know what to do.

***

"Papí?"

"Mi'ja? What are you doing here? You have classes today, no?"

"I have one later today. I'll be gone soon. I just wanted to see you."

"What's wrong, mi amorcita?" he asked joining me at the kitchen table.

"Daddy? Daddy...I–," I started, my words stuck in my throat. "I just don't know what I'm doing wrong that makes everything so messed up like this," I continued, tears beginning to drain from my left eye.

My father said nothing; he just slid his chair closer to mine and gently rubbed my back as I laid my head on the table and sobbed. I couldn't finish my story. He didn't press for answers, he just let me be. I think he knew it had to do with Luca and he probably also knew that there wasn't much he could do to fix anything.

I didn't make it to class that day. I cried until my eyes would no longer open and then I fell asleep in my old room. When I woke, the scent of my papí lingered in the space. I could tell he'd spent a substantial amount of time waiting and watching me, protecting me from anything and everything.

"Good day, mi amorcita," my father whispered to me as I leaned to hug him over the couch where he was reading.

"Hi Daddy," I added, joining him on the couch, my arms still around him.

"How was your sleep?"

"Thank you," I responded, ignoring his question, because he and I both knew he watched as I slept.

"Are you up for talking?"

"I guess so," I rolled onto the couch, and planted my head into his chest, "It's Luca."

"Is there more?" he pressed.

"All we've been doing is fighting. Every conversation turns into a verbal sparring match that I inevitably lose. I lose if I participate. I lose if I ignore it. And when I try to figure out the problem, he won't talk to me," I said fidgeting with my fingers. "It's like he shuts down and everything is, 'oh it's nothing,' or 'don't worry about it,' or 'you can't help with this,' but I never hear what it is that's making him so obstinate…and I just don't know what to do Daddy."

"First calm down," he told me, clearly sensing the anxiousness that was working to overcome me once again.

"I'm calm."

"Have you and Luca had this conversation?" he posed, lifting my chin so he could see my eyes.

"I told you Daddy; he won't talk to me. And believe me, I've tried. It's like he just woke up one day and decided he didn't like me anymore," I said tossing my hands in the air and letting them fall into my lap.

"The other day he said that he was tired of doing 'this' but he wouldn't go into what 'this' meant, and he got upset when I asked if he wanted to break up with me…which I thought was a completely valid question," I continued looking down at my hands.

"Noe…. relationships, they are like a journey. Or better, they're like any of the stories that you escape to every

168

day. The initial chapters introduce you to your protagonist and their supporting characters – that is, you learn your significant other and come to know the important staples in their lives, including the characteristics that make them, them," he said talking with his hands to chart the progress of my stories.

"The subsequent chapters highlight the good times and then somewhere about three fourths of the way through, you generally read and vicariously experience a valley – the character's low moments. During those times, your protagonist struggles and maybe for a time, things don't go her way, but ultimately, by the time you reach your ending there's resolution of some sort. Lessons are learned, and if written well, your character grows. You know why I said this to you?" he lifted his eyebrows to me.

"Because you know I like reading, so this metaphor would resonate. But I –"

"Noe, you're a very smart young woman. I would not use such an obvious comparison to prove any kind of point," he interrupted.

"Listen more closely. You're hearing my metaphor and thinking that you're the protagonist. This, mi amorcita, may not necessarily be your story. What you're experiencing might not have much to do with you and the development of *your* character."

"Well, then what…you mean?"

"Yes. This is *his* story and as his novia, you are –"

"A supporting character."

"Yes. Support. And as much as you feel confused right now and as much as you want to live in the moments where you've felt scarred, think about the life and the role of the supporting character."

"But how do I support him when he won't talk to me?"

"Noe that is an answer that I cannot give you. This will be one that you can only gain from –"

"Him," I finished. "Daddy, this is probably going to

be one of the hardest things I've ever had to do."

"Do you care for Luca?"

"Very much so," I answered softly.

"Do you care for your relationship with him?"

"Of course I do," I said looking up intently.

"Then why –"

"Am I shirking from something I need to do *because* I care for him and for the us that we have...?"

"That's my girl," my dad said smiling and patting my thigh.

"I learned from the best," I added leaning my head onto his shoulder. "Can I start supporting after dinner?" I called up, peering at him through my eyelashes.

"How about a cookie and a glass of milk for the road?"

"I'll take it," I added wrapping my arms around him and squeezing tight.

***

"Luca," I called as I found him sitting under my tree. He was exactly where I'd have been at that time.

He didn't answer; he just looked up, met my eyes, and reached for my hand. I let my hand meet his and he gently pulled me on the ground next to him where we sat, shoulders touching, pinkies entwined.

"You found me," he began after some time. "I'm so sorry. I love you so much. I don't know what's wrong with me."

"It's not that easy, and you know it. We can't be that couple. What's going on with you?" I asked leaning toward him, nuzzling my head in the crook of his neck.

"I don't want to bombard you with my struggles. It's not fair," he whispered into my hair. "Luca, that's what I signed up for. Your trials are my trials, and if you exclude me it's like you don't trust me to support you and that's a whole different problem. I'm here for you, but it only works if you let me in."

"I love you so much, and I don't want this to ruin anything," he retorted, voice quaking with anxiousness and sadness.

"Luca, there's no way to not ruin things. Wait, no, that's not how I meant it. Don't think about ruining things. Oh my gosh, look at me," I continued, as we turned toward each other.

"Yeah."

"Tell me. No holds bar. No limits. Just do it…and any other cliché or slogan that means tell me what's up."

"I'm so lost MC. I don't have anything figured out and I'm supposed to know what I'm doing by now," he said laying his head on my chest.

"Who said? Who determined that you're *supposed* to know what's going on in your life? Where's this rule book?" I asked stroking his hair and rubbing his back.

"MC, don't make light. I'm serious."

"As am I. Luca, please take it from me, a girl who has moved schools and changed majors more than anyone should be able to over the course of the past three years. It's okay," I added leaning over to kiss his ear.

"No, it's not. I'm no quitter," he sat up huffing.

"Luca, who said that it has to be all of that? What's so wrong with changing your path if it no longer makes sense for you? As long as your new direction exists and it's the best thing for you, you should do it, and do it freely."

"MC, you and I are completely different. For you that's fine, but it's not alright for me and my path. I have a path, a clear one, and I can't get sidetracked."

"What's making you feel sidetracked?" I asked, sidestepping his double standard in search of a better discussion.

"You know I love you, right?"

"Yes," I answered hesitantly. "Wait, me? It's me? You feel like I'm pushing you off your path? How?"

"I never said that!"

"But you're not denying it either. Luca, how? What have I done?"

"I... I don't know what you want me to say. I don't know what to do. I just don't know," he responded pushing up to stand.

"Luca," I pleaded tugging him back to his seat. "There's not something I'm looking for you to say, and the only thing for you to do is talk to me. Tell me what's going on in your head."

"You know what? I'm just overwhelmed right now. I'm not making any sense. We're fine, right?" he asked looking at me, eyes full of sadness and longing.

'We're fine, right?' I replayed it repeatedly in my head. He wouldn't talk to me. He wouldn't tell me anything. He was fine. His eyes were blank and his demeanor downcast, but he was 'fine'. We were 'fine'. I stopped pressing him for fear of upsetting him. I just tried to continue being his supporting character. We stayed beneath my tree a while longer, not really saying much of anything, just taking in the day's air.

Luca became himself over the course of the next couple of weeks. I continued to ask feeling questions that he continued to dodge. I told myself that I couldn't be angry with him or with our situation, and eventually I fell into my groove somewhere too.

***

"You have to be nice this time."

"What do you mean?"

"Harper please," I begged.

"If he can't take the heat then…"

"MC, we promise to be on our best behavior," Hayley interrupted.

"Thank you, Hayley, you're not who I'm worried about."

"Look MC, I don't know why you're freaking out but if you want me to, I promise I won't make your poor excuse for a boyfriend cry today."

"It's not about tears, it's about comfort Harper. You have a way of sucking all levels of comfort out of a space. I'm just asking if we can keep you at a 5 instead of a 10."

"If you insist…"

"I insist," I shouted. "Don't you Hay?"

"Hayley don't incriminate yourself," Harper interjected. "MC, I don't get why you always go to such great lengths to make sure no one says anything that might upset your precious Luca."

"It's not like that Harper and you know it. You're just always so mean to him. He really wants to get to know you all and he can't unless you lighten up. So please…can you?"

"Fine."

"Fine will work."

The three of us unhooked our seatbelts and exited Harper's jeep. We opted for lunch at Buffalo Wild Wings instead of our usual froufrou brunch spot to help make Luca feel a bit more comfortable. I'd told him to arrive 45 minutes later than we'd arrived to get Harper on board and to get settled for our meal together. Inside we got a booth, ordered drinks, and contemplated the menu as we waited for Luca to arrive.

"We've been here almost 2 hours and he's not here," Harper growled, spying a clock behind us.

"What time is it?" I asked fishing for my phone.

"It's nearly 2," Hayley spoke.

"Well I told him to get here close to 1:30 so he's not *that* late."

"Do you think we should check on him?" Hayley's concern chimed in.

"Yeah, shouldn't someone ask him why he's choosing to disrespect our time?" Harper added.

"I meant, to make sure he's okay," Hayley corrected.

"Yeah Hay. Um, I'll be right back."

Harper huffed as I scooted from our booth and made my way to the bathroom. I could feel her disapproving gaze the entire walk. Safely inside a stall, I pulled out my cell phone and worked to reach Luca. It's not like him to be late and not say anything. The phone rang and rang, going to voicemail each of the three times I'd called. I returned to the booth hoping to see him chatting idly with Harper and Hayley, telling them of his near-death experience or some uncharacteristic traffic during his journey, but he was nowhere to be found.

"Well?" Harper snarled.

"Well what?" I called back, taking my seat.

"Did you get him on the phone?"

"I went to pee. My phone is dead now anyway. I can't call him."

"Do you want to use mine MC? You can just check on him. I'm getting awfully worried."

"Thanks Hay, but I don't know his number by heart and besides, I think he might've told me that he wouldn't be here today."

"What? He told you he wouldn't be here today, but we're waiting for him?" Harper said.

"Yeah. Um. But it's not like that. We talked last night, and I was half sleep, but I think I vaguely remember him saying that we'd have to reschedule."

"You do huh?" Harper asked incredulously.

"Yeah. I think that's what it is, and that's why he hasn't called to let me know. Because we talked yesterday," I tried to make myself sound believable.

"Oh, well great. We can reschedule. Can we order now?" Hayley asked eagerly.

"MC you expect us to believe that story?" Harper snapped.

"It's what happened," I stressed. "Let's eat."

The three of us dined in a haze of discomfort. Harper sat fuming and only made conversation with Hayley. Hayley tried to speak with us both about nothing in particular, but it was just too hard to participate. After we paid our bill no one wanted to stay any longer. Harper dropped us off at our apartments, and though I was the last to get out, I ran toward the door to avoid the pain of any further conversation.

***

"MC is that you?" a voice called from the bedroom.

"Wha'? Who?"

"Luca. It's me, Luca. Where've you been?"

"What do you mean, 'where have I been'? Where have you been? You were supposed to have lunch with Hayley, Harper, and me. We waited for you and you never called, texted, or anything," I spoke sternly, seething, but trying to remain calm.

"I got busy," he said nonchalantly, turning up the volume on the television.

"You got busy," I echoed, finding him comfortably on my bed.

"MC, I'm watching," he chided.

"Luca, please," I began turning off the television to get his attention. "We talked about this yesterday. We were all going to have lunch. What happened? I had to tell some outlandish story to Harper because she was all over me."

"Since when is it my concern whether or not Harper is pleased?" he added jovially.

"Luca, please be serious right now. Where were you? Why didn't you call?" I questioned taking a seat next to him on the bed.

"Are you really upset by this? I thought you would've had a better time without me. You know Harper and I always fight."

"I know you fight, but you not showing actually made things worse. You've just given her more reason to say terrible things about you."

175

"But you know I'm none of those things," he noted stoically.

I hesitated, working to choose my words appropriately. It is true that I don't think he's uncaring, chauvinistic, or worthless – Harper's go-to descriptors, but it's getting harder and harder to defend him when he does things like this.

"Why are you thinking? Do you now *agree* with her?"

"It's not that, but…"

"Why is there a 'but'?" he asked with growing furor.

"It's not a 'but', but…"

"There it is again."

"Stop interrupting or I'll never get past it."

"There shouldn't be a 'but' to get past," he screeched.

"Stop getting upset. It's just like…I don't know. Look at today. Look at the situation you put me in."

"That has nothing to do with your thinking that I'm selfish, listless and a bigot."

"I never said any of that," I yelped, sliding closer to him. "Look at me," I pulled his chin up to see his face.

"It's not what you said. It's what you didn't say," he tugged away and moved from the bed.

"Where are you going?" I called after him as he stormed from my bedroom.

"Wherever."

"Why are you upset?"

"I thought we were past this?"

"Luca, what are you saying? Can you please stop moving and look at me? Talk to me."

He made his way to the couch and plopped down burying his face in his hands. When I saw him earlier, he was protected by his genial cloak of boyish charm. Somewhere in our conversation it'd fallen away, and he was a big ball of mush.

"I don't want to go back to fighting with you all the time," he sighed.

"Why do we have to go back there? This was

supposed to be an easy conversation. It doesn't have to be a knockdown, drag out fight," I said to him in my most soothing tones.

"But if you think I'm all those things.... that I'm the monster Harper paints me to be.... then I don't..."

"Luca, stop it. I already told you I don't think what she does, and she knows that. I wouldn't still be with you and I wouldn't still love you if I felt that way about you."

His eyes sagged with sadness as I joined him on the couch and wrapped myself around him.

"MC, do you love me?"

"Yes."

"Do you know I'd never do anything to hurt you?"

"Yes."

"Do you forgive me?"

"Yeah. I do."

"Will you grab me a bowl of ice cream?"

"No."

"What do you mean 'no'?" he asked.

"Well, I love you and all but I'm still mad at you," I giggled. "Sitting with Harper for three hours was sheer torture."

I tossed a pillow at him and tried to jump from the couch, but he grabbed hold of me and buried me kisses until I gave into his request.

Ebonii Nelson

From the Desk of _____ Noe Cortes

August 3, 2010

Tomorrow I will see Dr. Logan. He will ask for my journal and he will read this page and those preceding and he'll inevitably ask me why there's a huge gap and then he'll ask me why this one is so incredibly short. Then when I dodge each of those he'll venture to a conversation about Matias and whether or not it's healthy or really how I'm feeling about any and everything. We'll talk about why I refuse to go to the Speed Dating thing with Harper. It's going to be so much that I'm not ready for...or rather, I don't want to go through it because I know what's coming.

Wednesday, why are you doing this to me?!?

Chapter 15

"Harper."

"MC, quit stalling. Let's hear what unethical situation you've gotten into. I feel I must applaud your lack of scruples," she says offering me snaps in applause.

"Usually I'm on my own when it comes to making slightly questionable moral compass decisions. You are human. Praise baby Jesus," she says playfully, offering a prayerful pose and head nod toward the heavens.

"Harper, why do you have to be so loud all the time? If you want, we can go somewhere for lunch, yes?"

"This must be really serious," she pauses as she makes her way into my office. I close the door subtly behind her as she proceeds to rearrange some of my furniture. I watch as she pushes a small couch and a chair I have against my bookshelves to create an open space on the floor. Moving steadily she closes my blinds, shuts down my computer and makes her way back to the cleared floor space. She sweeps her hair into a quick chignon and takes off her shoes. Watching somewhat in awe, my ears tune in to her first words.

"MC...please come. Sit." I oblige as she continues.

"We're not going anywhere. We're not eating lunch. We're actually going to spend some quality time coming to an understanding of what has been going on in your life for the past month. I want this to be an open dialogue so I will do my best to be open-minded and inviting.

But MC," she pauses, places her hand on my right shoulder and gives me a death stare.

"If you decide that sharing isn't something you'd like to do today, I can and will make this a more painful process," she closes with an eerie smile.

For a moment I am strangely frightened by the level of seriousness this conversation has reached, and Harper's tone is unlike any I've ever gotten from her.

"So where exactly would you like me to start," I ask.

"At the beginning."

"The beginning is really hard to describe."

"Try," she answers quickly through gritted teeth.

"There are no stipulations on how long this story has to be, nor do I care whether or not the phraseology – as you like to say – is proper. I can't be a friend to you if I don't know what's going on with you. Seriously MC…tell me what's up," she ends, affability returning to her tone.

"Oh my goodness. Well, you already know that Matias came two months back. He's on a fellowship and he's here really to check out the academic world. When he came on, he had two options of where to set up shop. He could work with me and Joyce here or in the Administration building. None of that really matters, except that it sets the stage for how I even matter to him," I begin hurriedly, trying to take advantage of her sure to be short lasting geniality.

"Alright. Background painted. Continue."

"So there was one day I was here, and I almost had a full-fledged panic attack and I didn't really know why. I went outside to catch my life," I say pointing toward the door as I mentally replay that day's events. "During my episode, Matias walked up, and we engaged in a calming banter before we came inside. All was normal but during his time with me he did this weird staring thing."

"He stare–"

"I know, explain the staring thing," I interrupt. "Dr. Logan and I have already been here. I don't know how to explain it. It was just his look at me was more than a look. It was like he was seeing clear past me," I try explaining, willing her to understand. "It made me nervous, but also strangely enraptured. I started to yearn for that uneasiness and that elevated my nervousness. Oh, it also didn't help that he has no rules about personal space."

"So you liked him. How have you progressed?" she asks dryly.

"Harper, I don't know how that's easy for you to pick out. I don't think I liked him at that point. I didn't even know

180

him then. Besides that…he's technically my boss so I tried to avoid him at all costs."

"And we both know whenever you start avoiding someone, they're always available and magically appear everywhere ….so, when did you next encounter him?"

"I hate that you're so smart sometimes. I feel like this story would flow quite differently if I were telling Hayley."

"Thank you for the compliment. Think of me as helping you. I'm assisting you in energy conservation. If I already know bits and pieces, you can skip forward."

"Energy conservation," I say picking at a piece of fluff on the floor before continuing. "Okay…well…so the next time I 'encountered him'," I resume, "was when we had a lunch together. We ended up going to Bella Vita for lunch."

"Bella Vita? As in Luca's Bella Vita?" she asks leaning in closer to me with her repetition.

"The one and only," I add matching her lean. "So naturally I was–"

"Confounded, to say the least," she interrupts matter-of-factly. "That's bad business. I don't even know if I could…wait. Keep going."

"Right," I say breaking free of the tangent trance we'd fallen into. "I was lost and confused but I couldn't say that. I couldn't say that was the place that marked the last Valentine's day I'd had with the then love of my life and he damn near proposed to me before the untimely, yet well-timed expiration of our relationship," I say quickly furiously taking a breath. "These things I can't possibly say. So I didn't. I was instead ultra-weird, and he kept eyeing me and being uncomfortably close to me all the while looking undeniably handsome."

"What happened at the lunch?"

"So he starts asking me about my hopes and dreams, what brings me to work and what wakes me up every day," I continue using my fingers to count each of the recounted questions.

"Shell shocked, you were?"

181

"Of course. I don't know how to – wait, huh? How did you know?"

"MC, my feelings are hurt that you think that I wouldn't know how you work. As expressive and verbose as you are, you have a way with saying a ton of words about everything except yourself," Harper recites gently pushing me.

"I can't say whether you avoid self-talk because you're afraid of yourself, or you feel others don't really care, or because you really just don't know. But I do know that you don't do well when people ask pointed questions that require you to really explore and explain the inner depths of MC."

"Wow. Harper I am without words."

"Be without them later. Keep the story going."

"Always the sentimental one," I frown and watch Harper as she does the same. We stay engaged in our frowning contest until she sticks her tongue out, I smile and am forced to continue.

"Well…I failed, like you said, and I couldn't really respond to any of his questions. I was in a fog, so I left and exploded on Dr. Logan. He was quite comforting. I really love that about him. Even in his firmness and professionalism he's calming and reassuring," I add endearingly.

"So I rehashed what'd happened and he started asking me similar questions which stressed me out even more. It was all very counseling-y."

"Wait, your counseling session was…. counseling-y? This has to be something new. We must alert the media. Dr. Hale is doing his job."

"Really, with the sarcasm? And Dr. Hale? Harper, we both know that's not his name."

"MC I would love for you to call the man by his…. stop that," she protests, "I'm not going to indulge in this tangent. Finish. Story time. Go."

"So I left."

"Wait, you left? I'm confused. You were just talking."

"Oh I didn't have an appointment and someone with

one came, so I had to leave. I resolved to work on myself and get to a normal state of functioning. We had our girls' lunch, remember about Cirque du Soleil?"

"Right, your new perspective on life."

"Exactly."

"Hold on. Why didn't get give us **the** story about Matias that day?"

"I mean…technically I did."

"Technically, you didn't because you left out a ton of details that I am only now receiving. What gives?"

"You know Hay is so sentimental and I didn't want it to seem like a bigger deal than what it was. It's really not that serious."

"MC, I try my hardest to stand by you in everything. But I have to say, on behalf of Hayley too, we're your best friends. We're practically your sisters, and it's hurtful to know that you'd offer us a makeshift story of your life, but then expect us to serve as your accountability partners for this new life journey you're on. Where's the trust in that?"

"Harper, I didn't mean to offend anyone…but…you called me crazy that day, didn't you? What about that would invite me to share more with you?"

"I will defend myself in saying, had you actually replayed the story as it happened, I doubt my response would've been the same. If you only give me the highlights – the drama, then I can't help but have a dramatic response."

"I guess."

"No guessing. I'm serious. If we can't be around for each other, then what are we doing? I don't want you to think I'm going to judge or not take what you say seriously. I want you to feel just as comfortable as I do with you, letting me into your world."

"I apologize. I was grappling with a ton and I didn't want it to seem more than what it was. I feel like I have this reputation of having things put together and I didn't want to taint that."

"MC you are delusional if you thought that we thought

you had all your cookies in the cookie jar. You are certifiably insane, but that's what we appreciate most about you. You're our words and our brain, Hayley's our heart, and I'm the brawn. That's how we work, but we can't work if everyone isn't offering what they can."

For a moment we share sentimentalities amidst our silence, and we lean in for a rare hug.

"Alright enough with the mushy; finish your story," she breaks.

"No need to bask in our tenderness, on with the apologue," I respond gallantly.

"As long as you're aware of how things work around here," Harper chuckles.

"Okay, that next week I was absorbed in work and by the time Wednesday came I needed Dr. Logan to help me stop avoiding the inevitable." I start to get short of breath and I can feel my mouth get that watery feeling you get just before you vomit. Despite my queasiness I force myself to ignore the violent hunger pangs in my stomach and continue.

"Breathe."

"Thanks. I needed that. At work the next day I had to interact with him. I helped him clean up. As I helped shelve books, I turned to find my nose in between his pecks," I say placing my hand in front of my face much like his pecks were.

"He totally digs you, and that's totally inappropriate. From a legal standpoint I feel like we should really look into the philosophies TIC has regarding fraternization. But that will come later. Keep going," Harper encourages offering circular 'keep moving' motions with her hands.

"We sat and talked about our feelings for each other then he suggested we meet for lunch."

"Another one?"

"I know...yes, another one."

"And..."

"He walked me out to my car and then he kissed me on the cheek and that was that. We had lunch the next day, and every day since. We've gone on outings and we frequently talk on the phone. We have spent more time together than I can tell you, and each day I'm with him I get more and more drawn into him and the idea of us. Just this weekend we went to Hideaway Park and we had lunch and we talked, and we danced."

"You danced?" Harper gasps, understanding the severity of the situation at hand.

"Yes, we danced, and it was lovely, and he's lovely and well, everything feels…. lovely. After our conversation earlier today he came in and we danced again, and he told me he adores me, and he wants to quit here and work full time as faculty so we can date officially."

"Oh goodness, what did you say?"

"Well, I told him that I was okay with him doing what he felt he wanted to do and that we could date then–"

"What? Then what? You can't stop with a then," Harper pauses, gasps and adds, "did you guys? Eew…where? Here? Are we sitting in it? It doesn't smell like anything," she starts to sniff. "No smell. What's with the 'then'?"

"You truly are a special individual. We didn't do that. Geez Harper, what kind of person do you take me for? We did kiss, and it was the most passionate and heavenly thing I've ever experienced, until you friggin' called and interrupted."

"Good thing I did. My best friend was about to fornicate right here in this office if it wasn't for me. You do take after me in some ways. I'm so proud."

"You are a mess. Well, that's all of it. That's my story and that's why I've been anti the idea of going to speed dating. And I think it's a waste of time because you can't learn anything significant about anyone in that short time."

"Honest blog."

"Proceed."

"I know you're more grown up and things are different, but I can't help but feel like things aren't all that different."

"Aren't all that different from what?"

"Luca."

"What? How on earth does Luca fit into this picture?"

"MC, you have this wonderful way of inviting some very whimsical men into your life. I don't know how you do it. But you definitely have a type. They are otherworldly and I think that's how they get you."

She pauses briefly mulling over some things in her head before she proceeds.

"You, I think, crave the experience of other that you're too scared to just get on your own, so you live vicariously through these guys. Don't get me wrong they're always handsome and nice and sweet, but they're always wrong for you. Matias fits that mold and I know you don't like to revisit the past, but like with Luca, babe it'd probably be better to just walk away."

"I never understand this. I told you the whole story and you mean to tell me all you got is that he is a repeat...a Spanish version of Luca? How? And what do you mean I have a type?

Luca and Matias are nothing alike," I cry out with confusion and hurt.

"Be honest with yourself MC. Both foreign born. They were both initially appreciative and not frightened by your awkwardness. With Luca it was the dance thing and with Matias it was the weird porch thing. They both developed these premature infatuations with you," she proffers.

She notices as my mood doesn't soften and sharply continues.

"My goodness they move fast, and though you're usually slow and methodical, with them you too seem to move fast too. Flirting early, giving into their advances, and opening yourself to them so quickly and freely. Matias is a re-run."

"Harper that's not true. Matias is different. He's older, much more mature, and he really sees a part of me that I don't even think I have seen."

"He's older and more mature by default. You're also older and more mature, except when it comes to romantic relationships. And the other part business....you know yourself better than anyone else, and you know full well all of the crap that you say Matias sees, you see, and you know well. And if he knows anything about people, he can tell that you thrive on that kind of shit," she says and quickly throws her hands up before I can respond.

"Forgive my language," she concedes rolling her eyes. "But, he can tell that you yearn for another to recognize the complex nature of your personality and as someone who is clearly into you, he also knows that he should probably appease that part of you to ensure that he has a shot."

"You make him sound like some sort of con artist."

"Con artist no, but he's also no dummy, so I still stand by the notion that he pays attention to his audience and he caters to them – which is not a bad thing. MC, I love that you love love and romanticism and fairy tales, but as much as I know you – Middle Name Maries for life – I don't think that your guy is this Prince Charming you're expecting. I feel like he's just different than what you're imagining."

"I appreciate your honesty, but I respectfully disagree."

"MC, can you do me a solid?"

"What?"

"Two things really: I know you think that I'm anti love and I'm eternally negative, but please in your quiet time think about what I'm saying with regard to your love choices. Second, as we've already learned you're involved, but can you please just come with me to Speed Dating. This is not about you continuing your search for love, this is about you being a friend and having my back. Can we try that?"

"I can do that. I can. Love you," I nod reassuring the both of us.

"More."

"Alright, details please."

"Middle Name Maries are back," she says with a smile and extends her hand for a high five.

"It's in two weeks at the House of Blues downtown. I'll dress you so you don't embarrass me, and we can ride together if you'll drive to me. Sound like a plan?"

"That's fine. Although I would like to say I am more than capable of dressing myself. Thank you very much for your vote of confidence."

"Of course you are."

My day finishes with Harper – Middle Name Maries, what we called ourselves in grade school when we realized we shared a middle name. The two of us shut down the office and part ways – her to a young lawyer's reception and me to my apartment. I don't want her to be right about her assessment of me and my loves, but I know Harper and more often than not Harper knows best.

From the Desk of _____ Noe Cortes _____

August 3, 2010

I can't get Harper out of my head. She told me that I have a "type" and my "type" is inherently wrong. She said that Matias is a re-run of Luca and I should not give into my apparent infatuation for him. She said that my Prince Charming is a type of guy that I wouldn't think of and then she used "Middle Name Maries" to talk me into going to this speed dating thing with her. What is this type? She described it perfectly, but I want to believe that that's not the truth. Sure both Luca and Matias were well versed in the ways of the world beyond that which I have seen, and they were both very into me very quickly, but I don't think that means that Matias and I have to end the same way that Luca and I did. I just don't. It can't be that easy. And if it is, why don't I see it? And who is this other type of guy she's talking about is the right one for me?

There's no other. Shouldn't a potential suitor be infatuated with me? Shouldn't he appreciate me for my quirks? Should he be caught up in the rapture of love, to coin an Anita Baker phrase?

She's totally wrong and I won't have it. I won't.

She sounds just like I feel Dr. Logan will tomorrow. I hate them both. This is absolutely absurd. Why is it that I can never just be and be happy with situations as they are? Why do people consistently look for things to be wrong with the things, or in this case people that make the most sense to me? This is so frustrating.

Chapter 16

"MC?" Luca called from his bathroom.

"Yes sir?"

"Mamma just called and said that my dad is pretty sick, so I'm going to head up to see them this weekend."

"Do you have anything due for class? You cleared everything with your faculty, right?"

"My dad is ill MC. He could die for God sakes, why are you lecturing me on being responsible?"

"There is no lecture here Luca; I was just making sure that while you're attending to this stressor, you're not inadvertently creating a new one. Calm down," I said making my way next to him, staring at our reflections in the mirror.

"Don't tell me to calm down," he practically yelled, leaving the bathroom, and pacing in his bedroom. "Why can't you just support me?"

Our fighting banter had come back to haunt us. Luca's graduate program was coming to a close and he was trying to decide where he'd do his externship and he was still in counseling with Dr. Levi. I hated her; she seemed to help Luca blame a lot of what went wrong in his life on me. I was too clingy, but then I was too distant. I was too overbearing but then I wasn't attentive enough. I supported him in all the wrong ways, and I was simultaneously a distraction. We never had good days when he had a session. It was always, Dr. Levi says this, and Dr. Levi says that. I'd never met her, but I surely wanted to punch her in the face. Luca started distancing himself more and more. He always volunteered for extra hours at his internship, and he randomly joined a tennis league – when he'd never played a game of tennis in his life.

In the thick of it I found myself filling in the gaps left by Luca's new activities. I picked up some extra shifts working with my mom at her studio. I did jazz before class, intermediate ballet Tuesdays and Thursdays at lunch, and advanced lyrical and modern just after dinner. We barely saw one another, and when we did see each other, in an effort to avoid an untimely verbal sparring match, we kept our dialogue to pleasantries and platitudes.

"Luca," I spoke slowly, walking toward him and making sure to breathe and choose my words wisely. "How can I support you? How can I better this experience for you?" I added, sliding my hands atop his shoulders, beginning a comforting massage.

"Are you patronizing me?" he asked indignantly as he stood expressing disgust with my gesture and verbiage.

"Luca," I began. "I'm trying really hard to be what you need me to be. I'm not patronizing you. I'm not mocking you. I'm not, not supporting you. I want to be there for you and asking how, is the only way I know to ensure that I actually do that. Please. Tell me what you would have me do."

"Well," he huffed, "I just need some space. Some time to get my wits about me."

"To get your wits about you," I began to joke at his uncharacteristic cliché usage, but quickly remembered the severity of the present moment. "Fine," I added collecting my belongings. "Do you need a ride to the airport?"

"No. I'll have the shuttle come pick me up."

"Okay. Luca?" I called as I made my way to his front door.

"Yeah?" he asked, not yet emerging from his bedroom.

"I really don't want what we have to be broken, and I'm doing all that's in my power to hold us together," I sighed still inching toward the door. "I know we're not technically fighting because this seems to be a continual conversation, but whenever we've fought we said if there was more bad than good we'd part ways so we could preserve the friendship," I grabbed hold of the door frame to support me as I continued, frightened of the words exiting my mouth.

"Do you think there's more wrong with us than is right?" I asked through a whisper.

"I just need some time," he said still nestled within his bedroom.

I didn't know what was happening to us. During what seemed like the dissent of our relationship I actively tried to use all the things we discussed in my psychology classes to work on how we communicated with one another and how to best manage our relationship, but none of it worked. He wouldn't talk to me and I was lost and what was worse is that I started to hear a nagging voice in my head that sounded a lot like Harper's saying, "I told you so."

***

That's good girls. Alright, after the chasse I want to see a flick kick, or developpe battemate whatever you want to call it, right into a stag then jazz run off stage. Yes? Try that. And 5 – 6 – 7– 8.

"Marie Cortes?"

"Yes ma'am?"

"Come visit with me."

"I'm right there. Keep it going. Run it again and then when I get back, with music. Liliana, watch your back leg on that stag."

"Yes mama," I said making my way into mama's office.

"This class is over in 10, no?"

"Yes. It is. Is there a problem?"

"No. Do you have a private with Liliana or Mia today?"

"No. What do you need?"

"Nada mi'ja. As you were. See me before you leave, yes?"

"Yes," I nodded and returned to my dancers.

Something's up, I thought to myself walking back to the studio.

"Let me see it. Con música. Ms. Jana can you hit play on that track? It should be ready; number 7."

As Jennifer Lopez's "Get Right" played loudly I watched as the girls put their smooth and lyrical to the hard, brass rhythms of the song. Getting lost in the expression of it all was very soothing – so much so that I lost myself in it as well.

"MC? MC? MC?"

"Who? What?" I exclaimed a bit entranced.

"How was that? Would you like us to run it again?" asked one of my star pupils Mia.

"No it was good. Please come back Thursday with a 15 – 30 second solo," I began, waking from my brief reverie.

"Actually let's do 30. And make the second half of it group dance. Okay. Here's what I mean. Your solo is 15 seconds, then you'll have another 15 seconds of dance that all the girls will do, but each of you is to come up with your own different 15 second thing. Does that make sense?"

"Yes ma'am," they all responded in union.

"Good deal. Get some rest, and if you haven't already scheduled your individuals, please visit with Ms. Jana. I think right now I only have openings tomorrow and Friday."

As my girls left the studio, I made my way into the little office mama cleared. I wrote down the instructions that I'd just given the girls as to not forget it and walked back out to the studio to start on choreography for the rest of the song.

"Noe Marie?" my mom called.

"Ma'am," I called not yet emerging from my space.

"Here, please."

I loved how my mama always had a way of omitting certain verbs or subjects…. or really meaningful parts of a sentence.

"Yes 'am," I asked making my way into one of the small studios. We only really used this studio for private lessons or individual choreography.

194

"Maria…" she began as a song started to play –
Humble Me from Norah Jones. And then soon still silent, she
began to dance.

Enraptured in the lyrics 'truth spoke in whispers will
tear you apart' I felt myself join in the graceful expression.
Up chaine, plié, passé, half jump, slide down, toe rise and
reach. Coupe turn, step twice to fan kick and step out. Chaine
to relevé, soutenou, piqué, step down.

I'd never really danced with mama. I learned it from
her – watching and studying her but never in tandem. Not
like this. When we stopped, we each lowered ourselves to
the floor and sat in silence.

"What's going on with you?" she asked sincerely.

"How do you mean?"

"You told me so."

"I'm confused," I said pulling my feet toward me in a
butterfly position and stretching.

"Your dance."

"Mom, really I'm fine."

"Noe this isn't one of those moments where you
tell me you're fine and I leave you alone. I love that
you've been more active in the studio, but you and I both
know it's very uncharacteristic of you. What has brought
you here?" she asked signaling me to stand with her as she
made her way toward her office.

"It's nothing really mom," I said following behind
her. "I know that you need help and I could use the extra
money, so I just decided to help."

"Noe Marie, it is no secret that you and I bump
heads often. I think it is the me in you that causes us to
disagree. *Because* we are similar, I might get it."

"Mom, really…it's nothing like I said before.
Or…I don't know what the problem is really. So I can't
talk to you about anything. I'm just here to work," I sighed,
sitting in her chair as I dropped my head in my lap.

"Noe? What is this with Luca?"

"Why does any of this have to be related to him?" I

mumbled from my lap.

"Look at me," she asked coming to sit next to me in an adjacent chair.

"Yeah?" I asked peaking up from my lap.

"Noe,"

"Mom…"

"You feel like you can't find answers that you feel should be clear and you are trying everything you can think of to no avail."

"Mom…"

"You feel lost and you're trying to drown yourself in things that once brought you happiness."

"How do you know all of that?"

"Noe, we are one in the same. I know I don't know all the ins and outs of your relationship, but try this on for size: there are some things in this world that cannot be rationalized, analyzed or controlled," she said reaching out and lifting my chin so that our eyes met.

"For women like the two of us that can be extremely hard, but we have to yield to that truth. Whatever you're going through cannot be fixed by you alone."

"I know that I can't do it alone, but I don't know how to include him in the conversation. He doesn't seem to want to be an active participant. And everything that I know says that he has to engage."

"You have to let go Noe. The things you do in love don't always make sense. You have to let go of your theories and flow charts and just let your heart guide you. Be there for him and, and, and trust that he'll see the love in that."

"I don't even know what that means. What if he doesn't get that?"

"Noe, do you know that saying, 'if you love something let it go; if it comes back then –"

"Yes, I know the saying. And I hate it. It makes no sense. It's not reassuring. Why would I let go of what I love?"

"Noe I'm not going to try to make you believe that love makes sense. It doesn't. Before you find it, it's elusive and mysterious. When you're in it you feel untouchable and euphoric. And when you think that you're about to lose it, it's a feeling like none other."

Mama became very animated at the thought of love and understanding it. It surprised me and I felt oddly closer to her knowing that she too had perspicacious and sanguine ideas of love.

"There's no other feeling in the world that can be so different, so don't try to understand it. The one thing you can know for sure is that it is a two-way street. Right now your love is strained with Luca. The more you try to hold him, the more you will run the risk of suffocating him and losing that which you treasure most. He's probably just as lost as you are, and your attempts at rationalization and trying to fix it are poison," she continued.

"Poison mama? I just don't...I don't," I attempted, starting to sob uncontrollably.

"My sweetheart," she started, leaning in, and pulling me into an embrace. "I hate that with this type of lesson I cannot offer much more than my two arms of love. It hurts now, but there are lessons to be learned in all that we experience. You know that. All things work together for good."

I lost my words and collapsed in my mother's caring arms. I'd never shared much of anything with her before; my secrets were always saved for my papí because he always understood. But that day was different. That day she and I spoke the same language and we seemed like we were written from the same code. She shared her love for me in a way that I desperately needed.

***

"How's Louie?"

"Ha ha, Louie," Hayley chuckled uncontrollably.

197

"Seriously Harper, he's not a fan of it, and I can't say I am either. Give it a rest. His name is Luca," I gnarled.

"Grr. What's got your panties in a wad?"

"Sorry Harper. I haven't spoken to Luca since Tuesday when I left his apartment, and tomorrow he'll be well on his way to San Francisco to visit with his parents. His dad is sick," I sunk deeper into my chair.

"Why haven't you talked to him," Hayley asked innocently.

"Because he's a douche and he's starting to let his douche-bag tendencies show more often," Harper responded flippantly.

"Harper!" Hayley scolded.

"No. I keep quiet all the time. This isn't a new funk MC. I feel like you're on this perpetual rollercoaster where *Louie* is the conductor and is deciding how fast you should go and how everything should be and that's not right."

"This is ridiculous. I come to you not for you to tell me how stupid I am for being in a relationship and not for you to tell me how much he sucks, but for your support and you always do this. You go on this rampage against men and about how they're all no good, just because you don't have one," I moaned turning away from both Harper and Hayley.

"MC, you don't mean that," Hayley said fearfully, reaching for my hand atop the table.

"Don't worry Hayley. Thank you for telling me how you really feel MC. Forgive me for not wanting to deal with your shit anymore. Forgive me for not feeling sorry for you when you willingly entered into a relationship when I warned you. Forgive me for not yielding to your constant whining and being a pushover to some idiot who doesn't give a rat's ass about you or your relationship. You know what, fuck this," Harper sighed, violently rose from our table and retreated from the restaurant.

"MC... we can't be like this," Hayley said standing to depart. "I need to go make sure Harper is okay."

Who was she to talk to me any kind of way? She was always saying things like she knew. She didn't know. This wasn't an inevitable. It was totally avoidable. And I wasn't being controlled by Luca.

I sat, trying not to cry; ruminating after I'd effectively offended and utterly embarrassed one of my closest friends. I didn't mean any of it; I just didn't want her to be right in this way. She was so adamant that Luca was no good for my life. So I needed her to be wrong. I wandered out to find Harper and Hayley sitting on a bench just outside the restaurant.

"Harper…. I'm sorry."

She continued to sit as if I'd said nothing to her.

"Okay. You're right. You're always right, and I honestly didn't know what to do with it. No, I knew what to do with it; I just didn't want to hear it – not now," I conceded and lowered myself onto the ground behind the bench.

Staring through the grates of the bench I convinced myself to press on.

"I know you advised against this relationship, but I want it and I still believe that Luca and I are good together. And even if what you're saying is right in this moment, it doesn't erase the fact that I care for him very much, and I don't want to experience what I have been at his behest. And I feel shitty in general and listening to you just ugh," I rambled. "But I value our friendship and I love you so much and I didn't mean much of anything I said, and I would be more than fortunate if you would forgive me."

"Alright. But let me tell you this," she said standing and turning toward me, looking me straight in the face. "If you do that again, regardless of how long we've known each other, I will punch you in the mouth. Are we clear?"

"Yeah I agree," Hayley started. "Except for the punching part. But you definitely can't start turning on us. We're each other's support. If we destroy ourselves how can we expect to survive?"

"I promise I'll be better. I'm at my wits end and for some reason it was just easier to empty on you guys. I know I keep saying it, but really, I'm sorry. Forgive me?"

"Of course," Hayley sings.

"You've been warned," Harper growled.

"Well, can we go back inside and finish our lunch?" Hayley questioned.

"You mean start right?" I joked.

"Oh, yeah...let's start lunch," Hayley laughed.

"Bring on the vodka. I have a feeling we're going to need it for this conversation."

"What do you mean?" Hayley asked Harper.

"Well...MC here is going to tell us what's going on in la la Luca land. Considering she attempted to mar a 16-year friendship, I know it's going to require some booze."

We laughed and returned to our table. I dished about how Luca and I did nothing but argue, and I told them about my moment with mama. It helped talking to them, but I really wanted and needed to talk to Luca. I didn't know if that meant calling him or letting him have his space as he requested.

I had sleepless nights at home as the number of days since I'd heard Luca's voice or seen his face grew. Sunday night my phone rang – an all too familiar ring tone.

"Hello. MC?"

"Luca. Hi."

From the Desk of _____Noe Cortes_____

August 4, 2010

Dr. Logan, this is for you. I know that today you're going to ask me lots of questions about my progress. Have I gotten anywhere with my soul searching? Have I written anymore with my dissertation? Have I done anything remotely beneficial to my life and mental well-being?

Absolutely not.

I have been completely useless and completely overwhelmed by the déjà vu that my life appears to be taking. I can't help but remember when Luca and I were on the rocks. That's not what's going on here at all, but Harper's warning is there...I have that weird sinking feeling...and something very strange is my water.

I was floating blissfully along before Harper barged into my office and before you (which you will today) decided to go and ruin the only patch of good that I have to hold onto. I don't want to talk about it. I don't want to think about. I don't even want to do anything about it.

I seriously don't understand why I have to have these moments when the thing that brings me some of the most happiness turns out to be the same thing that will cause my demise. What about any of that is fair? I'm a good person so I can't understand why all these bad things keep happening or threatening to happen.

Dr. Logan, I'm ready to quit.

Dr. Pepper.... stat.

Chapter 17

"Dr. Logan I think I'm cured."

From the bathroom at his office I'm rehearsing for my session. I am nervous about this afternoon. I cancelled our appointment last week for the first time ever and I feel like he may be angry. But cancelling was good. I'm doing much better. At work I have a rhythm. Matias and I are on a nice path toward…I'm not exactly certain where we're headed, but I know the path we're on has forward progress. My dissertation…well, I've paused a bit on that, but where I stopped it looks great. I'm back to being a normal adult again.

"Who are you kidding?" I ask staring blankly into the mirror.

My life's a ball of mess. No one likes that I'm with Matias. I don't have anything to write with this dissertation. I don't like my work, but it pays the bills, and all I want to do is dance with Matias and let him read to me and be blissfully carefree.

"Get it together MC. You can't let him see you sweat. Let's do this," I say pointing at my reflection in the mirror.

I make my way out of the bathroom, down the long sterile corridor and back to Dr.

Logan's waiting room. So far, I've sweat through my shirt and my cardigan and I just feel like I am having heat flash after heat flash. This shouldn't be this difficult.

"Noe, Dr. Logan will see you now," Julia calls out.

"Right, yes of course he will. Thank you. It's 3 o'clock. It's time. It's now or never. It's…let's do this."

"Are you alright dear?"

"Great, peachy. He's just right beyond this door here. Make a left. He's the second office on the left. I know this. I've done it a million times," I say to myself willing each leg to take a step as I make my way to his space.

"Noe? Noe, why are you hanging outside the door? Come inside."

"Dr. L-Logan."

203

"Yes, 'tis I," he announces in a most Shakespearean way, chest protruding and lifting his arm toward the ceiling.

Dr. Logan is in rare form. He's wearing gray slacks, and a gray vest covering a white button down with his sleeves rolled up just above his elbows. He's wearing an unusually bright canary yellow tie and as he parades around like Demetrius from a *Midsummer Night's Dream,* I can't help feeling this peculiar and alluring tingly feeling awakening from my lower belly. His joviality, almost attractive, temporarily alarms me.

"Dr. Logan?"

"Yes, come in. Why haven't you had a seat?"

"Are you okay today?"

"I'm magnificent. Why? What's up with you? Why are you looking that way? Noe, sit. What's going on with you?"

"Dr. Logan stop telling me to sit and stop freaking out. I'm fine."

"You're…. fine?" he repeats, finding his way to his seat and rolling close to me, facial expression turned up with disbelief – his playfulness quickly fading.

"I'll sit if that makes you feel better. I've just…it's just I've been here for a while and I have been sitting for all of that time and I'm just tired of sitting."

"You've been here for a while? What does that mean? Our appointment is always at 3 o'clock."

"Yes it's at 3, but I came early."

"Early? More please."

"I came in just 60 minutes early or so –"

"You got in an hour early?" he asks completely dumbfounded. "Why Noe? Why, if nothing's wrong, why would you come an hour early for an appointment that never changes its time?"

"I just needed to," I whine a little.

"Is this because you cancelled your appointment last week?" he asks sliding his glasses up on his face.

"No. I just – Dr. Logan, I don't think you're hearing

me."

"I hear you Noe. I am listening to you and I will ask
you again, what's going on with you?" he finishes rolling
closer to me in his chair and lifting my chin so we're eye to
eye. "Talk to me…please."

"I don't think I can," I say beginning to cry.

"What are the tears about?" he begins, handing me a
Kleenex.

"I just had…I practiced this speech for you that I was
going to say, and now it's all messed up. I don't think I can
say it."

"A speech? What for?" he asks puzzled, his voice just
above a whisper.

"I need to be cured Dr. Logan."

"Cured? What do you mean? You don't have a
disease."

"I want to be better. I want to not need you, but I do. I
need to see you and speak to you and to have you tell me that
everything is going to be okay and that's not okay."

"Noe –"

"No, let me finish. Today I was gonna tell you about
Matias. You know we're in a quasi- relationship now? We
haven't had the talk to make it completely official, but I see
him and have lunch with him regularly. We hang out on the
weekends and he wishes me a good morning and evening
every day. He hugs me and I let him kiss me at work – *at
work,*" I try shouting through my tears.

"That's how much I don't care. And I was afraid to
tell you." I look up at him and try to make out his expression
through my steadily falling tears, hoping it would give me
courage to continue.

"I cancelled last week because I knew you would ask
me about things and I know you've read my journals, and,
and, and you know things. You would look me in my eyes
and tell me in that Dr. Logan way that it's all a bad idea and
then you'd be the 50 millionth person to tell me to cut it out,
and I am just not ready for you to say the same. I want

someone to be on my side. I'm falling apart and it's not fair that I've been coming here for this long and I'm still falling apart," I close wiping my nose and dabbing clean parts of the Kleenex at my eyes.

"Noe, when have I ever made you feel like you couldn't tell me something? That I might respond in a negative way, in a way that makes you feel shameful?" he asks, sitting next to me on his couch, placing his hand lightly in the center of my back, as I've leaned over placing my face in my hands.

"I guess you haven't, but I just feel like everyone feels the same way so why wouldn't you?"

"That's not how we work in here. This is a space for you to come clean and even if I have a differing opinion on a situation, I'll always leave you to your decisions. Can we at least talk about what's going on?"

"I suppose so. You promise not to judge?" I ask turning to make eye contact with him.

"You have my word," he continues not blinking, his gray eyes, searing into my soul – his hand still resting on my lower back and face inches from mine.

"Alright," I begin leaning away from him and shaking myself free of his trance.

I discuss with Dr. Logan my days with Matias – our conversations, our spot, his romance, us dancing, our interaction in the office, everything. I also let him know about Harper, her premonition, and our fight.

"She was right with Luca and I thought…I mean me and Matias…we're not nearly in that same space, but like I told you she said that he's a rerun. What am I supposed to do with that?"

"Why do you feel like there's something you have to do with it? Why does it matter what Harper's opinion is of any relationship you're in?"

"Because it does."

"Use your words."

"Dr. Logan she's one of my best friends. Sometimes I

think she can see things I can't always see. She was dead on
the first time and aside from the hurt of the broken
relationship, I don't want to go through another 'I told you
so' moment with Harper."

Exasperated I stand and make my way toward one of
Dr. Logan's all too familiar bookshelves. As I run my hands
across the spines of the literary works, I feel each character
offering refuge, their stories freely emanating from their
pages.

"Okay, so that answers the question of why you feel
her opinion matters," he calls from the couch, "but why do
you feel like because of her premonition you now have to take
action?"

"Have you ever read Pride and Prejudice? Lizzie gave
Wickham a chance and thought Mr. Darcy was bogus when
he tried to warn her about him? She was *sure* she knew
Wickham and that Wickham was a good guy."

"I'm familiar with the story."

"Lizzie was wrong. Mr. Darcy was right. Wickham
was a jerk with an eloquent tongue. Lizzie was crushed.
That's why it matters. That's why I have to do something.
Harper is my Darcy," I say whipping around to Dr. Logan.

"How is she your Darcy?" Dr. Logan asks, still seated
on the couch where I'd left him, his eyes serious and
concerned.

"Dr. Logan I don't know how to answer that."

"Then answer the original question. Why do Harper's
words make you feel as though you must now take an action
when it comes to your relationship with Matias? What's really
the impetus? The motivation? The driving factor? The –"

"I get it. I understand what you're asking," I shout at
Dr. Logan annoyed by his method of questioning.

"So?"

"Why do you always expect an immediate answer?
Why can't you just give me some time?"

"You're getting time right now. You're stalling and
pretending to be confused by my questions when really,

you're refusing to allow yourself to tell the truth and answer. I know you secretly hope I will get so frustrated with our back and forth that I stop pressing you, but that will never be the case."

I turn away from Dr. Logan and slowly move toward one of the room corners. His words are violent as they hit my ears and I want to get away, get absorbed into the folios amidst the shelves.

"There's no winning with you," I say just above a whisper and bury my face in my hands resting against a shelf.

The couch sings as Dr. Logan peels himself off and I hear his slow and steady footsteps walk toward me. He stops to my right and I can feel his breath on my neck. It's cool and smells of spearmint as he rhythmically breathes in and out.

"Noe," he starts, his breath nudging my hair slightly. "Don't go where you're going. This isn't a game I'm trying to beat you at. We both want the same thing for you, but that means you can't give way to your default responses of avoidance or that what-ifing thing you do so well."

"It's harder than you think."

"Can you please look at me?"

I oblige and turn my eyes over my shoulder, examining Dr. Logan as he casually leans on the shelf of books, his eyes instantly fixed on mine.

"Talk it through with me……please," he continues.

"Dr. Logan, I don't trust myself when it comes to love. I want it and need it so badly and fall into it so deeply that I don't think," I pause caught up in the rapture of my words.

"I don't think that I see anything clearly and nothing makes sense. And that scares me. I used to love that feeling of temerity and intrepidity. It was exhilarating and enlivening, but I always lose when I do that. It's not real life and it sucks. It hurts like hell to run up against a parapet of love and that's what always happens when you throw caution to the wind. So I can't do it anymore," I say exasperated, shaking my head in confusion.

Dr. Logan reaches out to me but I visibly tense.

"I need to listen to what those who mean the most to me say because they've been right. Right? So when Harper says, 'your dude's a douche run away' shouldn't I figure out how to run away? That makes sense, right?" I continue.

"Noe you shouldn't let the past control you. History teaches us lessons to use for the future; it doesn't depict what a future episode will look like," he says briefly gazing out as if watching a bird take off before returning his eyes to me.

"You should consider looking at your past experiences and working to understand the lessons you were to learn. There's a slew of information to glean from your past. Use that to help you improve your next time around," he adds furrowing his brow and gently massaging his temples.

"You're abstract art, not paint by numbers. Instead of defining exactly where your colors will go and what they will be, use your past to help sharpen the colors you use," he closes voice barely above a whisper.

"How?" I cry wrought with frustration. "I don't know how. I don't even completely know what that means, what you're telling me. All of the words I get, but the practicality of it all is a giant blur."

"Why do you feel that way? Is it because you've never tried to live a life that makes you happy? Because you take every facet of everyone you know into consideration when making decisions that most directly affects you?"

"That's not true."

"It's not? Why do you care whether or not Harper approves of your relationship with Matias? A guy you say makes you feel alive, he believes in you, and makes you happy."

I turn away from him because he's lost his compassion in exchange for this instigative fire.

"Don't turn away. Stop running," he snarls grabbing at my arm.

"I'm not running," I yell inadvertently, my heart rate

quickening and my palms sweating.

"Then what are you doing? Answer my question. Why don't you of all people seem to give a rat's ass about *you*?" Dr. Logan responds matching my tone and volume, the bass of his words reverberating in the inner hollows of my aural cavities.

"I don't know," I moan, eyes running with tears, as my legs buckling, forcing me to slide toward the ground.

Dr. Logan reaches out and catches me during my dissent and follows me to the floor. We sit in comfortable silence only interrupted sporadically by sniffles.

We stay sitting and not speaking for a while. Dr. Logan sits, my back to his right arm, and continues to offer encouragement flowing through the slight rubbing of my arm.

We see the steady flash of the red light of a new patient and hear the dull hum of the alarm signaling the end of my session and Dr. Logan releases his hold on my arm and places his hands at his side.

"Are you alright?" he asks his voice seeping with embarrassment.

"I'm fine," I say stirred by his abruptness, standing, and willing myself back to reality. "I'll go."

Dr. Logan follows suit and stands as I walk back to his couch and collect my things. I decide not to look at him as to not encourage a closing conversation. I don't want to talk about what just happened and I don't want to get an assignment, I just want to go.

He hesitates, making me feel as though I will get out successfully. "Next week?" he asks.

"Right, next week," I say reaching for the doorknob.

"You *will* come back?" Dr. Logan asks unexpectedly appearing at my side, hand covering mine preventing my escape.

I nod imperceptibly.

"Noe," he begins more forcefully, pausing until I look up at him. "Next week?"

"Next week," I echo.

"At 3 pm," he continues latently daring me to look away.

"I wouldn't have it any other way," I reply, fudging a smile.

"Okay then," he says returning my forged smile before he releases my hand from beneath the captivity of his and opens the door.

I walk like a zombie through the corridor, the lobby of the office, into the elevator and onto the sidewalk. My stupor carries me most of the way home and I am only awoken by my mother's all too familiar ring tone – Kanye West's "Hey Mama".

"Hey mama."

"Where are you mi'ja?"

"I…" I start, stopping in my tracks and looking around for something familiar, "I don't know."

"What do you mean you don't know? I'm not calling because I need you to do something Noe; I just want to know how you are. You don't have to lie to me," she spits her cheeriness quickly deteriorating.

"I'm not lying mom. I really don't know where I am," I sputter with growing tension in my knees, my heartbeat increasing, its thud growing louder thundering in my ears.

"Noe! You're not making any sense. What are you doing? How did you get where you are? What's wrong with you? Do I need to come get you? Are you alright?"

"Calm down mom."

"How can I calm down when you're telling me you're lost? You don't sound well."

"Mom!" I interrupt her. "Please. I'm fine. I just left Dr. Logan's and I was thinking, and I guess I just haven't exactly been paying attention to where I was walking. But it's fine. It's still light out, I'll just go backward, and I'll be…it'll be good. Please chill out. I'll be home in no time."

"Noe, what do you mean chill out? I don't speak this hip lingo. I didn't know you were going back to see Dr. Hale."

211

I put her on speaker phone while seriously examining my surroundings. I can't exactly remember which way I was walking when she called so I don't exactly know which way would be the reverse. I should be panicking slightly but I'm not.

"Noe! Are you listening to me? Are you there? Noe?!? Answer me!"

"Mother!" I roar. "I'm sorry; I didn't mean to yell at you. I hear you but I have a lot floating around in my head and I'm just not in the mood for talking. Can I please call you back when I get home? Would that be okay?"

"You're sure you're alright?"

"I'm sure. I promise."

"Call me as soon as you get home and not a minute later."

"Not a minute later," I finish and hang up.

I find my way back to Dr. Logan's office building and recall that I'd driven myself to the appointment. I find my car parked across the street from the building and I make my way safely to the driver door. Dr. Logan's window opens to this edge of the street so I can't help but imagine him peering out and eyeing me as I finally make my way away.

Whether being surveyed by Dr. Logan or the squirrels I start up the car, turn the radio off and spend some time with my thoughts the whole ride home.

From the Desk of _____Noe Cortes_____

August 11, 2010

I don't know how so many great things can disintegrate so quickly. I feel like a violent, supposedly dormant volcano has erupted all over my life and then when the one person who could rescue me came around, a bald eagle came and shat in both their eyes, blinding them and leaving the both of us to perish.

I can't be with Matias anymore, but I don't know why not? I mean, I know why not. It's because Harper said so and she's right more often than she's wrong. And then Dr. Logan, my supposed savior got blinded by all these other factors that honestly, I just don't know what to do.

My sessions are supposed to help me to feel calm, but after today's I just feel lost and shaken and I want for Matias because with him I'm never like that. He and I can make sense damn it. Can't we?

Chapter 18

"Luca. Hi."

"How can you be so cavalier with Sir Douche-ster? He's been M.I.A. for God knows how long," hissed Harper from my couch.

When I couldn't sleep, she'd come over to keep me company.

"Is that Harper in the background?"

"Yeah. I'm sorry about that," I said stepping into the kitchen away from Harper's spying ear.

"Don't apologize for me. I mean every bit of what I'm saying," she yelled.

"Will you please," I yelled back at her. "Luca, you were saying?"

"My dad is good."

"Good. That's…that's really, really…. good."

I didn't know what to say to him or how to behave with him. I wasn't sure where we were or what would become of us, so I just managed repeat myself a lot and stutter and stammer through my words.

"MC?"

"Yeah?" I asked, my voice rich with anxiousness and anticipation. "I'm sorry."

"No, I'm sorry."

"No MC. Let me," he started, taking a big breath.

"You shouldn't have to be sorry. You've done nothing wrong. You never do anything wrong. You've been there for me and have been more to me than anyone else and all I seem to do is make you cry. You used to be such a light, and now I think I've killed that."

"You haven't. You can't take responsibility for all of…I mean for everything. In a relationship it takes two you know…"

"That's just it. I haven't really been playing fair. I haven't been treating this like a 2- person relationship…"

"You've been going through a lot recently. It's

understandable."

"Please don't make excuses for me. It's not okay. I don't like it for either of us, but I promise I'll get better. I'll be better."

"Luca…"

"I'm serious. I want what we had. I miss us. MC?"

"Un huh?"

"Can you stay with me tonight?"

"You want me to…"

"Or I can come there. I just want to be with you…tonight."

"No, I can come. Just let me get a bag."

"Okay, I'll be waiting."

I didn't know what to make of Luca and his words and his request. I was on autopilot and I didn't really want to understand I just wanted, like he did, to be with him that night.

"Harper, thank you so much for coming over but I'm on my way out for a bit, so it's okay for you to go now," I spoke with rapid fury.

"You have got to be kidding me," Harper started dumbfounded as I moved back and forth between the living room and my bedroom, quickly packing an overnight bag.

"Harper don't be so dramatic."

"You're packing a bag? What for? For him? Are you going to see him tonight? What did he say to you? MC! Answer me dammit!"

"Harper, I don't want to do this right now."

"You don't exactly have the option."

"Actually I do. This is dumb. I already know you don't approve, so what does it matter why I'm packing a bag or what he said to me?"

"Noe Marie Cortes…"

"Seriously?"

"I can't believe you're being this girl. Just 20 minutes ago you were on your floor wallowing and talking about 'what have I done?', 'why me?', 'I don't understand'."

"Your point…"

"You can't keep doing this back and forth thing. You can't give him chance after chance to screw you over," she said chasing after me.

I rolled my eyes and scoffed at her commentary, continuing to pack.

"You're giving him permission to be selfish, and only think of himself, and to just take advantage of your niceness. Why? He's not even that freaking awesome. He's just averagely attractive with an average brain and a less than average everything else," she continued.

"Let it go Harper. Just leave it. Why can't you just…." I started embittered and drained, sitting on the bed staring at her as she towered in the doorway.

"Why can't I just what MC? Not tell you my opinion? Not, not, not…"

"Support me," I said pointedly, barley blinking at her.

"Wha…? You don't think I support you?" she asked walking toward me, stopping at arm's length, just short of my bed.

"Harper you never have. From the first time I talked about him it's always been about him being wrong for me and how he's this terrible, awful guy, and about how stupid I am for trying to make it work. It's just too much and I don't need this shit from you."

"I'm sorry you feel that way," Harper added, wiping a single tear from her cheek. "I'll see myself out," she quipped turning to leave.

"Harper don't leave angry."

"MC, you know what, I'll give you what you want. I'll shut up about Luca. And since I suck so much at supporting, don't look for me to be there when this happy ending you've concocted never comes."

With a slam of the door she was gone. I finished packing my bag and departed for Luca's. The drive to his apartment proved interminable. I blasted Natasha Bedingfield

216

the whole way, desperately trying to drown out Harper's monologue that seemed to echo from all the crevices of my mind.

"MC, thank God you're here. What took you so long? Are you okay?" Luca asked, pulling me in at the waist, lifting my chin to see my eyes, his filled with trepidation.

"I'm fine."

"You're fine?" he repeated not persuaded.

"Yeah. Harper was with me at the house, so I had to wait for her to go, but I'm good. I'm great. How are you? How's your dad? How was your trip?" I asked him quickly, subtly handing him by bag - willing the conversation to go in a new direction.

"Come inside," he ushered me in taking my bag. "MC, talk to me. I know Harper doesn't like me, and I guess I can't blame her. I know her words matter to you. She's your best friend. What's going on with you? Come sit with me."

I obliged, made my way to the couch, and sat beside him. He immediately resituated me across his lap and engulfed me in his arms.

"She just doesn't get it. She says I'm ridiculous and what I'm doing, what we're doing is stupid. I don't want what she says to matter. She's wrong I know that, but it's all just so frustrating," I explained resting my head on his chest beneath his chin.

"Harper's just protecting her friend as any good friend would. It's true I haven't exactly been the best boyfriend."

"How you can agree with her?"

"It's not that I'm agreeing with her, I just know that I want to be better, so I can understand how someone from the outside can look at us and see me as the bad guy. I'll accept the criticism and I'm working on changing," he said, tucking my hair behind my ear.

"I told you. I don't want to be that guy anymore. I don't want to be distant and cold and uncommunicative. I'm ready to be the guy you need me to be."

"I love you so much," I murmured in response.

217

"I love you too," he requited leaning over to kiss me.

For the first time in a long time I kissed back, and in our exchange, I could feel our passion return. The chemistry that I thought was lost forever was back with fervor and it took all that was in me to calm my loins and not release all of me to him. Coming up for air, Luca lifted and carried me into his bedroom and gently lay me across his bed. He removed my shoes – leaving my socks to keep my feet warm. With ease he slid off my jeans, lifted my shirt over my head and from his drawer he pulled out a Tiffany blue teddy.

"I got this for you. Consider it an early Valentine's Day gift. I couldn't wait until next week."

"It's gorgeous Luca and totally unnecessary. I brought a t-shirt and some of your boxers."

"Bambina," he started.

"Yeah?"

"Babe, I hate to say it, but the shirts and my boxers......not sexy."

"Ugh," I feigned shock and consternation. "I thought you liked when I wore your clothes."

"Sure, I love it when you wear clothes that hide your beautiful body and smell of my man scent. Hyper-enticing."

"Well, I love your man scent," I purred crawling toward him. "How about we save this teddy for next week when it was intended? Tonight I'll go as I am," I added tugging at his shirt pulling him closer to the bed.

"Are you sure about that," he asked wrapping his arms around me, his hands cupping my behind. "You know what all this uncovered skin does to me. Besides, won't you get cold?" he added trailing kisses up my neck to my mouth.

"With you next to me, I can't get cold. And you let me keep my socks. I'll be good," I laughed mid-kiss.

"You're such a goof," he added lifting me once more, my legs wrapping around his waist. "We have got to get some sleep. It's a school night," he finished looking at me seriously.

"Gee dad, thanks for getting my hopes up," I spoke

mock disappointedly.

"Ms. Cortes, please don't make me call your bluff," he said lowering me onto the bed once more.

"I wouldn't dream of it."

Luca disrobed and joined me in his giant bed. He curled up behind me and we fit together like two perfect puzzle pieces. My wonderful, romantic, insightful, thoughtful, beautiful Luca was back – and it felt good.

***

"MC, what happened?"

"Nothing happened. It is what it is. She's mad. She's ignoring me and even her mom won't talk to me."

"Mrs. Harrison won't talk to you? That's bad. That's real bad."

"Hayley, I'm exaggerating. Mama Harrison knows that her daughter is an extremist. She just told me to wait it out."

"Something had to have happened for her to be this upset. Walk me through it please."

"Welcome ladies, my name is Michelle and I'll be your waitress today. Can I get you something to drink?"

I needed to talk to my best friends about Luca's valiant return. Harper sent me into exile so that left Hayley to tackle my breaking news on her own – which meant On The Border. OTB calmed her so I was hopeful that she wouldn't freak out nearly as much as Harper did.

"I'll have diet coke."

"And I'll have a Dr. Pepper please. And can we have chips and salsa too?"

"Sure, I'll bring that right out."

"Whoa, chips and salsa. What's with the extras?" Hayley asked.

"What do you mean? This isn't that abnormal."

"MC, you are the cheapest person I know. Appetizers on a random Tuesday night aren't exactly characteristic."

"What the heck happened Sunday? You gotta tell me."

"Hayley…"

"Either you tell me, or I'll hear it first from Harper."

"But you know when she's mad she misconstrues everything."

"So open your mouth then."

"Ugh, when did you become such a hardass?"

"Oh, Harper's been giving me lessons. She's a hard-a ologist," she chuckled in true form. "Okay out with it."

"Here are your drinks, and your chips and salsa. Do we know what we want, or should I give you some more time?"

"Let's order!" I chimed.

"Fine. I'll have the chicken fajitas. No chimichangas. No enchiladas. Gosh. Wait. Is there a way that I can have all three?"

Laughing a bit Michelle responded, "Actually, we have a sampler where you can get the chimis and the enchiladas, and in place of the burrito you can get the fajitas. I'll just have to add an extra dollar, I think. How does that sound?"

"Perfect!"

"How about you?" she turned to me.

"I'll have the beef fajitas. Can I have corn instead of flour tortillas?"

"Sure."

"Is that extra?"

"No."

"Great. Oh, and I don't want rice or beans or guacamole or pico de gallo. Could I instead have the salsa verde?"

"Yes. No problem. Will that be all for you two?"

"That's all."

"Okay, I'll get that started."

"Thanks Michelle. Alright, MC, you've stalled for long enough. It can't be all that bad. Just tell it to me straight."

I took a few deep breaths and looked around for nothing

in particular before I resolved to tell her the story.

"So it's no secret that Luca and I have been on a bit of a rollercoaster ride. But that's what's normal. In relationships there are peaks and valleys. Just like our friendship, you know," I began speedily watching Hayley as she nodded in recognition.

"Well Sunday Harper came over and we were watching TV and vegging out. Okay, maybe at some point I got a bit emotional and experienced some minor bouts with tears but that's how I discuss."

"What do you mean minor bouts? And MC you don't cry. I cry. On the emotion continuum I think you can outlast Harper when it comes to crying."

"You're exaggerating a little bit. I cry. I choose to ration my tears and use them for truly distressing things."

"You're deviating."

"Fine. I bawled my freaking eyes out because I hadn't spoken to Luca and I couldn't figure out what was going on with him. And Harper was there to experience it. I'd gotten a hold of myself and we were good and then my phone rang."

"Oh boy. Who was it?"

"Hayley, really?"

"Right. Keep going. Tell me what he said."

"Well he just said 'hi'."

"Hi?"

"I mean what else do you say when you answer the phone?"

"Don't get defensive," she scolded putting her hands on her hips, "Finish the story."

"I'm sorry, I didn't mean to. So we exchanged pleasantries then Harper started getting louder and meaner when she heard me say his name. He eventually asked me if I would stay the night with him."

"Oh, MC you didn't."

"What do you mean 'oh MC, you didn't'? What's so wrong with it if I did? What is it with you and Harper?"

"MC…"

"Go ahead and get ready to be on her side because it seems like you're going to be just as disappointed as she was."

"So you went?"

"Yes. He asked me to come over and I said I would. I love him and I want to make things right. What else would I have said?"

"No."

"It's not that easy Hayley. You don't get it because you have Connor. You don't ever have problems. Not that I'm envious of that because I'm not. I'm just saying you don't know. What? Why are you looking at me like that?"

"I'm not looking at you like anything. I'm listening. Please finish your story."

"I don't really see the need. Let's go ahead and jump to the part where you concur with Harper and tell me I'm an idiot and he's no good and I'm asking for bad things to happen, blah, blah, blah," I continued making taking motions with my hands.

"I'm not going to do that. I promise."

"I hear it in your voice. I wish someone would see things from my side for once."

"MC, I'm sorry I'm making you feel uncomfortable. I'm here for you. You know I support you. Please finish your story."

"I jus-, I just want it all you know," I began, eyes leaking. "He called me, and he sounded so much like the Luca that I fell in love with and I miss him, so I went. And you know what; I'm not ashamed of that. It was the right thing to do. It was."

"What happened with Harper?"

"While I was packing my bag, she started yelling at me and I just got tired of hearing it, so I told her that she didn't support me."

"MC you didn't."

"I did. That's what I felt. I just want to be happy again."

"I get that, but…"

"No buts. I feel like it continues to have to be you two or him and I don't get why just once it can't be both. It's not fair. And it doesn't matter right now. I said what I said. She didn't like it and then she just left."

"MC…"

"I know she's hurt, but I am too. Why is it okay for me to let her make me feel like trash and not say anything? Huh? Why does that make sense?"

"You know that's how she loves though. She's blunt force, never one for tact."

"That's not okay though. I can make an exception for her and the way she makes me feel, but I'm not allowed to express how I do? That's ridiculous. I don't tell her how to live her life.

She goes through guys like toilet paper and no one says anything, so why can't I ask for my friends to let me do what makes me happy and be okay with it and at the end of the day even if they can see the future still let me….just let me."

"I'm sorry MC."

"What?"

"You're right."

"What do you mean, I'm right?"

"You're right. We should stand by you no matter what."

"You mean that?"

"Yeah. You make sense. I'll try to talk to Harper and…we'll just see. We're okay."

"I'm so happy to hear you say that. Thank you so much," I said leaning in and squeezing her with affection, tears flooding my eyes.

"Hayley, my shirt's we-… are you crying?" leaning

223

away I checked my now tear-soaked shirt sleeve.

"You know how I get. I'm sorry."

"Don't be sorry. Where's our waitress?" I said wiping my eyes

"I'm so sorry," Michelle came from the corner. "You all were having a moment. I just didn't have the heart to interrupt."

"Thank you," Hayley and I said laughing a bit.

"Here's your sampler, and for you the fajitas. Everything look okay?"

"Yes it looks good," I responded.

"Great. Enjoy your meal."

"MC?"

"Yeah?"

"You're a mess, and I love you."

"I love you too."

From the Desk of _____Noe Cortes_____

August 30, 2010

Today is a much better day than yesterday and the days before that. I still don't know where I'm headed with Matias and I feel like I've lost a part of myself. She's wandering and I can't find her, and she can't find me, or maybe she isn't looking. That's it...she's not looking for me because where she is, is where I should be too. It's probably a better place for me that makes sense.

Where are you?!?

I don't even know what this journaling thing is supposed to be about anymore. This seems more like a means for me to wallow more and fall more deeply into this hole of misery and solitude. I thought I had it all figured out. I really did. I thought that I was nearing cured.... but I...

I could go around in circles like this...I thought this but it's really that. I feel like this when I should feel like that...this and that...black and white.... either.... or.... it's a bust. I'm a bust.

Chapter 19

To: "Noe Cortes"<nmc@sharemail.com>
From: "Harper Harrison
home"<hmharrison@sharemail.com>
Subject: DON'T FORGET ABOUT TONIGHT!!!

MC,

Tonight is the night! You should be prepared and ready to go no later than 6:05 pm. Please arrive at House of Blues no later than 7:17 pm. You can still take me up on the offer to help dress you and apply your makeup appropriately. This night has to go swimmingly well. Actually, I'm being dramatic right now. I am just anxious about the new experience we're about to have. What am I saying? I sound like Hayley...worse, I sound like you. Anyway, as you didn't respond to my text messages, phone calls or other emails I've sent about this I can only assume that you're receiving them, you're alive and you're still coming. I know you wouldn't dare

back out.

Coral dress. Nude pumps. Black blazer. Flowing curls (if not, do the bun thing). Just liner and mascara tonight. Dangly gold earrings if it's down. Giant gold backed studs if it's up. Done. See you there.

- HH

I'm not terribly excited about tonight with Harper. Since my breakdown with Dr. Logan I haven't exactly returned to normal. Matias is even catching on and keeps asking me what's wrong. I've cancelled our lunches for the last week and I've been keeping a watchful eye on his schedule so I can conveniently create meetings for myself when his are scheduled to end. I can't really explain why I feel compelled to avoid him, but I do…well I have. I'm confused about whether or not I should be happy. I want to be but a small rumbling in my soul says don't do it and strangely enough my soul sounds a lot like Harper, so I have no choice but to listen.

Brrring.

I hear my all too familiar text message tone mark the arrival of a new message.

> Leave at 6:05 pm. Arrive at 7:17 pm. Don't be late.
> *12:30 p.m., 4 Sept*

> Are you even getting these texts? I'm serious. Don't be late.
> *12:50 p.m., 4 Sept*

> Do you want me to come over to help? What are you doing? Don't be late.
> *1:45 p.m., 4 Sept*

> At some point I'm going to need you to acknowledge my messages or I'll be forced to call the authorities.
> *3:30 p.m., 4Sept*

Harper had slowed her incessant text messages about tonight's events making me feel less anxious. I'm sure tonight won't be nearly as disheveling as I fear. This is good. This is great.

I get up from my bed where I've been laying all morning and into the afternoon and make my way to the kitchen to finally complete a text message to Harper.

227

> I'm alive. I've gotten ALL your messages. I'm still good with doing everything on my own. I will see you at 7 at House of Blues.
>
> 3:40 p.m., 4Sept

It's nearly four in the afternoon and I have done nothing all day. The Oxygen channel has been playing rom-coms and I along with my most esteemed bear friend have been taking in all of them. I'm in my oversized gray TIC sweatshirt and navy dance shorts. My hair is tied in a messy bun atop my head and I haven't had the strength to put on my contact lenses, so glasses adorn my face. I look like my college self after an intense time of studying for finals.

My kitchen is in even more disarray than I am. In addition to Matias I have also been avoiding dirty dishes, cleaning, cooking, and bathing as it seems. With a deep breath I take in the most melodious aroma emanating from my pores.

Despite my obvious personal hygiene issues I opt for some chocolate chip cookie dough ice cream, an ice cold Dr. Pepper and caramel corn for a pre-dinner appetizer as I turn on the tube and settle onto my couch for the last hour and a half before I have to get ready for tonight.

The Wedding Planner is on and I appear to mimic her as she settles into her apartment watching Antiques Road show, except she's a lot cleaner than I am. I sink into the couch just in time to hear frantic rapping my door.

"MC?" I hear a faint calling behind the door. Matias? He can't see me like this.

"MC? Are you in there? Wait, I know that you are in there. I can hear the television. Can you open up? I am worried about you. MC?"

I am not prepared mentally or physically for Matias. I

don't even remember when I last brushed my teeth. Why is he here? He's seen me at work. He knows I'm not ill. What's happening?

"Matias?" I call peeling myself off the couch and lowering the volume on the television. "Yes, MC my love can you please let me inside?"

"Matias, I'm okay, you don't have to come inside. Thank you so much for checking up on me. That's very kind of you," I stall moving frantically about the condo attempting to make sense of my mess.

"I'm not going to leave you. I would like it at this moment if you would let me inside so that I might see that you are alright for myself," he says more sternly.

"Matias are you sure that's what you want to do? I could be awfully ill," I mutter walking up to the door, placing my ear on it. I can hear his breathing. It's frenetic yet full of calm.

"MC," he calls sounding stymied and downcast.

"You don't need to worry," I say opening to door to a sad-eyed Matias.

Even a doleful Matias is a handsome one. He's wearing a short sleeved gray polo that carefully grazes the tops of his biceps and subtly outlines his abdominal muscles. He has on the darkest wash jeans I've ever seen, that fall neatly atop some white pumas.

His dress is uncharacteristically casual which actually reminds me a lot of Dr. Logan and it's unnerving how much more attractive it makes him to me. He smells of caramel and fresh linen, so as he rests his hands on either side of my door frame, I don't know whether to wrap myself in him or add him to my coffee.

"Oh my goodness I have missed your face MC," he says rushing toward me and pulling me into hug and taking in my scent.

I miss him just as much I realize silently against his passionate assault.

"What is wrong? Are you okay?" he asks still holding

me tightly, searching my body with his hands.

Why are you so concerned? It's so adorable. I think continuing my internal dialogue.

"May I please come in?" he finally asks releasing me and standing back in the doorway.

Fuck it. "Yes, please," I say.

"Your home…it looks," he stops struggling to find words to use for the post-tornado appearance of my condo. "It is very different from the last time I was here."

The last time you were here, we didn't really spend time in this room, I want to mention, but I resist.

"Right, it was different – cleaner. I've just, it's that I've. I'm planning on cleaning it today actually," I say looking over my shoulder behind me.

"Which is why I really must get to it. You've seen me and you now know that I wasn't lying about being okay, so you can just leave. Thanks for coming," I speak rapidly working to usher him back outside the door his seductiveness releasing me from its clutches.

"You have just allowed me in. There's no way I'm going back out there. I still don't know that you are okay. I haven't been able to see you or speak to you and I am beginning to worry. Have I done something wrong to offend you?" he asks walking closer to me.

"Oh gosh no. We've just both been, you know, busy," I respond turning my back toward him, which seems an odd gesture standing in a doorway.

"Well then what is it?" he asks more insistently moving just behind me and grabbing hold of my arms above my elbows.

"It's more than meetings. It's something else. You don't even talk to me as you did before. What have I done?"

"Nothing," I sputter with mild annoyance. I try freeing myself from his grip. He doesn't allow it, but instead turns me to face him.

"Then tell me, what's wrong and how can I help to rectify it?"

"It's not you. It's me, really. I think I'm overwhelmed with work and I just need a break and some alone time. You're amazingly wonderful and I know you don't deserve this type of treatment I just, this is the only way I... I'm so sorry Matias," I finish beginning to weep.

He loosens his grip and pulls me into a loving embrace raining kisses all over my face and neck.

"Please talk to me MC," he begins between kisses, his breath hot against my neck. "I am here. I can help you. You don't have to do this on your own."

"I think I need to," I continue tears picking up speed.

"Why? I do not understand it," he adds pulling away and lifting my face so that our gazes lock.

"Because," I stammer before his lips meet mine and I find myself in a passionate caress rendering me speechless and limp.

Our slow and passionate kisses give way to quickened and aggressive ones as Matias lifts me and my legs wrap themselves around his waist. He moves beyond the threshold of my open door, kicks it shut and feels his way through my living room past empty take-out containers strewn about the floor and the mountain of unwashed dishes in the kitchen sink to my bedroom. His legs meet the edge of my bed and with alacrity and deference he peels off my sweatshirt and my dance shorts as my fingers graze his scalp and lightly tug at his hair. He lays me atop my bed still maintaining lip to lip contact, kicks off his shoes and pulls off his jeans. He disengages briefly to pull off his polo, but he returns swiftly.

Matias interrupts the fiery passion of our lips to peer down at me. I stare back up at him taking him in.

He leans into me, gently nuzzles my neck and whispers into my ear, "I love you more than I know how to express it."

I can't find the words to reciprocate. They have lodged themselves within my throat. All I can do is weep. He wipes my tears saying, "That'll do" and we lose ourselves in one another.

***

I lay in a pool of serenity when I finally come to as Matias
and I engage in some post coital spooning. Matias continues
to stroke my thigh and the combination of this motion and his
sweet warm breath on the back of my neck sends electric
charges up through my loins. I'm brought from my reverie
when I see the clock flash five. As much as I don't want to, I
remember my night's obligations – speed dating with Harper
– and shudder. Attuned to my sudden realization Matias
asks,

"What is wrong mi amor?"

"I just remembered something I'm meant to do
tonight."

"What is it? Can it be rescheduled? We have not
properly relieved you of your stresses," he says not
recognizing the innuendo embedded within his words.

"I can't reschedule it. It's too important."

"Important? What is this important?" he asks.

"Speed dating," I say succinctly rolling over to find
him sitting up on his elbows.

"Eh, speed dating? I am confused."

"It's with Harper."

He maintains a confounded gaze.

"A few weeks ago Harper came to visit and asked me
to be her support when she goes to this event. It's called
speed dating because you have short one-on-one
conversations with a number of different people and you see
if you have anything to talk about or if you have a
meaningful connection to potentially start a friendship or
relationship."

"Ah, I understand it. Why though are you going? Have
I not made my intentions clear?"

He has such a boyish nervousness about him that I
almost want to play with him a bit and tell him that I'm going
so that I might have options in the event that things don't

work out. I abstain from the obvious opportunity and instead let him know the truth – or at least part of it.

"I am going as pure support. I'm going to make sure Harper doesn't make any poor decisions. She's pretty bad at picking quality gentlemen."

"And you're sure you must go?"

"I have to. Believe me I tried to get out of it, and I was met with the wrath of Harper. It's just one night though."

"Can we be together when your night it is finished?" he asks brushing a stray hair from my face.

"Is that what you want?"

"Of course it is what I want. MC this week without you has been very lonely and I meant what I said earlier. I love you and I want nothing but to be with you each and every night. I want to love away your worries and kiss away your pain. I want to be all that you need and more and I'm ready to start that now. I want all of you now," he ends forcefully, drawing me closer to him at the waist.

His powerful words render me speechless. All he says are all things that I've only dreamed of hearing and yearned for someone to mean. In all my wanting I don't think I've ever thought about how I might respond or what I might do. I've been avoiding so much for so long that I don't know how I feel about any of this anymore. I always thought such a declaration of love would free me to proclaim my requited love song but as I lay looking at Matias, I'm anything but emancipated.

"I can see that I have upset you," Matias seeing my face turned up in contemplation comments.

"No, I'm not upset just caught a bit off guard. I've never had anyone say such things to me," I confess.

"That is a shame. You are a bright light in a world that is dim. I will not coerce you to respond for I have had much time to think, but I would love it if I could at least spend time with you this evening. I have missed you in my life."

"I would love that," I utter, and he kisses me atop my forehead. "But I first must go so that I can come back," I say

233

Ebonii Nelson

lightly attempting to remove his hand from my hind parts.

"How much time do you have until you must be away?" he asks holding firm to my lower limbs.

I turn my head away from him and stare back at the clock – 5:15 it reads. "I still have to shower, and I have to be out of here in 50 minutes – Harper's rules."

"I can help with some of that," he says, a glint of mischief in his eyes.

"I'm sure you could," I add again working to tear his hands from me, "but we both know I wouldn't leave if you were to do that."

"Arg, I've been foiled," he finishes laughing.

I back out of the bed and head to the shower. I bathe and like a good boy, Matias stays in the bedroom. After I'm clean and shaven inside the bathroom I examine my face searching for reason, answers, and clarity for all that has occurred. This makes everything alright. He's here.

He wants to be here. He wants me and he has made his intentions clear. I should be elated right now.

I moisturize my face and carefully apply my plain eye make-up. I shake myself putting on an expression of happiness and exit the bathroom. Matias has returned to his lustful splendor and has not only made my bed, but the amassment of soiled and discarded clothing has disappeared. As I oil my body and put on my night's attire, I hear the sweet sound of Matias' beautiful voice. He's singing an unfamiliar Spanish song that is wistful and romantic. I dress quickly and exit to the living room.

"You are beautiful. Are you sure this is the ensemble you would like to wear tonight? It may be hard for uh, the gentlemen there not to fall prey to your allure."

"You're too kind. This ensemble, hair, makeup, and jewelry are all mandates from Harper Marie Harrison herself. If I were to alter anything, I would pay for it supremely."

"Well as much as I do not like it, I suppose I will be okay with it," he says with a coy smile.

Matias walks toward and meets me as I'm putting on

234

my earrings and finding my shoes.

It's 5:55 and I'm making excellent time.

"Mi amor," he says, "are you sure you have to go tonight?" He kisses me softly on my neck beneath my chin. I nearly topple over onto the couch. He quickly grabs me and braces us both against the back side of the couch.

"As enticing as your offer is," unhinging myself from his vice grip I continue, "I really do need to get out of here if I ever have hopes of returning."

I do a little dance hopping on one foot mounting one shoe and then the other. I land, both shoes on, at the door and I call out to Matias.

"I'm going."

"So I'll see you when you get home?"

"Yes you will."

"I will be here awaiting your return."

I make my way out and down to my car. Sitting inside the 2008 gray dodge avenger I take a moment to think, resting my head on the steering wheel. I don't know what I'm feeling right now. If you'd have asked me a week ago, I would've said I loved Matias and I loved him even more because I liked the person I was when I was with him. But now I'm so confused, and that confusion just makes me nauseous and uneasy. I don't know what to do or think now. The clock reads 6:03 as I turn on the ignition and I have no choice but to reverse out of my garage and head toward Harper.

During the drive to the House of Blues I sit in an uncomfortably abrasive silence. The radio is turned off and the streets are fairly clear but the ruckus whirring inside my brain is almost too much to handle.

'I love you and I want…' I hear Matias say.

'He's a re-run…' Harper's voice echoes.

'Why don't you of all people seem to give a rat's ass about you?' Dr. Logan's bass reverberates amidst the grey matter.

I don't know what's wrong with me or why I can't

shake all of this uneasiness. Harper never likes anyone I'm with and it's never bothered me before, so why now? Like Dr. Logan said, Matias does make me so happy and he loves me so why shouldn't I affirm it and my own emotional sentiments and love him back? He's good for me, he really is. I haven't done my pro/con list, but I just know his pros outweigh his cons.

"This is your life Noe Cortes," I hear myself saying aloud. "Do what Dr. Logan says and stop caring so much about what everyone else thinks and is feeling, and care about yourself," I continue with stronger resolve.

My personal pep talk ends as I arrive at the House of Blues. It's exactly 7:15 when I pull up to the valet booth and I'm proud of myself, finally basking in the glow of my entire transformation today. Suddenly I can't wait to get back to my condo. The valet takes my keys and I make my way up the stairs into the foyer of the venue. For a speed dating event it seems awfully sparse of speed daters.

"Welcome to tonight's Appeteasing event! May I have your name?" the host asks.

"My name?"

"Yes. I need to fill out a name tag for you."

"I can't do that by myself?" genuinely confused I press him for answers.

"Well, it's standard that the host collects information from each attending guest. It's, it's protocol."

The gentleman, who I can see is named Ron, retorts, his painted smile beginning to sag.

"I guess if you must. My name is…"

"Noe Cortes. First name N-O-E. Last C-O-R-T-E-S. Trust me you did not want her to tell you her name."

"Harper?"

"In the flesh. Thank you for being on time." She leans in to hug me.

"Right. I think I'm nervous and I'm not even here for me," I say fidgeting with the ring on my right ring finger.

"Well get un-nervous," she snaps. "An anxious Noe is

an awkward Noe and an awkward Noe is capable of one of
two things: being clumsy and embarrassing or being so
awkward that it's endearing and either way it's bad news for
me so get it together!"

"Stop with the Noe first please."

"Whatever."

"Thank you," I say taking my name tag from Ron.
"Harper I'll do my best to make you look good," I fake a
smile and bob a curtsy.

"If it makes you any less anxious," Ron's voice
crackles as he enters our conversation uninvited, "I think you
look amazing," he closes, eyes zeroed in on Harper's chest.

"Thank you," I add looking warily between Harper
and Ron as she begins to turn her face in disgust. "Tell the
man thank you, he gave you a compliment."

"Right. Let's go MC," Harper violently tugs my arm
and ushers us away from Ron's prying ear. "The audacity of
some people," she huffs loudly still within earshot of Ron.

Walking out of the foyer into a new room I see loads
and loads of hors d'oeuvres and people. Harper explains to
me that this is the appetizer room and essentially just for
grabbing food and beverage *not* for mingling. That's
apparently reserved solely for the main event. I take the
liberty of grabbing some wings and taquitos and the cutest
miniature wieners doused in barbecue sauce. Harper
admonishes me saying none of my foods particularly agree
with my ensemble. She instead opts for a tall glass of white
wine.

"She really is serious," I whisper aloud taking in all of
Harper's attire.

Tonight she pulled out all the stops. Ron was right.
She is surely hot shit. She is wearing a skintight buff dress
that ends just at the tops of her knees. The dress has cap
sleeves and this dark blue fringe lace at the bust line which
boasts the most unbelievable cleavage. She topped it all off
with the same shade of midnight blue Louboutins – no doubt
custom made. Her hair is understated, yet elegant. She can't

pay a curl to stay in it so it's bone straight and pulled into a ponytail with a swoop bang across her right eye. She's got massive diamond studs in each ear, which makes me happy I chose not to wear mine, and a matching tennis bracelet. She also painted her fingernails. Well, she put on a clear coat, but that's more than she usually does.

"How's that?"

"Oh nothing. The food's great. Are you sure you don't want to try anything?"

"Stop being gross and chew your food. And don't come near me. You're a walking hazard to this dress," she dictates with disgust.

"Oh my goodness chill out. I promise I won't embarrass you and I won't taint your precious ensemble. You're safe," I say sucking the barbecue sauce off one of my thumbs.

"Can you finish so we can go inside?" Harper asks impatiently, not really paying much attention to what I'd been saying to her.

"Okay, last bite," I say stuffing my face in a most unladylike fashion. "You're making me nervous again with your rushing."

"Sorry. Let's walk. This is new for me too. I've never felt this vulnerable before."

Harper and I walk into the main room as we hear the announcer beginning his opening remarks.

"Good evening all and welcome to tonight's Appeteaser! Tonight is about good fun and making connections. The rules are simple; you all will notice the room is set up in a horseshoe. On my word everyone can have a seat *almost* anywhere you like," he chortles at his attempt at a joke. One or two others join him to encourage his continued explanation.

"Well, ladies you will find a placard with your printed name at one of the seats located in the inner part of the horseshoe, and gentlemen you will claim the chair along the outer horseshoe that bears the number on your nametag. At the sound of this gong…"

Gooooonnnnnnng. He quickly demonstrates.

"You'll begin your exciting conversations. You'll have exactly five minutes to converse before the gong sounds again. This is important: gentlemen you will be the only persons traveling. As you all end your conversations make sure to make note of your favorites on your score cards."

He picks up a score card and demonstrates what men should be looking for as they make their rounds before continuing.

"Gentlemen you can do this by noting the table number of the lady or ladies of interest and ladies check out your fellow's number adorned to his nametag. At the end of the night you will turn in your score cards and we will send you official contact information. We ask that you please refrain from taking your own personal information. We want to ensure the integrity of this event and make sure no matter what it's an enjoyable time for all. Alright, that's enough of me. Any questions?"

"Okay, between guys let's chat. Or not chat but have a sign you know. Like we can say "Dude or Dud" and then give the number so the other person knows who not to worry about." "That can work, but whose standards are we going by?"

"MC, mine. Duh. I brought you. You have a boyfriend remember."

"Right. How could I forget? So, Dude or Dud. Got it."

"Let's get started. Ladies find your places and gentlemen make your way toward a table of interest."

Gooooonnnnnnng.

The gong sounds and we're off. Harper is seated on the other side of the room, her back to me, foiling our plans for consorting with one another. My first date is with Joshua of San Diego. He's an import here as an investment banker. He's 35 and enjoys manga. Strike one. Date number two is Paul or is it Peter? I can't remember. He's a cute red head with a heart for hymns. He knows the entire New Testament by heart – King James Version of course. His dream is to recite it for the Pope in Vatican City. "Noble goal," I tell him and watch him beam with pride.

Strike two. I am starting to get parched and to feel like this was a terrible idea and obviously a ploy to punish me for some inane reason. As the gong clamors again I mentally prepare for what will probably be catastrophe date number three when I hear a familiar voice.

"Hello Noe."

"How do you know my," I say raising my head to come face to face with Luca, "name?"

***

"How was the event?" Matias asks pouring me a glass of wine.

When I get home the house is immaculately clean, and a meal is ready made for me. He takes my belongings and invites me to sit. Matias is a true romantic and has candles ablaze. We eat spaghetti Bolognese, French bread and he serves a delicious red wine. For dessert he serves me chocolate mousse and raspberries. It's magical.

Over dinner I spill the beans about bachelor number one and bachelor number two and Matias just laughs, his hearty laugh so tender and sincere. He asks me about my distance, and I try to avoid his interrogation but with each touch of his hand – on my knee, inner thigh, collarbone, across my cheek, he coaxes it out of me.

"So all of this is because of Harper?" He looks at me quizzically.

"Yes and no."

"How do you mean it? Is it not a yes or a no?"

"Okay yes, because when we spoke, she just told me to be careful and not to rush into anything," I lie with ease.

Why does Matias need to know that Harper called him a re-run of my ex-boyfriend, whom I absolutely loved and have not yet completely told him about? This is for his own benefit that I shield him from these awful truths.

"But no, because I'm the one who went way too far and started panicking about it."

"Well, what about this Logan fellow? Is he someone special to you, no?"

Is he jealous?

"Dr. Logan is just a family friend I guess you could say. He's someone I go and clear my head with. He understands me and always has been good at calming me down."

"And with him there is nothing more?"

"What do you mean is there more? What are you thinking?"

"I'm just wondering because I think you've mentioned him before."

"Like I said I talk to him, so he can't help but be around."

"MC, I would like very much if you could talk to me."

"I can. I mean I will. It's just sometimes it's easier with Dr. Logan because we have a history. Not like that," I add quickly looking as Matias' expression turns to one of mild panic and suspicion.

"If it will make you feel better, I'll tell you."

And just not let you know when I speak to Dr. Logan. Clearly that'll be the only way for us both to maintain our sanity, I think to myself.

"Would you like that?"

"Very much so," he snarls scooting toward me on the pillow carpet arrangement he's created on the floor.

"Do you not want to hear anymore," I ask backing away from Matias much like a spider watching his eyes flicker with an ignited passion.

"I think I don't need any more. The problem is solved, and the only thing left is for me to –"

"It is?" I inquire extending my arms against Matias' shoulders as he's now towering over me.

"Yes. I am okay with it. It is normal and healthy for

women of your age to take much of their friends' opiñones into consideration. Time was all you needed so I'm glad you got it. And now Dr. Logan is gone. All is well."

He continues to nuzzle me at my neck and behind my ears while I lie still, ruminating over his words.

What does he mean 'women of my age'? He's not that much older than me. Sheesh. There I go again. He's just showing care. He's more than right and I'm wrong and I'm totally missing out of this pleasurable experience that's been created specifically for me.

"I love you too," I say snapping myself back into the moment.

With my utterance his pace quickens. He gently pushes me down on the pillows and migrates south. I'm still in my dress from the speed dating event. With his teeth and thumbs he hikes my dress up grabs me at the hips to pull me closer and plants a supple kiss on the inside of either thigh. He begins a dance that fills me with euphoria and renders me aphonic, wrought with exquisite pain on the brink of erupting.

Without missing a beat still sliding my dress up past my shoulders and eventually over my head I feel his lips on my stomach and he draws a river of lithe kisses up my abdomen resting momentarily on each of my breasts until our mouths meet.

"I love you more," he interrupts before enveloping me in a crescendo of ecstasy and total bliss. We release almost simultaneously and collapse against each other before drifting off into a calming slumber.

It's 3 am and for the second time today we lie entwined. Matias' head rests across my chest and I can feel his heartbeat and hear the soft murmur of each and every breath.

Unfortunately, I am wide awake and no longer feel blinded by the rapture of intimacy. Instead I can't stop playing and re-playing one of tonight's conversations in my brain.

'Hello Noe.'

'Luca? What are you doing here?' I asked with a mixture of horror and excited curiosity.

He leans closer to me across the table.

'Oh, I saw you come up and I thought, my God that woman is beautiful, I wonder who she is, and then I got in and I saw it was you."

From the Desk of _____ Noe Cortes

September 4, 2010

For the love of all things sweet why? Why is he back? Why is he here? Why was I there? Why? Why? Why? It's Harper's fault and she doesn't even know it. She has brought even more clouds and severe weather to my life's forecast than I can handle.

I was in my dark space from before with what to do about my mounting feelings for Matias but everyone else's warnings off of him. Then now...I was finally feeling gray...a comfortable gray and then this. My past has literally come to haunt me...but that's not how it felt at all.

It was the furthest thing...and that's wrong. Right? Luca – my first love and unfortunate first heartbreaker is back. And he wants me. He's admitted no wrongdoings but something about his presence says that this time things could be different. I say this time so definitively. Should there be a next time? What does this mean for me and Matias? He just told me he loved me, and we just shared in our first consummation of our all-consuming affection.

Was I lying to him when I accepted his love? Does Luca's appearance and my questioning change everything? Does it mean anything? If I allow Luca to come back into my life what will that mean for Matias? Everyone was anti-Matias...but everyone, well Harper mostly was also anti-Luca so maybe this is replacing one bad for another. But since I have a history with him shouldn't that mean that I'm more prepared to handle anything Luca could bring my way?

I didn't even want to go.

He still has a stronghold on me. He still excites me. He still knows exactly which buttons to push and I love it.... still

I don't even think Dr. Pepper is fixing this thing

Chapter 20

Today is Valentine's Day I thought to myself as I stood examining my every curve and feature in the mirror.

"Noe Marie, you look good girl."

The day was set up to be nothing short of wonderful. It was unseasonably warm, and I was sporting some casual chic – dark wash boyfriend jeans, a black and white striped tank, my new red blazer, and some black pumps, on my way to breakfast with my papí.

Since I was a little girl, he always made a point to show me that I was his number one girl. In the privacy of the library, our favorite room in the house, we'd have a heart shaped cinnamon roll with hot cocoa that had mini marshmallows in the shape of a heart floating on top.

After breakfast I had class then an early rehearsal for the valentine's showcase with the girls at the studio. Later I would have gift exchange with Harper and Hayley at my apartment, and then they agreed to help me get ready for the romantic evening Luca had planned for us that night. It was all going to be perfectly magnificent.

***

"Happy Valentine's Day Jackson!" I sang pushing past my brother and into the living room.

"You're so chipper and it makes no sense," he muttered, slamming the door, and following behind me.

"Why are you so…. not? Don't you have some bimbap on standby to dissatisfy tonight?"

"MC I only date ladies of class, thank you very much. Tonight, is no different, but unfortunately I have an issue."

"Issue? Whatever do you mean? Did you accidentally over commit?" I laughed.

"Actually MC," he began sinking into the couch, burying his head in his hands. That's exactly what's happened and it's not okay."

"What do you mean it's not okay? Jackson you do that all the time. You hardly ever have one girl at one time. You should be a professional at this. Jackson? Jack? Are you crying?"

"God, no! I'm not crying. It's just…. it's just this time it's different. I don't *want* to be double-booked."

"How's this time different? You actually like one of these girls?"

"Yes actually, I do. Her name is Kennedy. I don't know why you think that's so out of the ordinary."

"Jackson you can't be serious. You've never thought twice about a girl ever in life. Wait, except for Madison Reamer from next door when you were nine. Kennedy…"

"I'm serious. And why do you keep saying her name like that?"

"I can't help the irony that both of their names are Presidents."

"Wha-? MC, only you would find something so nonsensical. Thanks for your help," he grumbled, standing to leave.

"No, please sit," I pleaded tugging at his hand. "Let me see if I can help at all. I promise I won't laugh again. I'm so pro the Jack and Kennedy show. Oh gosh…and I didn't mean to rhyme just then. It was totally accidental. Please Jackson, tell me."

"Are you sure you're serious?"

"As a heart attack."

"Fine. So I met Kennedy last year. She was here doing a summer program working in the engineering lab. I was there too last year with Professor Cleiborne. Anyway, we didn't really work on the same projects, but we were around, and I would talk to her periodically when we had mixers and meetings for fellows."

"Okay, so if you didn't really talk to her, how do you know you like her?"

"I thought girls were good listeners. You defy statistics once again."

247

"I'm so sorry. I do that all the time. I'm listening I am. Go on," I urged.

"The guys and I would play lacrosse after work. We had open games and she would play. And MC, she can *play*. Afterward she would sometimes come with us to whatever bar we went to. I don't know, and I just thought that maybe we could. But I was being stupid and then she went back to Vanderbilt."

"Okay, so I have a couple of questions. I'm just a bit lost. Did you ever talk to her when you were around her for the entire summer? How do you even know that you like her? That she likes you? I mean, how did you even get to having a date with her now?"

"You're on overload. Chill out. We spoke sporadically like I said in the lab and of course we would trash talk during games. She's a pro, which means I love her. I mean, she's cool," he quickly amended, his face flashing crimson.

"At the bars afterward we would talk too. I mean that's how I knew she was at Vanderbilt, and she thinks she might like to come to Texas and so that's how she tried to get into a lab out here. The lacrosse thing she picked up in high school and plays intramural at her campus," he continued nervously running his fingers through his hair, his light eyes emblazoned with passion.

"I think that's probably all we were able to get. She rarely stayed the whole night at the bars, and I was never able to speak coherent sentences with her. It was alarmingly annoying, yet refreshingly peculiar for me. In my silence I was able to hear her speak, and she speaks so eloquently, but I also probably looked very Rain Man when I could barely get a complete sentence out."

"Jack, you are throwing me for a huge curve right now. I don't think I've ever seen you without your suave. I'm, I'm, I'm, I don't even know what I am. I don't have words. Who are you?"

"Are you making fun?"

"I'm really not. I just have never seen you or heard of

you being the way you described. It seems unnatural."

"It *is* unnatural MC. You just don't understand. Everything about her disarms me. She's ridiculously smart and nothing about my intelligence matters to her."

"I'll pretend like that's not a misogynistic statement."

"Shut up. You know what I mean. She's athletic, yet feminine and oh my god, she's hot. And nothing I do impresses. It's like she knows all of my moves before I make them. I should be deflated, but I'm exhilarated and drawn to her like a moth to a flame," he continued, his eyes glaring with an ardor.

"Jackson, I am so not used to hearing you say words like exhilarated or use similes and be this engaged in one girl. This is serious?"

"Yeah, and I don't know what to do. But I know whatever I do it can't be ruined by one of my regulars on a mis-scheduled non-adventure. Oh, I'm ruined."

"Jackson, you're not ruined. You just have to do something you've never done."

"What's that?"

"Cancel."

"Cancel?"

"Yeah. Simple. You like Kennedy. You hope Kennedy likes you, but you'll never know if your date is interrupted by one of your idiot boxes, so you cancel with dummy number five billion and give yourself a chance with the one who could be *The One*."

"You know my cancellation policy though."

"You don't have one."

"Exactly."

"You make no sense. If you like this girl, why would you risk ruining it for some stupid girl who humors you by laughing at all your jokes, telling you you're a god, and doing all but begging you to bed her. Don't you want to be excited and challenged and fulfilled?"

"But with Melody it's a sure thing. I know exactly what to expect and I know exactly what I'm going to get."

"You're scared," I shouted aghast and accusingly.

"Why are you yelling?" he retorted, leaning over, and covering my mouth with his hands.

"I never thought I'd see the day," I mumbled through his fingers. "How does it feel big bro?" I laughed licking his fingers.

"You really are a sadist you know?" he said wiping his hands. "I'm not scared. You just don't understand the situation."

"I'm not a sadist. This is just weird. I don't know how to take you in this way. What do you mean it's a sure thing with the airhead but not with Kennedy? How did you get this date with Kennedy anyway?"

"Well, it's not exactly a date per se."

"What *is* it?"

"Cleiborne and Tazaki are presenting our work this week at a conference. Kennedy was Tazaki's fellow that summer. Kay and I are co-presenters as major contributors. So she's here for the week. Yesterday as we were wrapping up Cleiborne invited the two of us to this social event with other engineers for tonight. She's going so I *have* to go."

"Jackson?! This isn't even a date. It's a work outing. What are you thinking?"

"I don't know. This is all I can do. I know; it's a disaster. So I shouldn't go right?"

"You idiot. This is not a difficult situation. Duh you should go. You need to find that Rico Suave in yourself and invite her for something individual for the two of you for tomorrow. You can't do this engineer thing and that's it. It's ludicrous. What's going on with you?"

"I don't know. You're making it sound so easy. I'm not you MC. I can't do the awkward thing and land some girl. I have to be prepared and able to communicate. I have to figure out how to woo her because she doesn't seem to notice that I exist. This is exhausting."

"Jackson, I know it's not easy and I hate that I make it sound that way. And you're wrong you know about the awkward thing. It's just as hard for an awkward girl as it is for a guy who usually has it all together. Look, it's simple: if you see someone you like then you've got to go for it otherwise you'll never know what could have been and you will probably kick yourself for years to come. This is good for you."

"Good for me? How?"

"Well, it doesn't allow you to use a trick to get to a girl. You have to actually want to know her and put in just as much energy as she does. It's like for the first time in your life you can experience what girls experience on a regular basis. This is great news!"

"I'm glad you're excited about it. I still don't know what to do. What do I say to Melody? What will I say to Kennedy? How will I convince her to go out with me tomorrow?"

"With Melody that's not that big of a deal. I am not condoning hurting her feelings, but you've got to be honest with her. Tell her that you accidentally double-booked your night and you can't go out with her and tell her that you don't like her. In a nice way. Stop wasting your time with frivolous girls."

"Okay. Cancel with Melody. What about with Kennedy? How can I show myself to be irresistible?"

"First, stop doing that. You jumped back into arrogant Greek God mode. That's not attractive. Keep going with the honest bit. Offer her some punch at this shindig. Ask her things you care about. Ask her about her. Listen to her and show her that you're not the definition of vanity. When the time is right, again with the honesty, tell her that she interests you and has since last summer and that you'd love to get to know her better and see if she'd like to go with you to dinner tomorrow. It'll be simple. Take it one step at a time. Don't freak out. Or if you do freak out, just go with it. You'd be surprised at how some of the best things come out of freak outs."

"Are you sure?"

"More than you know. You're actually a really great guy when you don't put on your usual show," I offered, gently punching him.

"Thanks," he said, standing and kissing me atop my forehead. "Wish me luck."

"Luck."

I watched as he trailed off into the kitchen and I couldn't believe that he wanted advice from me. It was a nice change of pace.

"Mi'ja, are you here?"

"Yes papí. I'm here. I was chatting with Jackson for a bit."

"I didn't hear any yelling. Are the two of you okay?"

"Yes, actually. We're perfect."

"Well in that case, happy Valentine's Day."

"Happy Valentine's Day to you too!" Springing up from the couch, I hugged my dad, gave him a kiss and he ushered me into the library where our breakfast was waiting.

"Papí, I think I love today even more than Christmas or my birthday."

"Well, have a seat. I hope that this day turns out to be all that you would have hoped for and more."

"Thank you," I affirmed breathing in the sweet smells of my cinnamon roll and hot cocoa.

"So what do you have planned for today that makes you so excited?"

"Nothing special. Can't I be excited just because?"

"Noe?" he responded incriminatingly.

"Dad, I can't tell you everything all the time. Besides, much of it is a surprise to me. I have class, then I'm going to the studio to watch a rehearsal, and of course Harper, Hayley and I will do our gift exchange, and then Luca has a surprise dinner planned."

"You, Harper and Hayley doing alright?"

"Yes. Don't start trying to get hyper serious today daddy. We're fine. This is tradition and we're good."

"As you wish. And Mr. Bianchi? Do you have any

252

inkling of what he might have set up for you?"

"Not a clue. And that's amazing. I'm so nervous I could spit."

"Well I'm happy for that."

We sat in silence for much of breakfast. Before I left, we talked about new books he was reading and my plans for spring break. Afterward I made my way to campus. I didn't have very many classes but while I was there campus seemed to hum with a warm-hearted effervescence. It was almost magical. Time flew by quickly and I was off to the studio.

"Good afternoon ladies."

"Hi," they answered in unison.

"Today is going to be quick. I just have time for three run throughs then I've got to skedaddle. Ready?"

"We're ready."

"Before we start, the girls and I have a surprise for you. Can we give it to you?"

"Noelle, girls, that's very sweet of you all. Sure, let's do it."

"Okay, you sit, and we'll get it together."

I sat while the girls recited an original poem and gave me a corsage. It was lovely. Our rehearsal was quick and painless. They'd obviously practiced and were ready for their Sunday afternoon showing. I bid them adieu after an hour and headed to my apartment to meet Hayley and Harper.

"Oh my gosh, you're gunna love my gift for you!"

"Hi, Hayley. Have you been here long?" Hugging her briefly, I fished in my purse for my door keys.

"Goodness no. Connor just dropped me off so he could go prepare for my surprise tonight. MC, I told you, you should put your keys on the same key chain as your car keys, this way you won't always have to dig around for them."

"Yes, you have told me that, but I love the adventure of sorting out my purse. It's really okay. Anyway, what are you and Connor doing tonight?"

"Oh, it's a surprise!" she giggled.

"Right, I know it's not a surprise. Neither of you can hold water. Ah ha!" I shouted, finally unearthing my keys. "Here they are. Let's get inside."

"Well, he's going to cook dinner, Hayley continued. "I'm not sure what though. And I think we're going to do some crafting and make s'mores in the fireplace. Ah, I'm so giddy. This is the best holiday of the year."

"I'm so glad that you're so happy. Have you heard from Harper?"

"No. Not today."

"Are you sure she said she was coming? We've been all weird since, you know."

"Stop panicking. She said she was coming, and things are not weird. They're fine."

"Alright, I'm just nervous. I really want us to be back to normal."

"The fun has arrived," Harper sang walking through my front door. "You should really consider locking that. It's dangerous out here you know."

"Hi Harper!" Hayley squealed.

"Hi Hayley. Noe. What are you two gossiping about?"

"No gossip Harper," I retorted, ignoring her formal usage of my name. "We were talking about Hayley's not-so-surprise surprise Valentine's celebration with Connor."

"Right. So let's get this show started. I've got places to be, people to see."

"Oh, you're not staying?" I asked.

"For what?"

"Remember? We were going to help MC get ready for her evening with Luca."

"It's totally fine Harper. I didn't realize that our evening plans were so closely scheduled. After gifts you can jet out. You can go first if you need to. That's not a problem at all."

"MC kill it. You're doing too much. I don't need to go first and I'm not meeting Ethan until 8 or 9, so we have plenty of time. I didn't think you still wanted all opinions," she retorted coldly.

"Great, no, please stay," I added.

"See, I told you things weren't weird."

"Hayley, utshay upway easeplay," I muttered through gritted teeth.

"Good job on the pig Latin MC. And things were weird. I'm just deciding not to let them continue this way. We're fine. Sit. Drinks. Gifts. Chat. Go."

After our initial inelegance as a group and Harper's dog-like commands we moved on with the rest of the afternoon. Hayley crocheted Harper and I berets, socks and fingerless gloves all adorned with hearts. Harper gifted us jewelry – a soft gold chained sideways 'h' for Hayley and for me a sterling silver knot ring. They were both gorgeous. For the girls I gave them a mixture of store bought and hand-crafted goodies – heart shaped picture frames with a picture of the three of us from our New Year's girl's lunch and a letter. I wrote each of them a letter sharing my thoughts of our friendship and really how I would take our sister love over any man's any day.

"I hope y'all don't think they're lame. The gifts you got me are obviously a lot better, but you know," I noted.

"I don't think this is lame. I love my picture and my letter," Hayley cooed.

After reading hers, Harper quickly stood and said, "Let's get this primping underway." This would be my and Luca's first Valentine's Day out. Last year, he had a class on Valentine's night so we just did something small at his apartment. And the year before that we were so new to each other that we didn't make a big deal out of the day. This year, with a new and more motivated Luca, we were really going to make a big splash.

He had been the Luca I'd fallen in love with for almost two weeks. He kept saying he wanted to make up for lost time and that he really wanted to show me how much I meant to him.

It was so romantic. In honor of how special I'd hoped

the night would be I bought a new dress and all the accoutrements. I had a sparkly gold mini dress. It had three-quarter length sleeves and it hugged all of my curves perfectly. I had black tights and black six-inch Jennifer Lopez platform pumps. I wore my hair down, with some giant ringlets and had some over-sized diamond studs for my ears. Harper painted my nails a devil red and she did a smoky eye for me. To finish it off I had a small black rectangular clutch with gold clasps. I was good to go when my knight in shining armor came to fetch me at 7.

"You look gorgeous MC," Hayley blubbered as she started crying tears of joy.

"Yeah, you clean up nice. Now, don't do anything I'd do. You're better than that," Harper added.

"Eek. I hope Luca likes it too."

"If he doesn't, he's a blind idiot."

"Thanks Harper. Will y'all lock up for me?"

"No problem. Harper and I can get it."

"Oh, and Harper I hope you have fun with Ethan tonight. Don't be too mean to him when he gives you a subpar gift. And Hayley, save me a s'more…or really just a marshmallow."

"I'll do my best. You know how I feel about crap gifts though," Harper chided

"Hugs!" Hayley cooed.

"Yeah, hugs are appropriate Hayley."

We hugged it out, all on the brink of tears, just as Luca came rapping at the door.

"Good evening ladies. Oh gosh, are you all alright? What's happened?" he asked nervously as I opened the door to our blubbering.

"Nothing. We're all fine. We just had a moment. I'm ready. Bye."

"Have a good night MC," Harper and Hayley called as we departed.

Luca took my hand as we made our way toward the car, and Harper closed the door behind us.

"I'm so excited for tonight," I beamed, squeezing tight to Luca's hand.

"Me too. I hope you like everything."

"I'm sure I will. I know I will. Ah, I love you," I gushed kissing him as he helped me into the car.

"There will be much time for that later. Let's go."

He drove us to a part of the city I'd never been before. I felt like a child on a family road trip and it took all my strength not to ask, 'are we there yet?'

After what felt like an eternity we pulled up to a very small, hidden restaurant with string lights all around. The valet quickly came to the door to help me out.

"Benvenuti a Bella Vita. How might we serve you today," a fast appearing host asked. "Reservation for Bianchi."

"Right this way Signore."

"Signorina," Luca remarked opening a path for me. "Gratzie."

The host led us through the foyer that was open to the beautiful night air. It was warm with little to no humidity, so the night was welcome. The hum of couples and families roared and whirred as we made our way through the restaurant. We finally stopped near the back of the eatery in a quaint and private half-circle booth. As we got situated, he opened a bottle of wine for the two of us and noted that our waiter would be around soon.

"This place is absolutely gorgeous. How'd you find it? I don't think I've ever been here before," I said looking around, properly taking in the space.

"It's a little secret of mine," Luca winked. "I'm glad you like it."

The waiter, Michael – pronounced Meek-hale, came, and took our dinner orders. I stuck with a simple rigatoni Bolognese and Luca was more ambitious with veal parmesan. The food was out quickly, and the aromas made our mouths water. Over dinner Luca and I chatted affably about everything under the sun – school, internship for him and the studio for me, my girls and his friends, the rest of the semester and graduation. We had a heavenly crème brûlée for dessert and before I knew it Luca signaled it was time to go.

"This has been absolutely amazing. Thank you."

"Don't thank me just yet. It's not over."

"There's more?"

"Of course, there's more. My love for you is more than a fancy dinner. Tonight, I show you exactly how much you mean to me," he said helping me into the car and hurrying around to the driver side.

We drove again to somewhere that was unfamiliar, but I didn't care. The surprise of it all was a startling aphrodisiac. This time when we parked there was no restaurant and no valet.

Instead we were stopped at a small dock. White Christmas lights were draped along a canopy of trees, and candlelight flickered through the windows of an attached boat house.

"Oh, my goodness Luca, this is absolutely beautiful. What are we doing here?"

"I told you tonight is for you. And right now there's only one thing that I want," he started, walking toward the boat house and flicking a switch that began a version of 'The Way You Look Tonight,' - the one by Harry Connick Jr.

"What is it Luca wants?"

"I want to dance," he stated plainly, meeting me, taking my hands in his, "with you."

"You know me too well."

Luca always knew to parrot my favorite lines from my favorite movie 'The Wedding Planner'. It made everything that much more perfect.

"Your happiness is my happiness," he whispered to me, pulling me tighter into his dance frame. "You are absolutely ravishing and it's taking every morsel of self-control I have to not have my way with you right now."

"My dear Mr. Bianchi, I must warn you that my fair maiden Harper did warn me not to go into uncharted territory on this night. Maybe it'd be better if I did my best not to tempt you," I finished and leaned my head back to see his face more clearly.

"Well then you best not speak, look or even smell the way you do, because it's all having a beguiling effect."

"Alas, I don't know if there is anything I can do to suppress your yearning. It might just be easier to allow life to unfold as it should."

"A woman after my own heart," he retorted smacking me lightly on the rear.

"Ha, I bet," I laughed laying my head on his shoulder. "I love you."

"I love you too. I don't think I can say it enough Luca, this is magnificent."

"Only because you are."

We danced quietly for a while longer, Luca lightly singing into my hair as we twirled. At the close of the audio he whispered to me once more. "Let's go home babe. I have one more gift for you."

I couldn't fathom another gift. I felt like the night had already been enough. It was more than anything I had ever imagined and made for the best Valentine's Day I'd ever had. I'd dozed in and out of sleep during the ride overwhelmed by the excitement of the day. Safely at his apartment, Luca lifted me from the car and carried me across the threshold, noting that one day we would do this again as husband and wife.

"That sounds nice. I'm sorry I fell asleep," I said sleepily. "If it makes you feel any better, my dreams were all about you."

"I wasn't offended. I like watching you sleep, but hearing that does make me feel better," he said placing a supple kiss on my lips.

"Do you think you can stay awake just long enough for me to give you your gift, or would you prefer it tomorrow?"

"Today. I can be awake. I want it today."

"That's my girl."

He made his way into his bedroom, laid me on the bed, and went off to get my gift. While he was gone, I took the liberty of disrobing and changing into the teddy he'd given me last week.

"I'm almost upset that I didn't get to undress you, but you look so exquisite in that negligee that I can't find it in me to get angry," he growled returning to the bedroom.

"Shall I join you?"

"I wouldn't have it any other way."

Quickly stripping to his boxer briefs he joined me on the bed with a small bag. "Noe," he began, sidling next to me and lifting me atop his lap side saddle.

"You make me nervous when you call me by my given name," I said awkwardly.

"Don't be nervous, but I do want you to know how serious I am about this."

I nodded encouragement and understanding as he began again.

"I want you to know that I care so much about you. I think I love you more than I ever knew I could love another person. You're supportive and caring. You're generous and exciting. You're everything a guy could want in a partner, in a friend."

He readjusted nervously and breathed deeply taking in my scent before he continued. "I know I haven't always been the best boyfriend and I'm so sorry for that. I hope in time you can forgive me. I know that I am better than I have shown you and I will continue to make that up to you for as long as you will have me."

"Luca, I –"

"Wait, let me finish. I got this for you, to show you really and truly that you're my everything."

From inside the bag, Luca unearthed a gorgeous ring. It was platinum, with a simple three-stone setting. The middle stone, a princess cut deep dark blue diamond with two smaller square white diamonds on either side. He bent the ring down to reveal some small writing.

"This is you Noe – my past, my present, and my future. With you I feel complete."

"I don't know what to say. This is more than anything I could've ever imagined. It's almost, no it is too much. I don't deserve this," I muttered pushing his hands away.

"MC let it be. This is what I want for you. I was lucid when I bought it and I'm definitely in my right mind now," he added pulling me harder against him and hoisting the ring back into my face."

"You're sure?"

"Just say you'll wear it."

"Of course I will."

"I love you, Noe Marie Cortes and there's nothing that could ever change that," he proclaimed almost as a mantra, sliding the ring onto my left ring finger. It was a perfect fit.

"Luca we can put it on a different finger."

"No. It means more. It should be worn there."

"You're fantasmic," I proffered swathing him in kisses.

"I don't know what that means, probably because it's not a word," he tittered, "but I think I like it," he added taking my face in his hands and slowing my kisses to more furtive and fervent ones.

Overridden with ardor and impassioned vigor the night ended with zest, pleasure, and calm. He was mine and I was his, and through no coaxing he made his intentions known. All that we'd gone through before was to get to this point of pure and utter euphoria. It was more than worth it.

From the Desk of _____Noe Cortes_____

September 5, 2010

I'm going. I am going to go. I have to. It's the only way I can figure out what's going on here. I don't think it's going to damage what I have with Matias. If nothing else if could strengthen it or worst-case scenario it could highlight the fact that we're not meant to be together and maybe it would settle this terrible knot I have in the pit of my stomach. Maybe it'll chase away the nightmares that seem to haunt me at night.

Am I doing this all wrong here?

I can't think about it. I just need to go with it. This is what seems right. It makes sense and I feel like I need to do it.

It's done.

Chapter 21

"What do you mean you're confused?" Harper asks agog and annoyed.

"Yeah MC, I'm confused too. None of this makes sense," Hayley adds.

"Well then you both understand perfectly."

"Don't try to be cute. This is abso-fuckin-lutely ridiculous. I know you like JLo and all, but I didn't think you would attempt to challenge her record for dumbest romantic decision ever."

"I think what Harper means," Hayley tries, "is can you just walk us through what happened so we can understand why you're even considering this."

"I thought I had."

"You thought you'd done what?" Harper probes angrily. "Explained in enough detail."

"Not particularly," Hayley eeks.

"Oh, for the love of all things sweet. So, it's like this: Harper and I are at the Appeteaser and rotations have started. I see boring Joshua and Paul or Peter or whatever his name was, and then him."

***

"Luca what are you doing here?"

"I was leaving Hooters and I couldn't exactly remember where I'd parked my car. I moved past the valet booth and then I see this woman. I think to myself, 'My God who is that woman?' I didn't have much else to do so I slipped inside," he says, accent still thick, sending a shiver up my spine.

I listen to him intently all the while scanning his face for any remote signs that he's joking. As I replay parts of his story to myself I can't help but get swept away in the familiarity of his accent and the memories that are immediately triggered when he licks his lips, musses his hair or even pauses briefly in a smile.

"It wasn't until Peter was doing his recitation that I realized my goddess was you," he continued, his eyes fixed on mine, locking me in place.

"You were there, well here, obviously being bored to death by ye olde English and likewise I was less than engaged in my conversation with Ella the taxidermist. At the sound of the gong I followed instructions and I'm here."

"I can't, I just, I can't believe that you would go through all of this. Why?" I inquire.

"You took my breath away out there. I couldn't pass up an opportunity."

Opportunity? I think, intrigued by his word choice.

"Why were you at Hooters? I thought you were otherwise involved."

"Happy Hour," he retorts succinctly.

"Well, what now?"

"We're speed dating."

"You know what I mean. We obviously already know each other. I don't know where to go from here."

"That's one of the things I've always loved about you."

Loved?

"You have this uncanny ability to work yourself into the most adorable tizzy. Calmare," he finishes reaching for my hands and clasping them atop the table inside his.

Goooooonnnnnnng.

"I know it's against the rules but meet me tomorrow outside the bookstore. You know the one," he says briskly slightly standing, my next speed date tight on his heels.

"What?" I ask unexpectedly breathy

"Don't think just say you will."

***

"You said you would meet him today?" Hayley asks.

"You are the biggest dumbass on the face of the planet. Why do you do this to yourself? Luca could give two shits about you and you're willing to throw away a relationship, albeit another wrong one, for him?" Harper asks, her face turned up in disgust.

"I'm not throwing away anything by just meeting Luca, Harper. It changes nothing with Matias."

"I know you, and you're incapable of just dipping your toe into the pool of possibility. You always have to cannonball in to find out if it's a good or in this case, a TERRIBLE idea."

"MC, Harper's right."

"Et tu Hayley?"

"High five Hay," Harper says holding out her hand. "It's about time you left the delusion depot with MC. Welcome to real fucking life."

"I thought friends were supposed to support each other."

"Your friends are supposed to tell you when you're fuckin' up. And MC, you're fuckin' up."

"Love."

"What Hay?" I ask ignoring Harper.

"Friends are supposed to love you no matter what."

"Thanks for the clarification," I respond snidely, rolling my eyes.

"You're most welcome," Hayley beams truly pleased with her contribution.

"I'm just going to talk to him. He just popped up out of the blue. What if he's in trouble? What if he needs me?"

"Do you hear yourself? You sound supremely idiotic. There is no 'what if he's in trouble' or 'what if he needs me.' That's not your problem. You're not in a relationship and you're not even friends, so he can deal with his personal circumstances all on his own."

"Why do you really want to go?"

"Yeah," Harper joins incredulously "good thinkin' Hay."

"This is it," I say, my voice betraying me and cracking.

"Just tell us," Hayley pleads sounding uncharacteristically exasperated.

"It's...I..."

"Just spit it out. It can't make you sound any dumber than you already do."

"Thanks for that vote of confidence Harper."

"Come on MC. Just spill the beans. We can't really help you unless we know what the real issue is."

"I've always thought he was my forever," I finally yell averting my eyes from the both of them searching for the rest of my words. "We found each other too soon. And with his abrupt and amorous declaration I just figured our time could be now. I'm not jumping into anything I really am only going to talk."

"But MC you do realize that with these hopeful thoughts floating around this talk is dangerous. You're already susceptible to any conversations regarding dating and relationships with him because it's something floating in your head. Don't be a dumbass; don't go."

"What do you mean don't go?"

"Hayley, can you help her understand? She's getting on my nerves." Harper stalks into the kitchen to refill her mug of coffee.

"MC, please know that we support you as an individual, but we can't help but think this may not be a great decision. It's like you going to the Dr. Pepper factory and saying you're not gonna try anything, you're just gonna walk and enjoy the tour. It's technically possible but highly unlikely. Does that make more sense?"

"I suppose so, but why do you all have no faith in me?"

"Your track record sucks for one," Harper exclaims emerging from the kitchen. "And secondly, when you say things like 'I figured our time could be now' it doesn't take a rocket scientist to decipher that you're going into this looking for an excuse to re-connect with Luca."

Everything begins to blur as Harper's words and Hayley's agreement whir around me. I know what they're saying is right and I know that if I were to move into anything with Luca, I'd really hurt Matias, but I can't fight the desire that's welling inside me.

Brrip. The ping of a new text message comes in.

"Is that him?" Harper growls.

"I don't know. Maybe. Probably. Could be Matias, who knows."

"Go ahead, answer it. Hayley and I are dying to find out."

I pull out my phone, type in the security code and open my new message.

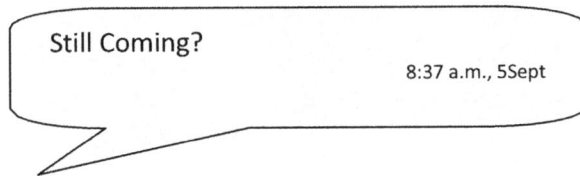

> Still Coming?
>
> 8:37 a.m., 5Sept

It's him. I don't know what to do. My body's already reacting as my pulse races and my palms begin to sweat. I feel like a member of a bomb squad trying to decide which wire to cut so I don't blow up the White House or something.

"Yeah it's him," I finally say to Harper and Hayley's questioning eyes.

"Well what'd he say?" Harper questions.

"Just asked if I'm still coming."

"Well, are you?" Harper and Hayley ask in unison.

"This is too much pressure. Yesterday when I said yes, it was simple and easy."

"Yesterday you were stupid," Harper says.

"Think about Matias," Hayley adds. "If you were him or if he were in this situation then what would you want him to do?"

"I gotta go. My brain hurts. This is too much for a Sunday morning."

"Make the right decision MC," Harper hisses.

"We love you," Hayley finishes.

"Yeah," I say standing and making my way to the front door.

"I'll call you later," I add to no one in particular and walk outside.

After I clear the door, I pull out my phone and respond to Luca's text.

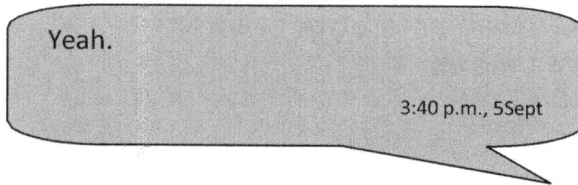

> Yeah.
>
> 3:40 p.m., 5Sept

I drive blindly and return to my condo lost in thought. I clamber inside and notice all the pillows from the night before are gone and the strongest aroma of bacon and waffles wafts enticingly into my nose.

"MC," Matias sings, "welcome home. I have breakfast and it shall be ready in a minute."

"Thanks," I say laying my keys and purse down. "I'm sorry I disappeared on you. There was a minor emergency with Harper and Hayley."

"Oh gosh, what is it?" he remarks, stunned in anticipation for bad news.

"Nothing really. Don't look so worried." Though I'm starving, the thought of food makes me feel a bit nauseous as I continue. "I'll have to step out in a bit. I'm going to quickly meet a friend who just got in town and I wanted to stop by the Farmer's Market today too."

"Well, after you chat with your friend would you mind if I joined you at the Farmer's Market?"

Shocked by his lack of questions with regard to my

friend I say, "Sure!" quickly before he has time to analyze any portion of my statement.

"Good. I have something I would like to talk with you about," he says beginning to plate our meal.

"You sure you don't want to start now," I ask warily as I begin carting the silverware, napkins, glasses, and fresh squeezed orange juice to the table.

"No, no. I think it will be good conversation to make at the Farmer's Market," he says smiling.

Matias brings the plates to the breakfast nook where we eat in virtual silence, both of us seated side by side in the window seat. With his right hand he strokes my thigh and uses his left to eat, drink and peruse the Sunday paper. Still feeling queasy I sit half-staring into space using a crossword puzzle to mask my anguish.

***

It's 11:45 and I've arrived at the bookstore early. I had to make a hasty departure from my condo because Matias' congenial disposition was beginning to make me question my decision to meet Luca. I grab a table and pull out a book I've read many times over – *Pride and Prejudice.*

"Settling for one of the classics today?" I hear the timbre of a male voice come from behind me.

"Luca, hi," I say with a smile.

"Oh, don't get up," he says putting up a hand interrupting my movement before he leans down and kisses my cheek.

"I'm so glad you came," he closes sitting in the chair across from me.

I place my book on the table and give Luca a once over. "What?"

"It's just that, well it's a lot of things. But first, why are you so surprised I'm here? I told you I'd be here."

"Well you never know. This was all on a whim so I just had a feeling that you might let greater reason prevail.

You know, let Harper talk you out of it," he says winking.

If only you knew, I thought to myself.

"Well I'm here now," I respond silencing my thoughts.

"I'm more pleased than you could know."

We exchange pleasantries until we flow right back into our old rhythm. Every so often I catch his eyes lingering on my face longer than could be called normal. And when I am certain he's no longer paying attention I allow my gaze to examine this version of Luca. The familiarity of our dialogue is enlivening. We get so comfortable with one another that our pinkies find each other across the table, and we sit fingers laced enjoying the good company and conversation.

"So, a math and science teacher?"

"Yeah. Not exactly what you and I worked toward, but you've got to believe me when I say it's the best thing I could be doing. It's better than anything I could've ever imagined."

"That's nice to hear. You seem very…I don't know…"

"Say it," he urges.

"You seem much more together and in a perfect place. It's nice to see you so happy."

"Well, you can't tell me that you're not equally as happy with how things for you have panned out."

"I won't say anything then."

"No really, tell me what's up. MC…. it's me here," he says tipping his head over to meet my eyes.

"I dunno Luca. Everything *should* be perfect, but I dunno."

"Stop saying you don't know. Tell me what you know."

"Everything's just too perfect and it's almost like it's perfect for someone else."

"How do you mean?"

"I mean…my job is great. I'm so close to being finished with my dissertation. I have a bo-…things with me

270

are good, but I…"

Brrrriiinnng. My phone rings and I immediately drop Luca's grasp.

"Hello?" I say almost whispering, turning away from Luca.

"Amor mio, are you returning soon?"

"Yes of course. I let the time get away from me. I'm sorry," I say working to cover my mouth as I continue.

"No apologies, I just wanted to hear your voice. I feel like a puppy. I've just missed you a bit and feel myself getting restless."

"I'm…yes. I'm coming."

"Okay. I will see you soon. Te quiero."

"Me too," I say coyly before hanging up the phone and turning back to Luca.

"So, you're going?" Luca asks with a wounded look stamped upon his face.

"Yeah. I didn't mean to….I…..I uh…I told a, a," I stutter searching for words, "companion," I continue with resolution regarding my word choice, "that we could go to the Farmer's Market today."

"Right. Companion," Luca remarks incredulously. "And this companion has a deep voice huh?"

"If you're asking whether or not he's a guy, then yes."

"And your companions, do they usually tell you they love you?"

"Luca, I…"

"You don't have to explain."

"I don't want you to think…"

"I understand."

"I don't know if you do. I know I'm here, but Matias is my…"

"Boyfriend. I know. I get it. I just popped up out of the blue. It makes sense you'd have a boyfriend. I'd be a fool to think you would've stayed and waited for me to get my act together."

271

"I don't know what to say."

"You don't have to say anything. Can you just do me a favor?"

"I suppose so," I respond cautiously.

"Just think of me."

"Huh?"

"I don't know how far in with this guy you are, but I feel like I have a fighting chance. So, can you, before you decide to get super serious with this guy, can you at least consider me? Second time around I could be good for you."

"I will," I hear myself saying before I've had time to properly comprehend what I'm agreeing to. "But I have a question for you."

"Yeah?" he asks hopeful and unassuming.

"How are you so sure you have a fighting chance?"

"Well you didn't tell him you loved him back. You called him your companion and never mentioned him in conversation. The MC I know can't contain herself when she's in love. And the kicker was…" he pauses dramatically.

"What?" I ask with vehement excitement.

"You came. Today, you're here which tells me that you felt what I felt last night which means you may feel what I feel right now. We make sense you and me. I won't pressure you, but I'm rooting for me," he says peering down at me with an alluring calm. "You should go. I don't want you to keep Matias waiting."

I am without words. I should tell him that I'm deeply in love with Matias and he loves me back and we dance and read and just enjoy each other's company and he's wrong about everything, but I can't. He stands and says "see you soon" before brushing my cheek with his lips and leaving just as he had come.

***

I perk up and put Luca out of my mind by the time Matias and I reach the Farmer's Market. Matias reminds me of why I admire the follow through and security he provides as opposed to the unpredictability that comes with Luca. Matias is so pleasant that it's hard not to love him more and get lost in his amenable manner. That's one of the things I adore most about him; his warmth is so contagious.

The Farmer's Market is downtown. I feel like Dorothy in Oz or Alice in Wonderland. Amidst the wrought iron gates, dirty metal, and bustle of the urban work hub there's this wholesome produce village waiting to be explored.

"So what fruits are you purchasing today?" Matias asks taking my hand in his.

"I'm going to see the berry man today," I answer guiltily tightening my grip on his hand.

"MC, I wanted to speak with you about something," he starts, breaking the speed of his stride.

"Sure." Breaking contact I make my way toward a delicious looking stand.

"Well last week I got a very important call."

"Call? About what? Work stuff? On a Saturday?" I ask not totally engaged as I'm picking at and smelling peaches and nectarines.

"I got a call from the Consortium."

"Oh, those guys that sent you here?" I inquire, briefly tearing my gaze away from the fruit I'm inspecting to look at him.

"Right. MC, do you think you could stop investigating the pears for one moment," Matias asks with minor irritation.

I stop and turn back toward him. We've wandered into a secluded patch of the market, so he and I are the only two people around. The only audible sound is the steady breeze blowing smells of fall all around us.

Matias carefully examines my face and steps closer to me. He brushes a hair from my face and catches both of my hands. His suddenly doleful demeanor makes me nervous and I can feel my heart skip a beat.

"The Consortium, they called and applauded the work I've done, and they asked me about maybe transferring to a

273

partner school in Cambridge and eventually on to Oxford."

Matias is amazing at all he does. He's worked wonders at TIC in just a short time. He has gotten professors on board with mingling with staff in meaningful ways and he's encouraged them, with some success, to participate in Student Affairs processes and invite students to engage in out-of-classroom academic endeavors. We have been incredibly lucky to have him.

"That sounds wonderful Matias. When will they need you? This summer? That could be an amazing summer vacation," I speak rapidly not picking up on the modest sadness in Matias' crystalline blue eyes.

"They actually want me to go next month."

"Next month?" I say affronted and snapping free of his hands. "What do you mean next month? Next month's like next week. How can they ask you to do that, move so quickly? And how are you so okay with agreeing to consider it?"

"MC please be calm. I did not tell you this to upset you. I have more."

"More? You have more? What else can there possibly be?"

"MC," he pleads wiling me to calm.

"I'm sorry," I say hanging my head in defeat.

"I want for you to come with me. I have no doubt in my mind that you would be a great companion for me and you are the only person I know who would appreciate the rich history and opportunity we have in front of us," he says lifting my chin toward him.

"I've actually already cleared it with your superiors, above me that is. They will consider it a sabbatical. You will just have to come home with some information about student conduct on the other side."

"You did what?" I hear myself asking with a much angrier tone than I anticipated.

"It seemed appropriate to do before presenting you the

opportunity. It would be the best thing for us. And it may help you with your writing rut on your dissertation," he continues either oblivious or in spite of my ire.

"Matias, this is all a bit much right now," I say shaking my head in confusion, trying to calm myself.

"It does not have to be. Did you hear me? I've got it all figured out."

"That's the problem. *You've* got it all figured out. What about me?" I question with fury, my eyes stinging with a mass of unshed tears.

"Why are you angry," he asks with genuine concern, drawing closer to me, laying his hands on my shoulders. "I thought this was good for the both of us. I thought you would be happy."

"Why would I be happy about this," I speak tears unleashed from their ducts.

"This way we can still be together. I-, I-" he stops at a loss for words.

"Matias…everything I know is here. What would I do if I were gone?"

"Everything like what?" he presses indignantly.

"Mama, Papí, Harper, Hayley, Dr. Logan. They're all here, unless you've made arrangements for them too."

"MC you can call your family and friends and they can visit. And Logan…I thought we discussed. You do not need him," he spits, his eyes briefly lighting with frustration. "We could have an adventure together. I really thought you would be pleased," he adds arms falling to his side in defeat.

"I don't want my whole of everything to become only you. How could you not know that I, that I can't," I struggle to get the words untangled from my throat.

"You can't; or you won't?" he asks with a renewed spirit showcasing a tone I've never heard from him.

"What difference does it make?"

"It matters. I do not know what is going on with you or what or *who* is causing you to respond this way. We've talked many times about going away on an adventure

275

together."

"What's with the emphasis on 'who'? And Matias that's the thing, we were talking!" I interrupt.

"It wasn't just talking. Our words were a recipe for the future, but it was real. This will be our future."

"What if I don't want this future?" I bark.

"You do not know what you want. This will be good for you," he retorts, huffing with frustration.

"No," I whine.

"I want to end this discussion for now," he says, his voice calming from the petulant tone of our ensuing argument. "I fear in our anger one might say things we do not mean and it's not allowing you adequate time to consider the proposal."

"Matias, what's there to consider? I can't go away with you," I say my tone unchanged.

"If that is truly how you feel and it's based on legitimate concerns, not diminutive evasion you've adapted to stay away from me, I will accept it."

"What does that mean you will accept it? I'm not a child."

"Then stop behaving as such."

He steps toward me like a raging bull.

"No means no, whether or not you deem my rationale sanctioned."

"The MC I know is not so combative. She's lovely and deliberative and she's honest with me," he says coolly, almost condescendingly.

"Well maybe you don't know me very well then," I scoff channeling the child he says I'd become.

"You today, you are not her and I cannot deal with this."

"You're breaking up with me?" I ask almost expectantly.

"No," he says annoyed, "But I can no longer be here with you. I must go."

"Okay. Fine. Let's go. But I'm not changing my

mind," I add crossing my arms and tightening my jaw.

"No. Alone. You stay."

Matias' head is hung low as he walks away from the patch of market, hands buried in his pockets. I stand and watch, my arms at my side, and keep my eyes narrowed on him until his tall figure disappears into the sunlight. I don't know what just happened. I don't know why I reacted the way I did, and I don't know what to do.

***

"Hale."

"Why do you answer your phone like that?"

"Noe?"

"I mean you could say hello. Or you could use your first name instead of your last. Logan makes a lot more sense. Or if you stick with a surname you could at least say 'this is Hale'."

"Noe?"

"'This is…' is a lot more appropriate."

"The 'This is' is actually implied with my current greeting."

"To what population?"

"Noe?" Dr. Logan calls more forcefully.

"What?" I yell back.

"Why are you calling me? On a Sunday? On my personal cell phone…that's reserved for emergencies only?" He places emphasis on the utterance of 'only'.

"This *is* an emergency," I call back indignantly.

"Please reveal the emergent qualities of your call," he says like a 9-1-1 operator.

"Don't mock," I say whining a bit. "This is serious. Can I meet you somewhere?"

"Noe…" he starts, preparing to decline.

"I could be a danger to myself," I say threateningly.

"Are you?"

"Of course not. I'm not a crazy person."

"Then what's this all about?"

"No. I can't like this. I need to see you and I want you to see me. It's the only way."

"I'm at my home and I can't exactly leave."

"It's okay. I can come to you."

"Noe..."

"Please don't say no. I wouldn't bother you unless it was real. Well I might, but I wouldn't be so insistent about it. You know that. You know me. Please."

"Okay" he says at a whisper.

"Oh my gosh, I love you. I'm in the car now driving west. I figured that's the general direction."

He laughs some until he finally guides me to his home. His directions are precise and deliberate, and I never once feel lost or abandoned. The soothing sound of voice calms me as I make my way through winding streets to his home.

When I arrive, I park on the curb, fly out my door almost forgetting to put it in park, and barrel down the driveway toward a relaxed and strangely mesmeric Dr. Logan. I'm so used to seeing him in his slacks that I have trouble catching my breath as I take him all in.

He's wearing loose fitting jeans that are just barely hanging at his hips. He's donning a black round neck shirt that hugs each of his tumescent biceps.

My barrel slows to a crawl when I see him stretch lifting his arms to reveal his beautiful stomach ripples, a faint southern traveling trail of hair and the hardest cut v-muscle ever. He's barefoot and wiggles his toes almost saying hello as I reach him.

"I'm here," I say short of breath partly from my light jog and partly from the breathtaking specimen before me.

"'Tis I," he adds sarcastically, lowering his arms from his stretch. "Shall we?"

He escorts me into the house through his foyer, past gorgeous mirrors, and black and white hand sketches of non-

278

descript faces and beautiful landscapes. His home is full of midnight blue and chocolate brown hues – warm and homey.

Inside, his couches are gargantuan and plushy making me feel like as soon as I land on one, I'm going to fall into deep slumber. His huge 72-inch flat screen is mounted along a wall above a wood-burning fireplace and floor to ceiling windows lay on either side of it. Along the adjacent wall I can see from my angle within the walkway a built-in bookshelf with books stuffed in as far as the eye can see. I am amazed at his collection. It reminds me a lot of my papí's.

"Do you want to inspect more?"

"Huh," I wince loudly, beaming with embarrassment. "No. I'll keep my word. This is business. Where shall we sit?"

"Just have a seat on the couch and we can see what exactly this emergency is," he boasts smiling a beautiful toothy grin.

***

"So, it sounds like you have some decisions to make."

"You say that so nonchalantly like it's easy. Did you even hear anything?"

"Yes of course I've heard it," he retorts. Noticing my disbelief, he pulls in a large breath and continues.

"Still rattled from our conversation and clearly not doing your homework as your capable counselor had encouraged, you've continued to avoid Matias. He makes an impromptu visit to your home where you make some hedonistic decisions giving your confidence a boost going into the *Appeteasing*, event," he says eyeing me.

"There, feeling recovered you dutifully engage with bachelor number one, number two and lucky number three takes you by surprise. In the flesh Luca Marcel Bianchi speaks to you and asks you for a follow-up meeting. You resolved to meet him and return to your condo to a waiting Matias. You consummate your revived relationship *again* and fall into slumber."

Dr. Logan looks so adorable. He's an excellent raconteur, very engaging. I think I better let him know that when he's finished.

"Early the next morning…well today, unable to sleep, you visit with Harper and Hayley who equally express their disdain for your decision to attend a follow-up meeting with Luca. Key element," he notes lifting his left pointer finger in the air.

"He texts you to ask for confirmation and though you hesitate, you agree. Later you return to your home for breakfast with Matias. With no set reconvening time with Matias, and as planned, you go off to meet Luca," he moves his hands in a darting motion.

"Waiting at a familiar bookstore you sit reading and are met by your intended. You both speak and catch up and your only interruption is from Matias calling to inquire about your ETA. You are now forced to reveal that Matias is your *boyfriend*. Luca offers a declaration of intentions and proffers some personal observations regarding the state of your relationship and the potential of a rekindled affiliation with him. A bit shaken you depart and rendezvous with Matias and you both head off to the market. In the market you peruse, and Matias discusses with you an opportunity he has along with a proposition for you."

He pauses slightly and sinks back into the side of the couch where he's sitting.

Throughout his story as things had gotten racy, he began moving closer and closer, sitting up slightly on his knees. His untimely interruption and movement away startles me.

"Go on!" I urge.

"I'm going. Without a soundtrack I need something embedded within my story to signify where the dramatics are located. It makes it more real," he says with a straight face though his aura is beaming with playful delight.

"Dr. Logan! Quit it. Finish," I whimper, swatting his

thigh in reprimand.

"Well, you and Matias exchange words in harsh tones – you lost in fury; him lost in unanticipated confusion. Enter Dr. Logan Hale," he says as a whispered stage direction.

"You phone and plead with me," he clears his throat, "I mean Dr. Hale to visit with you on his day off. He hesitantly obliges, you arrive and you both meet in anticipation of the cable and exterminator guys, respectively. So…. how'd I do?" he asks like a schoolboy awaiting his final marks.

"Aside from the theatrics, surprisingly……well," I say taken aback at his remarkable abilities to recreate and engage.

"So, what was that again about me not hearing?" he asks sneeringly.

"You don't have to be so snotty about it," I say, my voice bleeding with bitter disdain.

"There's no snot here. I just want you to acknowledge that you were wrong, and I want to point out that this was yet another attempt of yours to avoid responding to my inquiry."

"Dr. Logan you're so unreasonable," I whine just as the doorbell bellows down the corridor.

"I'll get that but note that I'm still waiting."

Dr. Logan walks to the front door and returns with a man wearing paint stained jeans and a short sleeved white button down that says AT&T on it.

"Noe, this is Andy."

"Hi," Andy says nervously.

"He'll be here repairing my satellite box."

"It won't take long miss. I jus' need tuh reset the switches then I'll be right outta yer way," he says revealing a Georgian accent.

"Noe," Andy and Dr. Logan call simultaneously.

"Noe," Dr. Logan begins again looking at Andy incredulously, "let the man do his work. I'll be in the kitchen scrounging up some drinks and a snack. Upon my return and Andy's completion I will be expecting your response," he says lightly – almost patronizingly.

He regards Andy and disappears into his kitchen. Andy attempts to make polite conversation, but his voice eventually disappears, buried by the sounds of Dr. Logan in the kitchen. I can hear his refrigerator open and close, cabinets open and slam shut, plastic packaging crinkle, the ping of buttons and the hum of the microwave.

I am confused about what Dr. Logan wants from me. I don't think he gets that I came to him for guidance. I need him to tell me what I should do. The microwave sings and the smell of popcorn envelopes the living room where I'm sitting lost in a cloud of thoughtless thoughts.

Almost like clockwork Dr. Logan returns with a bowl of popcorn, two cans of Dr. Pepper, and two cups of ice on a tray. Andy stands and meets him at the center of the room confessing,

"Welp, she's fixed."

"Just like that," Dr. Logan asks mock amazed. "Thank you very much Andy. I'll see you out."

"I hope whatever it is you figure it out and have a right good day ma'am," Andy calls tipping the brim of his imaginary hat and following Dr. Logan out the house.

"Here we are. Sustenance," Dr. Logan says returning and laying the tray of goodies between us.

"Thank you. I didn't know you drank Dr. Pepper too," I add popping open my can.

"You didn't think I always had cans just for you, did you? You will be happy to know that I appreciate all 23 of my flavors," he begins flashing a smile.

"Now Ms. Cortes…what have your thoughts been saying? You called this emergency meeting, so you need to use your words. Please," he finishes between gritted teeth.

"Dr. Logan, I'm really confused."

"Good start," taking a swig of his Dr. Pepper he readjusts himself. "More."

"I feel like I have everyone else's words in my head and I can't discern my own. I was fine with Matias."

"You were fine," he repeats.

"Yes. And then with that stupid speed dating thing Luca just had to show up. So, to me it's like a second chance thing, right? But again, with Harper and Hayley…Hayley! She's always on my side and this time she wasn't. Why did Luca have to be so lovely? Why am I so curious and stupid? And I was so rotten to Matias. I didn't mean to be that way. I care a lot for him," I say eyes darting from left to right as my words get jumbled jumping from subject to subject.

"May I speak?"

"Please. Shut me up!" I mock cry leaning over and burying my head in his thigh.

"I'm hearing a few things," he says lifting my head. "With regard to Matias you said you were 'fine' and you 'care for him'. Say more about this. You're big on phraseology so why those words?"

"I don't know."

"You do."

"Because that's real. We are fine. I am happy with him but…" I trail off.

"But what?"

"Is it wrong to feel like something's missing?"

"Nothing's ever wrong with feeling like you feel. When did this begin?"

"I guess the first conversation Harper and I had, and then my breakdown with you. Or maybe I knew deep down that he was just my means of escape because he was new and interested. I don't know."

"You know. Don't say you don't know just because you're scared. Push through that and use your words."

"Okay, I knew!"

"Good. And why did you move forward when you knew he wasn't exactly right for you?"

"Mary and Massimo."

"No Jennifer Lopez references please. Lay terms only."

"He has this way of always knowing what's best for

me. He is safe and he adores me. That sounds awful. I feel like such a loser. I'm a jerk. Jules and Kimmie."

"English please."

"It's from *My Best Friend's Wedding*. Jules kissed Michael in front of his fiancé Kimmie. But then when Michael ran after her, Jules she was forced to realize that Michael really is for Kimmie," I explain wistfully, remembering the movie as I explain.

"And then when Kimmie ran away and Michael thought he'd lost her; Jules came clean about all the underhanded stuff she'd been doing, and she calls herself pond scum. Then Michael's like, 'you're the puss that infects the mucous that cruds up the fungus that feeds on the pond scum.' And that's me. Horrible and disgusting," I say staring inexplicably into the distance.

"Noe, stop that. Focus," he says shaking me lightly. "You're only 'horrible' if you know what you're doing when you do it. You realize now so let's do something about it."

"Like what?"

"First things first. Luca. You said something about a second chance and him being lovely. What was appealing to you? What about his proposition captivated to you?"

"I already told you," I say aggravated, nearly jolting our drinks off the couch.

"Tell me again," Dr. Logan utters, carefully placing the tray on his coffee table.

"I don't know. I guess I just like the familiarity of it all. At the event we just fell back in sync. And moving backward seemed infinitely easier than moving forward. And this weirdness with Matias and our incompatibility or whatever you want to call it…it's just like why not. That's bad too. Ugh. Why am I so horrible?" I yell this last bit into a nearby pillow.

"Up Noe," Dr. Logan commands.

I rise at his call and stare wearily at him.

"I feel like I've created a mess."

"Clean it up then."

"I don't know how. I can't go with Matias but if I tell him he'll be hurt and probably think ill of me. I shouldn't get involved with Luca, but strangely I want to. I want to know what could be. What if all he needed was time? But what if I'm stupid? You know fool me once…that saying. This is too hard."

"Breathe Noe. Just breathe," Dr. Logan calls.

I close my eyes and repeat his words as a mantra silently.

"Noe. It's not too hard. You didn't walk yourself into any situation that you can't get yourself out of. Just breathe and think about what you can do. What you want to do. What you need to do."

"I can talk to Matias," I say with my eyes closed. "With Luca, I guess I can lay all my cards on the table and play it by ear. And with the voices. I don't know. I thought that was your job," I finish, opening one of my eyes to peer at Dr. Logan's expression.

"For a moment there I thought we'd made progress," Dr. Logan says swatting my nose lightly with a throw pillow. "With the exception of that last bit I think you've crafted a great plan for yourself. Now all you need to do is do it."

"Yeah. Do it. That's the hard part. I don't know if I…"

"You can. You can do what you allow yourself to do."

"Dr. Logan?"

"Yes?"

"Can I stay here?"

"Excuse me?"

"Don't look so disgusted. I don't mean forever. Just for a little while longer. I know I sound ready and technically there's not much more to discuss, but I'm not ready yet. Can I stay?"

"I didn't mean to look disgusted. I was caught off guard. While I do think that's well beyond the bounds of our professional relationship. You can stay for one standard length film, then you must go."

285

"Thank you," I say leaping out wrapping my arms around him in a hug.

"You're welcome," he grumbles uncomfortably.

"Can I pick the movie?" I ask sheepishly.

"I suppose. I'm going to order a pizza and see where my exterminator is."

"Wonderful! This is going to be so much fun. You won't regret it."

Dr. Logan stalks back into the kitchen taking the tray with our snacks with him. I hear the hushed sound of his voice as he calls his exterminator and orders our pizza. While he's out I choose, with ease a movie from Netflix. After a bit he returns, refreshes our Dr. Pepper's, and declares that the exterminator mis-scheduled the appointment setting it in his calendar for next month on the same day. He apologized profusely and vowed to come next weekend.

The pizza arrives rather quickly, and Dr. Logan dims the lights as I press play for our feature.

"Why?" he groans as the opening credits roll.

"Stop whining. You said I could pick. So shh or we'll have to start it all over."

We sit in silence engrossed in *The Wedding Planner*. I've seen it over 100 times, but each viewing makes me feel like it's the first time. I watch Dr. Logan periodically as he seems just as captivated as I am. He even misses his mouth once leaving pizza sauce on the side of his chin, but he wipes it away quickly hoping he's unseen.

The pizza is delicious and cut in an odd number of pieces. We get to the last one and generously Dr. Logan offers it to me and when I decline, he cuts it in half and we both share the final piece. As the ending credits roll, I realize it's time for me to go but I don't move hoping Dr. Logan won't say anything.

"Well, that was surprisingly enjoyable," he proclaims a little awkwardly breaking our silence.

"You've never seen it?"

"No. I hadn't."

"Then how did you pick up on the reference earlier?" I ask incredulously.

"You've mentioned the characters before. I just have a good memory that's all," he says almost too quickly.

"I suppose I'll believe that."

"As well you should," he says with resolve.

 "Well I guess…"

"You guess?"

"If I'm keeping with our deal…"

"If you're keeping with our deal?"

"I should go."

"Is that so?"

"What? No more Dr. Parrot?"

"You're so right it is that time. So sad to see you go," he says feigning grievousness, standing quickly and bringing up the lights.

"Fine," I say slowly unearthing myself from beneath the mound of blankets and pillows I'd had for the viewing. "What time is it?"

"Nearly six," he says helping me re-fold the blankets.

"Right. I'm sure…Matias…or someone will be wondering where I've gone."

I lay the last blanket down and make my way toward the door hesitating with my hand on the knob.

"Breathe Noe. Just breathe," Dr. Logan whispers materializing behind me, his breath hot against my neck.

I do as he suggests, taking in his sedative air.

"Thank you."

"Don't make it more difficult than it has to be. You are capable of doing as you must."

Dr. Logan watches me as I make my way across his driveway and to my car. Inside I crank it up and look longingly

back. He mimics taking a deep breath and I offer him a weak smile before I pull off.

***

I pull up to the faculty house where Matias is staying and peer at the beet red door. I re-play Dr. Logan's voice over and over again in my head. *'Breathe. Just breathe.'* And I convince myself to get out of the car, walk up to the door and ring the bell.

"MC?" Matias asks, surprised when he opens the door.

"May I come in?"

"Sure. Are you alright? I tried your condo earlier, but there was no answer."

"I haven't been at home. I needed to think. I had so much rolling around and I just needed some clarity."

"That is okay. Please come inside. Can I get you something to drink? Wine? Lemonade? Seltzer?"

"A regular water will do thank you."

Matias hurries off to his kitchen and I try to make myself at home on his sofa. The couch and chair in the living room are ornate and uncomfortable and everything looks so pristine it frightens me to touch.

"Here we are," Matias returns with a bottle of water and a glass.

"Thank you."

"So how do you feel now?"

"Much better." I take a drink of water and we stare at each other in a less than comfortable silence, thinking much more than we're leading on. "Matias?"

"Yes?" he answers quickly with anticipation.

"I'm terribly sorry for the way I treated you this afternoon. It was ugly of me and you didn't deserve any of that."

"I accept. I know that was very unlike you, so I was not too indignant."

"I'm glad for that," I say attempting to keep any sarcasm out of my voice.

"I am not trying to rush you. I am just curious. Have

you had time to reconsider my proposition?"

"Matias, can you come sit next to me?" He obliges.

His demeanor is calm, but something about him sings uneasy and it makes me nervous.

As he sits, I turn to him and he instinctively grabs my hands and holds them in his lap.

"I did think long and hard about what you've asked me. I care for you a lot and I appreciate the person you encourage me to be when we're together. But I can't go. I need to be where I am for me. It would be easy to pack up and go and it would probably be fun too, but it wouldn't be right."

"What do you mean it wouldn't be right? I love you very much. When is there ever wrong in that?"

"Matias, I don't. It's just that I…"

"You don't love me?" Matias asks wounded.

"I do, but no. I don't, not like you do. It's all my fault. I haven't been completely me with you because I like that we get along. I like not arguing. I like the adventure of everything Matias," I say freeing my hands and gingerly stroking the side of his face with my fingers.

"You're everything I've ever imagined making sense for me, and the thought of potentially ruining that with some of my many idiosyncrasies pains me. I mean I didn't even tell you about Dr. Logan and when you found out it didn't sit well with you. So, I guess in this regard you don't love me either. Not all of me anyway," I ramble.

"I do not necessarily agree, but I want to understand," he says grabbing my hand and moving closer into me, eyes filled with worry.

"I don't know wha…"

"You think what we have is a lie, and you don't feel as though it would work," he states inquisitively.

"I don't want you to think I'm making this up and trying to use that as a reason to deny your proposal."

"This doesn't make sense. The getting to know you process implies progressive revelation. You don't know all there is to know about me either, but that doesn't change the fact that I love you."

"But…"

"So, the real question is do you love me? And if you don't then why have you been pretending all this time? For my benefit?"

"I do care for you Matias."

"I didn't say care. I said love. Do you *love* me?"

"You're the Massimo to my Mary."

"What in God's name are you talking about?" he asks still squeezing my hand, eyes emblazoned.

"I'm sorry. Matias please don't be mad at me. It's hard for me to say all this. It is."

"It's that Logan fellow isn't it?" he growls grabbing me by the chin, making it so I can't turn away from him.

"What are you talking about Matias? Dr. Logan is my therapist not a lover!" I pull away from him and stand indignantly.

"Please don't go," Matias says lowering his tone and grabbing hold of my arm. "I'm sorry to have verbally accosted you. I'll be calm, I promise."

I carefully lower myself back onto the couch.

"I'm trying to do the right thing Matias. We don't make sense together, not really and it wouldn't be fair to you if I went because the parts of me you don't have, I'm not sure you ever will."

"What do you mean we don't make sense together?"

"I don't even know you. When we met you were suave and mysterious. Lately you've been clingy and overly romantic. Tonight, you've been nothing but enraged. It's too much."

"It is true I am upset, but I love you so deeply. And, and, the fact that you see me in all these ways shows that you *do* know me, just as I know you."

"Matias, you don't."

"Yes, I do. You are caring and deliberative. You have great artistic talent and you try hard to please others…even though you haven't figured out what pleases you. Is none of that correct?" he asks nervously.

"Yes, but…"

"But what? I know you. How can you say that I do not?"

"Matias, you didn't even consider me when you decided that you would move."

"I did consider you that's why I asked if you could come along."

"That had nothing to do with me. That was to help you. My lifelines are all here. The person you see that's mildly hinged is that way because of the people in her life. What would I do anyway, follow you around? I'd just be a puppy trailing behind you waiting."

"That's not true. There would be much for you to do."

"Like what?"

"I don't know. It would give you time to grow some and, well you say all the time that you just need to get away and start new."

"Maybe I do need to grow, but I'll do it in my own time. And starting over…I'm really good at starting over, but I can't do that. Not really. I have to be here."

"So, all of our months together…they have been laced with untruths? And the other night we shared together. It was all fake?" he asks hurt erupting from his words.

"Of course not. I do love you and I love being with you I just don't see forever with you." As soon as the words exit my mouth, I immediately want to take them back, but it's too late. The damage is already done.

"Matias?"

"No. Don't. You have said enough. I'm sorry I cannot be all that you desire," he says his eyes hooded and his voice low and detached.

"I never said that."

"And it was foolish of me to think that the one I love would come with me on my travels.
You are right. I was being selfish."

"Please don't do this," I try, leaning down to meet his eyes. "In another world it would make perfect sense. If I had been completely honest with you from the start, we would've never been here."

"What do you mean honest?"

"I have a thing for romance, and it was so easy to get swept up in you that I ignored the other things that make a relationship lasting. But when you asked me to go with you there was no way to avoid the reality of the situation."

"What is this reality? I still do not completely understand."

"I've not considered myself and what really makes me happy all while we've been together. I was comfortable getting absorbed in all the adventure that comes with you. So, I guess in that way I was being selfish."

"Meaning?"

"Matias the me you know is the person I want to be, she's not who I am. I am a walking, talking ball of anxiety who has absolutely nothing figured out but who doesn't really want someone else to decide it for her."

"And that is what I was doing?"

"It was, but it's not your fault," I reach out to him trying to showcase my remorse. "I allowed it."

"Is there anything I can do to change your mind? To make you consider continuing your growth process with me?"

"I don't think we should."

"And that I suppose I must respect," he says dolefully wiping his face with his hands.

Matias and I sit and chat a while longer before I bid him adieu. We arrange to visit with each other more before he leaves, but we reset our relationship on the friend dial. I'm so proud of myself as I exit his home and it takes all I can muster not to race back to Dr. Logan's and let him know of my triumph.

On the way home I call Luca and arrange to meet him the next day. There's uneasiness in his voice and I can't tell if he's picking up on the contents of tomorrow's discussion or if he himself has something going on. Instead of focusing on discerning his underlying feelings I opt for a long bath and peaceful slumber.

From the Desk of ___Noe Cortes___

September 5, 2010

Today has been one of great accomplishment. Matias understands, and tomorrow so will Luca and I'll finally have my real-life fairy tale. It's amazing to think that I actually was able to have a real-life adult conversation and not have it blow up in my face.

Harper and Hayley are so wrong, and I can't wait to rub it in their faces tomorrow.

On another note, it was very pleasant getting to spend the evening with Dr. Logan. It's nice to know that he's not so uptight all the time. That's just his doctor persona. He was actually quite...a lot of something I probably shouldn't write...so I shan't.

My bath was relaxing, and I must now sleep in preparation for my successful tomorrow. I'm on the precipice of take two of the Noe and Luca show. I think this time around it's going to be worth it to watch.

Chapter 22

"No, you don't understand," he said a bit flustered, wiping his face with his hands. "I love you so much. I jus-. I can't. I- I."

"You what, Luca? You're making me really nervous. Just tell me." I demanded anxiously adjusting the ring on my left ring finger.

"Do you love me?"

"You know I do," I shouted mildly affronted.

"Do I? You never tell me. But you know what you do tell me? That I'm not enough," he spat like a line of venom.

"When have I ever said that?" I interrupted exasperated by his outlandish assertion.

"I would never tell you something so horrible. Less than a month ago we both re-affirmed our love for one another," I said lifting my finger and pointing to my ring as a reminder.

"Luca, with you I've been nothing but supportive even though you choose never to talk to me about anything. You always talk to that stupid psychiatrist," my easy tone changed to one of indignation.

"She's a psychologist and she's not stupid," he yelled in return.

"Semantics," I muttered.

"You're starting to sound a lot like Harper," he retorted.

"And you're starting to sound like a crazy person. Seriously Luca, what's with this? You know I've never treated you the way you're saying."

"Okay, maybe you don't say it in those words, but I know that's what you mean," he added a bit deflated.

"Luca…you're not even making sense," I added rising from where we were seated outside the bookstore.

"What so you're leaving now? Just like that, not even give me a chance to speak."

"I'm not going anywhere. I'm just stretching – though I should leave with you being so combative."

"See. Do you hear it? That's what I was talking about. You're being you know," he said re-situating in his chair, his back to me.

"Luca."

"Wait, let me go."

"Okay. Fine," I said, my voice dripping with annoyance.

"I don't think I want to do this anymore."

"What?" I asked, confused, and unnerved watching as he continued to sit, never looking at me.

"I just can't. I can't be the guy you need me to be. I'm sorry MC. I wish I could."

His words send me through a whirlwind of emotions. I felt relieved that he'd finally opened up. I was angry because we were in public and he didn't even give me the respect of being in a private place. I was livid because we never talked about this, about how unhappy he was and about if we could fix it. I was sad because I knew he was already over us. I hadn't had a moment to make sense of it all and really decide how I felt, but he had. He'd gone through all the grief stages and was clearly at acceptance. I was near despondent because all I could think was Harper was right and I instantly felt alone.

***

"MC? Did you hear me?" Luca asks as I've drifted off, clearly cajoled by the déjà vu of it all.

"This isn't real, Luca. It can't be."

"I'm sorry. I know it seems like..."

"No," I start, interrupting what I feel is the worst pre-planned break up speech and full on crock of shit I could ever hear.

"You're not sorry and you haven't a clue what it seems like. I can't believe we're here again. It's a fucking instant replay."

"MC."

"No. No. No. No fuckity no. You're sitting. Again. I'm standing. We're in a quiet yet totally public place. You're strategically avoiding eye contact. And I'm accepting it. Again. You're saying contradictory statements in tandem – 'I care about you,' 'I'm not enough,' 'You're amazing,' 'You don't appreciate me,'" I say as if to myself, eyes darting as countless memories come rushing back.

He finally turns toward me seeing my mania and rises to speak.

"Don't Luca," I say raising my hand to his lips with more resolve than I've ever had. "You've always had control and this time it's going to be different. That scenario will not be replayed because I'm not that girl. There will be no tears. And you will not have the last word."

Fueled by all the hurt, fear and unsaid words of our first break-up, I continue, "I don't know what the deal is, but I know it lies in you. Last time when you bailed, I spent years of my life blaming myself for all that was broken. Years. I wasn't pretty enough. Too erratic. Too imperfect. I'm sure you can imagine how it goes. I did the self-deprecating classic break-up depression shtick. But truthfully it takes two," I say barely giving myself time to breathe and process all my words.

"And, and, an' you just gave up," I continue looking at him woefully.

He says nothing. He just stares at me blankly, his eyes full of confusion and I think fear at my outburst.

"But you came back. You came back," I repeat at a whisper looking from side to side searching for reason.

"I jus'…but no. I won't lie. I wanted a happily ever after. I wanted to believe all you needed was time. I was all, 'leave it and if it comes back' and…but I wasn't. I'm not her," I mumble, biting my lip and grabbing at my hair.

"Oh my gosh," I lip, chuckling a bit, "this is not all your fault, I'll admit that. We were clearly the Rory and Dean show, but I forgot at the end of the day, that relationship failed, and Jared Padalecki vanished only to be replaced by someone else."

"So, with the Gilmore Girls reference can I speak now?" Luca asks now agitated by my lengthy ranting.

"Is that annoyance I hear in your tone?" I ask, my retort dripping with pernicious sarcasm.

"It's just this is a prime example of…"

"Of what Luca? Why this time is it okay for you to kick me to the curb? I deserve it right?"

"Well…I just mean," he starts re-thinking his approach. "MC if you know what's next, what do you want from me?"

"I want you to respect me enough to just be honest with me. Tell me what's really going on, not some useless platitudes or clear jabs to make me angry. I'm reasonable and I'm mature enough to handle whatever you have. And if nothing else we've known each other so long that as your friend, as someone you care about even a smidgen, just be straight with me."

"I'm no good for you MC. All those years ago when we were first together you were too much for me. I wasn't ready for that kind of commitment. Your personality was overwhelming…in a good way, but even though I am older and I was doing the grad school thing…and I know I pursued you…I just wasn't ready and the more you asked me to be more, the more I wanted to run."

"Do you have any idea what kind of effect that had on me?" I ask, watching Luca as his eyes redden and begin to water. "I thought the world of you, and I was ready to go through whatever fire *with* you to make a stronger us…"

"But I never wanted that for you," he yells.

"So, you never loved me at all. Is that what it is or was or whatever?"

"I did, but…I just don't know. I don't think I could do it in the way you needed me to. I was just never good enough."

"Agh, don't with the self-deprecating jabber. This is a yes or no type deal."

"It's not that clear cut MC," he continues mussing his hair a bit in search of the right words. "You're the queen of gray how can you not know that?"

"Because when it comes to love quite frankly, I feel like it is black and white. If you love me, you'll work for me; if you don't, you'll run away. You chose the latter, so I just want to hear you say the words and not go on and on with this 'I'm no good for you bit'."

"Listen MC. I wasn't doing a bit. I'm…I'm not. You have this light…and that…. you just don't know how much…but that scared the crap out of me. I don't have that kind of freedom. Outwardly you seem calculated and routine and I'm like the quintessential off the cuff guy, but inside we're both just the opposite. So, I ran Noe. I couldn't be the reason your light never shined so it was just better for me to go. You can't possibly say we were in a good place. You were crying all the time."

"I'm not going to say we were in a great place. But all relationships go through peaks and valleys. I figured we were just in our valley and I was willing to find our way out. And I thought you were too. I thought you loved me enough to want to do that."

"I tried. After that Valentine's Day – The Valentine's Day, I wanted everything to go right, but I couldn't shake that feeling. My leaving had nothing to do with how much I loved you though."

"Luca, it has everything to do with that. The stuff you want you fight for. You persevere regardless of what you have to go through. For the things that aren't as important you let them fall by the wayside and you definitely found that you could do better without me."

"MC, I don't want you think…"

"Luca, I didn't want to be in a one-sided relationship with you. I know I love hard, but if you weren't in it the same way and you had to talk yourself into being in love with me then you should've said something. Don't you see how selfish that was to say 'she's just better without me' rather than talk to me about how our definitions of the way we loved the other were not the same. Because that girl you described…I didn't know her…I surely didn't feel like her…and when you just gave up on us, I felt so broken."

"You're right. I don't know what else you want me to say. You're always right. I was selfish and you were perfect and all this wrong was done to you," he says with a biting bitterness.

"Don't be that guy. I don't want a fight. I'm not looking to "win". I'm not even trying to be right necessarily; I'm just telling you what my vantage point was. And I want you to honestly tell me that you don't find any merit in any of what I'm saying and then I'll let it go."

"I guess I can see your point. But I never looked at it that way. I truthfully thought I was doing the best thing for the both of us at the time."

"And now? Why come back? To…to do it all over again? You've been out of my life for so long and it's taken just as long to rebuild myself up…and all for what? To end up here again?"

He pauses briefly with a look of puzzlement about his face before he responds.

"I didn't mean to drag you through the mud again. If I'm being completely forthcoming, when I saw you at the Appeteaser that day I'd just come out of a break-up and, and, and, then seeing you so into your book at the Bookstore took me back to a place that was familiar and great and I…I just wanted to be back in that space. I wanted the comfort that came with the old us. And I was regrettably presumptuous assuming that you would welcome me back…and when you did…"

"So, I was convenient. I was easy. I was a sure thing."

"MC…don't say it like that. Don't be mad. You wanted me to tell the truth. It wasn't like that. I mean I'm not proud of it, but I'm also not upset with how things worked out. We make sense together."

"What do you mean don't be mad and don't say it

"like that"? You just said it. I'm like a drive through and you were really hungry that day."

"Is there really a need for us to continue then? You tell me to be honest but then you get upset when I am, and I don't want that. I'm just...I'm sorry. I don't know what else you want from me."

"You know what? I'm sorry I made it so easy...wait...no...I hate that a part of me felt the same. It hurt not to be wanted so I leapt at the chance...at the thought of you recognizing the error of your ways. I always thought we made sense as a team, and I think I thought I was living in a real life rom-com."

"Wait, you're not mad? Is this a trick? You're not going to wait until I turn around and stab me in the jugular with your pen, are you?"

"Aren't we imaginative? H-Yeah! I'm pissed. But I get it." Remembering my conversation with Matias yesterday I continue. "We're both wrong...but strangely I needed this, and I feel like you did too. There was so much left undone from before and this time around, though tragically flawed, gave us the right stage to be honest with ourselves and each other."

With a glint of warmth in his eyes he voices, "Why are you so amazing? You, you take this shit show and create a total TV learning moment. Of that I am not worthy."

Staving off the smile that wants to break across my face I utter, "Stop saying nice things Luca." Forcing a frown, I continue, "I still have some choice words reserved for you that I'm trying to keep at bay. This is certainly a jerk face move and I don't need you agitating me."

"I'm glad you're so understanding. I know I messed up."

"So..." I start, yanking his arm down as I plop on a bench outside of the library where we've been debating. "What's up Luc? Who's this girl and why are you running from her?"

"Huh?" he squeaks.

301

"I know you. Don't try to get up," I say as he leans forward in preparation to stand. "Seriously...sit with me and I'll tell you how to fix what you shouldn't have broken."

"Am I really that transparent?"

"Shut up and tell me what's going on. Wait though...before we start, I'm going tell you that my almost photographic memory is never going to forget that you just cried," I utter offering my first smile of the afternoon.

"And after this...sensitivity training."

"Keep remembering.... you broke up with me.... twice....so honestly I'm entitled to be as insensitive as I want."

"Touché. Alright.... here's the thing..."

Luca and I sit on the library bench across from one another discussing the future he's too afraid to embrace. His more recent, real ex-girlfriend Audrey was a gem – young, gifted and very driven. She was motivated and likewise – as any awesome girlfriend would – motivated Luca. She supported him when he changed careers and he supported her as she came into her own. They were able to grow together and apparently being in the same place with someone and envisioning a forever with them is daunting, so Luca decided to flee.

I love and hate our process. It reminds me of how Dr. Logan and I talk – with ease and care. He says so much that's incomplete, but I get it and it makes sense without explanation...just like Dr. Logan always manages to get what I'm saying. It's like he can see the transcript of our conversations before we even make them. Unfortunately talking to Luca isn't all hearts and rainbows. It makes me feel that stirring of special feelings all over again and I force myself to resist the urge to envelope him in my most loving embrace. I know I can't as I hear him describe what he has with Audrey. It's the perfect love story and there is no way I could break that up. They're clearly meant to be.

"So.... you gotta go back," I say at the conclusion of

his story.

"Yeah, but what if she won't have me back."

"I don't know Audrey, but I know you, and if she knows you, she'll know this was a temporary lapse in judgment. I mean you'll clearly have to do a ton of clean-up because when you mess up you *really* mess up. You should write a book," I say winking. "But seriously," I begin lifting his head, so his eyes meet mine, "my guess is you'll be just fine."

"Thank you," he whispers leaning in to hug me. "I love you MC. I always have."

"Right back atcha," I speak a bit awkwardly at his emotional outburst. "Okay, then" I start, pulling away from him. "I must be off. I have an appointment at 3 o'clock. Stop running Luca," I add, standing to go.

"MC, I really am…you know I never meant to…"

"I know," I say, lean down and give him a small peck on the cheek, turn, and walk steadily down the pavement forcing myself to never look back.

***

"Dr. Logan, today I became an adult."

"Close the door please," he says, slightly dousing my enthusiasm. "What do you mean today you became an adult? I'd like to think that happened when you turned 13," he sits and winks at me clearly pleased by his attempt at a witty quip.

"Dr. Logan," I begin walking over to him and squatting so that we are staring directly at each other, "has anyone ever told you that when one intends to joke one ends up not being funny in the comical sense but more like the ass sense?" I finish beaming at him.

"Well whoever forgot to offer me that memo also neglected to send you the same one," he adds, matching my smile.

"Wakish," I say mimicking a whip, leaning back, and

303

shaking my hand as if I'd been hit. "Touché. When did you become so quick-witted?"

"You Ms. Cortes aren't the only one well-versed in the art of sarcasm. Now come on, have a seat, let's get to it," he says with a more serious tone as he gently swats me on the nose.

"Okay, Dr. Logan there's been a huge breakthrough," I start rising, making my way around the coffee table, and settling on the couch.

"Which is?"

"Cool it. You know I take my time painting the picture for you. I'm getting there. So, I told you about Luca correct?"

"Yes," he starts quizzically.

"Luca circa now, not episode one," I clarify. Seeing him nod I press on. "So, we were back on but then today out of nowhere he broke up with me."

"And you're happy about this?" Dr. Logan asks perplexed by the apparent inconsistency of my words and the smile that's plastered on my face.

"Well, yeah…but not at first."

"Forgive me for being at a loss for words."

"Don't mention it. You don't get it yet. I'm still explaining."

"Thank goodness for that," he mutters.

"How's that?" I question.

"Continue," Dr. Logan says clearly, adding a cheesy smile and a nod.

I recite my story to Dr. Logan in great detail, words spewing, neck winding and hands flailing about. I take him through my entire range of emotions and watch as he drifts close to me with each new phase of my story.

"Then I asked about his real ex-girlfriend and we talked, and I helped him figure out how to fix that relationship and now I'm here," I close concisely with a bright smile.

"Is that all?"

"What do you mean is that all? That was a hell of a lot of stuff and it was quite the breakthrough. So yeah...that's all...and that's like a big deal."

"I don't mean it's not a big deal, I meant was that all of the story you were going to share?" Noticing my blank stare, he adds, "You left out a lot."

"Because what matters is, I got to a place where I can have a conversation with Luca – someone who caused me so much turmoil and pain. And we talked about him being with someone else and I didn't gag or get all weird. It was as if I wasn't even me. I was this other me and she was completely just...I don't know, in control and confident," I add, mentally re-playing the series of events, nodding my head in awe of myself.

"I'm going to bypass the fact that there is value in the bits of the story you left out and just start with what you see as most important.

"I appreciate that," I begin sarcastically.

"That's unnecessary," Dr. Logan says putting his hand up. "Why do you think you were able to be this other you?"

"I don't know. It's...it's, it's...he made me so mad that I don't think I gave myself time to think about anything that was coming out of my mouth and I think I finally got to say all that was eating away at it about the previous break-up and once all that stuff was out, I could see more clearly. YouknowwhatImean?"

"I'm still with you, if that's what you're asking."

"Don't be so daft. You know that you know that's what I'm asking. Sheesh. So clearheaded me was totally able to see that he was clearly not being open about something...or someone rather, and I guess you just have to know him to know that a 'she' was the problem."

From the Desk of _____Noe Cortes_____

September 9, 2010

I really am immensely proud of myself; I think. I thought. I am. Today has been a crazy day. The last couple of days have been crazy and I'm really surprised at how well I'm doing with everything. I finally found closure with Luca and that feels really good. I didn't realize how much he was still controlling a lot of my life until I suppose...he returned, and I was not as hesitant about rekindling our flame as I should've been considering...Matias.

Matias...I think I made the right decision with him. I don't think we would have continued to work. We weren't working. I was losing myself in him. But...well...honest blog..... I don't know if I really did do the right thing. I mean what if Matias and I can work out now that Luca is out of my system and that I recognize that I was getting too caught up in him and now that he knows this too. I don't know.

He's leaving soon...like next week soon. I don't think I can face him. I don't think I want to really. I feel like

I owe him an apology especially now that the Luca thing is over and done with. Would that count as cheating, my brief episode?

I don't know. Maybe next week...maybe it's time for another grown up conversation. It's redemption season...or I'm going for a solution of absolution...

Maybe not.

Chapter 23

"It's Matias' last week at work."

"How do you feel about that?"

"I'm okay. I've fallen back into my rhythm this past week and a half."

"I agree, you have."

"You're right, I have," I repeat, not sure who I'm reassuring.

"What are you apprehensive about?"

"What do I have to be apprehensive about," I ask uneasily.

"Stop dodging."

"Dodging?"

"Yes. Enough with the echoing," Dr. Logan continues clearly annoyed.

"I'm not meaning to repeat you. I'm just thinking. I, I just don't know."

"That's something I can work with. There's something in that. There's something going on in that high-powered brain of yours that can let you know what you don't know, or why you don't know."

"Is that something that you're going to make me talk through right now?"

"Only because it is now 3:59 do you have a reprieve, but I want you to write it out. Think about it because his last day will be here sooner than you know it and whatever it is that's wearing on you will probably make its biggest appearance that day."

"Thank you for that prophecy Dr. Logan. I'll be going now."

"Next week."

"Indubitably."

I walk away from Dr. Logan's en route to happy hour with Harper and Hayley. Harper's going to tell us about Sebastian. He was her last match at the *Appeteaser.* and

apparently, they really clicked. He's lasted longer than most
– a whole week. He's German on his mother's side, and
Brazilian from his father. Apparently, he's a bronze, blonde,
green-eyed god, and Harper is absolutely smitten.

"MC!" Hayley sings as I find her standing outside the
restaurant.

"Hi, Hay," I call in response, hugging her as I do.

"Have you heard from Harper?" she asks.

"Of course not, but she wouldn't be Harper if she was
on time. Let's go inside and grab a table. She'll be able to
find us."

"Don't be so quick to traipse off without me," Harper
bellows walking down the sidewalk.

"We wouldn't dream of it," I scream acrimoniously.

"Harper, yay! We're so glad you're here. Now we can
get our seats together."

"I appreciate your enthusiasm," Harper cheeps
leaning down to give Hayley a hug and a peck on the cheek.

After my hug we separate and make our way into
the restaurant. According to *The Observer, The Spoon* is
the picture urban dining – whatever that means. They're
apparently known for their low-cost gourmet meals. Inside
the décor is very shabby chic with white linen everywhere.
Fresh air blows in from the open windows and it makes me
feel like I'm on a quaint patio in the heart of Paris or Spain,
or somewhere European.

"Welcome to the *The Spoon* ladies. Will this be all in
your party today?"

"Yes. There'll just be three today," I answer for the
group. "Could we have a seat on the patio maybe?"

"Certainly. Right this way."

The host leads us through throngs of strategically
placed tables, booths and small groups of people chatting
casually on this Wednesday evening.

"Will this work for you?" he asks peering at an
outdoor booth.

"Actually, can we have that table over there," Harper asks acerbically.

"If you have one open," Hayley adds attempting to intercept the daggers of Harper's tone.

"How about this one," he asks coolly, unaffected by Harper's attack.

"Better," Harper responds.

"Your server Nathaniel will be with you shortly. Enjoy your meal."

"Thank you," I finish as he leaves us to chat among ourselves.

"Harper are you okay?" Hayley asks.

"Yeah, Harper what's with verbally assaulting the wait staff?"

"It's nothing. I just wanted him to leave already."

"That excited about this story huh?"

"I am," she says giddily.

"Please share," Hayley says matching Harper's tone.

"Yes, please. I am almost frightened seeing you this way."

"Thanks MC. Always nice to know that I'm frightening."

"Oh, Harper…don't be so melodramatic. Tell your story. That's why we're all here."

Harper tells us when Sebastian sat down for their date, they shared their mutual disdain for all their previous dates – how appropriate for them to bond over negativism. They bonded over their Brazilian heritage and their other shared interests, as Harper so delicately puts it. In reality that means they're both sports junkies, both only children, both are career oriented but have higher aspirations beyond their current areas, and they're both giant romantics at heart. It was disgustingly precious to hear this story of unexpected love.

"That's fantastic Harper!" Hayley coos at the close of her story.

"Yeah. Who would've known this event could bring

two like-minded people together?"

"Are you being sarcastic?" Harper looks cross at me, her tone anything but light.

"Gosh no," I say.

Harper looks unconvinced.

"I'm serious. I recognize that I'm often sarcastic and my two most recent remarks could be construed as such, but seriously I'm happy for you."

"Well thank you," Harper says dubiously. "I don't think I really thought anything meaningful would come out of that night. I didn't even really know if I believed Sebastian when he told me he seriously wanted to meet up outside of it."

As I sit looking at Harper beaming with an effervescent glow of joy, I can't help but feel a pang of jealousy. Then I'm struck by a twinge of guilt for not being absolutely elated. It's so hard. I've just made the most adult decisions of my life and I was so happy about those but seeing Harper now and remembering about Connor and Hayley I suddenly feel lonely.

"Yo!" Harper yells. "Earth to MC! What's going on in there? Are you having a stroke?"

"Sorry I-, I-, I don't know where my mind was. What were you saying?"

"High/Low. I already went."

"Right. What was your high? I mean your low?"

"Are you sure you're alright honey?" Hayley asks with a concerned tone.

"Yeah. I'm good – great even. I just missed it that's all. Harper, if you wouldn't mind," I start returning to my old self. "Can you please say your low so I can get caught up on the conversation?"

"You seriously need a drink. Anyway, my low is now that Sebastian is around, I've kind of lost my edge. I think I'm losing my street cred around the guys in the office."

"Oh no!" Hayley exclaims.

"I thought you already heard this Hayley?"

311

"I still think it's a travesty," Hayley huffs.

"Street cred Harper? Checked out urban dictionary much?" Harper flips me the bird before I continue. "Why is it such a bad thing that you're acting like an actual human...with emotions?"

"MC, you know I can't slack off with the guys at work. I'll lose all the respect I've worked so hard to get. So, I need a course of action – a way to separate my two selves."

"First of all, you know you're terrible at separating work from play. Secondly, what respect are you losing? They always talk to you like you're their personal girl Friday."

"First to your first I am capable of separating if I really wanted to. I've never had a reason to separate. And second, even in their nastiness they respect the work I do, come on."

"A. There is no first of first. You're supposed to go to the next level. B. What now is the reason to separate? And C, how would you think they respect anything about you even when they say the terrible things they do to you?"

"Little A, I can say first of first if I want to. Little B, I need to separate, as I said before, because my adoration for Sebastian is making me somewhat emotional and the emotions are negatively affecting the way in which I am perceived at work, ergo I need to set some boundaries. And little C, they do respect my work because I am damn good at what I do and they recognize it," she says rising from her seat.

"By doing what?" I challenge rising to meet her.

Hayley's eyes are darting back and forth between Harper and I as we ping-pong through our conversation – matching each other tone for tone, our breath quickening as we begin a new response.

"Can I say something?" Hayley squeaks, lifting her hand as if she were in class waiting to be acknowledged by the teacher.

"What?" Harper and I ask simultaneously, turning violently toward her.

"Never mind," she answers, her lip quivering.

"No Hayley, don't," I start, knowing we've gone too far.

"Yeah, Hay...we didn't mean to..." Harper joins.

"You never do," she says her eyes starting to water

"You always do this, and I hate it."

"Hayley, where is this coming from?" I ask confused.

"Yeah, Hay we never knew that you were bothered by us."

"I'm not bothered by you. I'm bothered by the fact that you always fight. Why can't we just be nice to one another?"

"We're sorry," I say. "I don't think we ever thought about how you might be affected by this."

"That's just how we talk. We've always done that. The first time we met in the second grade we argued over the orange crayon and then we were best friends right after. That's how we communicate."

"But now you know? And even though you say that's how you communicate, it's not okay for me. It pains me to see you go at each other like you. It's ugly of both of you," she speaks sternly, almost yelling at us. "You're better than this and I'm tired of being in between the two of you when you go down that path of being nasty. It's unbecoming of the both of you."

"I'm sorry Hay," I say quietly, almost to myself.

"Harper?" Hayley questions.

"I got it," she snaps. "I'm sorry, yes," she quickly amends seeing Hayley's disapproval.

"Today should be a great day. Do you understand that?" Hayley asks.

"Great day, why?" Harper counters.

"Just because," I respond. "Hayley, we really are sorry. We didn't mean to be...I mean...we don't mean be the way we are," I add awkwardly.

313

"Right…." Harper says.

"Well I forgive you both. Now, may I go?" Hayley asks, quickly returning to her jovial disposition.

"Yes," Harper and I both say, still somewhat quiet from shock, scared to say that we hadn't finished our discussion.

"Well, I wanted to, wait…. actually…." she pauses dramatically looking from side to side at Harper and me.

"Spit it out," Harper finally says snapping back to her old self.

"I think I might do my low first."

"Okay…." I say expectantly.

"Right. Oh okay, goodie. Oh, this is supposed to be bad. I have a question."

"Seriously? Every time Hayley?" Harper sighs.

"Wait this time I think I should get a pass. Number one, you were both fighting. And B, my high is so high that I can't possibly bring it down with a low."

"MC you want to say anything about that list?"

"No. Hayley go ahead and do it your way. Right Harper?"

"Whatever," Harper rolls her eyes.

"Well yesterday Connor and I went to the Aquarium. You know I've never been there before?" she asks.

"Oh, no. I don't think we knew that. Did we Harper?" I say kicking her a bit under the table so she would pay more attention to Hayley's story.

"So I was super excited and we're walking around and we go to the part with the giant sea turtles and he tells me this story of how baby sea turtles are born on the shore and when they hatch they have to find their way back to the sea and then find their family from there. It was really fascinating."

She looks excitedly at us, shaking her head and smiling her most toothy smile.

"So, your high is that you saw some sea turtles Hay?

And that couldn't have a low? You, I will never understand."

"Harper, that's obviously not her high...well not completely. Go on Hayley. We're still listening."

"Thank you. Harper, I promise when I get to the punch line then you will definitely know
 okay?"

"Whoopee," Harper retorts spinning her finger in the air.

"Great! So, he tells me this story and he says the cool thing about the turtles is that it's like they have this internal sense that's like a magnet and they find their way to the current. It's magical. Then he stopped and he turned to look at me."

"And then what," I ask unexpectedly mesmerized hanging on her every word.

"Yes. Please get to the good part," Harper adds trying to conceal her own excitement for what will come next.

"So, he's looking at me and I just ask him what he's thinking, and he says to me 'Hayley' – you know how he sounds, so adorable," Hayley attempts to imitate Connor's voice as she recreates her experience. "He says 'Hayley, you know I love you very much and I must say all this time we've been together I honestly think you're my magnet.' I got kind of confused and I think he saw it on my face a little, so he sat me down on a little bench that was nearby."

"Only you Hayley," Harper scoffed.

"Finish. Go ahead, finish. What came next?" I urge.

"Well, I'm sitting, and Connor is kind of squatting on one knee, you know so we're more at eye level."

"Shut the..." Harper starts

"Oh, my good..." I interrupt

"Front door!"

"...ness!"

"What?" Hayley asks, baffled by mine and Harper's interjections.

"Nothing," I chant.

"Keep going," Harper fires.

315

"Alright, alright…so I'm sitting and he's squatting. I didn't know what he meant. He says to me, 'I think that all my life you were and still are the plus side of my magnet. It's like I was that baby turtle and I had to find my way to you. You're the first thing I think of when I wake up and the last thing on my mind when I prepare to sleep at night. You're amazing in every single way and I would love it if you would marry me.' Stunned I didn't know what to say."

"What do you mean you didn't know what to say? How did you not know what he was working toward? He was in the propose position."

"Harper shut it," I snap mock zipping my lips. "Hayley, what's next?"

"Well I just started crying. You know how I get emotional sometimes."

"Sometimes?" Harper hisses.

"Yeah," Hayley beams oblivious to the intent of Harper's biting comment. "So…"

"So what?" Hayley inquires blithely.

"Finish your story," Harper and I urge.

"Well, I cry a lot actually and Connor joins me on the bench and gently strokes my back until I calm down. Then he asked me again if I would honor him by being his wife. And I said yes! Look!" she bellows thrusting her left hand in both of our faces.

Her ring is absolutely gorgeous. It's a platinum band with a pearl solitaire and tiny diamonds that line the sides of the band. It's unique and charming and suits her perfectly.

"That's wonderful Hayley!"

"Yeah," I begin.

"We must celebrate!"

"Celebrate," I echo Harper suddenly lost in the intensity of the moment.

"Tonight. We dance. We drink. We live," Harper dictates.

"Wait, but what about MC. She didn't get to do her

high/low yet," Hayley calls.

"This is totally her high Hay. Right MC?"

"Right," I say mock jovially.

"Okay, so everyone we're going to Mambo. Tonight. Drinks at my place at 9. We'll head out and make it there by 10:30ish."

"Harper, wait. I can't tonight. Connor wants to tell the parents so I'm kind of booked. I'm
  sorry."

"It's fine."

"And besides, it's Wednesday and we all have to work tomorrow anyway," I add uneasily.

"So, let's go Friday night then. It'll be perfect. I'll work on the VIP list," Harper notes.

"This is wonderful. Let's depart then, shall we? We have loads to do before the week's end," Hayley sings.

Harper is giddy and offers to pay for all of our drinks. We collect our belongings give our hugs and go our separate ways. I walk back to where I parked near Dr. Logan's. I ride home in silence, my high and low whirring around seeking an escape.

***

"MC?"

"Yeah, it's me. Jack is Papí there?"

"I don't know I'm not his keeper," he responds sounding affronted.

"What crawled up your butt and died?"

"Do you ever think about anyone besides yourself? Do you? Other people around here have issues."

"Jack? Seriously, what's wrong?"

"Papí is here. I can put him on the phone," he interrupts tersely. "Jackson, what's going on with you? Talk to me…. please."

"I messed up MC."

"Messed up how? What do you mean?"

317

"Kennedy."

"Okay, what about Kennedy? You've been with her for like five years, what could you have possibly done to mess things up with her that you didn't do before now?"

"It's been five years, two months, three weeks and four days," he says with dart-like determination.

"Oh my goodness, did you cheat on her?"

"No! I'd never cheat on her. I love her."

"Then what is it?"

"I was going to propose to her," he bellows gruffly.

"What?!" I can't help yelling. "You want to propose to her? Jackson where did this come from? Why haven't you talked to anyone about this before?"

"It doesn't matter now because I messed it up and she's never going to marry me now. She probably won't want anything to do with me after what I did."

"What did you do? Have you told mama? You know she loves that girl. Hell, I love that girl," I plead.

"No, I didn't take the time to talk to mama. What would I say to her anyway? I'd probably mess that up too."

"Jackson, what did you do to my mama buffer?"

"I told her I didn't love her anymore."

"What?! Why would you say that? What were you thinking?"

"Don't yell at me. I know it was messed up."

"I'm not trying to yell. I just want to know what thought process went into you telling your girlfriend of five years, two months, three weeks and four days that you don't love her anymore," I continue, yelling inadvertently.

"It's not like it seems."

"Oh really?"

"I was trying to use reverse psychology with her."

"Reverse psychology? Do you even know what that means?"

"You know...I'd say something and then she'd do the

318

opposite and it would be good."

"You can't even explain that you moron, what would make you think that it would work in real life?"

"I don't know. It was supposed to be perfect and then she was going to get a little bit mad and then I'd...I don't know."

"You have to know. What were you thinking? Seriously, tell me."

"I was going to talk to her and tell her that I didn't think it was working and then she'd get all sad you know and go stay at Camille, her sister's house right?" he asks expectantly. "Anyway, so she'd be at Camille's, but Camille would know that I would secretly not dislike her, and she would help me with my plan to get her back."

"And?"

"And what? That's it."

"That's it? What do you mean that's it? What's the rest of it? What was your plan to win her back? What did Camille say?"

"Well, that's where I messed up."

"Jackson, please don't say what I think you're going to say."

"I didn't exactly tell Camille about the first part of the plan. I thought she would get it, but she won't even speak to me. She won't answer my calls and Kennedy won't answer my calls either and I just don't know what to do. I really messed up this time."

"Shit," I mutter.

"Shit? No shit. Don't say shit. Shit's bad. You don't shit. You have positive. Come on you watch all those goofy love movies, what happens in those? Give me something. No shit. Please no shit."

"Jackson stop saying shit, and shut up! Let me ask you one question, offer one factual statement and then we'll troubleshoot."

"Get on with it," he urges.

"Statement. My movies Jackson are just that,

movies. They're not real. Stuff like that doesn't work in real life. Question. How could you *not* include the girlfriend's sister in a plan that includes the girlfriend's sister?"

"I know; I'm an idiot. Where's my troubleshooting?"

"The only thing I need you to do is go to the jewelry store and get a kickass ring and I'll take care of the rest. Oh, and make sure you go with someone. Take JJ with you. He's a voice of reason and if you get close to another ledge, he'll be able to knock some sense into you."

"What are you gonna do?"

"Forget about it. Do your part and be ready to do whatever she wants for as long as she wants."

I forget my conversation with Papí because Jackson needs me more. I get a hold of Kennedy's sister Camille and have a sister-to-sister conversation to enlighten her on Jackson's inefficacious plan. Thankfully, she kind of understands and together we arrange to repair their broken relationship. Jackson's attempted relationship suicide temporarily distracts me from my own personal dilemma, but not for long.

***

"Good morning MC."

"Good morning Joyce," I say walking into the office.

"You know, today is the day before tomorrow," she says eagerly.

"That's right. That's usually how it goes Joyce."

"You know what that means right?"

"That tomorrow is Saturday?" I try at walking out of the conversation.

"No…that today is Friday. It's Matias' last day. Don't think I don't know that things have gotten weird between you two. If you ask me, I think you should just apologize for whatever work you refused to do. You have a way of being so stubborn MC, so just apologize so you don't

320

burn any bridges."

"Thank you for your concern Joyce," I say walking away from her toward my office, "but things with me and Matias are fine. All my bridges are fine, and I think he's going to be just you know, fine when he goes away."

"You really think I am going to be just fine," I hear Matias' voice as I round the corner to my office.

"Holy firec r a c k e r. For the love of all things sweet, Matias why?" I say grabbing my chest.

"I did not mean to frighten you. I was just coming in and I didn't want to interrupt your dialogue."

"And you thought this was a better option? Eavesdropping and then scaring the living daylight out of me. Of course, this is an infinitely more effective plan," I finish scornfully pushing past him and opening the door to my workspace.

"Please don't be upset with me. I need to speak with you."

"I'm not upset; you just scared me that's all," I finish with resolve, determined to remain calm, though my pulsating heart and sweaty palms haven't yet received the memo.

"Is it alright if I come in? May I close the door?"

"Sure. Sure."

As Matias closes the door quietly mumbling to himself, I make an attempt to self soothe. I rub my temples, practice breathing, and proceed normally through my morning routine starting with my office email. At the top of my inbox I have an undoubtedly calamitous memo from Joyce urging me to make amends. I love her but she is so meddlesome.

"Ah, Joyce," I mutter.

"What is that?"

"Nothing. What do we need to talk about?"

"It is my last day today."

"I know that," I respond succinctly suddenly at a loss for words.

"Can I speak with you?" He walks toward me, challenging me to meet his gaze.

"Yes, that's why you're in here right?" I do my best to turn away from him and avoid eye contact.

"Of course. It's just that, I am not sure what I can say to you," he says leaning down and pulling my chin up to meet my eyes.

"Just say it Matias," I almost yell snatching away from him. "Whatever it is you need to say, just say it." I stand and try to wriggle away from him, but he closes off my path.

"I would very much like for you to come with me when I go," he says to me earnestly.

"Matias you know that I can't do that," I try again to step away from him, but he disallows it.

"You can't or you won't?"

"What difference does it make," I bark starting to cry.

"It makes a difference. You told me that it is because we don't belong together. But that is not true," he pants, his words getting somewhat caught in his throat. "You love me, I know you do. Why can't you just admit that and come with me? I'm good for you. You *need* me."

"Matias," I say pausing willing my words to sound through my tears. "I can't. I just can't. I meant what I said. We're not each other's forever. I wish we could be, but we aren't." I feel my legs begin to weaken and Matias catches me before I meet the ground.

"And maybe I do need you, but I need to decide that, not have it chosen for me."

"Mi amor," he hums, cradling me as we rest against my wall.

"Don't Matias. Please don't," I say tears falling even more furiously as I bury my face against my bookshelf away from Matias' gaze.

"MC. I do not understand. How can you push me away but react this way?"

"Do you know how much it hurts to be here with you this way?"

"I think I do. It is the way I have felt since you left me."

"No, it's not. Matias you don't get it because you're the person I want so badly to want. But I…"

"You still don't," he completes my sentence his tender touch turning cold.

"No…. I don't," I breathe sinking further into the floor as Matias separates from me.

I continue to weep and Matias sidles in front of me. Still on his knees he bends down, cups my face, and kisses me delicately at the corner of my mouth as he brushes a hair from my face tucking it behind my ear.

I hear him say "I will carry you in my heart always," before he stands and leaves my office. I feel too weak to rise so I stay slumped beneath my windowsill on the floor. Not long after Matias departs Joyce comes in. She's reticent and comforting letting me continue to sob and rubbing my back until I've calmed. When I've quieted, she helps me up and I leave without a word. I drive indiscriminately to my apartment and inside I stumble into bed and fall into a deep sleep haunted by Matias' beautiful face, Luca's hurtful words followed by this blissful happiness for Audrey, and the abyss of loneliness that I've tumbled into.

Ebonii Nelson

From the Desk of _____Noe Cortes_____

September 15, 2010

He left and I fell apart today. He still wanted me and to
an extent I wanted him too but something in me says it's
not right. I don't love him like I should, but I want to. I
don't know what's wrong with me. I've been asleep since
I found my way back home sometime this morning. My eyes
hurt so badly, and my head is pounding.

I'm surprised I'm lucid enough to write right now.

I'm so tired of thinking about him...well...them. I
think of Matias and how he looked when I couldn't tell
him that I loved him in the way he wanted, deserved and
needed, and then I think of Luca when he told me the
same thing....he didn't love me like I loved him and it
shocks my system. I can't believe I'm that girl. I
brought someone or am bringing someone similar turmoil
to what I experienced so many years ago. I hate myself
for it...but I don't know what else I can do. What else
could I have done? To me it wasn't a lie while we were in

it. I didn't know. I didn't see it until Luca.

It's not my fault.

Everyone's happy but me. Connor, Hayley, Jack, Kennedy...and now even Harper and Sebastian. Harper...has a Sebastian. Ugh, I don't know anything anymore. I don't even know why I'm writing right now. Nothing makes sense in my head. It just hurts...I feel it daring to explode with each new thought...each new

Chapter 24

"Get up sow!" I hear a muffled Harper.

She must have let herself in because I can't remember opening the door for her. I want to speak, but my head is throbbing, and the light is having a menacing blinding effect on me.

"Shut up!" I croak grabbing a pillow and a handful of comforter over my head.

"We have partying to do for Hayley. What are you doing asleep at this hour? Didn't you go to work today?"

"Yes, I went to work today. I didn't feel good. I left early. In case you were wondering, no, this isn't helping my condition."

"Glad to know you have an excuse for looking like shit."

"Great so can we reschedule tonight to tomorrow so I can adequately hang out with my shittiness? By tomorrow she will have gone," I say sliding my feet near her to gently nudge her off the bed.

"No goes it. Tonight's the night. Get your sorry ass up and get in the shower," she says snatching my covers and pillow and slapping me forcibly on the butt.

"Seriously!" I exclaim writhing in pain.

"Yes seriously," she answers unapologetically. "These moments are few and far between and we've got to maximize them."

"What are you blathering on about?" I ask rubbing my hindquarters still averting my eyes from the light.

"This is about to be the end MC. The end of our time as the trio we know and love. Carpe diem."

"Oh my gosh Harper you sound like Jackson, pimping random clichés, hoping they sound right." I sit up and let my eyes adjust to the harsh overhead light. Harper drops my bedding at the foot of the bed and crawls to sit next to me.

"What's going on?"

"Nothing. Just a migraine."

"I know your migraine's name is Matias and I promise the only cure for you is to get up and come hang out with your best girlfriends."

"You think?"

"I know."

"Yeah."

"Let's do it. You get up and give Hayley today, and I promise tomorrow I'll let you wallow, eat ice cream and we can watch all those insipid love movies you like."

"*The Wedding Planner?*" I ask sprightly.

"I wouldn't expect any other selection."

"Love you," I say leaning so our foreheads kiss.

"More," she adds grabbing hold of my hand and giving it an affectionate squeeze.

Harper lets me sit for a little while longer before she sort of rolls me out of bed and into the shower. She gives me strict instructions to meet her and Hayley at her townhouse later that night. My shower manages to rejuvenate my body and I convince my mind to put my feelings aside for the sake of Hayley.

***

"I'm so glad you're feeling better MC. Harper told me that you weren't well. What was wrong?"

"Oh, it was just a migraine. I'm fine now though. Thanks for asking," I respond before downing a rum punch.

I'm not one for drinking; I prefer the mild sugar rush that comes with my Dr. Pepper. Today however the drinks seem to taste like sweet nectar begging me to ingest them.

"How many is that for you MC?" Harper asks breathing heavily as she steps off the dance floor.

"I appreciate your concern, but I'm delightful," I say concentrating so as not to slur. While I don't think I'm drunk, I am certainly on my way and I would hate to give Harper any ammunition to treat me as though I'm

327

already there.

"Are you sure MC," Hayley asks.

"What do you mean Hayley? You were just talking to me and I was fine. I am fine."

"Come walk with me," Harper commands, grabbing my right arm nearly knocking me off my stool.

"No. I don't want to," I struggle trying to wriggle free of her grasp.

"You need to come, now. We'll be right back Hayley," she finishes cheekily.

Harper dexterously uproots me from my chair and tows me to an alcove at the far end of the club away from Hayley, near the bathrooms.

"What the fuck MC? I thought we discussed."

"What are you talking about?" I ask confused still trying to release myself of her maniacal claws.

"This night is for Hayley, not you. She shouldn't feel obligated to babysit you. Stop being so selfish right now. Get your act together."

"I'm sorry," I say finally free.

"Don't be sorry just fix it."

"It's fixed," I say standing and staring at her my inebriety raging with indignation.

"Good now go in the bathroom, throw some water on your face and get back out here and be a friend," she says ignoring my ire as she walks away from me toward Hayley.

"You're not my mom you know?" I shout at her.

"What?" She whips around hands balled into fists at her sides.

"You're not, you know. And I never asked anyone to babysit me. I didn't even ask to come here."

"So why are you here?"

"I told you I didn't want to come here. I wanted to stay home tonight, but you made me come."

"Why are you here then MC?" Harper asks again a calming frustration radiating from her words.

"Because of you. Then you lecture me about caring about someone else. When have you ever put someone else before you? I'll tell you when…never. That's right. Not ever. You are always only ever thinking about numero uno. You know!" I finish thrusting my pointer finger in what I think is her face.

She briskly walks back to me, moving so fast and getting so close that I bobble a little, my equilibrium shaken.

"Fuck you Noe," she says coolly, before turning on her heel and walking away.

"Yeah me," I add nonchalantly when she's just out of ear shot.

With drunken and spiteful resolve, alone, and on wobbly legs I wander onto the dance floor. The humid air renders me breathless but entangled with all the partiers I start to get a sudden rush of adrenaline. As the rhythmic, bass-filled music bellows I am joined by interested gentlemen callers, each one touching me in just the right way and their bodies molding to mine as we gyrate to the music. My new friends bring me drinks to keep me amped up and as the night wears on I am soused in spirituous perspiration. I'm not sure when Hayley and Harper leave but I don't really care. I just know that I'm releasing myself of all the mess that's holed up inside, and it feels good.

"How are you getting home tonight?" a distorted fuzzy face shouts into my ear.

"However I get home," I muster.

"Let me take you home," he offers.

"Okay," I concede easily.

"Right now," he adds with consternation.

"What?" I inquire standing up straight no longer dancing as I try to reconcile what our conversation now means.

"I can't believe this. Come on," he continues grabbing me by the arm.

"Oh my goodness, no. This is not real. I can't. I have to find my friends. I have to find my stuff. I have to..."

***

"No!"

I sit up violently, drenched in sweat. I grab myself instinctively, trying to make sure I'm still me. I'm wearing a white tank top and some red basketball shorts with the SMU Mustang emblem at the corner. Both articles mine, but I don't remember putting them on. My mouth has gone dry and my hair is matted in a bun atop my head. I can't remember where I am or how I got there and the confusion of it all causes me to cry in my delirium.

"Breathe Noe. Just breathe. You're alright," a familiar voice attempts to soothe me, laying a cool damp towel across my forehead and rubbing my back.

"I can't. It's wrong. I'm...where? I have to find my, I have to find my..."

I drift off again unable to complete my statements. In my dreams I feel myself running with no end in sight. I keep running though I can't seem to catch my breath, and the more I gasp for air the faster my legs seem to run. I rise again and on autopilot find my way to a washroom. Eyes still closed I relieve myself and pain begins radiating at my temples. I flush and wash my hands and splash my face with cool water. In the mirror I finally open my eyes enough to examine my reflection I've lost some of my color and my skin has a sort of green tint all of a sudden. My eyes are bloodshot red, my mouth is like an acrid desert, and if it's possible a halo of nausea seems to hover over me. I dry my face with the hand towel and behind me I hear the male voice again.

"Are you feeling better?"

"Dr. Logan?" I ask turning too quickly toward the blurred figure standing robustly in the doorway. "Where?

330

How?" I can't manage to complete any of my sentences and begin to feel faint.

My legs bobble and he makes haste, appearing quickly at my side.

"I guess that means no. Come on, lay back down. You had a pretty full night."

"I don't understand."

I'm dizzily confused and as I blink, I see images of what I assume was the night before, but I can't manage to stream them together. The caring male guides me out of the bathroom and into a living room that shows vestiges of me. Everything about the space feels so familiar and at the same time incredibly foreign. Nuzzled in a couch, the man hands me a glass of ice water pulled seemingly out of thin air.

"There. That should help. Here, take these too." He hands me two aspirin and I toss them to the back of my throat and take another swig of water.

"Thank you."

"You're very welcome. After a few more hours I'm sure you'll be back to normal."

"Dr. Logan?"

"Noe?" he asks in response settling cross-legged on the floor so our faces are parallel to one another.

"You're him, right? I can't make out your face right now, but your voice...I know it. It's that voice. It's the three S's blended with a scoatch of d – m – v."

"The three S's," he repeats inquisitively. "Southern, sultry and sexy."

"And the DMV," he inquires further, quietly laughing.

"Disapproving, matriarchal virulence."

"You know matriarchal generally pertains to women, right?"

"See there it is...DMV. I think I love that...I do. I love you...that damn d – m...m – v," I say drifting back into an encouraging slumber.

***

"Are you dead?"

"Wha-?"

"See Hay, I told you she wasn't dead. She's up."

"MC," Hayley shouts at a whisper. "How are you feeling?"

"I'm not sure. I had this weird dream. I was dancing a lot. It was like I was on a meth high or something. But I was out and then some guy took me home with him. Then it flashed I was in a house. It seemed like mine, but I peed and then there was the guy again and he put me on the couch, and he gave me water. I kept calling him Dr. Logan, but he would never say. That's weird huh?"

I try peeking through slits made by my eye lids at my companions, but it's too painful. I raise my eyebrows in hopes that someone will answer my question.

"I've got news for you. With the exception of the crystal meth, your story was anything but a dream."

"Harper?"

"In the flesh."

"Hayley?"

"Yes sweetie, I'm here too," she says taking my hand in hers and patting it softly.

Harper and Hayley are sitting on the floor next to the couch. Harper's back is against its front, her right ear just beneath my chin and Hayley is sitting cross-legged in front of me.

"What do you mean it wasn't a dream?"

"Well, last night you, Hayley and I went out to celebrate her and Connor's engagement and you chose to get shit-faced and wreck our night."

"Harper," Hayley bites with disapproval.

"What Hay? It's true."

"She's ill," Hayley reasons.

"Bullshit! Anyway, we ran into your beloved Dr. Logan on our way out."

"You were going to leave me?"

"MC you obviously don't remember this, but you gave quite the little speech encouraging me to leave. It was a real shit show. You were being selfish and ruining Hayley's celebration, even if Hayley wouldn't say so," she finishes quickly cutting Hayley off just as she was about to interject.

"So, you saw Dr. Logan? How did you know it was him? You've never met."

"Well, I guess you can just say he happened to be the right guy at the right time in the right place because he saw me stomping away from our row and he called your name. I confirmed that the person he was seeing was in fact you and I asked him what the connection was. He was strangely tongue-tied, but I got his name out of him and I pieced it together from there."

"He's never tongue-tied. I can't believe he was out. I can't believe…what must I have looked like?"

"A damn fool," Harper offers.

"MC, you weren't that bad. I think you just needed to blow off some steam. For the record I was enjoying myself last night."

"Don't try to make her feel better about herself. She needs to feel bad right now. Real bad. Got that?" She says looking from Hayley then quickly to me.

"I still don't get the rest," I say baffled.

"I told him he could be responsible for you because I was over it. I gave him your purse, cell phone, and keys and I took Hayley to Jovie's."

"The cupcakes were amazing," Hayley reminisces fondly.

"So, you just left me in the hands of some random guy? What if he were a rapist or a murderer or something? Hayley, how could you just leave me?" I rise briskly to confront them both, but quickly return to the couch as the blood surge in my brain makes my head feel like it's going to explode.

"Don't go trying to guilt Hayley. You ended up in the situation you were in on your own."

"I'm sorry MC."

"You're not sorry Hayley," she says before turning to me, "She's not sorry. Hayley doesn't have to apologize. You brought that on yourself."

"You made your point. I still can't believe you just assumed the guy was legit though," I say.

"Logan wanted to stay there for you. And anyway I know a guy who works for Dallas PD and I told him to keep an eye on you, get a read on lover boy and to contact me if anything was fishy or when it was time I take you home – whichever came first. You were safe."

"Oh sure. You can say that now because I happen to be alive."

"Apparently you only got worse when we left," Harper continues ignoring my theatrics.

"Oh really?" I gasp.

"Really," Harper and Hayley say in unison.

"Logan said that you started downing whatever drink a guy would feed you and that at one point you were covered from head to toe in horny men, their roving hands and happy sticks."

"He didn't say it like that MC," Hayley admits.

"I know Hayley. I can clearly see Harper's creative liberties in this recitation."

"He might not have said it in that way, but I know that's exactly what he meant. He said he broke his way into the group and offered to take you home. When you obliged so easily, he'd known it was time for you to go. He brought you back here and probably let you puke your brains out. Then about an hour ago he called and told me that he had an appointment, you were still asleep and that you would probably appreciate friendly faces when you woke up."

"So, Dr. Logan was here? In my house? While I was drunk out of my mind? I can't believe this. I cannot believe any of this. How did this happen?"

"You were being totally self-absorbed which caused you to get pissy drunk that's how."

"Harper," Hayley snaps again.

"Wait, how'd he know to call you today?"

"Why does it matter? I'm waiting for you to apologize to Hayley for being a douche, to me for being a douche and to the both of us for being the douche master," she closes using her fingers to count my grievances.

For a moment I stare off into space unable to speak. Hayley mimics me a bit looking awkwardly amidst the silence and Harper relentlessly taps her feet against my coffee table. After some time passes, I shake from my musing and find some words to speak.

"Hayley, I sincerely apologize for spoiling your celebration. I had no intention of selfishly making everything about me. And I know you have no reason to accept it, but if you would believe me when I say I am truly repentant, I'd be more than grateful."

"And," Harper interjects gruffly.

"And," I begin boldly, "Harper I apologize to you too for the less than friendly words I had for you while you were attempting to speak some sense into me."

Hayley looks anxious but she doesn't move. She looks frantically from Harper to me, itching to say something.

"I suppose if you really mean it, we might be able to accept your apologies," Harper broods.

"I really do. I hate the way I was."

"We forgive you," Hayley says sprightly.

"Way to make her sweat Hay," Harper adds gently pushing Hayley.

"You were going to do an apology stand off? How rude," I mimic Stephanie Tanner.

"You deserved it MC. You were really not in a good way."

"Thanks to the both of you for not completely

abandoning me."

"Even though you don't deserve it, since we're all here, tell us what's going on? Who was that girl last night?"

"I'm ashamed."

"Ashamed? Why?" Hayley asks.

"Please do tell," Harper turns around to face me as I find the strength to sit upright on the couch.

"Please don't judge me or hate me."

"We won't," Hayley assures.

"I might," Harper amends.

"That'll do. Well, I ended up breaking up with Matias. It just wasn't right. He was perfect on paper and in real life, I thought, but just wasn't perfect with me. He asked me to go with him to Cambridge and Oxford though. He said he loved me and wanted a future with me. Again, with the perfect. It's like all of my movies. He said things I've only dreamed of hearing," I say rotating on the couch so I can look in their direction as I continue.

"It's like when Lorelei and Chris finally got together and of course they broke up and Lorelei was all like 'I want to want you' or something to that effect. That was me. Anyway, after I broke it off with him, I went to Luca. I actually did go see him that day after the Appeteaser."

"MC," Hayley gasps in surprise and Harper tisks and smacks her lips a bit.

"I know, I know, but I felt like I had to. Anyway, after I told Matias we couldn't, I went to Luca to talk about whatever he wanted to do. Before I could even get that out, he was breaking up with me."

"But you weren't together," Harper yells. "Unless…"

"No, we weren't."

"You better not…"

"So, I get hyper upset and we go back and forth arguing about this time around, but it was more about our original break-up. I think it was good for us. We aired out what was and then I helped him craft a plan to get back with his girlfriend Audrey."

"What?" Harper and Hayley ask together. Harper sounds much like an angry badger, and Hayley in contrast almost sounds positive and upbeat.

"Yeah, I know it doesn't make much sense, but trust me it's for the best."

"So, get to the good part. How does this all add up to you being a little shit at Hayley's night?"

"I'm getting there."

"Yeah, Harper she's getting there. Don't rush the story," Hayley beams.

"Thank you, Hayley. I thought everything was good. Wednesday I had my regular meeting and Dr. Logan said I should probably prepare for Matias' departure. I didn't want to because I just figured he would leave, and it wouldn't be that big of a deal."

"Of course, you were wrong. You're so naïve."

"Thanks for your critical assessment Harper. Friday gets here."

"Oh yay…it's time!" Hayley harks, tossing her hands up in the air and clapping rapidly.

"I get to work, and Matias catches me as I make my way into my office. He asks me again to come with him. He said he thinks I'm wrong and I'm running or something to that effect. I cry because I don't understand what's wrong with me. He's hurt. He leaves. Boom. Migraine."

"There's someone else," Harper states definitively.

"There's no one else Harper. What?"

"Yeah Harper, what?" Hayley parrots.

"Trust me. There's someone else."

"There's no one. Anyway, I went home. I was sad and depressed about Luca and Matias and I was jealous and upset about being jealous about Harper and Sebastian, then there's Jackson and Kennedy…"

"Jackson?" Harper starts.

"And Kennedy?" Hayley finishes.

"Yes. He's going to ask her to marry him. Jackson, my brother the ladies' man is prepared to settle

337

down. And there was also...."

"Me," Hayley whispers.

"Yes, Hayley there was you. I'm so sorry I didn't mean to feel the way that I did. I think it's great that you and Connor," I pause briefly shaking my head in disbelief. "I just felt like something has to be wrong with me if everyone around me seems to be making sense of their personal relationships. I went to the club and I didn't plan to get so ridiculous and I didn't plan to ruin everyone's night. I promise. Please forgive me."

"You're already forgiven," Hayley sobs a bit.

"Why are you crying," I ask starting to tear some myself.

"Because it's just so sad for you. Why are you crying?" she says.

"Because seeing you cry is making me cry. I don't know why," I rhyme unintentionally.

"Oh, my goodness you both are ridiculous. Suck it up."

"Thanks for your empathy Harper," I add sucking back my tears.

"The question I have for you Noe Marie Cortes, is who is the someone else?"

"What are you talking about Harper? There is no one else. In my entire story I told you there was never mention of a new someone."

"I didn't say there was a new someone because I know the someone is an old someone and I know who he is."

"Who?" Hayley asks sotto voce.

"Logan," Harper states decidedly.

"Dr. Logan?" Hayley mouths.

"That is crazy Harper. Where on earth would you get that kind of idea?" I ask.

"It's not crazy. Think about it, he knows you better than anyone and he's willing to put up with you and all of your insanity. He let you go to his house. And I told you he

wanted to take care of you last night when you were
sloshed. He was here with you all night. That's well
beyond his duties as your psychologist. I'm sure there's
some kind of code he's violating. I bet he's secretly guiding
you in ways that make you break up with all these other guys
just so he can be with you. This is perfect. I'm good."

"Crazy is what you are," I say.

"Crazy to you is genius to someone else MC, and I am
a genius."

"Harper, I don't know about that. It seems a bit
farfetched."

"Thank you, Hayley, it does seem farfetched, because
it is. Dr. Logan is just that, my hired mental health
professional. He pitched in last night because he clearly knew
that the two of you, no offense Hayley, weren't going to. It
was a helpful gesture and nothing more."

"Well, that takes care of him. Let's say he doesn't
have any ulterior motives. What about you? This could be
the answer to why you can't seem to stay with any other guy
that walks into your life. It's because you like Logan. How
about that one? Oh my gosh, I should be a lawyer. Well hot
damn I am one," Harper boasts rising and making her way
toward the kitchen.

"Harper you're wrong."

I say the words but inside I start reconsidering all of
my time with Dr. Logan – the facts that Harper so plainly
laid out. I don't think I've ever really thought about Dr.
Logan in that way. I will admit that he is very handsome,
and he does get me, and I do feel extremely comfortable
around him all the time. Sure he let me come to his
house and he did watch *The Wedding Planner* with me
and he did take care of me last night, but I don't think he
could possibly ever think of me that way.

From the Desk of _____Noe Cortes_____

September 18, 2010

Let this be an apology for all of the discord I have caused. It wasn't fair mature or nice of me to be the way I had been.

This is the start of a new month and can be my resolution...the start of something new in my life. With Matias and Luca, I grew. I learned about myself and I think ultimately, they really are better off without me. Having Hayley and Harper over earlier today definitely helped me get my bearings back.

I can move forward and be happy for the happiness that's coming to my friends and family and not get so downtrodden by where I am. Things are that bad for me. I have my health. I have a great family and friends that care. I have a home and food regularly. I have things people around the world are dying for. It's about perspective and I just have to decide to be happy and be content.

Oh.... thank you, Dr. Logan, for making yet another

exception for me and not letting me die or get abducted and raped last night at the club.

Now...please forget the state you saw me in and let's move forward. It's a new month you know. That was in the past.

Chapter 25

"How are you feeling today mi'ja?" My dad asks grabbing a jug of lemonade from the refrigerator.

"I'm doing well. Thank you for asking."

He sits two glasses down on the table and settles in the chair next to me. For a time, we just sit in silence, drinking our ades and taking in the scenery through the patio door.

"So, Noe," he starts breaking our comfortable silence. "How are you really doing?"

"I'm fine papí. I just told you that."

"I know what you've said to me, but I also know my only daughter and I know she is not doing so well, so please talk to me."

"It's nothing really daddy. There are just a lot of things changing and I'm trying to get used to the difference. Nothing major, I promise."

"If you say so. Have you spoken to your brother?"

"JJ?" He looks at me as if to say, 'you know that's not the brother I'm referring to.'

"No, I have not spoken to Jackson. Not since I helped him clean up his mess with Kennedy."

"He's very grateful for you, you know that don't you."

"Yeah," I say nonchalantly drawing circles on the wooden tabletop.

"I'm serious. Even if he doesn't say it, he loves you and appreciates how you helped him."

"Thanks for saying that papí."

"Noe Marie, so nice to see you," mama says walking into the kitchen and planting a kiss on daddy's cheek. "To what do we owe the pleasure?"

"No reason in particular mama. I just haven't been here in a while, so I thought it'd be nice to visit."

"It would've been nicer if you came with us to church this morning, but I suppose this will do."

"Thank you for your absolution," I mutter. "JJ and Jack with you?" I ask at a volume she can hear.

"They're in the living room watching some game on the television."

"Right. I think I'll join them. Please excuse me."

I stand and quickly make my escape. My mom seems to be in a mood and I'm not in a place to withstand her comments. In the living room, JJ is sitting in papí's reading chair and Jackson has commandeered half of our massive sofa. The television is on and I can't yet tell which sport we're watching.

"What are we watching," I ask having a seat next to Jackson on the couch.

"Right now, commercials. Move over."

He shoves me but I resist.

"You're warm and it's cold. I'll move in a minute. What are we watching after commercials?" I ask using all my force to shove him back.

"Blankets," he states not yet making eye contact with me.

"We're watching blankets?"

"No nimrod, blankets are what you use when you're cold, not," he pauses to do a sweep of his body, showcasing himself much like Vanna White would, "this Cortes Adonis."

"Wow, I can't believe this is what Kennedy chooses to deal with on a regular basis. Cortes Adonis is reaching a new level."

"I think the game is coming on," JJ calls with annoyance.

"What game?"

"The Giants and the Cowboys," Jackson responds turning up the volume of the television.

"Right, it's football season how could I forget. JJ what are you gonna watch?"

"Ha ha. I watch football, MC the better question is what are you gonna do? You know if you're around any longer you'll have to stay for dinner."

"JJ you genius. MC you *are* staying for dinner because we have guests coming, so get settled. Is that what you're wearing?" Jackson adds.

"Guests? What are you talking about? And what's wrong with what I'm wearing?"

"Guest. You know, a person who comes to visit someone else in their home. And everything is wrong with what you're wearing. You look like a hobo."

"Again, I'm not an idiot I know what guests are. It's Sunday; since when has mama been okay with guests coming over?"

"Kennedy is coming over now that she doesn't hate Jack anymore and duh, they're getting married in case you missed that memo," JJ answers.

"No, I didn't forget about Jack and Kennedy, but I didn't think that an impending marriage meant entrance into Sunday dinner. Oh, by the way Jack I'm still waiting on my thank you gift for saving your ass."

"Language,"

"Sorry mama," we all call in response to her disapproving tone.

"It's in the mail. And JJ my man has his lady friend Adriana coming over, we mustn't forget that."

"Shut up Jack!" JJ yells his cheeks turning bright red.

"JJ, who's Adriana? Why haven't I heard of her before? I'm not a hobo by the way."

"Well dearest sister, you're not the hobo you *look* like the hobo. Listen to the difference," Jackson teases, pointing at his ears.

I give him the finger to avoid mama's wandering ear and he mocks taking it and putting it in his pocket.

"In response to Adriana and her invitation to dinner, since you like to stay hidden you don't know of this femme fatale. She is a soccer superstar who has the hots for our baby bro."

"Jack, shut it. I'm serious," JJ cries, red travelling from his cheeks and taking over his face.

"She's still new," I say affronted.

"I think mama's just happy that JJ actually like's girls, so she was more than thrilled to say yes. Chill out baby bro. I'm almost done," Jackson says attempting to calm JJ. "MC, Adriana's actually pretty cute, she's quiet and she's smart. And right now, JJ is playing a little hard to get just like I taught him."

"JJ that's adorable," I squeal, my mild ire dissipating. I run and jump to his chair and sit on his lap.

"Adorable?" JJ and Jackson question disgustedly in unison.

"Sorry, you know what I mean. That's awesome."

"So, all that's left is for you to rustle up a guy and it'll be eight's company."

"I think I'll pass," I slide off JJ and start to walk toward the front door. "It's probably time for me to get going anyway."

"What's this I hear about you leaving," mama asks coming into the living room.

I stop, suddenly frozen. She always manages appear out of thin air at just the right time. She's got some mom sensor or something. It's too strange to be normal. I'm unable to find words so I just stare at her. Brooding in front of my brothers and me she's showered in golden sunlight. She's wearing a very girlish salmon colored sundress with white lace fringe. Summer has treated her nicely and left the faintest freckles on her cheeks, atop her nose and shoulders. My mom looks gorgeous and ethereal and almost makes me forget that I'm trying to escape.

"Noe Marie Cortes? Since when have you taken to ignoring me?"

Almost.

"Lo siento mama. I don't know where my mind was," I say clasping my hands together and backing toward the doorway. "But, I was going because I just don't want to disturb the nice dinner you all are having tonight. I am not dressed for it, so I'm just going to be on my way," I add

345

reaching blindly for the doorknob.

"I will not hear of it. You're staying," she declares making a move toward me. "Sunday is family night and you've been so busy with your own life that you haven't made time for us. Tonight, you dine with your family. Entiendes?"

"Yes mama. Can I at least go out to get changed?"

"No, but you may go to the grocery store for me. I need ingredients for a cake I want to make."

"Sure. Great. Got it. I'll be right back."

The jaunty spirit that had arisen within me during my romp with Jackson and JJ quickly dissipates as I walk out the door, get into my car and make sense of what I've just been committed to.

***

I walk despondently into the grocery store lost in thoughts. I can't figure out what to make of anything anymore. I look at the lemons and limes and think Hayley is with Connor. The green and red bell peppers yell Harper is with Sebastian. In the dessert aisle cupcakes taunt me with their sweet song of Jackson has Kennedy and JJ has Adriana. Even the row of fresh breads croons Luca has Audrey; Matias has Europe; and Mama is with Papí and I'm confused about everything. This weekend has been a blur and I don't know how to make sense of any of it. I'm turning into an alcoholic I think or at a minimum an alcoholic sympathizer. I need Dr. Logan because I know he'll bring some clarity to all of my situations.

"Just the eggs ma'am?" the check-out kid asks as I make my way to the counter.

"Yes. That's all."

"It'll be $2.12."

"2?"

"Yes ma'am. Two dollars and twelve cents."

She spits on me as she says cents. Her braces mixed

with a lisp gleak onto my face and the debit machine.

"Right," I say blatantly wiping her spittle from my cheek. "All I have is $3."

"Okay, out of $3. That means 88 cents is your change. Have a great day ma'am."

"Great day. Thanks."

***

Dinner comes and goes. First course is a garden salad with a raspberry vinaigrette dressing. Mama makes chicken cacciatore on a bed of linguine. It's delicious. For dessert we have homemade turtle cheesecake. It's kind of perfect but I can't stay focused on any one thing. Adriana seems very sweet and a perfect complement to JJ. Kennedy is her cheery, doe-eyed self and is hanging on Jackson's every word. And mama and papí seem to be in perfect rhythm too. Everyone is where they are, and things are just as they should be.

"That was a great meal Mrs. Cortes. Thank you so much for having me tonight," Adriana says.

"I agree; everything was delightful Mrs. C," Kennedy adds with less formality.

"I'll clear the dishes mama," I say almost yelling, standing, and collecting some of the dishes.

"I'll help," I hear Jackson utter following suit.

I walk back and forth to the kitchen in silence stacking the dirty dishes on the counter next to the sink. I turn on the water for it to heat as Mama, Adriana and Kennedy still seated at the table start with some girl talk and JJ and Papí sit in adoring manly silence. As my rote dish collecting ends and all the dishes are collected, I stare at the water falling from the faucet. Jackson scrapes all of the remaining food into the trash can and adds his dish to the pile.

"What's up with you MC?"

347

"It's…"

"And don't say nothing, because it's definitely something."

"I don't know Jack," I turn off the water and begin putting the scrap-free dishes into the soapy water-filled sink.

"You don't know?" he asks dubiously.

"Yeah. No. I don't know."

"Well let's rap it out."

Feeling like I'm going to implode I blurt out "Jack, everything is all messed up."

"Messed up like how?"

"It just is." I add dunking my hands deeper into the dish water fishing for a dish to clean.

"No, you don't get out that easy. You're not even saying any words. Come on you're supposed to be the one of us with the larger vocabulary. Say something."

"I don't know how everything got so screwed up. Everyone seems to be in this perfect place and my life seems to be in shambles."

"In shambles, how? And since when have you cared about how everyone else's life is going? You're a professional when it comes to blazing your own trail."

"Jackson I've blazed so much that I can't even find a trail anymore. I've messed up."

"How?"

"Matias is gone Jack. And Luca is with Audrey. And I'm all alone. Everyone seems to be making these great strides and I'm stuck going nowhere."

"Hold on. Hold on," he says grabbing the dish I'm washing and turning me to face him. "Where did Luca come from? Why does he matter ever?"

"I don't know when I became the girl who needs a guy to feel complete."

"Stop being that girl."

"It's not that easy."

"Why not MC? Neither of those guys were doing anything for you anyway. Luca is a grade A idiot who's never realized what he had in you," he says forcefully. "And Matias, no offense to him because he was cool and all, but he wasn't right for you. He was too knowing, too old. Yeah, he was old," he repeats seeing the affronted look on my face. "I'm glad you kicked him to the curb. And this not going anywhere...don't be ridiculous. You're a gem Noe, but you've gotta believe that and you've got to be okay with that."

"I want to be okay with that. I do."

"Do you? My little big sister wouldn't get down on account of some guy. And she wouldn't let other people's situations make her feel small or incompetent. When everyone was busy not transferring did you think anything was wrong with you then? No. When mama constantly attacked you about choosing and sticking with a major and a career path did you decide to pick something to make her happy? No. You did your own thing. When mama told you, you needed to go to therapy..."

"What?"

"Well you did, and then you went, so I couldn't really finish that one," he laughs and tosses a bundle of bubbles at me. "But you get the picture. You don't do what other people do simply because it makes sense to them. You do what's right for you in your own time and it works. Shake this off and just be you."

I grab my dish from him and go back to washing. He takes over drying the wet pile of china. We dunk and wipe, rinse and dry in relative silence, our gentle nudges every now and again picking up where our words had gone. When all the dishes are clean, dried, and put away we discard our gloves and cleaning aprons.

"Thanks Jack," I say fixing my arms around his before he has time to think.

"Anytime MC," he adds pulling his arms from beneath mine and wrapping them around me. "Anytime," he repeats planting a kiss atop my head.

***

"How are you feeling today hun?"

"I am great," I say resplendently and meaning it. "I actually brought some sweets for us today," I add lifting a grocery sack for Joyce to see.

"You sure?" she asks unconvinced.

"Yes. Look," I begin walking toward our break room. "Yesterday my mom made cheesecake. I know how much you love it, so I just had to steal some."

"Oh, I love it," she coos and swoops in to grab the cheesecake.

Joyce takes the cake and goes to the cupboard grabbing plates and utensils for us. She's babbling sprightly and has forgotten her concerned tone from my arrival. I take a moment to slide into my office and deposit my other belongings leaving her to buzz without me.

This is my first day back in a world that before last Friday was full of light, abandon and love. Lowering myself into my chair I start thinking about how I know it's going to be hard not to seeing him each morning reading and enjoying a bran muffin and orange juice. It will be hard not smelling his smell or hearing his cheerful voice and accent muddle through phrases in the most adorable way.

"Here's cheesecake," Joyce sings interrupting my ruinous musing with plates of my mom's dessert.

"Thanks."

"Bon appétit."

"Did I tell you that Jackson proposed to Kennedy?"

"No," Joyce's says astonished.

"He did. They haven't set a date yet, but mama's over the moon about it. She's finally going to get her perfect daughter," I say with my mouth full.

"That is just lovely for him. I'm so glad he's finally settling down," she finishes.

"Connor finally proposed to Hayley too."

"Your life seems just filled with good news."

350

"It does, doesn't it? And Harper finally found a formidable foe to date. His name is Sebastian. And JJ even, he has a little girlfriend. Her name is Adriana. I met her yesterday when she came to dinner. They're so cute together."

"MC honey, your time will come."

"Joyce," I start pausing briefly to gain control of my emotions, halting the sadness that's trying to escape. "I don't know that it will. But it's okay because I'm so happy for all of them. This is all just great; it really is."

We finish our cake in silence. I can feel Joyce staring at me as I try to log-out and re log- in to my email to offset the quiet.

"Can I take your plate," she finally asks.

"Sure. Thank you."

"You're welcome. You want me to order us lunch today? Student Conduct special?" She smiles weakly as I lift my eyes to meet hers.

"No thanks. I might work through lunch today so I can take off a little early. I feel a headache coming on."

"Are you sure you're…" she begins

"I'm fine Joyce…. really. Don't worry."

"Alright," she concedes and turns away carrying our dirty dessert saucers.

"Can you close it? I want to focus."

"Sure," she answers with a sigh and pulls the door shut behind her.

I stay working and plugging away all morning and through lunch. I'm so intense that I don't even get hungry like usual. I feel numb inside and my only recourse is to work.

***

"I'm so glad you could make it. Have a seat."

"I apologize for my tardiness. I'm not terribly

familiar with this part of town and I had difficulty finding somewhere legal to park."

"Oh, you could've parked anywhere. I know a guy."

"Right, well it all worked out."

"That it did."

"So?"

"Oh, I took the liberty of ordering you a drink. I hope that's alright."

"I don't tend to drink during the week. I like to keep a clear head."

"I…. see. Well, order whatever you like."

"I'm actually quite well, thank you. If you could, just help me to understand why it is that you asked me here. I'm not intending to be rude by the way."

"And I'm not offended so we're good."

"Your drinks ma'am. Scotch neat for you sir, and a lime seltzer ma'am."

"Actually, the scotch is mine and the other you can take back."

"Excuse me?" the waitress questions confusedly.

"I'll take the brown drink and my friend here doesn't want the other."

"Would you like something else instead sir?"

"No," he says pointedly.

"I could get you a drink menu if you'd like," the waitress adds looking at him longingly.

"I'm fine thank you." This time he peers up at her and smiles to show her it's okay to walk away.

Not understanding she continues "Sir, I…"

"For fuck's sake will you just order a goddamn drink," Harper hisses rubbing her forehead.

Taken aback he says, "I guess I'll have a um…a Dr. Pepper on the rocks." He flashes a smile and beams with pride for his clever order.

"Dr. Pepper on the rocks. Got it," she repeats sounding falsely impressed, turning back toward the bar looking tall and hippy, attempting to entice his eye.

"This is unbelievable."

"Can we?"

"Give it a minute."

"Huh?"

"Your soda," the waitress says abruptly re-appearing at their table.

"Thank you," he says.

"Yes, thank you. Actually, what is it Hannah?"

"Yes. I'm Hannah."

"Right, well Hannah we won't need you for the rest of the time we're here. No need for refills and we won't be dining, so if you could give Gil my regards and he'll put the drinks on my tab. Do you comprehend?"

"I think so."

"I don't need a think so Hannah. I need a strong yes or no."

"Yes."

"Great."

They look back and forth at each other for a moment, Hannah glued to the floor with a gaped mouthed look of horror.

"That will be all Hannah."

"Right," she murmurs and scuttles away still in a daze of confusion.

"So, you...." Harper begins.

"Yes, me."

"I think you need to be careful with the way you interact with MC."

"Excuse me?"

"Logan. Is it okay if I call you Logan, or would you prefer Dr. Hale?"

"Logan is fine. I'm not sure I'm following you."

"I'm surprised you don't know MC as well as you should considering she's been bearing her soul to you for the past two years."

"Is this a question of how well I know one of my

clients? I highly doubt that's at all appropriate."

"This is not about one of your *clients*," she says using air quotes. "This is about MC, the person and her well-being."

"As her psychologist, I assure you that the work we do in the privacy of our sessions *is* for her betterment."

"I don't think you get it."

"No, actually I don't. I've already unearthed that notion."

"Don't get so feisty," she laughs wildly. "If you knew her even a little bit beyond your practice you would see that she has a crush on you and honestly I think it's reciprocated."

"That's preposterous," he snickers, "I can't believe you asked me here to say something so absurd. The relationship that Noe and I have is purely professional and she knows that, and nothing I've done has confounded that."

"Does she? And you've done nothing to muddle the waters?"

"Yes, she does, and I don't appreciate you implying otherwise."

"All I'm saying is based on the evidence…"

"Evidence?"

"Yes, evidence. I'll walk away from MC's crushing behavior because you're a dude and as observant as you are, dude tendencies can prevent even the brightest from seeing what's so clear. We'll instead focus on you and your latent intentions," she says thrusting a finger in his direction. "Last weekend MC got pissy drunk and while I thought it was weird, I'm willing to believe in coincidence to explain why you *happened* to be in *that* club *that* night. But in her inane inebriety you volunteered to watch her and ensure that she was well."

"I…"

"I'm not done yet," she quickly interrupts. "You're probably going to say that since you have a relationship with MC and because we, her friends, were so undone by her behavior that you felt you had a duty of care to her. Right?" she asks rhetorically. "Okay, we'll go with that too. So, you get her out of the place when she's reached her limit and you bring her home. If I recall, before I departed, I believe we agreed that you would call me, and I would go to MC's apartment to her aid."

"But..."

"You didn't. That's correct. You instead stayed with her and nursed her and watched her sleep all night until you decided the following morning that it was appropriate to make the previously discussed phone call."

She pauses and Logan's jaw is clinched as he grinds his teeth, seething with indignation. "Interesting. If that's not enough, I have to ask, when has inviting a patient to your home ever been considered professional?"

"I've never invited Noe to my home."

"You haven't?"

"No."

"So, MC has never been to your house?"

"I didn't say that. I said I've never invited her."

"Semantics. You've had her over. You watched that insipid movie with her."

"What you're not mentioning is that she practically begged me to come over and I hesitantly said yes, not even giving her the address."

"Are you being serious right now? That's the worst argument I've ever..."

"And while she was there, we had a session. That's why she came. It was an afterhours emergency and we had a session. And *because* I know her well, I allowed her to watch a film that I know helps calm her. And afterward she departed. Plain and simple."

"It's not plain and simple."

"And I didn't call you immediately upon getting her home because as you so eloquently stated she was inebriated past the point of return and you were obviously already in a state of anger so I didn't see a need to re-

355

introduce you to an already toxic situation. No pun intended."

"Who asked you to do that?"

"The time I spent with her was, aside from the fact never going to be remembered by her, purely in efforts to ensure that she lived to see the next day, and though not technically within the bounds of my direct responsibilities, not encroaching upon the line of unprofessionalism. And Harper while I appreciate your concern, I would ask that you didn't call to question how it is that I do my job."

"Logan it's dangerous that's all I'm saying. I'm not calling you a bad psychiatrist."

"Psychologist."

"Whatever."

"They're different."

"Seriously, not caring. MC is on a downward spiral."

"I know that. It's my job to know it."

"Well Mr. It's My Job, you need to make it your job that her inevitable dissention is not made worse by your continued actions," she says sitting slightly straighter in her chair. "I don't know if you need to lie to yourself or if you haven't figured it out yet, but you have a thing for my friend and she's feeding off it like ivy on a fucking brick wall," she continues leaning in toward him. "And when she gets so low and her only refuge is you, in that moment she chooses to bear her soul, and it'll happen, I promise, if she hears you tell her that you don't feel the same she will be crushed."

"I don't understand what you want me to do."

"It's not rocket science. Come out of the MC closet or stay in, but pick one. If you're out, then obviously that offends some doctor-patient something or other. If you're staying in, then you're a professional...fix that shit. I don't need to see your like, lust, or love. Put that in a box; lock it up; and throw away the fucking key. Got it," she closes leaning back into her chair.

"I think so," he stammers, a blank expression written

on his face.

Harper drains the rest of her drink and excuses herself to the bathroom. Logan sits very still, palms glued to the tops of his thighs. He stares blankly toward the waitress kiosk. Seeing an opening, Hannah rolls her shoulders back and makes her way back toward the table.

"He's out of your league," Harper calls emerging from the bathroom causing Hannah to do an about face and retreat.

"Don't look so glum doc," she says hovering over Logan's shoulder. "MC is really awesome. But then again, you know that. You're doing the right thing. It's for the best." Harper says and slaps Logan hard across the back, jostling him slightly. His hands stay affixed to his legs and eyes glued forward. "Have a drink. I'm sure it'll take the stink off," she says as she finds her way to the front of the eatery and out the door.

Ebonii Nelson

From the Desk of   Noe Cortes

September 19, 2010

So, I backslid just a little today. But I was brought back which is all that matters.

I didn't realize how hard it would be and being at the house and being confronted by JJ and Adriana and Jackson and Kennedy and Mama and Papi even...I just wasn't ready for it. But I love my brother. He was ...well IS right. I don't need to try and live by other people's standards or ideas for me. I don't know why that's so hard for me to wrap my brain around. It's my life, right? I should be doing what's best for me and not being concerned with everything outside of me?

Well...what is it that I want? That's the question, right? I suppose I can use my resolution to do some soul searching and figure it out. I wonder what you're thinking about all of this Dr. Logan. What should I do? How should I start?

Chapter 26

"One for *Flipped*."

"Just one?"

"Yes. That's the Rob Reiner one, right?"

"Yes ma'am. That'll be $6.50."

"That's it?"

"Thursday special."

"Sweet. Here you go," I say happily handing the ticket guy, Carl, six dollars and fifty cents exactly.

"Enjoy your film."

I make my way through the lifeless and lackluster theater lobby. The stained furry red carpet hosts a malodorous musk that can't help but mingle with the aromas of stale buttered popcorn, roasting mystery wieners, and nacho cheese sauce. I bypass the refreshments settling instead for the illicit red vines I have in my messenger bag.

My movie is in theater three. I walk inside just as the lights are dimming and I find a seat along the aisle near the natural center of the room. I watch the screen blithely – a coming of age love story, the preview called it.

I sit intensely engrossed in the story of young Juli as she makes her way along a tortuous path of triumph, disaster, family drama and first love. I find myself almost crying just as the credits start to roll.

"Here you are," a gentleman I hadn't noticed before says handing me a Kleenex.

"Thank you. I don't know why I'm so emotional, you know? They're children," I add babbling and wiping my face.

"Yes, they were children, but they were experiencing things that even we as adults do every day, and I think their youth made it more tender and endearing."

"Oh my goodness, you're right. You're very good with words. You know you actually sound just like someone I know. It's uncanny."

"Do you think we should get going? I think the

cleaning crew would really love to get to their work."

"Oh, I didn't even think about that. Let's," I say standing to my feet with the help of the thoughtful gentleman's accommodating hand.

We emerge to the theater hallway, him first. My eyelids are bound from my crying episode and the harsh fluorescent lights nearly blind me as I try to force them open. I finally maintain open eyes enough to see my movie watching companion.

He's wearing some non-descript but nice navy and white canvas sneakers, vintage wash classic fit jeans that hug him in a way that accentuates his firm posterior, and a gray SMU college shirt that, like his jeans, manages to grip his golden and robust biceps.

By the time I make it to his face I am only able to see his bright smile and cavernous dimples before I realize that nice film comrade is not a nice stranger.

"Dr. Logan?" I ask abashedly.

"Hello Ms. Cortes," he responds casually. "It really was a nice movie wasn't it."

"I can't believe…I…oh my…I might be a bit embarrassed," I stammer feeling my cheeks warm at this finding. "For the love of all things sweet, why didn't you say so before? You let me babble on and cry…oh my. I cried."

"No need for embarrassment," he says grinning with amusement.

I find it hard to make eye contact with Dr. Logan even with his absolution. I cannot believe I hadn't recognized that the all too familiar and friendly voice belonged to a person that I have been more than vulnerable with for the past two years.

"You have time for lunch?" he asks oblivious to my internal berating session.

"Lunch?"

"Yes. Food. You do eat sometimes, don't you?"

"I do eat, but I'm really confused right now."

"What are you confused about?"

"What's happening?"

"We have both seen a film today. It's lunch time. I have hunger. I assume you might as well. I invited you along with me. Simple."

"I mean technically…."

"Are you hungry or not?"

"I am."

"Were you going to eat at this point in time?"

"Well…yeah."

"Good. Let's go."

"Okay," I respond dumbfounded and a bit caught off guard.

We walk side by side in comfortable silence to a location of which I am unsure. I didn't think to ask. I get so lost in my confusion that I accidentally brush his hand a couple of times. After each one I offer an apology hoping he doesn't think I'm doing it on purpose, but he never seems to get offended. He doesn't even offer an acceptance. He just smirks a bit and forges ahead.

I hate that his grin and each touch of his hand gives way to exciting pulsations of my blood. It's strange and I don't understand where it comes from, but it's there and only seems to intensify with each repetition.

"Here we are," Dr. Logan speaks after what has to have been 10 minutes.

"Where is here?"

"After you," he begins holding the door open for me to walk inside. "Welcome to Kincaid's burgers," he beams proudly.

"Kincaid's? Never heard of it."

"What? Noe you have not lived if you have not had a burger from Kincaid's. It's a good thing I'm here to rectify that."

"What do I order? I know it's a burger place but there so many," I ask as we make our way to the ordering counter.

It looks like an old-timey diner complete with short order cooks and greasy spoons.

"We'll have two bacon cheeseburgers, an order of fries, onion rings and fried okra. Two fountain drinks and if she's not full after that we'll come back for dessert."

I watch in awe as Dr. Logan engages with the cook-waiter who meets us. He seems so confident, suave, handsome, and wonderful and...

"Where shall we sit?" Thankfully, this question stops me from continuing down this path –My inappropriate and more inappropriate thought pattern.

"Oh, you're the professional here. I'll sit wherever."

"How about over there by the window?"

"Sounds perfect."

We find a corner booth made for two. The chairs are made of that funky diner plastic that squeaks and sticks to everything and the tables are topped with red and white checkered tablecloths. I sit so my back is to the window and I can be warmed by the sunlight cascading over my shoulder onto my face. Dr. Logan stays standing and after I'm situated comfortably, he leaves me with my thoughts in search of our fountain drinks.

"Order 315!"

"I'll grab it," I call to Dr. Logan across the restaurant quickly rising to return to the food counter.

"At the window honey," the cook says when I run up to him.

"Oh. Thank you," I say nervously.

When I get to the window, I see that Dr. Logan has beaten me and is grabbing part of our order that spills onto two trays. I grab one so he doesn't have to juggle both and follow back to our corner table.

We begin our meal in the same comfortable silence that we'd arrive. The burger melts in my mouth, savory and well-seasoned. The onion rings are amazing, and the fries are indescribable. I avoid the okra, but from the insatiable way Dr. Logan is devouring them, I'd say they too are delectable.

Somewhere in between competing for the last fry and sharing the most delightful banana pudding we fall into a comfortable conversation. We discuss the movie and I learn that he found it endearing and the best way to tell a love story – through the innocent eyes of child. We have playful banter discussing new books we've both read. I tell him of me choreographing my mom's show and he even asks if he might be able to catch one. He lets me know a little of him too. I learn that he dabbles in photography and had recently done a shoot at an outdoor dance performance in downtown. It's so easy talking to him that time just breezes by.

My phone buzzes jarring me and invading our conversation.

"Do you need to check that?"

"Do you mind?"

"No, go ahead. I'll put our trash away."

Be at Hayley's tomorrow early.
HH -
5:37 p.m., 24 Sept

Tomorrow?
5:38 p.m., 24 Sept

Yes. Hayley's pre-engagement engagement party.
HH -
5:40 p.m., 24 Sept

Harper's text message confuses me. I hate that she insists on sending such detail-less messages.

> Tomorrow?
>
> 5:42 p.m., 24 Sept

> Why are you confused? Girl's night tomorrow at Hayley's. Be there at 7.
> HH -
>
> 5:43 p.m., 24 Sept

> I'm there
>
> 5:44 p.m., 24 Sept

I don't exactly understand why we're pre-partying for an engagement party, but I oblige so I can return to my conversation with Dr. Logan.

"Is everything okay?" he asks sensing my apparent frustration.

"All is well," I smile willing him back to our rapturous duologue.

"I suppose that was our closing bell. I hadn't realized the time."

"Right. I suppose it is pretty late," I say dismayed.

We stand and exit the eatery just as we arrived, in silence. We walk back to the theater, this time with a slightly quickened pace and a significant distance between our hands. Ever chivalrous Dr. Logan walks me to my car and opens the door to help me in.

"Nice day today," he comments still holding the door though all parts of me are safely inside.

"Yeah," I agree leaning up to see his face, squinting into the setting sunlight.

"So, I guess I should let you get going," he adds moving closer and blocking the sun. "Right," I mutter kerfuffled by my newfound ability to see his intense gray eyes and caramel skin. My breath catches in my throat as I find myself forgetting how to inhale and exhale.

"I'll see you."

"Of course," I squeak.

"Of course," he repeats closing my door, putting his hands in his pockets, and flashing one last captivating smile before he turns on his heels and crosses the parking lot.

***

"To the future bride and groom!" everyone repeats after Mr. Martin's toast to his daughter and future son-in-law.

"Thanks daddy!" Hayley cries running to hug him.

The music portion of this very reception-esque engagement party begins leading with Hayley and Connor's favorite tune – Stuck like glue by Sugarland. They're so cute singing all the words –aloud and off key and dancing their own special jig – off beat. They're the most adorable couple I've ever seen, so cute that I get nauseous at the sight of them making heart symbols with their hands and stealing kisses as they spin in circles and pretend to surprise each other by being there.

"Bartender, I'll have a white Russian and a shot of tequila," I say turning away from the dance floor where more guests have joined Connor and Hayley.

I've been glued to the bar since finishing my speech and I've been trying to maintain the buzz I started at Hayley's pre-engagement engagement party at Harper's.

"Are you sure you want to mix those?"

"I appreciate your concern Mr. Bartender…"

"It's Mitch."

"Mitch. I appreciate your concern but I have a taste for those particular flavors so I would more than welcome your quick adherence to my request."

"As you like it."

"Great play."

"Huh?"

"Nothing."

"What are you doing all the way over here?" Harper yells.

"Oh nothing. I'm just getting to know Mitch here. Where's Sebastian?"

"Sebastian has been sequestered by Mr. Martin and your dad over there by the table-o- meat," she beams with excitement.

"Poor guy," I add somberly.

"Not really. He's loving it. When I told him that those two were like my 2nd and 3rd fathers after mine died, he was all too eager to get in good with them."

"Well…. that's just…great. It's really nice."

"What's wrong with you?"

"Nothing, really."

"Nothing really? I don't buy that for a second. You're sitting here all alone, all mopey. You just ordered the most disgusting drink combination and you're telling me nothing is wrong with you."

"That is correct. Absolutely nothing is wrong with me. I'll tell you like I told Mitch. I have a hankering for those flavors."

"Don't get so testy."

I am getting crotchety and I can't exactly explain why. This is a joyous occasion and I should be happy for my best friend and her fiancée, but I'm not. I should be happy for my other best friend who seemed destined for a life of solitude, but I'm not pleased with that either.

I look around the room grasping for a pleasant sighting and I can't seem to find anything that doesn't make me want to begin bawling my eyes out. Harper abandons me when she sees that Sebastian has been released from the care of the papa bears.

I stay perched on my stool sipping my drinks at first, but as the night wears on and the parents leave and no one seems to be left except couples, Mitch, the wait staff and me I start downing with the intent to blur and erase the night.

"Last call MC," Mitch says sounding thankful and liberated.

"When did I tell you my name?" I ask slowly and methodically concentrating on sounding out every syllable, willing myself sober. "I ne-, I never told you anything did I?" I hiccupped.

"Yes, you did. It was after the Mai-Tai but before the Chupacabra."

"Those sound terrible. That couldn't have been me," I say shaking my head and losing my balance.

"That's what I thought too, but then you asked for a 7 & 7 and a Skittle Bomb and you're magically still sitting so maybe you're on to something we both don't get."

"You're very funny you know?" I say abandoning my feeble attempts at feigned sobriety. "You're cute too Mitch. You know that?" I yell.

"Thank you. Do you want me to call you a cab or something?"

"I don't need a cab. I can get myself my home. I can myself hominy. I go. I can."

I am tired of Mitch and his recitation of my night's orders, so I unsteadily slink off my stool and make my way across the room. With my cell phone in hand I find an alcove beneath a set of stairs just outside the bathrooms. Everything is fuzzy and I feel my legs threaten to give, so I lean on a nearby wall for stability. With legs seemingly unhinged, I slide across the wall before gently collapsing into a corner.

I roll ever slightly over my shoulder, so my forehead

is against the wall offering pressure and relief from the pounding that's begun in my head. I unearth my phone from the vice grip of my left hand and start to dial a set of numbers on impulse.

"Hale."

"Again?"

"Excuse me? May I ask who's calling?" he questions equally confused and perturbed.

"Why d'you always answer your phone like that?" I slur.

"Noe?"

"Sí. Me llamo Noe Marie Cortes. Ene. Oh. Eh. Como el hombre con la barca," I continue words muddled. I feel myself start to dribble a bit, so I pause.

"Noe, where are you? What's going on?"

"Estoy a la fiesta de compromise de Hayley y, y Connor."

"En Inglés por favor."

"Dr. Logan?" I ask, out of breath. "You speaky Spanish?"

"Can you please speak English?" he asks frustrated.

"What?" I ask confusedly.

"Stop that."

"Huh?"

"Noe?"

"Yeah?"

"Why have you called me? Before you answer, please think and respond to this in English."

"Dr. Logan..." I whisper.

"Yes?" he asks expectantly.

"Hi," I giggle goofily.

"Hi," he responds dramatically less enthused.

We both pause and hold our respective phones in comfortable silence. My heart is whirring and I'm becoming strangely turned on by the voice I've been hearing on the other line. I imagine him sitting on his couch wearing his tight-in-the-right-places fitting v-neck tee, probably in gray or black, with is low-hanging jeans. It's Saturday night so he's probably wearing his glasses instead of his contacts. They always magnify his beautiful, icy gray eyes. Before I dialed, he was likely watching a light comedy and eating popcorn.

"Noe?" Dr. Logan asks, waking me from my reverie.

"Huh?"

"How are you?"

"I am…" I trail off, closing my eyes tightly trying to envision his image again, this time with me alongside.

"You are what?"

"I'm at Connor and Hayley's engagement party. I told you that already. I've been drinking a lot of soda, so it's made me harder to understand."

"Are you sure what you've had is soda?" he asks dubiously.

"You're so silly. Of course it was," I hiccup. "Mitch was tooootally good. He was sweet but kind of annoying."

"Okay…"

"You know something?"

"No, tell me something."

"I know all three of your names." I hold up three fingers instinctively as if he can see me.

"Okay."

"Logan Aaron Hale. That's a really nice name. Your parents are probably really proud."

"I'm sure they would appreciate your compliment. Noe, where is your party?"

"We're at the Lobe Mansion."

"Where?"

"You know…B-E-L-O."

"The Belo Mansion?"

"That's what I said."

"The one in the Arts District?"

"Okay."

"Okay?"

"Lawyer's a Harper and she used her connections to steal the place," I laugh.

"Okay, where is Harper?" he asks more hurriedly.

"I dunno. Probably with Sebastian. They're a couple you know. Like Connor and Hayley. But not me. Nope. I'm too wrong for people. What's that beeping sound? Is that your car? You know you shouldn't drive and be on the phone. It's dangerous," I sound like a small girl nicely educating her parents of safety rules.

"Thank you for your concern. Are there any others near you?"

"Well…" I drop the phone and tear my forehead away from the wall and slide along the floor to peer out from my nook into the main room where the guests are still gathered and mingling. It's hard to open my eyes so I can't really make out much. I vaguely recognize Mitch's figure still behind the bar. All the other people – couples, seem to easily blend into the décor.

"Noe!" I hear Dr. Logan yelling as I crawl back into my spot and bring the phone up to my ear.

"What?" I yell back matching his volume and inflection.

"Where'd you go?" he asks nervously.

"I went to see if anyone else was near me like you asked. Are you alright? You haven't been drinking tonight have you?"

"No. Where are you?"

"Huh? I can't hear you. Why is it so windy sounding at your house?"

"You said you're at the Belo Mansion?"

"Yesth," I say lisped.

"Where exactly in the mansion are you? Hi. No, I'm great thanks."

"Hi, okay. Wait are you talkin' to me?"

"Where Noe?" he asks with consternation.

"In the cute pre-bathroom corner," I giggle re-situating

370

on the floor in my cubby sitting cross-legged with my eyes closed.

"Excuse me, where are your bathrooms?" muffled I hear Dr. Logan exchange words with someone. I can't exactly make out what they're saying.

"Dr. Logan!"

"Yes?"

"Are you listening to me?"

"Of course I am. You said you're in a pre-bathroom corner."

"Wait, you're echoing a little." I pull my phone from my ear and shake it a bit in effort to eliminate the parroting.

"Noe…" I hear a voice call to me.

"Hi." I smile up at the voice, eyes still close.

I feel a gust of air as the person walks toward me and drops from standing to just in front of me. I smell a familiar smell – a man's scent.

"Hi," the voice responds to me.

"You sound just like Dr. Logan. He's on the phone with me. I just shook him though cause he started echoing," I speak goofily.

"You want to open your eyes?" the voice asks as a hand brushes some stray hairs off my face behind my ear.

I oblige and I see Dr. Logan squatting in front of me. He's wearing a honeysuckle yellow v-neck shirt, almost as I imagined, along with jeans that look very worn, but well kept.

"What are you doing here?" I ask gaily, desire growing inside me.

"I feel like I should ask you the same," he begins having a seat next to me so that his left thigh rests just under my bent knee. "Do you think we should get up from here?"

"I *need* to be here," I say determinedly pointing and looking at the ground.

"Okay," he says, his right hand lifting my chin to see my eyes. "What's going on in there? Talk to me. Why do we *need* to be here?"

"It's comfortable here," I say straightening my legs, so

371

they lay across his.

"Noe," he begins unstirred by our close proximity.

"Yes Dr. Logan…"

"What's going on with you right now," he asks scooting a bit closer to me so that the underside of my thighs and edge of my hindquarters are resting snugly against his thigh, our faces inches apart.

"I love you Dr. Logan," I say facing him, my eyes locked intently on his gaze.

"Let's explore why you think that, why you're projecting such special feelings onto me."

"Quit with the psychobabble. I do. I really do love you. I know it. And you love me too. That's why you're here right now. That's why you're always here."

"Listen to me Noe," he begins calmly. "You do not love me."

"Don't say that. I do," I say angrily. "I don't know why I never thought of it before. You get me. You're the first person I want to tell everything and you're the only person who knows how to calm me down and make me feel better. You drink Dr. Pepper just like me, and you're quirky in a different way, but just like me. I know your smell and the way your eyes glitter when you get excited or turn ice cold when you're angry or frustrated," I say leaning closer to him.

"I can guess what you're going to wear…like I knew today you'd be in a v-neck. We speak the same language. Think how many times we've been in your office and we utter only parts of sentences because we just know what the other one meant at the start or the end of the clause. And my friends trust you. That's why they left me with you from before, and…and, and my mom already loves you. That's how I know it'd be perfect. She's displeased with every decision I make. She already chose you, so I know she'd be fine."

There's a break in my monologue while I await a response. For a short time, he says nothing. He just stares at me. His eyes look sad and are losing their color. They're darting quickly left and right and I can tell he's having an internal conversation with himself. He's no longer relaxed and open. As his pacing eyes slow to a stop he becomes rigid and casually creates space between us. His change has an unnerving and sobering effect on me.

"Noe," he begins gravely.

"No. I don't think...I don't want to hear what you're going to say," I start, my voice catching as I'm shaking my head to dry up the tears welling in my eyes.

"You may not want to, but you need to hear me right now Noe."

"Why?" I whine.

"Shit, Noe," he says turning squarely in front of me, voice stern. "You do not care for me in that way. This is a manifestation, a uh, um projection of...an amalgamation of other emotions that are easily projectable onto me. Aside from that, it's inappropriate based on the *client-* counselor relationship we have established. It will not happen," he finishes. "I should've listened to her," he mutters rubbing his face and furrowing his brow.

He looks back at me and his eyes are no longer cold but filled with a sadness that matches my own as he waits for a response. Unable to speak and unable to contain them, tears begin to flood my eyes.

"I'll fetch Harper or Hayley for you. I- I I- need to go," he says confusedly, rising to go.

I sink further into the corner where we'd been discussing and weep myself into a stupor. I hear his words and the stab of his rejection on repeat in my mind.

"MC? Honey...it's Hayley and Harper," Hayley's motherly voice calls to me.

"MC, we saw your Dr. Logan out on the floor. We didn't even know you invited him," Harper adds.

"Is he gone?" I whimper through my tears.

"Yeah. He told us we should be with you, but he wouldn't say why. He was all disheveled and said he had to go," Harper responds.

"Honey, can you sit up and talk to us?" Hayley coos, gently stroking my back.

"What happened?" Harper asks pointedly.

I can't find the words to speak. Each time I think about words, my heart rate increases, and my face is surged with a river of tears. He left and isn't coming back. He doesn't want me, and I don't know how to make sense of that. Everything made sense I thought. And I thought he felt like I do, but he said no.

Harper and Hayley stop asking questions and just wrap their arms around me and rock with me as I sob.

From the Desk of ___Noe Cortes___

September 26, 2010

I am ashamed. I got drunk made a fool of myself again and now I may have created a problem that cannot be solved.

Dr. Logan, I'm so sorry.

Dr. Pepper peace offering anyone?

Chapter 27

"Buenas mi'ja"

"Good morning Papí. How are you?"

"Your father is well. How are you? How's my one and only?"

"I could be better," I answer honestly.

"Can I help?"

"Your voice is enough actually."

"Your plans today?" he asks hopping into a discussion we must have started telepathically.

"I'm having brunch with Harper and Hayley later."

"Qué más?"

"Nada. We may come up with something there," I respond softly.

"Come visit with your mother and brothers maybe?"

"Y tú, también? Yes. I'll try and come by when I'm done there. Can we have lemonade and talk about what you're reading right now?"

"Oh ho, book talk!" he calls excitedly. "We can, mi amorcita."

"Great. Well I'm going to go and get ready for my brunch."

"'ta luego."

"'ta luego Papí. Te quiero."

"Con todo mi corazón."

I hang up with some energy from my quick chat with my father. Harper, Hayley, and I have scheduled our brunch at Iron Cactus downtown at 11:30 a.m. It's barely 9:00 a.m. as I roll out of bed to make my way into the shower.

I turn the water on and let it run as I disrobe. In my full-length mirror I examine my whole self. There are 26 days until my 29th birthday and I feel like my face has begun to harden with stress.

"What are you doing with your life?" I ask aloud poking and lifting pieces of skin on my face and arms.

I turn away from the mirror and climb into the shower. I lean into the steady stream of water before I lay my head against the wall and allow it to cascade down my back. Though it pains me to have all the memories from yesterday rush into my subconscious, I close my eyes in search of a sense of calm.

***

"Hi," I say when I arrive at the Iron Cactus.

The air is strange. I feel like I've interrupted something as I look back and forth between Harper and Hayley. Harper's timeliness sends a chill up my spine and I nervously fidget with a string on hem of my shirt.

"Hey honey," Hayley begins with uneasiness in her voice. "How are you?" She eyes Harper and motions for me to have a seat.

"I'm fine," I respond hanging my bag on my chair and carefully taking a seat. "What's going on? It seems like I've interrupted something here. And you, Harper" I look at her. "You beat me. I think I'm scared," I end laughing awkwardly.

"Are you feeling okay today?" Hayley asks motherly – almost condescendingly.

"I'm fine. Thanks for asking. Have we ordered yet?"

"You are not fine," Harper says sternly.

"Well hello Harper," I respond sarcastically.

"Cut the shit MC."

"Harper!" Hayley snaps.

"Yeah Harper, what's with you. Maybe I should be asking you how *you* are."

"Do you remember last night?" Harper asks incredulously.

"Yes," I say hesitantly. "It was Hayley and Connor's

377

engagement party. I gave a speech. How could I forget that?"

"All that happened then you got drunk...again, invited your *psychiatrist*..."

"Psychologist," I interject nonchalantly.

"I don't give a fuck!"

"Harper, what the fuck?"

"Ladies!" Hayley scolds.

"MC you're not alright and you need some help," Harper continues.

"What are you talking about?" I ask, attitude growing more serious.

"MC the last couple of times I've seen you you've been drunk off your ass, crying over some issue. Since when have you turned to drinking? You don't dance anymore. You don't even really say anything substantive," she tosses her hands up in defeat.

"What are you doing with yourself? I don't even know who you are these days. You don't seem to care about anyone, and your actions are incredibly selfish. You look gaunt and sickly and you're a mess," she closes eyeing me disgustedly.

"We're just worried honey. You're not yourself and we just want to know what you're going through so we can help you," Hayley adds.

"You too Hayley?" I ask affronted. "Is that what you were talking about before I came in?"

"No actually that was something else," Harper spews.

"Well in the name of honesty, educate me."

"Harper," Hayley says worriedly laying a hand on Harper's shoulder.

"It doesn't matter now Hay," Harper says shaking Hayley's hand from her shoulder.

"What is it?" I ask annoyed.

"Last week I had lunch with Dr. Logan," Harper begins ignoring Hayley's plea, looking directly at me.

"For what? Why would you need to meet with him? Why did he agree to see you?"

"The 'whys' are neither here nor there. I met with him to discuss you. I know you have a little crush on him and because of his more recent behavior I felt like something needed to be said."

"Harper, I just don't think this is wise."

"Hayley sometimes confrontation is healthy and necessary. And within a relationship honesty is a great policy. So, we're killing two birds with one stone. Please let me continue."

Hayley doesn't concur, but she silences herself and re-situates in her chair.

"What current circumstances and what do you mean his behavior?"

"MC you were just re-dumped by your ex-boyfriend and first real love. This other oh-so- wrong-for-you love interest abandoned you and you're now surrounded by my newfound romantic happiness, Hayley and Connor, your brothers – plural, and you're still underwhelmed by your work," she starts to ramble in a way I've never known.

"I've known you for over 15 years MC," she continues. "I know you're feeling like shit. And…"

"And him? How does this matter for Dr. Logan? If anything, this is great business for him."

"As I was saying," she sneers annoyed by my interruption. "Your *psychiatrist* has an unsightly admiration for you, and I do not think in your state, not to mention illegality, it's the smartest."

"So, what did you say to him?" I ask huffily, nervous in anticipation for her response.

"I called him out on his inappropriate lusting and though he denied that, I told to him cut it out."

"You said what? Cut what out exactly?" I shout gruffly.

"MC please calm down."

"Hayley did you know too? Did you agree with her doing this?"

"No. She just told me, but I don't think you should get

worked up."

"How can I not get worked up? I've just been told that one of my best friends has been doing some reconnaissance work behind my back, sabotaging my relationship. I mean, my, my, my thing with my *counselor, psychologist*. This is inappropriate and I can't believe you did that."

"Cut the dramatics MC. He obviously didn't listen to a goddamned word I said to him because he was there, at the party…. with you. The little fucker," Harper spits.

"You told him I had a thing for him?" I ask.

"Did you even hear you just a second ago? You just said your 'relationship.' MC, you don't have a relationship. You have a contract-b a s e d association – the most platonic form of connection."

"I know the bounds of our relationship Harper."

"Do you? Because the way you speak and the way you behave certainly doesn't look like you understand the bounds of your relationship," she adds mockingly.

"You also told him you thought he should avoid me?"

"Not exactly the message, but ignoring semantics, yes. That is also true."

"Hayley what about this wouldn't cause me to be unconscionably irate?" I attempt to bring Hayley onto my side.

"Don't go getting upset with Hayley. She agreed with you that I shouldn't have gone to him without your knowing. She defended you even though you've done nothing but ruin her special days, selfishly drawing attention to yourself."

"I do not feel like you've ruined my days MC, please believe that," Hayley tries.

"I believe you Hayley and I'm also very upset with myself for my unintentional attempts at stealing your thunder. And I'm also sorry that you're always in the middle of my and Harper's fights and that today will not be different."

I turn to Harper standing and struggling to grab my bag to leave. "Harper, he heard you loud and clear," I say directly leaning into her still fiddling with my bag.

I finally loose my belongings and speedily make my way toward the exit. I walk out to the street unable to fully process what I've just heard. I look right and up the hill in the direction of my car, but I don't feel lucid enough to drive. Instead I turn left and walk deeper into downtown.

Memories are jumping back into my mind mending themselves together and things are starting to make sense. When he said he should've listened to her, he meant Harper. I can't believe she would do that to me and mask it in care. I'm not gaunt looking. I'm in transition.

I walk on autopilot willing myself not to cry and find my way to a familiar ballet studio. I know this place. My mom used to teach supplemental classes here when her studio was just getting off the ground. The non-descript gray lettering of BALLET SCHOOL towers over the tall brick building. I open the door and go inside up the monotonous set of stairs. On my climb I hear Tchaikovsky's Swan Lake and calm calls – demi-plié, degage, relevé. At the top of the stairs I instinctively drop my bag, exit my shoes, and join the young teens at the bar – fondu, frappe, developpé, battement tendu. One of the cadres looks like she's prepared to eject me, but a woman I remember, Madame Cicely, wearing her black leotard to everyone else's pink, raises her arm signaling stop to the teacher as she continues her calls and at the ballet barre

I bend and flex, extend and retract and get lost in the fluency of it all.

As class ends, all the students offer their gratitude, pack up their belongings and disappear. I blend into the background of the studio, not yet ready to escape the sanctuary.

"Thank you Madame Cicely, for allowing me to stay. I know I am not properly dressed, and I recognize my tardiness and abrupt entrance may have caused more of a disruption than I intended, but..." I ramble as she approaches me.

"It is okay my darling," she interrupts with her French accent. "Can you help me out before you go?"

"Definitely," I oblige sprightly.

"Madeleine you can go. Noe here is going to help me close up," she says to the woman who earlier wanted to dismiss me.

"Thank you Madame Cicely. I will see you tomorrow afternoon." Madeleine quietly and swiftly makes her escape and Madame Cicely turns back to me.

"Noe, grab those paper towels and the spray bottle. We'll clean the mirrors." For a short while we squirt and wipe, concentrating so as not to leave smudges.

"Your form is nice Noe Marie. Your flexibility is questionable. I can tell you've been out of practice, but you dance very well. There's much talent harnessed within you still."

"Thank you," I cower with embarrassment.

"I noticed something else about your dancing today." I look up silently inquiring further.

"You danced much like you're carrying a load. What brought you here today?"

"Wow Madame Cicely..."

"Cicely. You're old enough now, and you're no longer one of my students."

"Cicely," I say a little awkwardly. "You don't waste much time with small talk."

"We did that when we cleaned the first mirror. Enough of the pleasantries."

"Right," I add.

"So, out with it. Dancers are terrible at concealing their feelings during dance."

"Cicely can we stop cleaning for a minute?"

"Yes, we can," she stops, walks to the center of the floor, and takes a seat.

I follow suit and join her.

"I really don't know what's going on with me. I just feel really lost and confused, and I don't know what to do with that. I feel supremely out of touch with *me* and I don't know how to fix it. I came here today accidentally but it felt good to be free for the moment."

"I'm not going to ask you to explore more of these feelings verbally with me, but I want to encourage you to pour more of it out in your dance, and then spend some time with yourself really exploring all that you've released. The dance is just the release. It doesn't bring about the resolution that you want…that you *need*."

"But how will I know…"

"Stop thinking about it. Just do it. Treat it like you did today. You didn't stop to ask where we were in the warm-up you just jumped right in and let the motions come to you. Do what you do best and allow your resolution to come organically."

***

"Good afternoon Julia. I know I'm a little early, but I wanted to come and just zone out, or zone in or whatever before session. I don't know if he told you, but Dr. Logan kind of got mad at me and so yeah I wanted to mentally prepare for whatever is waiting for me, if that's okay," I finish noticing the less than pleasant expression on her face.

"Actually Ms. Cortes…"

"It's Noe. You know that."

"Ms. Cortes," she continues resolutely. "I have some correspondence for you today and your session this afternoon will be with Dr. Reagan Piper."

I take a letter from her and open it immediately. It's short – only 3 sentences.

```
Noe —
Due to present circumstances it has
been brought to my attention that
you may be better suited for a
different clinician. I am entrusting
the rest of your care to my
colleague, Dr. Piper. This is for
the best.

Hale
```

I read it over and over searching for semblance of something that makes sense, but it's typed and not printed. Everything about the letter is cold and vacant and re-reading it slowly renders me empty and forlorn.

I look over to Julia and she avoids my gaze undoubtedly because she knows what my *correspondence* says.

"I don't understand."

"Ms. Cortes," a friendly voice calls as the door to the counseling corridor opens. I nod noncommittally whipping around toward the voice.

"Welcome. Please come this way. I'm Reagan Piper, Dr. Hale's associate."

She's bright and cheery and warm in an almost insincere way. Her chestnut brown hair falls just beyond her shoulder blades framing her oval face. Her eyes are a faded blue beneath her perfectly manicured eyebrows. She has very high cheekbones and when she smiles, she reminds me of Jennifer Aniston.

As I walk behind her, and she makes insouciant and undeniably inane small talk, I notice her almond colored sheath dress and black cardigan. She's wearing smart, black kitten heels and yet she's still tall – very statuesque.

"Please have a seat anywhere you feel most comfortable," she says holding her door open for me. I notice when she says comfortable, she makes sure to pronounce it as though it were two separate words: comfort and able. I'm annoyed.

"Thank you," I almost whisper.

"As I was saying, Dr. Hale has taken the liberty of providing me all of your notes on progress and where you are in your action plan with him. Though this may seem abrupt, it's actually quite common. There are times when change is helpful for clients so that they can accomplish the most in the most efficient way. In this case, Dr. Hale thought that with some of your trials you might find it easier to identify with a woman. Does that make sense to you?"

"No, actually it doesn't. Thank you for asking," I utter revealing my annoyance as it's increased with her flight attendant-like enthusiasm.

"Oh," she says taken aback, not expecting my response.

"It's just, you're new which means we have to start all over again," I drone, spinning on my feet wanting to explore but seeing nothing to investigate.

"I assure you this modification in treatment will seem like a seamless process," she says stepping in front of me halting my circumspection. "Although there are some glaring differences between myself and Dr. Hale," she continues, "he's a man and I am not, and he's from the South and I am not, we use similar techniques and I can emulate him enough to get us going before we morph into a plan that will help you make the most progress. Does that ease your anxiety a bit more?" she asks beaming with pride from her response.

"What do we do today?" I ask avoiding her question, sidestepping her, and sitting on her uncomfortable red leather couch.

Everything Dr. Piper starts saying sounds like gibberish. I can't believe Dr. Logan is so upset with me that he fired me, and he didn't even have the decency to tell me in person. He gave me a letter and pawned me off on this big ball of pseudo sunshine.

"Could you excuse me? I really need to pee," I blurt

interrupting her glee.

"Oh, well…I suppose I can't ask if it's urgent…"

"Technically you did, and it is. I know my way around. I'll be right back," I say quickly and exit her office before she has time to prevent me from going.

I walk out of her office and wander past the door to the main corridor to Dr. Logan's side of the suite. It's 3:30 which is squarely during my time so I can't imagine that he's busy if he's here. I carefully examine the frosted glass of his door to try to see shadows with no success. Feeling more curious I press my ear against it and hearken for hushed voices.

I lean further into the door and close my eyes willing him to appear, willing my memory to conjure up his voice. "I had to. You did. You had to do it for her sake and yours."

I jump back at the apparent power of my thoughts. The voice I imagine in my head is definitely emanating from beyond the door.

"You didn't have to do it how you did Logan. That was stupid and passive and, and, and stupid."

I want to open the door and call to him that he can undo what he's done, that it's not too late.

"Logan don't beat yourself up. You did your job. It was grossly inappropriate. She's impetuous and, and, and flighty and…It has to be this way, despite what you might…"

I walk quickly away from his door not wanting to hear the conclusion of his ruminations. He's made up his mind and seems content with it. Besides, he sounds like mama calling me 'impetuous and flighty.' How dare he. He's giving himself a pep talk to justify what he did. I arrive back at Dr. Piper's and pace briefly behind the door trying to calm down before I slip into her space.

"Noe," she says sounding surprised that I returned.

"MC actually. Took longer than anticipated," I offer a shoddy excuse feigning consideration for her time before I sit again.

"Not to worry. It's probably just a nervous bladder.

386

Unfortunately, it's 3:50." She hesitates expectantly.

"Right," I begin slowly. "I have 10 minutes left."

"Oh no," she says disconsolately. "Ms. Cortes…"

"It's MC. Well you know, Noe. N-O-E, but pronounced like Noah, the man with the boat. I know that's a b…"

"*Em-cee,*" she concedes radiating some irritation. "As I was saying, sessions are 50 minutes. The 10 minutes that would complete the hour are held for the psychologist – me," she notes placing her hand to her chest. "It allows time to construct notes and prepare for subsequent sessions."

She finishes this last bit in a hurry noticing my attempt to interrupt following her self- identifying as my psychologist.

"So, what you're saying is…"

"It is now 3:57 and I do have another appointment at 4 pm," she smiles as she opens the door signaling the appropriate response for me at this moment would be to leave. "Make sure to schedule your next appointment with Julia," she adds, feigning a smile.

I get up and depart as Dr. Piper would have it. Through clamorous silence I also exit the building.

"I can't believe he left me with her," I declare aloud. "What the fu…" I begin running my hands through my hair unable to make sense of what feels like a breakup.

I walk blindly to my car, open the door, sit, and clasp my seatbelt anticipating a departure.

I reach into my glove compartment and fish out my phone. I search the home screen for messages – a text message, voicemail, missed call, but I come up short. I instinctively begin dialing a familiar number and listen to the hum of its ring.

"Texas International College, Office of Student Conduct, this is Joyce."

"We should really reconsider this greeting Joyce," I say playfully.

"Hey hon'. I wasn't expecting you."

"I know. I wasn't expecting me either. I'm going to do some work out of the office so can you do me a favor and route my phone to my work blackberry and cancel the meetings I had for the rest of the week and into next week?"

"I don't exactly understand MC," Joyce begins her voice full of nervous anxiousness.

"No need to worry Joyce."

"But I am MC. You haven't really been yourself the past couple of days, this past week you know?"

"I know I've been a bit out of it, but I promise you have nothing to worry about. I have some things to do and it requires me to be out of the office. I wish I could tell you more, but I can't. I just…" I pause, it growing more difficult to maintain my jaunty tone. "Things are great Joyce. Can you help me?"

"I can," She hesitates.

"Thank you. Don't worry please," I plead. "I'll see you when I get back."

"Be well sweet Noe."

I hang up and drive steadfast to my condo. There's so much running through my mind. It all serves as fuel as I climb my stairs two-by-two, open the door and barrel into my bedroom.

From my closet I grab a duffel bag and start tossing in shirts, and pants, socks, and underwear. From the bathroom I grab some toiletries and hair ties. I get some bottles of water and granola bars, my iPod and mini speakers and head back toward the front door.

"I think that's it MC. This is all you need."

I speak aloud to myself quickly checking off items from my mental checklist. I'm going away. I not sure where and I don't know for how long but I know I have to get out of dodge and do like Madame Cicely says – let a resolution come to me organically…whatever that means.

From the Desk of _____ Noe Cortes

September 29, 2010

This is stupid. Writing right now in this is dumb. I highly doubt there'll be a need for me to leave it with Julia for Dr. Piper.

This isn't about them. This isn't about anyone but me. Everything is falling apart around me and right now I'm the only one who can be here for me. Dr. Logan is out. Harper and Hayley...I can't handle them right now. Harper with her 'I told you so' and 'get your life together'...Hayley's incessant worry...I can't take any of it. I can't go home...Jack has his own thing and new life to plan. JJ is JJ and would know nothing about where to start. Papi.... I don't even think there's anything he could say to help...and Mama...I don't want to hear her remind me of my obligations as an adult or hear any of her cold and insentient remarks.

I'm so confused about everything but there's one thing that's blindingly clear. I have to go. Gotta move.

Chapter 28

I wake to the incessant ticking of a clock just above my head.
I open my eyes and re-live the last few days. After finding
out that my best friend purposely sabotaged my
relationship with Dr. Logan, I went to visit him and clear
up any misunderstandings. Instead of doing that I was met
with a memo – a Dr. Logan proxy, and the insipid Dr.
Reagan Piper. I listened to Dr. Logan's ruminations
reminding him of his great decision to end all contact with
me then I left. I took an informal leave from work and I
packed up my things and I drove south. I don't know where
or for how long, I just know I drove until I felt like I should
stop.

I ended up here. I don't know where here is exactly,
but I think it's best that way. I'm lakeside at a remote camp
retreat center. When I saw all the signs pointing toward it
something tugged at my heartstrings, so I followed. I spoke
with Diane and Pierre Kellog, the owners, and convinced
them to allow me to rent one of her cabins. I told Diane I was
a dancer-writer looking for a place to do my craft and I
assured Pierre that my activities wouldn't cause him to lose
any profits and if they did, I would leave. I don't know
what either of them saw in my eyes, but they agreed to the
stay in exchange for teaching a dance class for the duration. I
willingly obliged and unpacked my new life.

***

"Dr. Logan Hale please."

"D'you have an appointment sir? What's the name?"

"I don't actually have an appointment. He is…or he
was my daughter's counselor, and I'd hoped that he might
be available to meet with me today."

"He doesn't generally do walk-ins darlin' and
because of confidentiality rules I'm afraid there's probably
not much he can say to you anyway. What's the daughter's

name if I may pry?"

"Sure, her name is Noe. Noe Cortes. I'm not sure if
you are familiar with her. I'm sure there are a number of
people who frequent your space."

"Do you want to have a seat?" Julia asks with a
sudden hurriedness in her tone.

"That is no problem. I will be right over there."

There's no one buzzing around in the lobby.
Everything's quiet and uncomfortably sterile.

"Dr. Hale says he has a free hour right now and he
will see you if you have time."

"He will? That's absolutely perfect – really wonderful.
How do I find him?"

"He'll actually come for you."

"Great."

The non-descript spa music in the lobby has a
numbing effect that isn't so much relaxing as it is rueful.
Awaiting Dr. Hale's entrance, time seems to pass in
alternating slow and quick spurts.

"Dr. Hale," he calls standing as a tall gentleman
appears in the doorway. "My name is Ricardo Cortes. How
nice to meet you. Thank you for agreeing to visit with me."

"Hi Mr. Cortes, right this way. And feel free to call
me Logan. Dr. Hale is more or less reserved for my clients,"
Logan says holding the door open.

Logan and Mr. Cortes make their way down a
short corridor to Logan's office space nestled in a modest
corner of the suite.

"My office is right in here. Please, have a seat
anywhere you like. I'm intrigued about why you are in need
of consult."

Mr. Cortes enters and as if on impulse takes a
walk around the office, examining the bookshelves and
generalities of the space before he joins Logan and takes his
seat.

"Noe is very much like you."

"What makes you say that?" Mr. Cortes says hands placed neatly in his lap as he peers at Logan.

"I have been privy to Noe for quite some time and there are some characteristics that you exhibit that I've seen in her."

"That is very interesting to hear. I've always thought her to be more like my wife."

Mr. Cortes closes his statement and he and Logan sit allowing their silence to swell. Neither of them blinks much. They just exchange wary and inquisitive glances at one another.

"How might I help you today Mr. Cortes?" Logan asks.

"Ricardo."

"Beg pardon?"

"Please call me Ricardo. While we do not know each other well, I would like for us to converse more like friends."

"Well then, Ricardo," he almost mutters before clearing his throat and sitting up straighter in his seat. "What brings you here today?"

"Noe."

"She asked you to come?" Logan raises his brow in promise and leans forward.

"Not exactly. She has gone and it appears that between her mother, me, her brothers, and her two best friends, we do not know where. I don't know if she's still been meeting with you regularly, but I know that for a time you were someone that knew the inner workings of her life and she trusts you. Do you have any idea of where she might have travelled?"

"Are you sure Harper and Hayley don't know where she might be?"

"I have not spoken with them, but based on the information my wife delivered me, no, they do not know where she might be."

"I don't think I can be of much help to you. Noe

and I no longer have a relationship, and if we did, doctor-patient confidentiality regulations would preclude me from doing so," Logan says stonily.

"Something is wrong," he says definitively, looking at Logan expectantly.

"You're worried about her? This is very uncharacteristic of her, but I don't think you should worry. Noe has never been without her wits, so I'm sure that wherever she is she is safe. Give her some space and some time and she'll come around."

"That's not what I am referring to."

"I'm not sure I understand."

"Something is wrong with *you*," he adds pointing and looking directly at Logan.

"With me? Mr. Cortes…I mean Ricardo, I am perfectly well," Logan says breaking eye contact.

"No, there is something wrong here. When I mentioned my daughter's name to the woman in the front office, I was immediately granted access to you. When you mentioned that Noe's behavior is somewhat reflective of mine you said so with a tone of reverence and longing," he begins standing and making his way onto a sofa closer to Logan.

"Ricardo…. I don't know what you'd like me to say right now." Worry spreads gradually about his face just as his posture deteriorates.

"But then something in you changed," Ricardo continues. "It's as if you mentally reminded yourself of something and then your words were distant and cold when you told me that you couldn't help me. And you used the word relationship. Relationship…" he repeats. "Is there something I should know young man?"

Logan sits staring at Ricardo. His eyes begin darting and his leg jostles up and down creating a steady beat against the hardwood floors. He looks up and parts his lips as if to speak but loses momentum as his hands graze his scalp and he stands and walks toward his bookshelf.

"Young man?"

"I really don't know where she is sir."

"I believed you when you said that before, but I still believe that there is information you are not sharing with me that may help me to understand why she might've gone," Ricardo utters more aggressively.

"Sir..."

"Logan," Ricardo interrupts sternly, standing as he does.

"She and I may have had words," Logan begins warily.

"You *may* have?"

"We had words and I said some things that she didn't agree with. But in my defense," he stammers, "she was intoxicated and belligerent and I didn't know what else there was to do," he groans wearily.

"Now it is my turn not to understand. Please explain it all to me."

Logan recounts the girls' night and his caretaker role afterward before describing in modest detail his and Noe's conversation at Hayley and Conner's engagement party and his memorandum he'd left with Julia. Ricardo interjects often, asking for details and clarification, making his way closer to Logan each time.

"I apologize if I've caused this. But I...I don't...I can't..." he stutters, changing clauses in search of the best one.

"Do you have feelings for my daughter?"

"What?" Logan exclaims briskly crossing his office past Ricardo, toward his desk.

"I am not sure that the behavior you have described to me is necessarily appropriate within the context of a professional relationship like the one you and my daughter had."

"With all due respect sir, I don't think that you are in any place to analyze my behavior," he says standing in the corner behind his workspace.

"I do not have the education to analyze as a counselor or as a psychologist like you do, but I can speak on the grounds of being a father and at the very least a gentleman who's found love," Ricardo orates evenly, slowly encroaching upon Logan.

"Mr. Cortes," Logan begins with trepidation. "I don't know what to say. I…it's just that. The things you are saying. They can't be. They're not…It's not." He struggles to complete his sentences.

"No worry," he relents. "You have a good heart young man, and I appreciate all that you have done with and for my daughter," he speaks turning toward the door.

He stops with a hand on the knob, "there are things you must come to for yourself. I am not one for popular culture, but my daughter she has me watch those romance films she enjoys. In one a young boy faces his internal bouts with love. Maybe you're familiar with it?"

Logan shakes his head in dissent.

"The young man he says, 'love is about finding courage inside of you that you didn't even know was there.' He's a smart kid that one. Thank you for your time."

Ricardo exits quietly thanking Julia as he departs. Behind closed doors, Logan slinks to the ground in his office reminding himself to breathe and replays Ricardo's intuitive comments and the unclaimed ardor growing inside.

***

"What are you doing with your life?" I ask myself aloud.

"How's that?" Diane asks. I hadn't noticed her presence in the room with me.

"Oh nothing," I sigh and take another spoonful of cereal, cowering over my bowl.

"So, tell me again how you found your way here."

This really won't be *again* because in all the times the Kellogs have asked, I've never once given them a straight answer to this question.

"Have you ever needed to just get away? You know, clear your head a bit?"

"Well...no," Diane looks at me quizzically, her mind clearly churning in hopes to find a similar sentiment.

"Oh."

We return to our peaceful silence and I finish my breakfast while Diane puts away the dishes that are left in the dishwasher.

"What's the schedule like today?" I ask.

"We're actually on a break for the next week and a half."

"Bummer." I've actually been enjoying the classes I've taught. The kids really love it and they remind me of how simple life should be and it's refreshing.

"Oh, you'll need the rest. I promise. I'm surprised you haven't burned out yet."

"I don't mind it at all. I love it actually. Back home, I sometimes teach classes at my mom's dance studio," I smile longingly. "I don't know what I'm going to do with my time now."

"You should just relax a bit. Mr. Kellog and I will be leaving this afternoon actually to take a mini vacation of our own. Pierre's sister has a timeshare out in Arkansas."

"Are you sure you don't need me to vacate while you're out?" I ask walking to the sink to clean my breakfast dishes, catching her before she exits.

"No. Don't even think of it. You will house sit," she says resolutely. "It will be your way to pay your room and board while we don't have campers," she laughs and offers me a wink.

"Right," I say attempting to chuckle.

"Really dear," she walks back toward me and lays a hand on my shoulder. "I'm not exactly sure why you landed here...heck based on your explanations, I'm not even sure you know either. Take some time to yourself. It'll do you good."

"Yeah," I add solemnly almost as an afterthought as Diane disappears leaving me in repose.

***

"I had an appointment today?"

"Where?"

"I went to see Logan Hale."

"Noe's Psychologist, Dr. Hale?"

"Yes."

"Why?"

"What do you mean, why?"

"I didn't even think Noe was still going to see him."

"Well she isn't," he leans over, turns on his bedside lamp and sits up in their bed.

"What is it Ricardo?" she asks worriedly.

"How have you not noticed...we've failed her," Ricardo's brow furrows and his eyes fill with sadness.

"Why must we have failed her?" she slides up to his level. "She's 28 years old. She's an adult and doing for herself. Besides, Noe is strong. She will pull through. She just needs time."

"She may be an adult but she's still our little girl," he says wiping his face in desperation. "And Caroline, she's not you," his tone strengthens as he turns to face her, worry written about him.

"I know she's not me," she begins, shaking from his tormented gaze, "but what else are we supposed to do? She's not here. She left of her own freewill and chose not to speak with either of us."

"How can you be so nonchalant about all of this?"

"I'm not nonchalant. You see her as your little girl and the two of you have this secret language you share. I respect that, but you know the two of us have a different type of relationship," she peers up at him wistfully. "As much as she mirrors your mannerisms, very much of my thought processes live within her. And I know that I sometimes need a little me time to allow greater sense to prevail."

"I suppose you are right. There is one other thing…"

"Yes…"

"Logan, he…"

"What?"

"There is something…"

"What?!"

"There is just…"

"Ricardo Cristobal Cortes-Andrada…. *finish* your sentence," she says quickly sitting up next to her husband.

"I don't know exactly what it is."

"Just tell me what you think. Speak your thoughts and I'll make sense of it."

"I think there is something or there was something between him and Noe."

"What did he say?"

"He didn't say much of anything and that is how I know."

"I don't understand. It sounds like you're speculating, and that's a pretty bold assumption to make."

"No, no. This is something I just know. His face lit up when I mentioned Noe and then something changed in him and he quickly closed up."

"Are you sure his behavior couldn't have been because he encountered a bad memory? She's never spoken of him. Not just not in a romantic way, but not in a professional manner either."

"I know what I know to be true."

"What did you say to him?"

"I didn't tell him anything too direct. I encouraged him to be courageous."

"What if that's not it at all? Or what if it is and he's not willing to *be courageous*? Then what? What are we going to do Ricardo?"

"Yo no sé, mi amor. I just don't know," he says laying back down slumping into bed.

"She will be well," she says leaning over him to turn out his light and lightly kiss before nuzzling against him. "I'm sure of it. She is strong."

***

> Meet me at Pierce Park by the barbecue pavilion at 2:00P
>
> 9:37 a.m., 19 Oct

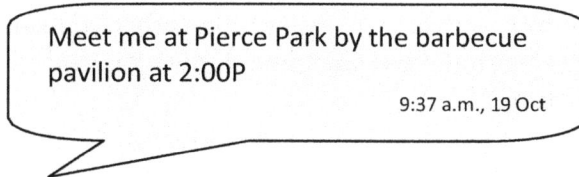

"Do you know why we're here? What did his text say again?"

"Hayley, it doesn't say anything," Harper responds frustration growing. "It just says be here. I don't know why he wants to meet me. But you're here so you can make sure things go as they should.

"Do you think he knows anything about MC?"

"Hayley I don't really want to tell you to shut the fuck up because I know foul language hurts your feelings, but if you don't shut the hell up, fuck will be closer than you think."

"Good afternoon," he says interrupting them.

"Hi. I brought Hayley with me this time. I figured it'd be safer this way."

"I don't know what you mean by safer, but I suppose this works better anyway. Hello Hayley."

"Hi," she responds nervously.

"Would you like to tell us why you've cryptically asked us to come here?" Harper asks.

"I'm prepared to explain. Could we have a seat?"

They make their way toward a set of benches beneath a covered pavilion. He fidgets, alternating between the hem of his shirt, his collar, and a small blade of grass he grabs when he takes a seat. Harper sits unfazed to his right and a wide-eyed Hayley flanks him on the left.

"The last time the two of us spoke Harper," he begins

uneasily, "you said some things."

"Yes," she responds expectantly.

"Hayley are you aware of this conversation?" he asks.

"I know the important parts, and I know what came of it," Hayley replies.

"Of course you do," he mumbles. "Well today all I wanted was to say that there were things that you said that were right and then there were some things you said that were definitely wrong."

"Okay," Harper says questioningly. "I'm supposed to care about this why?"

"Do you know where Noe is?" he asks with more confidence.

"No."

"Do you Hayley?"

She shakes her head no.

"Do you know anyone who knows where she is?" he asks addressing both Hayley and Harper.

"Can't say that we do," Harper answers sarcastically.

"And you don't find this problematic?"

"No. She's a grown ass woman. She can go wherever she damn well pleases."

"Dr. Logan-er...Hale..." Hayley begins.

"Call me Logan."

"Logan," she restarts, "do you know where she is? Harper has a funny way of displaying her worry."

"I don't know where she is, but I know that part of why she might have disappeared is because of me. And part of why I responded the way I did is directly because of you."

"Me? Again with being a grown ass..."

"Harper, please cooperate," Hayley chastises.

"Logan, I apologize for my apparent nonchalance, but I just don't see what the big deal is. When we met up last time I was doing what I considered my best friendly duty and letting you know that her feelings for you were unhealthy and that your actions were inadvertently encouraging her," she utters judiciously. "I don't see the problem. If she chose to be offended, that's her issue. I can't fix that."

"Do either of you know what happened at the engagement party?"

"No," Harper and Hayley answer in unison.

"Well things got heated and we both said a number of things. I left in haste. She came to my office last week and I just couldn't. I made her an appointment with my associate in hopes to better meet her needs and that was the last I have heard of her."

"What's with all the vague story telling? What did you say? What does any of this have to do with our previous conversation? Why do you have me here?" Harper spews.

"Logan?" Hayley counters noticing his hesitation.

"It's just that…" he tries.

"Just say it, will you. I guarantee you it won't be a surprise, and if I am going to judge you, I will tell you outright. No guessing," Harper urges.

"Yes Logan, please don't be frightened to say what you are thinking. You're obviously worried about MC and so are we. If you have an idea of where she might be that would be great," Hayley adds sweetly.

"I don't know why this is so hard for me," he mutters, wiping his face with his hands. "I don't know where Noe is," he booms abruptly.

"So let's hang this shit up and go find someone who does."

"Harper, shh. There's more."

"So I don't know where she is, but I just feel like I have to come clean and you two make most sense."

They all look at each other. Hayley filled with hopeful optimism, Harper's face marred with a scowl and Logan's worry and apparent anxiety spreading throughout his entire body.

"That night at the engagement party…wait, before

401

that. The night you all were at the club and I took Noe home. She told me she…"

"Loved you? Just say it. I told you. I knew it already. Shit, you already knew it. You know why? I already told you," Harper yells.

"Harper, can you do me a favor? As ironic as it may seem I'm not too keen on being vulnerable and the words that are slowly making their way out of my mouth aren't exactly things I've readily embraced."

He waits in anticipation of a retort, but Harper just sits, eyes wide.

"Can you just give me a small break and listen? Let me get it out in my own time."

"Sure," she says pointedly.

"Thank you. Like I was saying, that night she was out of it and through her delirium she would wake and say random things."

"Things like what?" Hayley asks.

"The three S's and D – M – V…disapproving matriarchal virulence."

"That sounds like her," Hayley adds.

"She also told me that she loved me, but she wasn't in her right mind. I laughed a bit at her temporary dementia, but I honestly thought nothing of it."

"So, moving forward to the engagement party…" Harper attempts to advance the conversation.

"Right, the engagement party," he readjusts himself in preparation for the close of his story.

"Earlier that week she and I ran into each other at the cinema."

"Purely coincidental?" Harper asks dubiously.

"Yes. It wasn't planned," he responds forcefully.

"The only things Noe watches alone are those ridiculous romance movies. So you're telling me that you voluntarily paid to see a chick flick without a chick?"

"Why does that seem odd?"

"I think it's lovely," Hayley says smiling.

"You would," Harper addresses Hayley. "I want to believe you Logan, but it just seems too happenstance for me."

"I am telling the truth. Those movies calm me oddly enough. They're very light and don't require much thought."

"You can say that again," Harper guffaws.

"If it makes you feel any better, she was just as surprised as you are. She could barely function when she noticed my presence. But since we were there afterward, we went to lunch together."

"Wait. Did you ask her to lunch or did she ask you?"

"Why does it matter?"

"Oh it matters," Hayley adds, voice rich with concern.

"I think I asked her."

"Um-hmm," Harper gnarls.

"We had lunch and then we parted ways. Hayley's engagement party I think was the next day. I didn't know what was going on when she called me. I was so worried that she was out and alone, like maybe you'd left her again."

"You were worried?" Harper poses.

"Naturally. So I went down there to see for myself."

"Even when she told you where she was you felt compelled to come to MC's aid.... again. Wake up!"

Ignoring Harper's comment, he continues, "I get there and she's a mess and, on the floor, and she's talking out of her head again. She tells me that she loves me. She says it seemingly soberly, and even when I tell her she's misappropriated her feelings she just said it more."

"Why are you surprised?" Harper interrupts.

"I told her no. I told her it was inappropriate. And I just remember thinking about the conversation, the warning that you gave me Harper, and I had to get out of there."

"Did you tell her what I said?"

"No. I may have mentioned that I should've listened to someone, but I don't know. I was so confused."

"What happened next?" Hayley asks anxiously.

"Well...nothing. I was you know...and then I didn't

know what to say or what to think. I figured I needed to plan ahead so I wrote her a letter and I transferred her care to my associate."

"Logan, can I please speak?" Harper begins calmly.

"I'm not sure I'm prepared to listen."

"Hear her out. Sometimes she makes sense," Hayley proffers.

He nods offering permission.

"First, that was a jackass move leaving a fucking note. Second, and I'm being super serious right now...how can you *not* see how much you also care for MC? It may have taken her getting drunk to help her see, because she too was in denial, but at least she said something. You're walking around here lying to yourself and what sucks is that you look like shit running from what makes sense."

"See what I mean," Hayley beams. "I agree with her assessment. It's obvious that you don't just see her as a client of yours. There's more."

"I know," he says, voice heavy and low.

"You know?" Harper instigates.

"I do."

"You do what?" Hayley joins.

"I love her," he mumbles.

"You what? Your leg hurts?" Harper mocks.

"You're Ben-Hur?" Hayley adds jovially.

"I love her!" he shouts.

"Shit yeah," Harper responds tossing her hands into the air.

"But I've...I don't know what to do with that. I'm not supposed to love her or even like her but everything about her is endearing and loveable. She challenges me and when she's not in her manic states she demolishes my protective coat of armor and I feel free," he pauses wistfully.

"Why didn't you say any of that to her?" Hayley asks.

"I couldn't. She was drunk. We were out in public. I didn't..."

"He's a guy Hay. They're the lesser form of our

404

species because they're slow to do everything."

"I don't know what to do now though. She's gone and even if I knew where I doubt, I'd be her favorite person." He hangs his head and rubs his thighs drying his now sweaty palms.

"What did the letter say?" Harper asks.

"Huh?"

"The letter you said you left at your office," Hayley fills in.

"I shouldn't say," he mumbles embarrassingly.

"We already know your shit stinks so just come clean already," Harper encourages.

"It said, 'Due to present circumstances it has been brought to my attention that you may be better suited for a different counselor. I am entrusting the rest of your care to my colleague, Dr. Piper. This is for the best.'"

"Is that it?" Harper screeches.

"Yeah," he responds hesitantly.

"Oh no," Hayley says.

"You fucker," Harper starts. "Are you stupid? Who leaves a note like that?"

"Why so cold Logan?" Hayley asks.

"Look, I don't know. It made sense at the time. I panicked. I...it happened. Can I fix it?"

"Assuming we find her first?" Harper asks.

"Obviously. Are you always this...this...."

"Congenial?" Harper offers.

"Yes. You get used to it," Hayley adds.

"This is something that should probably get addressed. I know a good therapist."

"I don't know how I feel about that. If he's anything like you it could be a problem," she laughs. "Seriously. I'm being serious right now...."

"Thank you," he says.

"I don't think all is lost. We've just got to get her back here; then you've got to lose your pride and your ego and go whole hog. She likes all that romantic comedy shit, so you'll probably have to pull some of that out of your ass too to woo her back."

"Just be confident and be honest and there's no way she can resist," Hayley adds.

"Play your cards right because you're the first guy that makes sense for her and I might just like you Hale."

"Thank you?"

"You're welcome."

***

In my three weeks away I've had time to figure some things out. I've had time to dance with students who are full of innocence, life, and untapped potential. It's been life changing. They show me what's important. They breathe into me in a way that nothing before them had. In my down time I write, and I scour the local bookstore filling my head with new stories.

Doing so much I absolutely love helps me see a couple of wrongs in my life. I hate my job. I never said it before because it never made sense and I knew that everyone desperately wanted me to reach normalcy and I think I wanted that for me too. I don't want to get my PhD, or at least not the PhD that I'm presently working on. I want to have a life that embraces my eccentricities and lets me share myself and my talents.

I am my own meaning maker, and it's time I start actualizing.

October 19, 2010

Diane & Pierre,

Thank you so very much for opening your home to me, taking a chance on a stranger, and allowing me to find myself.

I never thought the best kind of therapy I could find was honestly just taking some time to engage in the things that make me most happy and to take some much needed me-time.

You two have both been a blessing to me, and I hope that I have been able to help you as well. I must return to my life now. I need to hopefully right some wrongs and get on a track that makes sense for me.

I know that I've never really shared how I managed on your property, and Diane, the truth is as you said, I honestly don't know. I just drove and here is where I landed.

I truly appreciate you both.

Noe

Also...I left some goodies for you in the refrigerator. I hope Arkansas was as restful as you'd hoped. Best wishes for the rest of your fall camps.

Chapter 29

"Good morning Joyce!"

"MC? Is that you?"

"In the flesh," I say, channeling Harper and showcasing myself like Vanna White.

She jumps from behind her desk and rushes toward me. She envelopes me in the biggest bear hug I've probably ever experienced, and I feel the wet from tears that have suddenly sprung to her eyes.

"I didn't know what to think," she squeaks.

"Don't cry Joyce. I told you I was going to come back," I say working to free one of my arms and pat her back.

"I know that's what you said but it was all so abrupt. And everyone was just so worried, and I didn't know what to say to them."

"I'm sorry it had to be that way."

"Don't ever leave me again."

"I really am sorry Joyce. I know that doesn't fix anything, but I don't know what else to say. Please stop crying," I implore her, attempting to lift her head from my neck.

"Let me just get it all out," she retorts, squeezing me tighter.

After near 15 minutes of intense hugging, she frees me and heads to the bathroom. I brought breakfast because I knew she was going to have this sort of reaction, so while she's out I set up a little morning picnic for the two of us.

"Joyce, I have a surprise for you," I say as she returns. "Actually, I have two. Come see one of them."

"Oh MC, you're never going to believe this, I've been practicing my Spanish."

"Well where is it? Why aren't I hearing it? Por qué no me escucha?"

"Lo siento," she begins enunciating each and every syllable. "Yo tengo un perro. Es un Labrador."

"Que bueno. When did you get it? Cuándo adquirió el perro?"

"Ad- key…"

"Ad-key-ree-oh. It means acquire."

"Like get. Ad-key…" she starts mouthing the rest. "Right. It sounds like it too."

"Pues, dime. Tell me. Cuándo?"

"En la semana pasada. Mi amiga, Jenny…" she fumbles trying to remember words she wants to use. "I don't know how to say it," she sighs. "Last week, my girlfriend Jenny's dog had puppies and she couldn't keep them all. It was either I take one or the puppy was going to the shelter. I couldn't bear it."

"Pobre perro, pero estoy felíz que él tiene una casa buena. I'm glad he has a home with you," I echo. "Cúal es el nombre del perro?"

"El nombre," she repeats whispering a bit searching her memory banks for its meaning. "That's name right?" She asks excitedly.

"Yes ma'am. Cúal es, what is, el nombre del perro?" I ask repeating my question.

"His name is," she begins, "Oh, right, se llama Felipe."

"Felipe, qué bueno. Your Spanish is really coming along." I pause just shy of the break room.

"What's wrong?" she asks nervously.

"Nothing. I just hope you're surprised," I respond mock pleasantly.

"Well, why are we waiting?" Joyce asks exigently, as we approach the threshold of the break room.

"Have a look," I say.

She peaks around the corner and her eyes widen before threatening to release a flood of tears once more. "It looks lovely!" she coos.

"I'm glad you think so. Go on…sit down."

We feast on breakfast tacos, fruit pastries, muffins, assorted fruit, sausage, bacon, and orange juice. She gives me updates about her daughters, Morgan, and Heather. Morgan's boys, Kenneth and Edison just started fourth grade and are struggling to understand fractions. Elise, Morgana and Julianne, Heather's girls are on the dance team and are making their recital circuit soon. She lets me know that during my absence absolutely nothing occurred, and she reminded me of Matias' forwarding address.

"Joyce," I start uneasily during a lull in our conversation.

"Yes ma'am," she responds jovially.

"I have a second surprise for you."

"So far I am loving your surprises. What's this one?"

"I don't know if you're going to be as pleased by this one."

"Why? What's wrong? Are your parents okay? Your brothers?"

"Calm down Joyce. It's nothing bad like that. Everyone I know is okay…well they were okay as of a few weeks ago. I doubt things have turned upside down since then."

"I'm glad to hear that," she sighs with relief. "Then what's the problem?"

"This is really hard for me to say, but you're like a mom to me, so I want to tell you what's going on with me," I say taking a moment for a couple deep breaths.

"While I was gone, I had a lot of time to think and make sense of some confusion I had in life. I realized that even though it was an accident, I needed to take that break."

"I'm not sure I follow."

"Joyce, have there ever been times when you thought I just didn't make sense in this job?"

"Well yeah, but that's just you, you're quirky. It's, it's endearing. You and the job don't have to make sense because you do it well."

"That's just the point. It should make sense," I say.

She blinks in anticipation of what I have to follow. Her face, once full of worry at the start of my story, softens as I fidget and prepare to bestow my surprise upon for her.

"I really hate my work Joyce," I let out a sigh of release. "I think because I wanted to try to be normal for a bit, I became blind to my unhappiness until Matias. We probably shouldn't have, but we began a relationship."

"That's not news honey. You two are as discreet as a dog in heat. And the sexual tension between the two of you…you could cut it with a butter knife."

"Joyce!" I call out taken aback by her straightforwardness.

"I will refrain, but I'm happy to have my assumptions verified."

"Matias for a time was good for me. He was so worldly and experienced, and it encouraged me. It was exciting even though it was never going to work."

"Never?"

"Believe me, there is someone much better suited for him. A person who wants his guidance and love and his perspicacity and…"

"But you two were so perfect together," Joyce interrupts confused and hurt.

"For a time, I guess. Honestly, Matias did not challenge me to figure things out or do for myself. With him I was morphing into someone that lived to love him instead of living for myself. Does that make more sense?"

"Somewhat," she responds questioningly.

"He's like the professor that you have a crush on. You think the conversations you have after class about Kafka show how much you have in common," I say looking wistfully out.

"You start dressing in a way that you think mirrors his wardrobe, and you take everything he says as golden and law, all the while missing out on experiences you could have to catch up to his level of intelligence. And you miss out on you or someone that wouldn't need you – not that Kafka professor asked this of you, to become this other person that you're inadvertently becoming," I finish turning back to Joyce. "Does that help?"

"Yes. I think I understand, but I thought he was good for you."

"He was, but *I* want to be good for me and get to a point where I can be good for someone else too."

"So what does this all mean then?"

"Joyce, I'm resigning from my post here."

"What?" she asks in disbelief.

"I had a meeting earlier this morning with our Dean and I let him know, effective immediately I will no longer serve as Assistant Dean of Students."

"You're...leaving? All because of Matias?" Her words get stuck in her throat and she grabs the sides of her chair beneath her.

"No, not because of Matias. The end of our relationship did stir some things up, but I'm leaving because of me," I say scooting my chair and closing the gap between Joyce and me. "It's what's best for me."

She examines my face, searching for traces of uncertainty.

"It's okay Joyce. This is good," I add encouragingly.

"As much as it tears my heart up to see you go, I know you're doing the right thing," she answers shaking free from her initial shock and disbelief.

I lunge from my chair and hug her tight around her neck as tears flood my eyes.

"Thank you. Thank you for understanding. Thank you for not making me feel guilty and thank you for your blessing."

"My sweet Noe," she rubs my back as I start heaving with growing relief. "You don't need my understanding, any guilt or my blessing. You're more than this. You're more than the stars and the moon combined, and I've been waiting for the day when you realized it. I just didn't think it would be today."

"I love you Joyce," I whisper.

"I love you too."

***

It's Wednesday and a past Noe would be preparing for her weekly session with Dr. Logan. Instead I'm mentally preparing to forego my session and leave him a note. Joyce and I cried together much of the morning. And when we took a break from crying, we began sharing 'remember when' stories and reliving our years together which initiated more crying.

    Our tears and stories were so long-winded that I didn't manage to properly collect myself for the drive to Piper & Hale. In the car the radio is silenced in effort to convene my thoughts and courage to do what I've prepared to do. Last night I sat down and crafted a message to Dr. Logan. I don't know what prompted the letter-writing, but I went with it.

October 20, 2010

Dr. Logan,

    Please do me a solid and read this in its entirety. I know you've probably had enough of me and my idiosyncrasies, but this is my last attempt to communicate with you. I promise. I leave this memo for you with a heavy heart but a positive spirit. I don't want to cause you any more turmoil so I decided this would be the best way to let you know where I am. I want to sincerely apologize for taking advantage of the kindness you've always shown me. I want to also apologize for overstepping my bounds as a client of yours. You must know it was never my intent to behave inappropriately or make you feel uncomfortable.

    I wish so badly that I hadn't misbehaved to the point where you didn't even think you could face me and tell me that you thought it better for me to continue my treatment with Dr. Piper. She's different by the way. I don't know if our types of different mesh well.

In the name of honesty and forthrightness I want you to know that I appreciate all you've done for me and whether or not you realize it I always listen and I really think I've grown. Seriously, your voice is constantly in my head seeming so real. That fact makes it hard to tell you that I'm planning on transferring to another counseling center. This way you don't have to avoid me, and I can start over somewhere with no history — probably with a woman so I don't run the risk of repeating this experience.

While I'm sorry that my actions brought about the demise of our much appreciated and very necessary relationship, I am not apologetic regarding the sentiments I expressed to you. I'm learning to be more honest with my thoughts, wants, needs, and desires and oddly enough I think that night of drunkenness started it all. I'll say regardless of this outcome I wouldn't take back anything I said. I meant it — pauses, punctuation, and all.

Read the extra pages I've attached. I think you'll appreciate them...maybe. I couldn't leave forever without turning in my homework.

For the love of all things sweet.... Be well.

Noe Cortes

"Good afternoon Julia," I say mock jovially.

"Hi," she responds, her voice full of uneasy surprise.

"Don't be nervous. I'm not here to cause a scene." I watch as her face relaxes. "I actually wanted to cancel my appointments from here on, and I'd be most appreciative if you could deliver this," I say handing her the printed envelope, "...to Dr. Logan."

Her face contorts with confusion as she hesitantly takes the letter I'm holding out for her. "Thank you," I add as

I slowly back away and wave before exiting.

***

"Hi," Harper says with intrigue not yet taking her seat.
"Hi," I repeat.
"Well hey!" Hayley bellows making her way to the setting, following suit, and remaining upright.
"Well…. hey," I echo looking from Harper to Hayley in confusion. "You want to sit?" I proffer.
"You're sure we should," Harper asks dubiously. "You're not going to have us tied down to torture us, are you?"

"Such a vivid imagination Harper; you should go into creative writing," I say mockingly. "Sit down would you. I'm not going to bring either of you harm.

They warily take their seats and we order a round of waters and iced tea from our server. Harper and Hayley take turns looking at one another, telepathically imploring the other to speak.
"So what's this about?" Harper finally breaks the stillness.
"Yeah, MC this is a bit frightening," Hayley adds.
"Frightening? I'm so confused. Listen to you two. Our girl's lunches are normal. This," I make corralling motions with my hands, "is just us returning to…well…us," I finish shrugging.
"So you're not upset with us?" Harper asks incredulously.
"Well I'm not jumping for joy about these last couple of weeks, but we're good."
"I'll take it," Harper says succinctly.
"Me too," Hayley adds smiling and leaning across the table to hug me.
"So…. what's up? Where have you been? What brought on this calmer version of you?" Harper interrogates.

I explain to the two of them my first uneventful meeting with Dr. Piper and of Dr. Logan's monologue behind closed doors, him justifying and reassuring himself I wasn't good for his life. I describe Diane and Pierre and my drive to the middle of nowhere. I tell them all about my returning to campus and resigning from my post…and my letter to Dr. Logan.

"You quit your job?" Harper asks affronted.

"Yes."

"And you're okay with that?" Hayley asks a follow-up.

"Very much so. It's the best decision I've ever made."

"I'm so happy for you," Hayley starts, tears glistening in her eyes.

"Wait. In addition to being jobless you also broke up with your therapist. The only person who knows how to keep you sane?" Harper interrupts, still baffled.

"I don't know if break up is what I would call it, but yes I turned the page on that chapter. Or whatever would sound more natural as a metaphor," I ramble awkwardly. "Damn it! Harper," I say springing back from her disturbing blow across the left side of my face. "What the hell?"

"Just making sure you're real."

"Next time can you ask me my birthday or something else equally less painful?" I ask massaging my face.

"So what's next?" Hayley asks.

"I know, but I don't exactly know."

"Explanation…" Harper asks.

"Well, I know that I want to explore some avenues that bring me happiness, but I don't know exactly where to start. It's all very liberating but frightening at the same time."

"I think that's so exciting that you're throwing caution to the wind MC," Hayley says supportively.

"I want to join with Hayley, but I think you may have made some hasty decisions."

"Harper, don't be a negative Nellie," Hayley chides.

"This is good for her."

"Hayley and Harper, I appreciate both of your forms of support. Harper, I know it's scary for you to make sense of in this nebulousness," I start outlining clouds above my head. "But you've got to believe that this is right, and this is going to work," I plead laying my hand on hers.

"Bullshit. I'm not scared. You're talking crazy," she says, eyes searing into me. "There is no this. You need to figure out the this. Then I'll think about taking you seriously."

"Fair enough. I'm a work in progress."

"Ever the unfinished masterpiece," Harper murmurs.

"How's that?" I ask.

"Harper, why don't you…" Hayley begins winking not very subtly.

"Why doesn't she what?" I ask in confusion.

"I have something for you," Harper calls.

"A gift?" I inquire, sitting up radically straighter, instantly shaking my confusion for excitement.

"It's not from me."

"I don't get it," I slump deflated.

"It's from someone else. Someone you know," Hayley attempts to clarify. "Don't try to guess; just open it."

"Do you know what it says?" I ask taking the letter from Harper.

"I am quite an investigator, but I don't read other people's mail," Harper responds offended.

"Besides, we were under strict instructions not to do so," Hayley adds smiling.

"Thanks for your honesty Hayley."

I take the letter and examine it. It's a plain white envelope. The only visible markings are the letters that make up my name, printed in the center. In all capital letters I can instantly tell who the memo is from.

"Well…. open it already!" Harper urges.

I look up at both Harper and Hayley, still fingering its seal. I'm nervous and feel my heart rate increase steadily.

"Do you want us to leave?" Hayley inquires.

"No," I attempt a light laugh. "I don't know why it's taking me so long to just…do it."

"Breathe Noe," Harper says.

"Yeah, just breathe," Hayley adds.

I do as I'm told and open the letter. It's a plain sheet of yellow legal paper. Three lines from the top in black ink I find four short words, a period, and a question mark.

FORGIVE ME. MEET ME?

I fold the paper back in threes and return it to its envelope before placing it in my bag.

Though they beg and plead I refuse to let Harper and Hayley know what my letter says. As curious as they are and relentless as they could be, they both leave it. I don't ask Harper how she managed to get hold of the letter and I do my best to put the four words out of my consciousness as we continue our lunch as though no time had passed.

Sebastian and Harper are still going strong. She has met his family and vice versa and she asks if it'll be alright for him to join us for my yet to be planned birthday celebration. I am overrun with excitement for her and of course oblige with the birthday request. Likewise, Connor is continuing to be just as wonderful of a fiancée as he was a boyfriend. We end our time together settling on Houlihan's for my birthday dinner – quiet, cool, and sophisticated, and go our separate ways.

***

"It's so nice to have our whole family here."

"Mom!" Jackson, JJ, and I all sing together. She's uncharacteristically emotional and none of us know how to react.

"Leave your mother alone," Papí says lovingly, wrapping his arms around her and pulling her close.

"She's crying dad!" JJ says in protest, pointing at her newly saturated face.

"You try going for such a long time without having your children all with you and you see if you don't cry," she squeaks.

"Mom, don't be so dramatic," JJ starts.

"Yeah, Mamí you make it sound like we don't live in the same state and like one of us went to war or something," Jackson says laughing.

"You laugh Jackson Antonio, but Noe just came back so it might as well be true. And before she'd gone that's what it felt like each week when I had to beg her to come over for dinner," she says pointing in my direction, "and these days you're either out with Kennedy or she's here."

"Ha ha, she hates her," JJ giggles.

"I don't hate her; it's just sometimes I want my own children here. It's selfish really, but I want you and only you," she closes turning into my father's chest and sobbing even more.

"We got it mama. We're sorry, but we're here now so let's enjoy it," I jump in not sure whether I'm rescuing my mother, my brothers or myself from what would happen if the conversation continued.

Papí ushers mama to the bathroom so she can get cleaned up. JJ, Jackson, and I get started in the kitchen. For dinner tonight we're having a little bit of all of our favorites. Pot roast for Papí, steamed broccoli for JJ, roasted new potatoes for Jackson, macaroni and cheese for me, and for dessert turtle cheesecake brownies for mama. Mama returns and takes command of her troupes and we pour, stir, wait, and taste until the meal is complete and the table is set.

We all have a seat with wide eyes and eager bellies, ready to feast.

"Jamal Joaquin are you going to bless the food?"

mama asks.

"Mah!" JJ calls in protest.

"I will do it," my father bellows laying out each of his palms, inspiring the rest of us to join hands, bow our heads and close our eyes.

"Gracious Lord we come to you this day giving thanks. We give thanks for this meal and for the love that we have around this table. Please offer your grace to each and every person seated here today," he says giving my hand a special squeeze, "in whatever way they need it most. And finally, bless the food we've prepared together for the nourishment of our bodies. In your most precious son's name we pray..."

"Amen," we all ring in unison.

We drop hands and our dinner commences. We gently pass dishes from left to right, and we fill the space with idle chatter. JJ talks about his soccer playoffs and that there will be scouts from college and summer programs all over. Jackson of course has wedding talk and he discusses the trials and tribulations his fair Kennedy is experiencing. Mama reminds us of the fall recital fast approaching, right after Thanksgiving. She eyes me throughout waiting for me to volunteer to work with her once more. Eventually we get to Papí and he's uncharacteristically excited telling us about a new client he has at work – a partner with Random House. He tells us how he and Yanis Laurent, a new Vice President on the Acquisitions side of the South African office have a play date to discuss some new manuscripts.

"Ricardo, I thought you were hired to handle his money," mama says gingerly.

"That's really nice Papí," I say delighted for him being able to do something that excites him.

"Gracias mi amorcita. Now it is your turn," he says to me.

"Well, I actually have some really exciting news for all of you," I begin tentatively. I look at everyone, nervous to continue.

"Well? Out with it!" mama bellows impatiently.

"Yeah, get a move on," Jackson cosigns.

"Take your time," Papí adds calmly.

I offer him a gratuitous glance before I continue. "I quit my job," I say with jazz hands.

For a time no one says anything. Everyone stares at me waiting for me to carry on.

"Is that all you're going to share with us Noe Marie," mama asks, her ire flaring.

Breathe, Noe. Just breathe. I think to myself. With renewed calm I tell mama, Papí, Jackson and JJ of my impromptu sabbatical and my resolution. I tell them in detail how I resigned from my post at work, walked away from the dissertation I was supposed to have finished, and was blissfully happy with what would become my life of travel, dance and writing, either as a Fulbright scholar or just a wayward traveler with a set of skills.

No one speaks really. They just sit and stare at me with eyes that look a mixture of grief- stricken, confused, secretly excited and house a general fondness. Mama is the first to break the silence as she calmly pushes herself from the table, walks her dishes to the sink and leaves the room.

I quickly follow and leave the Cortes men to discuss among themselves.

"Mama," I call to her.

"How could you Noe?"

"How could I what mom?"

"How could you abandon everything you have? Everything that makes sense? And for what? Frivolous, irresponsible, childlike fantasies with no returns," she says calmly, eyes never turning away from me.

"Why do you think that way?"

"I think because I know. You are ruining your life with an impetuous decision like this."

"How can you be such a hypocrite?" I ask bitingly.

"You do not speak to your mother that way," she snaps.

"Why is every decision I ever make always the wrong

decision? You did the same things and look where you are now," I wave my hands around all we have. "Do you mean to tell me that your studio, Papí, me, Jackson and JJ are no returns?"

"You will respect me in my house," she adds.

"I do respect you. I love you and I want to please you so badly, but I can't do it the way you want me to. I hate that you have no faith in me, and you think..." I pause. "You know, I don't know what you think," I breathe out exasperated and sink into a nearby chair.

"I have faith in you," she whispers coming closer to me and dropping to my feet. "And I do consider you and all the many blessings that I have as great returns. I did not mean to imply otherwise. It's just that," her voice catches, and she grabs hold of one of my hands. "I don't want you to struggle the way that I had to. You have great talents, more than me, and I just don't want to you to miss out on laying a more supportive foundation than I ever had."

"Mama," you had an accident, that's the only reason you had to struggle," I say sliding out of my chair to the floor with her.

"But I wouldn't have fallen so hard if I had nurtured other skills in preparation for the 'what if' that unfortunately came to be."

"Mama...I love you so much and I'm grateful every day that you not only nurtured my creative side, but you encouraged me to do well in everything else. You're so strong mama and self-sufficient..."

"My darling," she interrupts.

"No mama let me finish. I know it's hard to see me want to follow in your footsteps, but please know that you, and Papí," I add endearingly, "created a very capable young woman and more importantly your footsteps created a path of success that I can't wait to follow."

She and I take turns crying and consoling one another

until we reach the end of our individual troughs of tears. We silently rise and wander to the downstairs bathroom where we clean our faces and brush our hair. We giggle at the sight of ourselves all red-eyed and puffy in the mirror and we engage in a loving embrace.

After they've cleared the dishes and put away the leftovers, Papí, JJ and Jackson come to find us as we exit the bathroom. Papí kisses each of us on the forehead and Jackson and JJ let us know that dessert is waiting.

We all return to the kitchen to brownie slices on small saucers adorned with glasses of milk. Our conversation picks up where it left off, everyone welcoming my tentative plans for my future.

From the Desk of _____Noe Cortes_____

October 24, 2010

I'm back today re-purposing this journal of mine. I came clean with my family today. The last people that needed to know that I am a new me and the new me is absolutely amazing and ready to be happy, in whatever way that means. Mama took it surprisingly well. Okay, after her initial shock and anger she got it. Well...I think she gets it.

I think our talk will hopefully mean that our relationship will be different and better. All this time while I was growing up, she saw herself in me, and she didn't want me to go through any bad times like she did. She was attempting to protect me all the years telling me to avoid dance and go for something that "made sense". Now it all makes sense and I love her for her concern, and I love her even more for understanding why I need to do what I'm doing now.

In 5 days I will have another birthday, and I think this week is setting up my 29th year in a way that I can't help but be excited for.

This is good. For old time's sake.... celebratory Dr. Pepper.... stat.

Chapter 30

Today is the first day in a very long time that I feel completely free. I'm free. I can be all that I have ever wanted to be. And the lack of concreteness that such an opportunity presents me is surprisingly not scary.

Yesterday I spent time with my father roving through his library and highlighting prime locations to contain in my destination log. At nightfall we took a walk to our secret park – a place that though in the city, is frighteningly quiet and still at night. It holds one of the only clear patches of the starry night's sky.

***

"¿Tú sabes qué?" he asked me during our walk.

"No. ¿Qué Papí?" I asked saying my part in the reprise of our recurring tête-à-tête.

"Tú eres mi orgulla y te amo con todo mi corazón."

"I love you too papí," I cooed reaching, grabbing hold of his neck, and pulling him down to kiss his cheek.

"Do you know something else?" he asked, stopping, and offhandedly taking a seat in the grass, patting the ground beside him.

"No, I don't," I responded joining him on the ground.

"I think mi amorcita that you are going to have a marvelous adventure," he said wrapping his arm around me as I leaned my head into his neck.

"You think so? I hope it's not terribly lonely," I said.

"Lonely? Never," he said voice rich with melodramatic surprise – borderline sarcasm.

"I'm not joking," I said nudging him in his stomach. "I'm going away, and I'm not scared, but I just thought…you know, I don't know. Even though before now I never had a plan like this, now that it's here I think I thought I'd have some kind of travel partner."

He turned his head and peered down at me with eyes I

couldn't decipher.

"I know it sounds silly," I added looking down and plucking a blade of grass from beneath me.

"Nothing you say is silly. It sounds like you had someone in mind maybe?"

"Daddy don't pry?" I pushed him again.

"What is this pry? I'm just asking a simple question. Are you telling me you cannot answer?" he chuckled, leaning back into me.

"How do you always know things Papí?" I asked looking up at him. "Yes, I *had* someone in mind – had being the operative word. I made some poor choices and now as much as it probably wasn't likely before, it's definitely not a possibility now."

"You've upset Harper and Hayley?" he asked surprised.

"You know just as well as I do that, I'm not referring to Harper or Hayley, and you also know that I'm too smart to walk into your trap. I won't say who. It's just as well…it probably wouldn't have worked out anyway."

"How would you know?"

"I just do," I said returning my eyes to the ground. "There are some things you just know…you know?"

"Maybe...Noe?"

"Hmm?"

"Look at me."

I readjusted and turned toward him.

"Do you remember when we watched that film together?"

"Which one?"

"The love story in New York with the young children."

"Little Manhattan?"

"Yes, that is the one. The young man in the story…"

"Gabe…" I interjected.

"Yes, Gabe. In his youth he managed to say some

very profound words; words I've found myself proffering to others in times of need."

"What do you mean? Words like which ones? I hate Rosemary Telesco," I joked.

"No, he says some eloquent words about courage. Young Gabe says, 'love is about finding courage inside of you that you didn't even know was there'."

"How do you remember that?"

"Incredible words, this young man says. How can you forget?"

"Anyway...I don't know dad. How would you say that line helps me?"

He turned away from me and lay on his back searching the sky for stars never answering my question. I eventually followed suit and joined him on the lawn, snuggling up against his protective arms. We stayed for some time, and before I went home, he kissed he me on my nose, and was the first to wish me happy birthday.

***

Today is a special day for many reasons. First, it's my 29th birthday – my golden birthday. I turn 29 on the 29th day of October. It's also a day that I wake up feeling more than prepared for the next chapter of my life's quarto.

It's mid-autumn though it's clear the weather hasn't yet caught on. Leaves of trees have turned their own hues of rouge and russet but there's a warmth to the air and a spirited calm that usually only comes with summer.

It is in such a calm that I find myself in the design district outside the LuminArte gallery sitting at a wrought iron bistro table. I'm in my low top red chuck taylor's, jean shorts and a ribbed white racer back tank. My hair is sprawled atop my head in a messy bun and I've littered my tabletop with cans of Dr. Pepper, French vanilla pirouettes, travel books of Spain and my MacBook.

"It looks like you're having a picnic for a 15-year-old boy," a southern drawl makes from behind me.

"That might be what I was going for," I say looking up from one of my books to see a man.

He looks to be about 6'1" with an athletic build. He's wearing dark jeans and a gray V- neck t-shirt that caresses each of his bicep bulges.

"It could be hazardous to your health since you're not exactly a 15-year-old boy," he says stepping out of the sunlight revealing more of his stubbly, bronzed profile.

He has caramel skin, a low-c u t brow, slight 5 o'clock shadow, and perfectly shaped eyebrows cradling the deepest gray eyes – eyes so full of history and care.

"Since when do you care about my health?" I ask unassumingly.

"I don't know what they are called, the spaces between seconds – but I think of you always in those intervals. Salvadore Plascencia said that you know."

"Look who's been reading," I say unmoved.

"I know of no greater happiness than to be with you all the time, without interruptions, without end," he adds stepping closer.

"Kafka."

"What?"

"That's Kafka."

"Right. Love is about finding courage inside of you that you didn't even know was there."

"What?" I look up sharply at his newest reference.

He starts to sway slightly from side to side and wipes his face, looking more and more uneasy and suddenly unsure.

"What I mean is..."

"You want to have a seat while you figure it out? You're making me nervous with all the sashaying," I say convinced I misheard his last quote.

"How are you so calm?" he asks quickly taking a seat

430

and wiping his furrowed brow. I slide a Dr. Pepper his way and pop open the can.

"Thank you," he sighs. "I uh, I got your letter."

Not expecting his commentary I draw away from my can and pull the pirouette I'd just tackled from my mouth.

"Yeah and I think it's good," he continues with my full attention.

"It's good?"

"I mean it's great."

"It's great?"

"I mean you wrote it," he says almost impatiently. "No, I don't mean it like that." He lays one of his surprisingly soft and sweatless hands atop mine. "What I mean is I'm really happy that you've made the decisions you've made. You're travelling?"

"That's the plan," I say holding up one of the books I'd been perusing.

"And dancing?"

"Yep."

"That'll be good."

"Great even," I add smirking.

"There was one part of the letter I didn't read though."

"Why? It only makes sense to read it. I'm pretty sure I said that. No, I'm completely sure that *that* was a directive – to read the letter in its entirety."

"Yes. It was, but I wanted to, you know, ask you the questions in person."

"You did?"

"Yeah, I mean yes. I did. I do."

"So?"

"Will you answer them for me?"

"This is grade A weird."

"Please."

I turn away from him, close my eyes and take a deep breath. Breathe. Just breathe. I think to myself.

"Alright, ask me now."

I slowly and methodically recite my answers to some pointed, soul-searching questions Dr. Logan'd asked me months ago, but before I was too preoccupied to answer them. As he asks me now, I grip my seat with unfettered vigor. I remind him that before now I didn't know exactly who I was and the parts I knew I didn't always like and that I felt like the girl I didn't like was always driving people away and messing things up so I didn't want to show her.

Reliving my writing process and the emotion of my response sends pulsations of anxiety through my veins. I find myself dancing a bit in my seat. I take time to open my eyes and look out into the distance before continuing with gusto.

I tell Dr. Logan of my fears of rejection and how the thought of not being able to completely predict an outcome I wanted was crippling before I stop to breathe, close my eyes once more and return to my list.

"The thing that scares me most about me is that I'm all I've ever needed. I've always had this dream this fantasy that there was someone somewhere out there who held the key to me or the other piece to my best friend's necklace you know?" I ask using my hands to air draw a necklace that only I can see.

"Obviously through a various bit of experiences I have found a strength that I only ever thought was with someone else. I am more than enough and am capable and it doesn't freak me out anymore to own that."

On a roll I start fidgeting, my legs quaking with fear. I continue to tell him about feeling like I should always know and that I never before did things that made my life smile. I stop my restless legs and begin rambling, answering questions he never asks, getting anxious again.

He nudges my drink toward me, and I dramatically grab a swig to help me continue slamming the can back on the table after I've received my jolt. I tell him about my lack of attending to my soul and pleasuring myself and we finally get to his last question.

"And number one…"

"What is your passion?" we say in unison.

"Love. And its many forms. I know that's my most ambiguous answer but it's real. It's honest. It's true. It's the only thing that comes so freely and I've just had to learn how to share it and figure out what to do with it," I say rising slowly from my seat.

"It's why I was scared. It's why I do any and all that I do. It's that thing that no one can explain but everybody needs and wants. That's what my whole life is about."

I find myself standing as my monologue comes to a close. I feel strange having verbalized my responses and turn to get a sense for what my male partner is feeling. With my eyes adjusting to the light I see that he looks stupefied.

"You're looking at me and you're not saying anything. You're saying nothing. I know it all sounds crazy. That's why you were supposed to *read* it."

"No, no, no, no. It's not, it doesn't sound crazy at all. I understand. I, I…Noe I… I'm so glad you're not my client anymore."

"That's an interesting segue. Wow, Dr. Logan I knew…" I begin crashing back into my seat, looking to grab a pirouette to shove in my mouth but making contact with Dr. Logan's hands instead.

"Logan. Just…. Logan," he remarks grabbing my hands tighter.

"Okay, Logan…well crap. I don't even remember what I was going to say. I've been…"

"Do you want to know the first thought I had when we first met?" Loosening his grip, he uses his hand to lift my chin, so our eyes meet.

"I hadn't, but now I'm intrigued," I say swallowing hard.

"Wow. Just wow. I could tell you were flustered but even with all that nervous energy you shone through as,

433

wow," he says speedily with an air of nostalgia. His eyes seer into me, and though I'm certain he's aware of me I am not sure that he's really seeing me.

"Logan, I don't know what you're saying."

"Your mother said you were like a precious flower lost in a desert storm. I didn't exactly understand what she meant. I knew she was a dancer, so I just figured it was her artsy way of saying you were lost or depressed or, or, or, just you know...a perfect candidate for therapy."

"My mom said what?" I ask affronted.

"But then I saw you and it all made sense. You couldn't have cared less about anything I told you that first day. You just wandered around studying my bookshelves and just being you," he adds with a smile.

"Logan I..."

"I'm almost finished, I promise," he continues nervously scooting his chair nearer to mine awkwardly as he's still holding onto one of my hands. "I know that when you came in that Wednesday you were there for me to help you, but every week for the past two years you've been helping me. I hated turning you away at Hayley's party and then leaving you that letter with Julia, but it wasn't right yet. You were vulnerable and I couldn't take advantage of that and honestly I wasn't ready to admit what'd you become?"

"What I'd become?"

"Noe, because of you I regularly stock my home and office refrigerators with Dr. Pepper."

"But you..." I jump in.

"I know I said otherwise. I lied. What are you gonna do?" he shrugs. "I use phrases like 'for the love of all things sweet.' And I find myself reading more and more just to keep up with you."

"Hence the Kafka and the Plascencia?"

"Yeah," he concedes blushing a bit.

"But what was the other one? I've heard it before."

"Your dad?"

"My huh?"

"Noe I," he interrupts then hesitates some. "I know the curves of your face," he recites. I feel tears start to sting the backs of my eyes as he continues.

"I know every fleck of gold in your eyes. And I know that that day in my office was the best one I've ever had. P-please say something."

"Steve," I beam as tears flood my eyes.

"And you're my Mary and you…you've become what wakes *me* up every day."

"What are you saying?"

"I'm saying…" he looks down briefly and takes both my hands in his. "I'm saying…my mother's name is Jane and my father's name is Micah. She's a nurse and he's a pilot. I have one sister, Sidney, who is an art teacher and lives with her English professor husband James in Tennessee with their son, my nephew Liam. I love romantic comedies and doing crossword puzzles," he continues sliding closer to me, my hand still locked in his.

"I'm saying…I dabble in photography and have a secret wish to quit my practice, take pictures and teach it full time. I played lacrosse in high school and I sucked at it. I…I…" he says stammering all at once."

"You're saying?" I call trying to help him find his words, nervous by his sudden anxiousness.

"I'm saying, Happy Birthday."

"What?" I call, jumping slightly at his deviation.

"You know you've never once asked when my birthday was. Of all the questions you've asked me, intrusive as ever, not once."

"I'm sure you'd never tell," I laugh a little, freeing one of my hands, wiping my face and sniffing back my emotional snot. "Wait. I'm so confused. Can you please focus?" I ask turning into him, so my knee grazes the top of his leg.

"Breathe. Just breathe," he says with closed eyes, leaning closer to me so that the hem of his shirt brushes my sun-kissed thigh.

"I am breathing," I give a quippy retort.

"That's for me," he says, opening his eyes smiling.

"Oh sorry. Breathe then. Close your eyes and just breathe."

"That day two years ago was Wednesday, July 24th."

"Yes, I remember."

"*My* birthday. You were the best birthday present a person could ask for."

"I was..."

"You were and have continued to be and if you would accept it."

"Wait!" I yell, putting a hand to his lips and the other on his chest.

"What? This is kind of a crucial moment. Usually you're pretty impeccable with timing. I can't say so much on this one," he mumbles through my fingers before grabbing hold and lowering them.

"No, it's just that I want to focus completely on all you're saying, but your elbow is digging into my thigh and it hurts. I can't really concentrate on you because my leg is falling asleep."

"I'm sorry."

"No problem. Let's just get re-situated."

The two of us stand and stack all of my books. Logan clears the table of all the trash I've accumulated. We reorganize our chairs and reacquaint ourselves in them.

"Comfortable now?"

"Hold it," I start with both my feet on the floor, mine and his legs alternating.

Still uncomfortable, I try crossing my right over my left and resting my right arm on the table. I rearrange again and settle for sitting cross-legged, hands resting on Logan's thighs.

"Now I'm ready."

"You sure?"

"Don't patronize me. Go on with your speech man," I threaten playfully.

"I feel like it's lost some of its appeal and the original mood of the moment."

"No, it's all still here. You're Steve. I'm Mary the Wedding Planner. I'm sitting on my tree, tossing out brown M&M's. Heartbroken and unknowing, but secretly hopeful. See look at my face," I attempt to go through a variety of emotions to evoke heartache and feelings of being lost but also hopeful.

"Why are you only eating the brown ones?"

"Be serious, come on now. It's my birthday, you have to."

"You're not going to finish it? Come on you know you want to," he teases, holding up a finger, threatening to poke me in my side.

"Because someone once said they had less artificial coloring because chocolate's already brown. And it kind of stayed with me."

"You kind of stayed with me. And, and today, um on this October 29th, I would love to be a gift to you."

"That's not in the…wait what? Are you saying what I think you're saying?"

"Well that depends on what you're thinking."

"You are secretly funny you know that? What I hope you're saying is you fancy me and can't possibly imagine the rest of your days without me. You want to be like….my boyfriend."

"I'm not thinking that."

As a reflex I punch him in the side, and he feigns hurt. I pull back to strike him again and he starts to laugh. He grabs my face in each of his palms and I can smell the minty freshness of his breath.

"What I mean is I'm not thinking all of that. In that way," he says still laughing.

"So, some of it's right?"

"Yes. Parts."

"Parts of it? Which parts?"

"I may be a closet comic and I may as you put it 'fancy you'."

"Is that it?" I ask incredulously still between his hands my arms flailing about.

"I may in fact only be able to think of you each and every day and I may have envisioned countless days in the near and distant future with you."

"So that only leaves one thing. Boyfriend. How much sense does that make? For the love of all things sweet will you stop with the round abouts. My stomach is tied up in knots."

"You really are more than the sum of your parts," he smiles, his hands off my face now only our foreheads are touching. "Instead of calling myself your boyfriend and you my girlfriend I think we..."

"We what?" I yell almost unexpectedly. "Always so difficult. This should be the easiest yes or no ever," I sigh turning my head.

"Breathe. Just breathe," I hear him whisper in my ear. "We're only really just meeting one another, you know really getting to learn a different type of us," he continues using his finger to turn my face toward his so we can see one another. "For now, we can just be... a work in progress."

I beam as he coins my personal phrase, for us. He smiles his charming smile, takes my head between his hands, and kisses me tenderly. A kiss no story could ever describe but every bit as sweet as all 23 flavors of my Dr. Pepper.

From the Desk of _____Noe Cortes_____

October 29, 2010

"I love him, and it is the beginning of everything." (a variation of F. Scott Fitzgerald)

I will not say that my beginning started with a guy, but I will say that the middle is certain to be a little sweeter thanks to my new tag along. This is about to be my new travel journal. I was already in the planning stages of Spain when Logan's unexpected proclamation of love was unleashed. So he's coming with. We're going everywhere and we're going to capture everything. I'm dancing and writing and he's teaching, which apparently is what he's wanted to do for a while. He has a couple of contacts in Spain at a local university and he will be teaching Historical Photography (whatever that means) to High School seniors who are participants in a college bridge program. Pretty neat huh? He is wonderful, isn't he? Mama used some of her old contacts to help me along as well. When I'm not learning flamenco and some classical ballet, I'll be teaching master classes at a couple of dance companies mama used to travel with when she was younger.

Tonight Logan will join me, Harper, Sebastian, Hayley, Connor, Mama, Papí, JJ, Adriana, Jackson and Kennedy at Houlihan's for my birthday celebration, and tomorrow we will pour through books and books about travels and sights, those full of literature and brave and gallant heroes and heroines, and whatever else to plan our trip. I'm honestly the happiest little Noe that ever was.

This work in progress is coming along. Happy 29th birthday to me!

Made in the USA
Coppell, TX
25 April 2021

THE HAM WHISPERER'S
TECHNICIAN CLASS
LICENSE COURSE

The Ham Whisperer's
Technician Class
License Course

Andy Vellenga, KE4GKP

Andrew Vellenga
Alexandria, Virginia

ISBN-13: 978-1456484811
ISBN-10: 1456484818